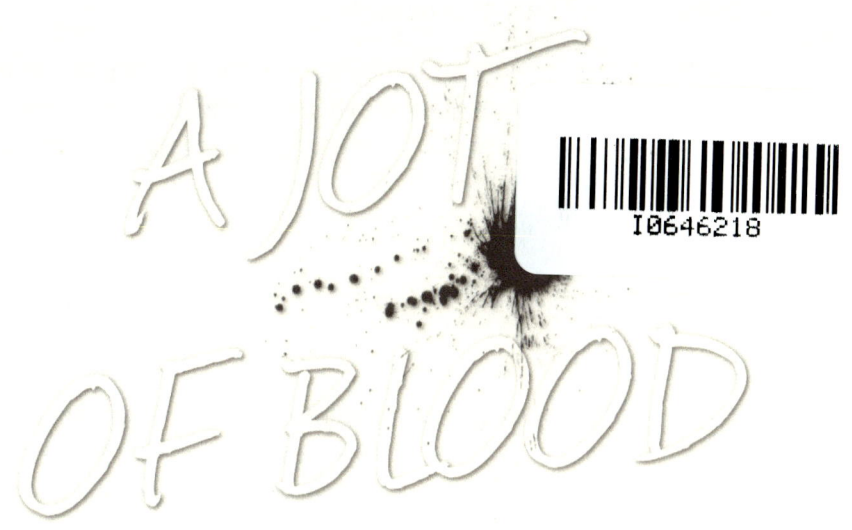

A JOT OF BLOOD

by

Katherine Bayless

SCRY
MEDIA

OTHER NOVELS BY KATHERINE BAYLESS

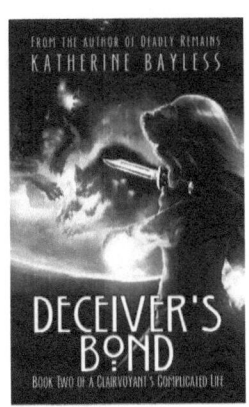

Theresa, Ryan, and Tyler

Never let the fear of making mistakes stop you from pursuing your dreams. Make your missteps, learn from them, and there will be nothing your hard work can't accomplish, especially if you're following your heart.

FOREWORD

Joy and apprehension …

That's what I'm feeling as I stand ready to release this book. *Joy*—because I love this story. *A Jot of Blood* is my favorite romp so far. Every moment I've spent at Coventry Academy, living inside Lire's sixteen-year-old head, has been an absolute hoot. *Apprehension*—because I worry that I'm about to disappoint some of you who were anticipating the fourth book in the Complicated Life series.

Touching on Lire's past while writing *Reluctant Adept* was the spark that compelled me to write this book. I wanted to know more about Lire's time at Coventry Academy. I wanted to learn what her life was like, meet her classmates and teachers, and experience the events that shaped her to be the thirty-year-old psychic I've gotten to know in my *A Clairvoyant's Complicated Life* series.

I also can't deny that living under the same roof with my three teenagers was a major catalyst. More than anything, I wanted to write a book that they'd be thrilled to read, especially my daughter and her friends. (No word yet on whether I succeeded.)

In writing *A Jot of Blood*, I followed my heart. I can only hope that you're up for coming along for the ride.

Since this story is set fourteen years in Lire's past, I elected to peg cultural and technological references to the year 2003, give or take.

-K-

ACKNOWLEDGEMENTS

A big hug and thank you to my test readers whose critiques I value beyond measure. Dave, Trish, Michelle, Sarina, Natalie, Kathy—you guys rock!

To Scot—my husband, my wingman, my soulmate—I love you. If not for you and your many talents, I'd never have published my first book. You've turned this hobby of mine into a professional endeavor and I am forever grateful.

And last, dear reader, I thank you for sticking with me. I write mostly for myself, but I publish because I hope that what I've worked so hard to create will inspire and entertain you.

CONTENTS

Tarry a little; there is something else.

This bond doth give thee here no jot of blood;

The words expressly are 'a pound of flesh:'

Take then thy bond, take thou thy pound of flesh;

But, in the cutting it, if thou dost shed

One drop of Christian blood, thy lands and goods

Are, by the laws of Venice, confiscate

Unto the state of Venice.

— *The Merchant of Venice* (4.1.305-312)

A JOT OF BLOOD

OF BLOOD

CHAPTER 1

Perhaps a little bad is called for

THANKS to all the showboating spellcasters, residual magic enveloped Coventry Academy's main walkways like the stench of bad cologne. It slid over my skin, irritating my eyes and tickling my nose.

Just your typical move-in day. Why bother carrying your stuff when magic could do all the heavy lifting?

Sneezing for the third time, I plodded toward Spencer Hall, the girl's dormitory, and the fresh air of my private room. If not for the three plastic storage bins that lurched and bobbed along the asphalt path in front of me, each one floating atop a column of spinning air, I'd already be through the front doors and halfway there.

I bounced my armload of boxes into a more comfortable position and tried to ignore how sweaty my hands had gotten beneath my formal length gloves.

Why couldn't I have been born a telekinetic? My boxes and I'd be sailing over everyone's heads, right now, instead of stuck here on this hot pavement.

"Move it, slowpoke!" a youthful voice called out, piercing my fantasy.

A Louis Vuitton duffel, powered by six shadowy appendages, swerved around me, shooting beneath the slow-moving baggage train to reach the dorm's front door.

The vortices, disturbed by the rogue duffel bag, sputtered and then evaporated, sending the three heavy-duty bins crashing to the ground, blocking the entire pathway.

"Nice going, butthead," a girl with a nasal voice complained.

"So?" her counterpart retorted. "Get up there and fix it, dummy."

"But—it's *her*."

Apparently, 'her' was code for 'the disgusting troll who swallows people whole when they get too close.'

I ground my teeth. Yet another classmate too dumb to figure out that skin contact with *anyone*, much less a spellcasting twerp like her, was the last thing I wanted. Why else would I be wearing these stupid gloves and my long-sleeved uniform on move-in day? It was almost ninety freaking degrees. Plus, I was holding a stack of boxes. What did she think I was going to do? Attack her with my face just so I could learn all her deepest, darkest secrets?

Gross.

"Move it, *noobkins*," a new voice commanded.

"But—"

"Get a clue. That's Lire. She's a clairvoyant, not an ogre with a taste for seventh graders," the newcomer scoffed. "Get out of my way. Here, I'll take pity on you, but only because you're obviously short on potential and long on dumb."

A girl, half a head taller than me, with long elaborately braided cornrows, appeared beside me on the pathway. Without her customary afro framing her face like a dark puffy cloud, it took me a moment to recognize Darla.

"Seventh graders," she said, shooting me an exasperated eye roll.

Turning her attention to the pathway, she muttered under her breath and flicked her pocket-sized wand at the three offending crates. All at once, they shot upward, spun in place, and then darted, one by one, down the path to land in a perfect stack to the right of the dorm's glass doors.

Darla raised the tip of her retractable virge to her lips and blew on it like a cowboy's six-shooter. "Catch you later, Lire."

With a dramatic toss of her beaded braids, she strutted up the pathway, her own train of baggage following behind her like a string of obedient ducklings.

I didn't spare a glance for the incoming seventh graders. I could tell by the boldly stenciled 'Dawson' on their containers that they were Jessica's younger twin sisters. If I turned around, they'd stick their noses up at me, inevitably following the example of their snooty popular sister.

I breathed a sigh of relief when I strode into Spencer Hall's air-conditioned lobby. Even with Dad's help carrying the heaviest boxes, my long-sleeve oxford stuck to my back like an unyielding second skin, and I'd probably be able to squeeze a pound of sweat from my underwear.

I tried not to grumble as everyone else ambled through the dormitory halls wearing shorts and tank tops, their sun-kissed skin mocking me.

Here I was at Coventry Academy, America's most respected private school for the magically gifted (or afflicted), and I still stood out like a black magus at a Glindarian witch convention. With my strawberry-blonde hair, green eyes, and pale skin, I wasn't exactly the stereotypical wicked witch, but you sure wouldn't know it by the way most people treated me.

Reactions were always worse if I took someone by surprise, which happened a lot, especially in the school's crowded corridors.

Case in point, I hadn't taken more than three steps into the lobby when Miss Blonde-and-Popular, Amanda Olander, came a whisker away from plowing into me. Gabbing with her friends, she glanced up at the last moment and practically jumped out of her flip-flops when she found me in her path. She and her minions scurried to the side, shooting me the stink-eye the entire time.

I watched while they gave me the widest berth they could manage. *Melodramatic much?* They knew darn well my gift needed skin contact.

Gift. I rolled my eyes at the irony. No doubt Amanda, snooty-booty sorceress of light, viewed her magic ability as a gift. Out in the real world, she could easily pass for normal.

Not like me. Gloves were a necessity. But I was done with hiding.

"Coming through!" Boxes raised like a battering ram, I marched down the busy corridor.

Dad arrived with his own burden as I unceremoniously dropped my load to the right of my door. He waited patiently, holding the large plastic cooler he'd carried in from the car while I searched for my key. At this end of the hall, near the storage and laundry rooms, things were notably quieter than the rest of the floor.

My magic familiar, Red, popped out of his specially outfitted pocket in my cross-body bag to hand me my room key. His six-inch-tall teddy bear body scarcely fit with all the stuff I'd crammed into the main compartment.

"It appears a fellow clairvoyant will be your neighbor this term," he said, gesturing to our left with his pudgy black paw, drawing our attention to the door sandwiched between mine and the eastern stairwell.

An array of neon yellow caution signs had been affixed to the closed door's wood surface. They were the same ones that could be seen on mine.

PSI-FREE ENVIRONMENT
DO NOT ENTER WITHOUT FULL SKIN-SUIT

VIOLATORS WILL BE LIABLE FOR CONTAMINATION CAUSED BY UNAUTHORIZED SKIN CONTACT.

It wasn't that long ago that nobody knew what psi-free meant. But then Gwyneth Paltrow did that famous Oprah episode about healthy living and suddenly, it seemed like everyone wanted products that'd never been touched by a living soul. Even Nabisco had jumped on the bandwagon. Not that I was complaining. Somewhere in my stuff was a box of psi-free Oreos that had my name all over it.

"Another clairvoyant. How nice," Dad said. "I'm sure you'll be the best of friends."

Somehow, I avoided making a face. I'd only met one other clairvoyant in my life, back in the second grade. He'd been three years older and a big fat jerk, so I refused to get my hopes up about this new girl.

I examined the neighboring door. Ever since seventh grade, when I first moved here from Coventry's elementary school campus, the room next door had been used for storage. Now, drywall dust coated the hallway's gray carpet in a three-foot swath, a lockbox hung from the nickel-plated doorknob, and the threshold's off-white casement was dinged and scuffed.

"Looks like they're not done with the psi-free resurfacing," I said. "I wonder when she's moving in."

Dad shifted the cooler in his arms, resting it on his left hip. Although his hair was more salt than pepper these days, he was still fit and strong, his lean, sinewy physique wrought from years of tennis. "After I set this down, I'll have a quick word with Headmaster Simmons, see what I can suss out."

I opened my door but stopped cold at the unexpected sight of the slant-front desk on the opposite wall. I hadn't seen the Colonial American antique since appraising it for Ben Gibson at his shop at the beginning of the summer. The desk had been my first professionally paid reading for him, and I still got goosebumps thinking about it.

Again, I marveled at my luck this past summer. How cool was it that I'd been a paid consultant? Part-time, but *still*. How many just-turned-sixteen-year-olds could say that?

Dad nudged me inside with the cooler and set it down near my small refrigerator. When he turned toward me, I stared at him, blinking away my blurred vision.

"Did you think I wouldn't call Ben?" he asked while absently tugging the cuffs of his psi-free gloves to snug them tighter on his hands. "That desk is all you talked about for at least a fortnight."

"Until it sold ... " I forced out.

He nodded, his easy smile revealing the crescent-shaped dimples at each side of his mouth and the fine lines around his gray-blue eyes. "Until it sold."

I would have thrown my arms around him, but I remembered Red, who'd scrabbled his way up my arm to perch atop my right shoulder. My familiar's powerful aversion spells were there to discourage anyone from getting within touching range, ensuring that his fuzzy black body always remained psi-free. I didn't want to get close enough to make Dad flee my room in horror, so I bounced up and down on the balls of my feet instead.

"Thank you, thank you, thank you!" I squealed, clapping my hands together, and then pranced to my desk.

It wasn't psi-free, but that was okay. I'd already learned its secrets — the intimate thoughts of dozens of people, most of them long dead.

Until I began touching antiques, I hadn't realized that performing psychic readings could be useful, much less something I'd enjoy doing. Granted, not all the memories were happy ones, but they were almost always fascinating.

Earning two bucks an item plus minimum wage at Ben's shop had been an eye-opening experience, in more ways than one. I now knew, without a doubt, what I planned to do with my life, what I wanted to do for a living. I was going to get my degree in art history and become the most renowned antiques appraiser in the country, maybe even in the whole world.

For the first time ever, I'd felt empowered, and it was a feeling I wouldn't relinquish without a fight. From then on, I'd worn my black gloves proudly.

And this desk had brought that about.

"Isn't it pretty, Red?"

"Indeed. And I know how much it means to you. Your father is a perceptive man."

"Perceptive ... bah," Dad said. "She could hardly speak of anything else."

"Oh, be quiet." I mugged at him. "I thought you were going to see Mr. Simmons." Just because I refused to get my hopes up didn't mean I wasn't curious about my new classmate.

"That I am." He stopped to yank my abandoned boxes into the room. "I'll grab the last of your things from the car on my way back."

"'kay. Thanks, Dad."

By the time he returned with my final moving box, more than thirty minutes later, I'd finished stuffing my refrigerator with the psi-free items we brought from home, my laptop was setup on my new desk, and my suitcase sat half unpacked on my bed.

Dad dropped his burden next to my open suitcase. "That's it. Enough snacks and goodies to see you through until Thanksgiving. I parked your Vespa in its locker. Enjoy it. *Fais attention à toi.* Always the helmet. *Tu m'entends?*"

Dad's native French always came out when he wanted my attention. *Look after yourself. Do you hear me?*

In other words — be careful.

Duh.

"*Oui, bien sûr papa!*" My '*yes, of course*' came out with considerable exasperation. "You said it about five hundred times on the way here and at least a thousand before that. Don't worry. I'll never ride without my helmet. I'm not stupid. Besides, I don't want to get a ticket and lose my license."

Earning the privilege had taken me fifty practice hours and a five-week class over the summer. My sweet sixteen and the ninety-two percent score on my DMV driving test topped off what had been the best summer of my life. My brand-new red motor scooter? Icing on the cake.

"*Bon, tu m'as compris. Alors, tiens, elles sont à toi.*" *Good, you get me. So, here, they are yours.* He dropped my Vespa's keys into my waiting palm. "You know the rules. Weekends only."

"I know. I know. No further than town and no passengers. I remember."

"*Très bien.*" *Very good.* "Now ... don't you want to know about your new neighbor?"

"Yes, but you were too busy nagging me."

"Her name is Diedra Yamaguchi, and I'm pleased to report she's in your grade. Her mother is an attaché for the U.S. Consulate in Tokyo. They're currently in Japan, but she's scheduled to start sometime before Thanksgiving. Construction should be done in a week or two. Mr. Simmons thinks you and Diedra will get along well. Apparently, she's a real firecracker."

A firecracker, huh? Coming from a Rowan warlock headmaster who dressed in three piece suits and often addressed the students as 'master' and 'mistress,' that could mean just about anything. Now I for *sure* wouldn't get my hopes up.

My grunt must have sounded skeptical because Dad shot me one of his looks reserved for when he thought I was being difficult.

"Need me to reopen the water valve for your washer-dryer?" he asked.

"Jeez, Dad. I've lived here how many years? Pretty sure I can twist open a valve."

"*Ah bon?*" His cheeky 'is that so?' was accompanied by his amused chuckle. "I should hit the road. If you need anything, or even if you don't, take pity on your old dad who likes to feel useful now and again." He squeezed my upper arm, which was safely covered by my sleeve. "*Sois sage, d'accord?*" *Be good, okay?*

"When have I ever not been good?"

"Then perhaps a little bad is called for, no? I want you to have fun. But not so much that I get a call in the night from an angry headmaster." He raised his eyebrows and looked at me sternly. "*Tu m'entends?*"

I rolled my eyes but couldn't stifle my grin. "Yes, Dad, I hear."

He held open his arms, and I gave him a careful hug, tilting my head to keep the exposed skin of my face away from his clothes.

"Look after her, Red. Don't let her eat every meal in her room, *d'accord?*"

"I will do my best — as always," Red said from his position on the top of my desk. "Drive safely, *Monsieur.*"

Dad turned at the door to smile at me. "See you both at Thanksgiving."

"*Merci, Papa.* I love you. Call when you get home so I know you got there okay."

"*Bien sûr, ma pucette. Moi aussi, je t'aime.*" *Of course, my little flea. I love you too.*

The classic French endearment always made me smile (a flea, really?), but this was goodbye. I swallowed the lump in my throat.

"Bye, Daddy," I rasped as he closed my door behind him, leaving me alone with Red.

I continued to unpack, biting my trembling bottom lip as I struggled to avoid thinking about Dad driving the three hours to our empty house.

If not for you, he'd be going home to Giselle and Mother.

I shook my head. Even after nine years, my older sister's cruel voice still rang in my head, blaming me and my "abnormality" for breaking up our family.

You'd think I'd have gotten over that by now, especially given how many times Dad had gone out of his way to reassure me (often in fervently spoken French) that the divorce hadn't been my fault.

Sniffling and feeling raw, I hoped Red wouldn't give me a hard time about avoiding the refectory this weekend. Dealing with the school's cafeteria during Monday's forced lunch period would come soon enough.

Despite my newfound confidence, my stomach clenched at the thought of the boisterous dining room. For the first time in years, I was friendless. My BFFs, Sheri, Viv, and Javier, had graduated last term. Ever since, I'd been dreading the start of school, convinced that I'd be spending my remaining two years at Coventry with Red as my only confidant.

It made it especially difficult to stop my plaintive hoping that the new girl and I would hit it off. In fact, I alternated between wishing she'd show up sooner and pleading, *Please, God, let her be nice, let her like me,* in my thoughts.

So much for not getting my hopes up.

CHAPTER 2

Two freaks and a testy guard dog

WITH the hike from American Civics and its classroom at the furthest end of campus, I arrived at the refectory behind the sixth-period lunch stragglers. I hitched up my backpack and grimaced. My shirt was damp where I'd gotten sweaty beneath the weight of all my binders. The Pacific Northwest's infamous winter gloomies couldn't come soon enough. This eighty degree stuff was killing me and my stupid gloves didn't help.

As the dining hall's heavy wood door closed, I darted inside on the heels of Ted Mason, our school's star basketball player. But instead of following his size fifteens through the archway to my right, I paused, allowing my eyes to adjust to the dim lighting, and relished the cool air.

My stomach rumbled at the smell of chicken and something tangy, most likely Mrs. Godfrey's spaghetti sauce. Glancing to my left, I confirmed what I expected to find—the dining room crowded with juniors and seniors—most of the room's tables already at capacity.

For a moment, I wavered, half tempted to skip lunch and head to the library, but my rumbling stomach demanded that I stay. Besides, my mouse days were over.

"Clotilde!" Mrs. Godfrey beamed at me from behind the plexiglass sneeze shield, her hazel eyes radiating warmth through her bifocals. A lock of graying brown hair had escaped her customary hairnet, curling below her left ear. "Good to see you, honey. What can I getcha? We've got a new supplier for our psi-free pasta and cheeses, this year. Good stuff. I've got linguini or cheese pizza ready. Veggie wrap, of course. Or I could whip you up an omelette. You name it kiddo."

Behind me, two of Amanda Olander's minions, Trina and Jessica, snickered after one of them uttered my given name sing-song.

What are they —third graders?

I'd been going by Lire for the past five years, but Mrs. Godfrey had known me from kindergarten as Clotilde and darned if I couldn't convince her to call me by my nickname instead. There were times I wanted to strangle her.

"Pasta, please, Mrs. Godfrey. You know how much I love your sauce," I replied with forced cheer. But much as I tried to hold my chin high and my shoulders square, the weight of ridicule pushed down on me with a gravity all its own.

"Here you are, honey." Mrs. Godfrey handed me a plate with her linguini and red sauce, steamed broccoli, and a side of garlic bread. "All psi-free, don't you worry."

My stomach growled, and this time my smile came more easily. "Thanks, Mrs. Godfrey. It smells awesome." I only hoped I didn't lose my appetite between here and whatever seat I managed to find.

I snagged a psi-wrapped bottle of water and trudged to the dining room.

"May I sit here?" I asked Nancy, even though I knew her answer would be 'no' as soon as she and her friends had noticed me moving in their direction. I ignored the bead of sweat trickling down my side as humiliation seared a blazing path across my cheeks and neck. Hers was the third table I'd approached. Shania and her clique of witches had been the first. They'd shot me down with hardly a blink, just three tables over. And then there was Stephanie and her cadre of shifters. I could still hear their furious whispers behind me.

"No, um, sorry. We're saving it for ... someone," she replied, glancing apprehensively at her friends who shot her wide-eyed glares whenever they thought I wasn't looking.

"Okay. No problem," I said cheerfully, moving away. Darned if I let them see the cuts they'd made.

Near the large picture window that overlooked the ornamental garden, I noticed Trina and Jessica sliding onto the empty bench at Amanda's table. Judging by their animated discussion and canary-eating grins, they were twittering about a cute guy. Much as I wanted to roll my eyes, I couldn't blame them. If Sheri and Viv were here, I'd be doing the same thing to them. And Javier would have beaten me to it.

For the millionth time, I wished they hadn't graduated.

Walking slowly, I scanned the room for an empty seat at a table that wasn't populated by small-minded jerks and their spineless minions—no small task. At the back wall, though, I spotted several openings at one of the smaller, four-person tables where a guy I didn't recognize sat alone, head bowed over a book.

No guts, no glory.

Even when I stood inches from the edge of the rectangular table, he didn't look up. From this angle, standing above him, about all I could see was his messy brown hair, broadly-hunched shoulders, and a school uniform that practically bulged at the seams. I couldn't tell whether his large size was thanks to too little exercise or, perhaps, too much.

Sticking out from the cuffs of his long-sleeve oxford shirt, his beefy hands gripped a massive trade paperback. I craned my head to read the title: *A Game of Thrones*. It sounded vaguely familiar.

"Mind if I sit here?"

"It's taken," he said with an unyielding voice that matched his bulk. The jerk didn't bother to look up at me.

Okay, yes, there was another tray centered across from him, but only pizza crusts and some raw carrots remained, so that person had finished and hadn't bussed his or her spot. But even if they came back, this was a four-person table. Still more than enough space for me.

Odds were that he'd seen me coming, spotted the gloves, and purposely buried his nose in his ridiculously thick book in the hope that I'd get the message to stay away. Clairvoyants need not apply.

I ground my teeth together as the heat of indignation threatened to turn my vision red.

I had as much right as anyone else in this room to sit down and eat my food, which was probably stone cold at this point, thank you very much.

That's it. Done.

I'd reached my limit. The jerk could darn well turn tail if he didn't like sitting next to me. Let *him* find another goddamned table to sit at.

I smashed my tray down to the left of his, my pasta and garlic bread nearly jumping off the plate. I planted my butt next to him and then shoved him down the bench with my hip, forcing his ass to slide to the left and make room for me. It was lucky the benches were slippery. The guy was larger than I'd thought. I wouldn't have been surprised to learn that he was a defensive lineman on our varsity football team, although, not many of them would want to be seen reading a two-thousand-page book at lunch.

"What the fuck?" he sputtered, finally lifting his nose from his paperback boat anchor to glare at me with—*holy moly*—the most brilliant blue eyes I'd ever seen that weren't on a Siberian husky. "What the hell is your problem? I told you—this table is taken."

"Oh, yeah? Your ego's so large it needs three additional seats?" I slammed my water bottle down next to my tray. When he scowled, I snapped, "You don't want me sitting here? Then tell me, your highness, where should I sit instead? Over there?" I jerked my chin toward the empty space where my trail of humiliation had started. "Oh, my bad, Shania said that seat was *taken*. Okay, never mind. How about that one there, next to Stephanie? Whoops, no, so sorry—*taken*. Oh, but wait, what about that one there?" I shot him a glare so bitter he'd need an entire liter of Pepsi to wash it down. "Nope ... that one's *taken* too."

I rammed my psi-free fork and spoon through their protective plastic sleeve with more force than necessary. "Yeah, they're all *taken* — taken by empty fucking air, just like the seats across from you." *Jackass.*

I wasn't usually one to let fly with the F-bomb, especially with people I didn't know, but he'd already beaten me to it. And, boy, did it make me feel better, almost as good as smacking this jerk upside the head. Not that I had any experience roughing people up, mind you, but after enduring years of bigotry, I excelled at using my imagination.

A bark of laughter, followed by amused chuckling, came from nearby, but when I snapped my surprised attention to the guy next to me, his surly expression hadn't much changed. Although, now, he appeared to be more peeved than outright angry. Still, he wasn't the one laughing. No way was any sound escaping from between those tightly compressed lips of his.

A male voice replaced the laugh: "Real smooth, bro. Congratulations. She thinks you're a total asshole."

As I looked for the source of the cutting remark, Mr. Invisible went on to declare, "That clinches it. I like her already."

Crazy as it seemed, the voice emanated from across the table ... from the *empty* bench in front of that other tray. Straightening my back, I peered over the table's far edge. Maybe Coventry Academy had admitted a brownie or a leprechaun to school this year, although, from what I understood, they rarely left their private island.

Mr. Invisible snickered. "Don't mind him. He's still pissed that the author killed off one of his favorite characters, like *five hundred pages ago.* My name's Zach by the way. Don't bother looking — I'm an occultum. The dickhead next to you is Cal."

One of the Hidden? *Whoa.* That curse was unaccountably rare. Total invisibility, including their shadow. Supposedly, less than a few dozen people on the planet had it.

"Fuck off," Cal growled.

"With a roommate like him, who needs friends, right?" Even though Zach was invisible, my imagination conjured his smirk — the fleeting Cheshire Cat with his invisible smile.

It was hard to know where to look when he spoke. I alternated between staring at the leftover crusts of pizza on his tray and straining my eyes at the empty air in front of me, more than likely going crosseyed.

"So, you must be Lire, the school's one and only clairvoyant and chief contender for Brainiac of the Year. I've heard all about you. You and bookworm over there should get along famously."

He laughed and something smacked the table, probably his hand. "Dude, this couldn't get any better. A testy guard dog and the two freaks who can learn everyone's dark secrets. Together, we'll be feared by the entire student body. Take her royal bitchiness, Amanda, over there. That girl knows how to get *down* with the nasty. I mean, look at her, tossing her hair and whispering to her friends about Ted Mason's microscopic dick and how it curves — "

"Could you shut the hell up?" Cal snarled. "*Jesus.* That's the last thing any of us wants to know. *Christ.*" He ran his hand through his shaggy mane, combing it back to reveal a rockin' widow's peak for half a second before it flopped down to completely cover his forehead again.

Dark hair and amazing blue eyes. A stunning combination. Too bad the guy was such a grouch. If he ever stopped glowering, he'd be hot.

Zach laughed. "You have a point. Look at her. She's seriously spooked. You're not going to run away now, are you, princess? Wishing you hadn't shoved the big bad wolf aside to take his seat?"

Did that mean ... Cal was a werewolf? With their exclusive schools in Idaho and Montana, very few dub-dubs had ever attended Coventry.

I smoothed my pinched features, but there was nothing I could do about any lingering blush. *God.* Could this day get any worse? No doubt they thought I was a goody two-shoes. Which, honestly, I probably was, despite ingesting more than a few memories belonging to the opposite sex. I knew full well the things they did in private and what that —

Hold the phone ... Had he really overheard Amanda talking about the size of Ted's you-know-what as if she was an expert on the subject?

I smirked, gazing across the table at the nearby air. "Wow. You dissed both Amanda and Ted with that one rumor." I shook my head as I peeled the psi-free plastic away from my bottled water. "And it's the first day of school, plus you're new. Remind me to stay on your good side."

My brain finally caught up with my mouth, and I stopped to stare across from me. "But if it's all the same, being feared by the entire student body isn't my goal in life. I stay out of other people's business — a lesson I learned a long time ago. Most of them already hate me. I don't need for it to be any worse."

"And *I* learned a long time ago that judgmental assholes aren't worth my time," he scoffed. "They're sheep. We'll let the big bad wolf eat them for breakfast."

Next to me, Cal grumbled something unflattering under his breath, whether it was about Zach or 'the sheep,' I could only imagine.

Although I tried to fight it, my insides warmed at Zach's use of 'we,' as if I was already a part of their group. Having a werewolf as a protector sure wouldn't suck. I wasn't sure whether Cal wanted any part of that, though. He'd hardly done anything but grunt this entire time.

I tucked into my lukewarm pasta, but it went down with all the satisfaction of a ten-pound brick. Tapping my heel against the linoleum, I shook off my worry. How often did you meet an occultum, much less talk to one?

I jerked my chin in Zach's direction. "So, I have to ask ... how're you navigating the hallways without getting trampled? Not like you can wear hazard lights. Anything that touches you disappears, doesn't it?"

I didn't want to be so tacky as to peek under the table, but I wondered whether the bench where he sat had turned transparent at the contact with his butt. Did the ground beneath his feet shimmer with his every step? *Dang.* I missed seeing him eat his pizza. Although, it probably wasn't all that interesting if the slice disappeared as soon as he touched it.

"Automatic invisibility takes skin contact, *princess*, just like your touchy power. Stuff beyond that is up to me, but fuck if I'll wear warning lights like some kind of airplane tower or goddamned *bells* on my shoes." By his disgust, I guessed both options had been tried at one point or another. "That's why I've got double-dub, there, to run interference. Nothing beats a wolf's sniffer for seeing the invisible. Don't

17

be fooled by the muscles; he knew from across the room whether you took a shower this morning, what your panties smell like, and whether you're scared or horny. Still want to sit at our table, baby girl?"

Cal growled, clearly not happy with his roommate's reckoning.

I rolled my eyes and tried to play it cool. "I'll take my chances."

He'd been prickly, but that was okay. My questions had tweaked him, and we all had our ways of dealing with feeling like a freak.

I glanced at Cal with his book still cracked to the page he'd been reading when I shoved my way onto the bench. I wondered whether reading was his escape, same as mine — although, why he felt the need to bury his nose in a book mystified me. Cal was good looking, in spite of his unruly hair. He could undoubtedly hang around with whoever he wanted, and being a dub-dub wasn't exactly uncool, not like being a clairvoyant.

I downed a few swallows from my water bottle. "Where'd you guys go to school before this?"

"I had tutors the last few years. Effin' Rotterdamned before that," Zach replied, his voice dropping register at the derogatory name for Rotterdam. The exclusive East Coast academy must have been where the administration wanted him to wear lights or bells.

"What about you?" When I met Cal's gaze, I half expected him to growl and ignore me.

"Home schooled," he said, practically chewing each word.

I wondered why he wasn't going to one of the dub-dub academies, but his clenched jaw and shuttered expression told me the topic was off limits. *Crud.* I seemed to be on a roll when it came to bringing up sensitive subjects.

I peered at his book, which he'd rested against the edge of the table, still cracked open to his page at least halfway through the thick volume. "What're you reading?"

He glanced down, as if he'd forgotten about it. "*Game of Thrones.* It was nominated for the Nebula a couple years ago. You know it?" He sounded skeptical, and, for a moment, I wished like anything I *did* know it.

"No. What genre is it? I mostly read mystery and horror ..." Romance, too, but I left that out. I shrugged, adding, as if in afterthought, "And some manga."

A *lot* of manga, more like, but there was no sense scaring them away with my inner nerd.

My answer seemed to surprise him, and he scoffed, "Lemme guess: *Sailor Moon*."

"There's a lot of awesome shōjo manga besides *Sailor Moon*, furball," I retorted. "But, for your information, I also like shōnen and seinen manga too." Truthfully, I did have a weakness for shōjo, or young girl manga, over the ones targeted to guys, but I wasn't about to tell him that.

"Yeah?" He turned to face me, and my stomach did a flip when I met his wide-eyed gaze. His startlingly blue irises were each encircled by a navy-blue ring and laced throughout with silvery-white, which contributed to their brilliant color. Absolutely gorgeous. And, without the scowl, he had an attractive face, even if his nose was a touch crooked and his brows were so fuzzy I wanted to smooth my fingers over them.

"Have you read *Ghost in the Shell*?" he asked.

"Duh," I drawled. "Along with *Inuyasha*, *Astro Boy*, *Blade of the Immortal*, *Lone Wolf and Cub*, *The Rose of Versailles* … oh, and, of course, *Akira*."

Across from us, Zach groaned. "God, no, not another one. Please tell me you're not an anime geek, too. I don't think I can take it."

I grinned. "Sorry. But … yeah, 'fraid so."

Zach sighed. "It figures."

"What's your favorite anime movie?" Cal asked. He dogeared his page before closing the Herculean tome.

"That's easy," I boasted. "Everything Miyazaki's directed. *Kiki's Delivery Service* was the first anime I ever saw. Fan for life after that."

He nodded eagerly. "*My Neighbor Totoro* was the same for me, but then I discovered *Castle in the Sky*."

"Kill me now," Zach muttered.

I laughed. "Oh, come on. How can you not like anime, especially Miyazaki?"

"It's not that I don't like anime, I just don't live it, like some people I know."

"Shut up. I don't *live it*," Cal grumbled.

"Says the guy with the framed Cat Bus picture above his bed."

"It's a rare Japanese movie poster," Cal snapped.

Zach snorted, but before I could gush about Cat Bus, the ten-minute bell rang.

"Well, see ya 'round, princess," Zach said as I watched Cal unfold himself from the table.

Holy bench press, Batman.

Now that Cal was upright, I tried not to ogle the width of his shoulders or the way his biceps stretched the fabric of his crisply pressed shirt, particularly when he hefted his backpack over his shoulder. Cal might be a bookworm and an anime geek, but his body spoke to other more physical activities. Interesting, though, that he wore long sleeves on a warm day like today.

Wouldn't mind seeing him in a short-sleeve polo, I thought to myself, turning away before he noticed my moony eyes and fast-heating cheeks. Zach hadn't been kidding about his roommate having muscles. I hoped he'd exaggerated his account of the werewolf's sense of smell, though. I hated to think what my pheromones might be telling him at this very second.

"Yeah, okay. See ya," I mumbled.

Zach's raspy whisper came inches from my right ear as I stuffed my water bottle into my backpack, "We'll save you a seat at dinner."

At my startled gasp, he laughed, the sound growing distant as he walked away. Cal regarded me with a raised eyebrow and turned to keep pace with his invisible friend.

I hoisted my backpack from the floor while trying not to look as though I was eye-groping the werewolf, which was a challenge since my gaze was determined to have its way with him. Broad chest and shoulders, narrow waist, nice butt, plus he loved manga and anime ... Cal was the stuff of daydreams.

Maybe this year won't be so bad after all.

I glanced down at the table. *Gosh darn it.* They hadn't bothered to bus their dishes. With a resigned huff, I schlepped each tray to the dirty dish bay. On my way out the door, I cheerily waved to Mrs. Godfrey even though I was now running late.

CHAPTER 3

Welcome to English Comp, wolf boy

WITH five minutes to get to class, I hightailed it down the covered breezeway that connected the refectory to LARTS—the two-story Language Arts building that had been built two years ago in the same sort of deluxe-lodge style as the rest of campus.

I'd once overheard a teacher describe Coventry Academy's architecture as 'Northwest modern.' Somehow, the crisp lines, deep eaves, and wide windows fit with the lush, rolling landscape of the area. Maybe it was because of the rustic stone and stained wood siding.

After bursting through the double-doored entrance, I sped down the off-white corridor, passing a harried-looking freshman before I came to the stairs. If I had to be tardy for Professor Everhart's class, I'd picked the right day since everyone was still learning their new schedules. Although, when it came to *Neverhart*, I'd be lucky to get away with simply breathing.

Taking the treads two at a time, I landed topside amid dozens of students who roamed the second-floor hallway as they made their way to their classes, some in more of a hurry than others. I slowed to a crawl, falling in behind a group of sophomore girls. Eric Chen bolted past me, between the imaginary lines of traffic, and dove in front of the chattering girls only to be brought up short by something in front of him.

"What the hell, dude?" I heard him exclaim.

"No passing on the right," a familiar voice growled.

The group in front of me stopped dead, but between their heads I could see Cal who'd turned to scowl at Eric.

"What are you, the frigging hall monitor?" Eric snapped.

"No, I'm the guy who's telling you to back off, asswipe, because you're about to trample someone."

Eric barked out a humorless laugh. "Yeah? Your imaginary friend?"

Although traffic on both sides had ground to a halt with students gawking at the unfolding argument, I managed to squeeze past the girls in front of me to stand next to Cal. At seeing me and my gloves, everyone, except for Cal, stepped back.

"Hey, Cal." I eyed the empty space between Cal and the wall where I hoped Zach was standing. If not, I was about to look like a complete idiot. "Hey, Zach. Still in one piece?"

"You know it, princess," he replied. "Where you headed?"

Eric goggled at me, at Cal, and the empty space. "What the — ?"

"It's Coventry, Eric. Summer's over." I nodded toward my new friends. "This is Cal and Zach. Guys, this is Eric, pyromancer *extraordinare*."

Cal jerked his chin at Eric. "Hey."

"Dude," Zach chimed in, but if he planned to add anything else, it was cut off by the seventh period starting bell.

Eric jumped. "Crap. Uh, yeah. Guess I'll catch you guys later." After a brief hesitation to weigh his options, he skirted around me and strode down the center of the hallway, staying well away from the right-hand wall.

Show over, the other lingering students scattered.

"I've got English Comp," I said, answering Zach's earlier question. "What about you guys?"

"With Everhart?" Zach asked.

"Yep. You guys too? You're juniors then?" When Cal nodded, I started down the hall. "Fun times. Room 240 is this way."

Professor Everhart's disapproving glare greeted us when I opened her door. "Miss Devon, late I see. I trust you remember where your seat is."

Someone snickered. I think it was Shania. As I made my way down the aisle, I ignored the mix of smug smiles and pitying expressions from the kids I passed.

"You must be Mr. Mars," Professor Everhart said. "Is Mr. Carter with you?"

"Yes, he is," Zach replied.

"Good. Your seats are at the back. Follow Miss Devon. I don't tolerate tardiness, but since this is your first day, I'll refrain from giving you a referral." She looked down her long nose at Cal, her gray eyes narrowed by displeasure.

At the room's farthest corner, I sat at my ridiculous desk, the same one as last year, the one with the painted orange frame and the RESERVED FOR LIRE DEVON, CLAIRVOYANT sign glued to the chair back. For once, though, I wasn't the only one who'd been singled out by such treatment. The desk in front of me had a red base and sported a RESERVED FOR ZACHARY CARTER, OCCULTUM placard on the tabletop.

I nearly giggled at Cal's peevish expression as he walked down the aisle.

Unlike ours, Cal's desk frame was the normal gunmetal color, but there was a folded card on his desk reserving it in his name. The distinctive sound of paper being crumpled emanated from Zach's chair and I realized his placard had disappeared from his desktop. I might have been tempted to do the same, except Professor Everhart had virtually laminated mine to the plastic chair back.

Superficially, the professor's attention to detail might have seemed thoughtful, but despite her name, Professor Everhart was anything but kindhearted. Last year, under the guise of 'making Lire comfortable,' she went out of her way to single me out every chance she got, which made me feel *anything* but comfortable. Her zeal continually called attention to the unique danger I posed to everyone's privacy—the fact that I could learn a person's secrets by touching an object they'd previously had skin contact with.

So I wasn't surprised when her special treatment resumed as soon as she introduced herself to the class and handed out the course syllabus.

"Miss Devon, you may leave your seat to retrieve your psi-free copy of the syllabus I'm handing out. You remember where your box is, don't you?"

How could I forget? All the way across the flipping room so everyone got to see the show.

I strode to the front corner of the classroom and removed the topmost sheet from my conspicuously labeled, bright-orange inbox. The paper was, predictably, neon orange too.

"Don't forget to remove it from the protective plastic and leave the sleeve there. You remember …" She smiled and nodded encouragingly, prompting the entire class to watch my progress right along with her.

As I returned to my seat, Cal's brows had disappeared into his hairline, although it wasn't much of a challenge since his tousled hair virtually covered them already.

Welcome to English Comp, wolf boy.

Zach muttered, "Jesus. Is she serious with this crap?"

A few minutes later, while Professor Everhart read through the course guide, expecting us to follow along, a folded note appeared at the center of my open binder, the white lined paper standing out starkly against the orange of the syllabus. I unfolded the page, mindful of conspicuous crinkling noises.

One good thing about sitting in a solitary row at the back of the classroom was my lack of immediate neighbors. Still, I kept half an eye on Brad Perry, whose bulk practically overflowed into the aisle at Zach's right. Not that I thought the varsity football player would make a fuss, but with his size, just a turn of his broad shoulders to glance my way would draw Neverhart's attention.

Ever wonder what secret she's trying to protect? You know that's why we're sitting at desks that look like garage-sale tricycles, right? the note read.

Below Zach's messy printing, I wrote back, *That's the last thing I want to know. She'd shit kittens if I ever took a glove off in class.*

After refolding the note in half, I tapped my gloved fingers next to the rectangle. It disappeared from my desk a second later.

I smiled to myself when I heard his quiet chuckle.

Less than a minute later, the folded slip reappeared. Below my previous response, it said, *No doubt. And it wouldn't take much effort, either. Some sneaky-time together and you and I'll have her quaking in her boots, a steaming pile of mewling fur-balls between her feet. Just say the word, princess.*

I pressed a hand to my stomach as it took a dive. I couldn't decide whether I was excited or terrified by the suggestion that he and I were a team. *Together, you and I . . .* Warmth bubbled through me at his words until my little voice woke up from its stupor.

Moron. Invading your teacher's privacy is a sure-fire way to have zero friends for the next two years. Actually—scratch that—it's a first-class ticket to getting expelled.

This was the second time Zach had hinted about the two of us terrifying people with our powers. I didn't enjoy sounding like a prude, but it was time to nip this in the bud.

I jotted, E*ww. That's the last thing I'd ever want—Neverhart's thoughts in my head. Yuck. Not gonna happen.* I drew a frowny face with a tongue sticking out for good measure.

The note disappeared shortly after I refolded it.

I'd assumed we were done, but the folded page reappeared a few minutes later. I could tell by its shape, though, that he'd slipped me a new piece of paper. On it he'd drawn a picture of Neverhart standing in front of her desk in a bow-legged stance, a wet mass of furry kittens between her booted feet. It was so expertly drawn that a giggle slipped out my mouth before I could squelch it.

"Miss Devon, perhaps you would share with the class what you find so funny about my grading policy."

I froze, hand slapped to my mouth even though my hilarity had all but dried up, and shook my head. "N-n-nothing, Professor." I shrugged sheepishly, keeping my gaze firmly glued to hers. "Sorry."

Don't look at my desk. Don't look at my desk. Don't look at my desk, I chanted while praying like mad that Zach had removed the cartoon so Neverhart couldn't see it.

It took all my willpower to stay relaxed instead of draping my fore-arms over my open binder to hide the paper I hoped like hell had disappeared.

When Neverhart stepped in my direction, now scanning my sur-roundings for anything incriminating, my heart thumped loudly in my ears. Without a visible body occupying the chair in front of me, noth-ing blocked her view of my desk's surface. No doubt the cartoon's white paper stood out beautifully against the orange of my class sylla-bus. Damn her, printing stuff for me on orange paper!

The itch to cover up the contents of my desk had my fingers twitching, but Zach wouldn't be able to pull the page away if I did that. Somehow, I avoided looking down or slumping like a guilty tod-dler in my hard plastic chair. I was sure my expression had turned doe-in-the-headlights under the professor's scrutiny, though.

I'd have killed for Obi-Wan Kenobi's mind powers right about now. *These aren't the droids you're looking for. Move along.*

"You know my stance on disruptions." She glared at me over the top of her reading glasses, her gray eyes regarding me flatly. "If you're having difficulty concentrating, I can always move your desk to the front of the classroom. Although, I'm afraid by doing so, it would risk other students coming into contact with it."

"No, ma'am. That won't be necessary. It won't happen again."

"See that it doesn't." She returned her attention to the overhead projector and our boring syllabus.

I glanced down at my binder to discover that, as I'd hoped, the cartoon had vanished. At the top margin of my syllabus, however, pen-ciled letters began to appear, slowly, because Zach had to write them upside down so I could read them.

S ... O ... R ... R ... Y.

I glared at the word before blowing out a resigned breath and wrote in inverted letters, I ... T ... 'S ... ... O ... K ... A ... Y.

After waiting several seconds for him to read it, I sat back in my chair and tipped up my binder so it rested against the inside edge of my desk, depriving him of the means to communicate further.

We're done now. I hoped he'd get the hint.

Thankfully, he did. I made it through the rest of class without incident.

As I packed my binder into my backpack after the bell rang, Zach rasped at my ear, "Are you mad at me now?"

I jumped and almost gasped aloud. Cal stood in the aisle, arms folded, watching while he waited for Zach.

"No, I'm not mad," I replied under my breath. "But I'd like to avoid a repeat performance." I glanced at Professor Everhart, who eyed me from the front of the classroom. On my way to the door, I called over my shoulder, "What do you guys have next?"

"Advanced Art," Cal said.

I nodded, turning toward him once we were out in the hall. "That's around the corner." I jerked my thumb over my shoulder. "I'm downstairs. French III. I guess I'll see you guys later."

"You know it, princess," Zach replied, leaving me with another case of the warm fuzzies as he and Cal walked away.

Even though Room 104 was downstairs and on the opposite side of the building, I made it to class with half a minute to spare. Just inside the doorway, I stopped cold at the sight of a mountainous man standing at the front of the class, his thick forearms folded beneath his broad chest.

This was Professor Trapp?

Jeez. And I thought Ted Mason was tall at his measly six foot four.

My teacher topped Ted by four inches, at least, and outweighed him by ... I couldn't fathom how much. It was a lot to take in — dark-brown hair, trimmed beard, penetrating eyes, massive muscles, plus he was taller than Sasquatch's older brother!

They expected me to speak to this formidable man, on a daily basis? In French? My insides quavered at the thought.

"*Bonjour, Mademoiselle.*" As he greeted me, my teacher's keen gaze zeroed in on my gloves before coming to rest on my face. "Clotilde Devon, correct? Or is it Lire? *Est-ce que vous vous appelez vraiment Lire?*" he said, asking if I was really called Lire.

His deep voice seemed to rumble along the floor and up my legs, but at least he'd pronounced my nickname correctly—'lear' (instead of 'liar' or some other weirdness)—which made sense since it was French.

In the third row, Amanda Olander turned to scowl in my direction. *Drat.* Why couldn't she have quit French after fulfilling the two-year foreign language requirement?

I opened my mouth but had to clear my throat. "*Oui, Monsieur. Je m'appelle bien Lire. On m'a surnommé Lire,*" I replied, explaining that, yes, I really was called Lire. I went on to say that Lire was my nickname.

Jeez. Not only was I babbling but I also sounded like a terrified chipmunk.

Again, he glanced down at my gloves. "Ah—*Lire,*" he drew out my name, his understanding coloring the word. "*Je vois.*" *I see.*

So he got it. I 'read' things when I touched them with my bare skin. Maybe he'd remember it and I'd actually get through a full year without some boy calling me '*Clit*-tilde.'

The bell rang.

Professor Trapp nodded at me. "*Enchanté, Mademoiselle. Asseyez-vous, s'il vous plaît,*" he said, issuing the customary 'pleased to meet you' and urging me to take my seat.

"*Oui, Monsieur.*" I started up the center aisle, aiming for the empty desk I'd spotted in the first row.

As my professor turned to write several French phrases on the white board, I wondered what kind of magic he possessed. It wasn't a requirement, but most of the staff at Coventry were gifted or cursed in some way. My guess was a werebear. A shifter's physique didn't always correspond with the size of his or her animal alter ego, but every werebear I'd ever met had tilted the scales in the height-weight department. Take Brad Perry—the guy was my age and already built like a professional defensive lineman.

As it happened, I didn't have to wonder about Professor Trapp's ability for long. All because I tripped.

One second, I was gazing at my French teacher's broad back and imagining what he'd look like as a grizzly bear, and the next, my feet tangled and I hurtled toward the floor, my arms instinctively flinging out in anticipation of the unavoidable impact. Milliseconds before I crashed to the linoleum, a gust of wind exploded beneath me, buffeting the full length of my body and cushioning my landing. Instead of smacking the ground with all the grace of a dead moose, I came to rest as easily as a falling leaf, the cold floor and my blossoming humiliation my sole discomforts.

The mysterious gale disappeared as quickly as it had manifested, but when I pushed to my elbows and peered through my disheveled hair, there was no mistaking where the violent gust had come from. Professor Trapp stood rigidly at the front of the classroom, his right hand thrust outward, the spectral glow of his eyes betraying the power of his recent expenditure. He was a sorcerer—one with the power to control air. Only a sorcerer could unleash a spell with a single gesture and no focusing object or vocalization.

I scrambled to my feet, too embarrassed to consider how I'd tripped. Cheeks burning something fierce, I scurried to the empty desk up front, sorry I hadn't taken a seat at the back of the class instead.

Amid everyone's fierce whispering, I slid my backpack to the floor next to me, being careful to avoid jostling Red, who was tucked inside his specially made pocket. Slouching in my chair, I wished I could disappear like Zach. Politeness dictated that I thank Professor Trapp for saving me from a painful fall, but my blazing embarrassment kept me silent. I'd catch him after class.

"You, what's your name?" Professor Trapp demanded. For a confusing and terrifying moment, I thought his stern question had been directed at me.

"A-a-amanda," my nemesis stammered.

"Take your things and report to Assistant Headmaster Gibbs, at once," he ordered.

"What?" she cried. "Why?"

"Don't play the innocent, *Mademoiselle.*"

Professor Trapp glared at Amanda, who stared back, wide-eyed, her face so devoid of color that her pale brows stood out in stark relief. She shook her head. "I d-don't know what you mean. I didn't do anything."

He thinks Amanda tripped me?

I glanced at the aisle. True ... I'd stumbled near her desk. Frowning, I replayed the mortifying scene in my head and wished I'd been paying more attention to walking and looking where I was going, instead of dwelling on Professor Trapp's impressive size. I had a vague memory of catching my toe, but it could have been the fault of clumsiness, not necessarily something Amanda had done.

"I'm a Council-ranked airmaster, Amanda, not a carnival magician," he snapped. "When you move, the air moves."

Council-ranked? *Holy cow.* That meant he'd been tested by the Arcane Council. Only the top five percent of magic users qualified for the rigorous examination and even fewer passed. He could run for a council seat if he wanted to.

"Gather your belongings and go." His tone said she had zero latitude before he'd physically remove her, but Amanda continued to shake her head.

What a moron. There were times I wanted to slap her. Most of the time, actually, so why I should stick my neck out for her, I had no idea.

Now who's lying?

Amanda's bottom lip trembled.

Stomach quailing, I straightened in my chair. "*Pardon, Monsieur. C'était de ma faute et pas de la sienne,*" I said, quickly explaining that it was my fault, not hers.

He turned his furious glare to me, and I had to keep myself from shrinking in my seat. "I am not in error, *Mademoiselle* Lire."

As a ranked sorcerer, that was undoubtedly true. "*Oh Monsieur, je suis sûre que vous n'avez jamais tort.*" Oh, sir, I'm sure you're never wrong.

I continued, speaking in rapid-fire French, hoping the faster I spoke, the less likely Amanda or any of the other students would understand what I was saying. Unfortunately, it also revealed my fluency, a fact I'd downplayed since freshman year for the easy 'A' on my report card.

"*Je peux vous expliquer tout plus tard, mais je vous prie de laisser tomber ça cette fois-ci,*" I said, telling him that I'd explain everything later, but to 'please let this go, just this time.'

Sucking in a breath, I added, "*Je sais que vous ne comprenez pas, mais je lui dois ça. Au moins pour une fois.*" I know you don't understand, but I owe her this. At least once. "*S'il vous plaît, Monsieur.*"

He stared at me for a long moment before raising his chin. "*Il est clair que vous n'avez pas réellement besoin de ces cours.*" It is clear to me you don't need this class.

Eyebrow arched, he went on, "*D'accord, je vais oublier cet incident. En échange, vous allez être mon assistante pendant ce cours.*" I will overlook this incident. In return, you will be my aide this period.

Shaking his head, he flicked his hand dismissively. "*Mademoiselle Amanda*, since technically no harm was done, your friend has convinced me to allow you to stay. Do not make me regret it."

He turned to his desk to retrieve a stack of paper and then divided the pages, handing a pile to each of the first-row students, allowing us to pass the paperwork down. "Now then, the syllabus ..."

I welcomed the boredom. After that crazy adrenaline rush, I craved the downtime to simply slump in my seat, clear my head, and unclench my trembling limbs.

I'd mostly relaxed by the end of class, but the pall of the final bell reminded me that I was moments away from speaking to Professor Trapp, presuming I didn't chicken out.

Jaw clenched, I took my time closing my binder and stuffing it into my backpack, as all the other students escaped the room to pursue their after-school activities. When I couldn't delay any longer, I forced myself to approach the sorcerer, who sat behind his desk, eyeing me expectantly.

"*Monsieur*, I, uh, wanted to say thank you for helping me ... you know, earlier," I mumbled.

He sighed, leaning back in his swivel chair. "You're lucky I was paying attention."

I nodded.

"She deliberately tried to hurt and humiliate you," he said, his eyes flashing, radiating disapproval. "Why did you cover for her? You're right, I don't get it. Please tell me it's not because you don't want to rock the boat."

"I don't give a crap about that." I looked down at my feet, which I tried not to shuffle. "Well, that's not completely true. She's been awful to me ever since the third grade, and I'm sick of it."

Sticking the tips of my fingers into my front pockets, I met his steady gaze. "I made the mistake of using my power and tattled on her when I discovered she'd carved graffiti in the library bathroom. I was a stupid little kid, and I'd read a few too many *Nancy Drew* books." I shrugged. "After seven years, I figure this'll make us even. I got her in trouble, once, and, now, I've kept her out of it."

Shifting on my feet, I shook my head. "I don't know. It's dumb. After this long, it probably won't matter anyway. My *gift* makes people do weird things." I wiggled my fingers in the air.

"I know." He sounded tired but certain.

"You do?"

He nodded. "My best friend in school" — his breath caught and I might have missed it, if not for the momentary tightening of his mouth — "was a clairvoyant."

I puzzled over the inflection he'd placed on the final three words. Either they'd drifted apart or his friend was no longer a clairvoyant, which meant one thing since a psychic power wasn't something you could banish.

He stood and pulled out the top drawer of his metal desk. Unlike most of my teachers, he didn't have any personal items on display, not so much as a family photograph. Of course, this was his first day teaching at Coventry.

I watched him closely, working to decipher his expression. "*Was?*"

He nodded brusquely. "She died while we were in high school."

There wasn't much in his drawer. He extracted a set of keys and his cell phone, both of which he tossed onto the desk's laminate top. He leaned down to retrieve his black leather briefcase from the floor and began jerkily loading items into its various pockets. "Where did you learn French? Your accent is quite good."

I blinked at him, speechless, still tripping about his friend. The leading cause of death for clairvoyants, especially ones in their teens, was suicide — a fact that threatened to dredge up some very dark memories of my own.

Maybe I was jumping to conclusions. More than likely, she'd died from an illness or an accident. I wondered whether the two of them had gone to school here at Coventry. I examined Professor Trapp. Not a trace of gray in his dark hair and the skin above his beard was smooth, so he was a lot younger than Dad. Maybe late twenties? Coventry had been around for twenty-two years. I did the mental math. It was possible he'd been a student.

He looked up from his briefcase, his left brow arching upward, waiting for my answer.

I shook myself. "Oh, um, my dad was born in Amiens. My *grand-père* moved the family to the states when Dad was twelve."

"How's your written French?"

"Not very good," I admitted, wondering how I could steer the conversation back to the subject of his friend. Straight-out asking whether she'd killed herself didn't seem the best way to go about it.

"Then that's what we'll focus on. And, as classwork gets turned in, you'll help with grading papers. Starting tomorrow, you'll sit here." He gestured at his chair.

I started, and my eyes must have gone as wide as ping-pong balls because he frowned and asked, "Is that a problem?"

He sounded ... offended? My eyes grew larger with that impossible thought, which, if anything, seemed to annoy him because his frown deepened.

"Um, not a problem, no," I blurted, waving my open palms at him. "Not for *me*, anyway. It's just that, well ... even the teachers who *don't* make me sit at the back of the class would rather burn their desks than allow me to sit at them. Which is stupid, since my uniform covers practically every inch of me. And everyone knows that objects don't convey psychic imprints to other objects, so it's not like I can get all their juicy secrets from the seat of my pants or something."

Instead of making things better, my rambling explanation did the opposite.

"You have teachers who force you to sit at the back of the class?" His voice rose in volume until the last word ended in barely contained outrage.

'Neverhart' almost popped out of my mouth, but I clamped my teeth together.

"N-n-no. Forget it. Tomorrow, your desk. Got it." I backed away and then scurried for the door, trying not to trip in my haste. "See you tomorrow."

I fled before he could interrogate me. The last thing I needed was Professor Trapp making waves with my teachers.

For the entire walk back to my dorm, I couldn't stop thinking about my professor's best friend and the way his breath had caught when he'd mentioned her. For once, if people flinched out of my way as I hurried down the various paths and hallways, I didn't notice.

"I get that it's none of my business, but I want to know what happened to her," I told Red once we'd gotten back to my room and established that he'd overheard my conversation with Professor Trapp. I bounced onto my bed, crossing my legs to sit kindergarten style. "I bet it's because they were friends that he's not afraid of me. That's why he didn't think twice about telling me to sit at his desk."

"It is plausible. When it comes to magic, it is *rarity*, not familiarity, that breeds contempt. As to the circumstances of her death, perhaps you would do well to allow the truth to emerge on its own, instead of digging where your nose is not wanted."

I made a face. "Then I'll never find out. Teachers don't volunteer personal things like that to their students."

"A statement that illustrates my point rather succinctly, I should say."

Flopping back against my pillows, I folded my arms and mumbled, "Whatever."

Maybe there was a way to find out, without having to come out and ask. If she'd died here, while she and Professor Trapp had been in school, there might be a record of it in the *Coventry Courier*, the town's local paper. Did they have back issues in the public library? I nibbled my lip, thinking, and realized I was getting ahead of myself. First, I needed to find out where Professor Trapp had gone to high school.

"I know that look," Red said. "Why do you wish to know so badly?" He moved to the edge of my desk and sat. His pudgy legs dangled over the side as he studied me. "Are you curious simply because she was a clairvoyant? Or are you, perhaps, wondering whether she was a kindred soul, due to your own brush with death?"

I should have known Red would bring it up. How could he not? Memories of that horrible day, the day I'd nearly ended everything, had snagged my thoughts at the first sight of Professor Trapp's pained expression, its barbed hooks sinking deeper at the mention of his teenaged friend's death. It brought me back to a place and time I didn't enjoy revisiting.

"I don't know." I tightened my arms, hugging myself. "That is ... yes, it's made me wonder about her. I can't help but think — " Frowning down at my damask duvet, I blew out a breath. "I mean, if she did it, if she did what we're thinking — I can't help wondering if she might have stopped, if only she'd had someone like you."

Someone begging her not to take that step, not to jump off that cliff ...

No, Lire! This is not how it is meant to be! You are here for a reason, just as I died and my soul was cast about for over three hundred years —for a reason. You were that reason! Your father was meant to find me, just as I was meant to be here with you. We are both on this earth for a purpose, and God did not grant you life just so you could throw it away ... I love you, Lire. Step back. Please.

Maybe she'd have realized that there was something worth living for.

I looked up to take in Red's fuzzy face — his black button eyes, embroidered nose, and softly rounded ears, blurred by my tears and comforting in its familiarity. But it was the soul bound to the stuffed bear, with his unwavering kindness and forthright personality, who I'd truly come to cherish. John Redborn, nearest thing to a big brother as I'd ever know and the perfect companion for a social outcast like me.

"I love you, Red."

"Oh, my dear girl, you know I love you too."

CHAPTER 4

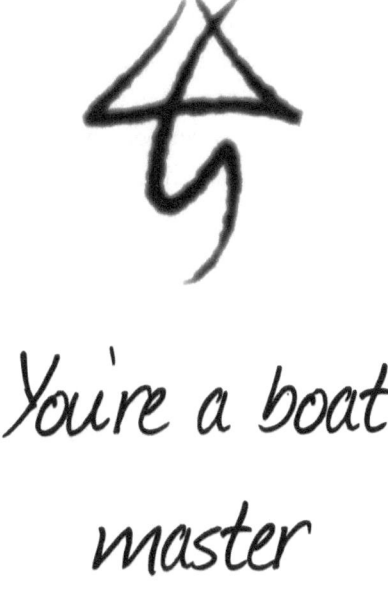

You're a boat master

DINNER for upperclassmen started at six. I left my room ten minutes late, but if it hadn't been for Zach's whispered promise to save me a seat, I might have opted for Cup Noodles. Even then, I hovered indecisively at my door for an embarrassing length of time, with my hand on the knob and Red safely zipped inside my cross-body bag, before I found the nerve to go out.

The remembered warmth of the afternoon radiated from the concrete walkway as I trudged to the refectory. Behind me, the setting sun filtered through the dogwood trees, painting everything in my path with dappled apricot-tinged striations that shifted playfully in the early evening breeze. This would be a decent night for a run.

I joined the juniors and seniors already in the chow line and tried to overlook the obvious nudges and furtive whispers at my arrival. Interestingly, though, instead of giving me a wide berth and then ignoring me, Ted Mason turned to consider me.

He jerked his chin upward, giving me that 'hey how's it going?' greeting that guys liked to do. He probably thought it made him look cool. Honestly, it did, and it was so unexpected that I glanced over my shoulder to see if he'd aimed it at someone else.

The two senior girls who stood a safe distance behind me in line whispered to one another, casting surreptitious glances my way. If Ted had directed the greeting at them, they sure weren't acting like it.

I think my discombobulation amused the sandy-haired werelion because he smiled at me before turning to put his tray on the stainless-steel serving line. Even Jason Vandermeir, his roommate and fellow basketball player, had looked at me thoughtfully, instead of scowling at our proximity.

Okay, that was ... different.

Not surprisingly, the dining room bustled with students, nearly every table packed and the room buzzing with conversation. As I scanned the tables for Cal, my hunger fled. What if Cal and Zach weren't here?

I spotted Cal's shaggy head at the far end of the room, at the same table where we'd eaten lunch. Shannon, a geomancer with short blonde hair and an annoying laugh, had taken my prior seat. Across from her, her roommate, Darla, perched next to Zach—or, rather, where I *suspected* Zach sat. Since he was invisible, who the heck knew?

I wanted to kick myself. *Of course* other girls would want to sit with Cal. How could I have not anticipated that? He was good looking in a rugged yet thoughtful way that made him seem dangerous and safe at the same time—the bad boy with a brain. Plus, he had stunning eyes and a killer body. He'd have a troop of girls going gaga over him in no time. I'd be lucky to sit at his table ever again.

As I stood there looking stupid, the voices around me seemed to get louder while heat rushed to my neck and cheeks. I distinctly heard my name mentioned in conversation, somewhere close.

Before I could abandon my tray in the dirty dish bay and flee, Cal leaned back to peer around the girl seated next to him. As soon as he saw me, he waved, beckoning me to their table.

With the two girls taking up space, there wasn't a spot for me. Why Cal aimed a puzzled, 'what are you waiting for?' look in my direction,

I couldn't imagine. What did he expect me to do when I got there, sit on his lap?

To my surprise, Cal was busy glowering at Shannon as I approached. "You need to move."

Darla said something I couldn't hear, and Cal all but growled at her, "I told you we were saving a seat. She's here. You need to go back to your table."

"Always good to chitchat, homies," Zach said as the two girls unfolded themselves from the bench. "I'll catch ya both later, you hear?"

Thanks to his flirtatious purr, both girls were smiling and looking smug as they walked away with their trays.

Zach was definitely the charmer.

"Sorry about that, princess. Dub-dub over there is just too sexy for his own good. Girls can't stand to see him sitting alone."

"Shuddup," Cal grumbled.

I took the now vacated seat next to Cal. "Thanks for saving me a spot."

"No problemo," Zach replied. "Besides, you're the girl of the hour. Everyone's talking about how you took on a Council-ranked sorcerer to keep Amanda from being expelled. I wanna hear all about it."

I nearly choked on my cheese soufflé. No wonder the whispering and sidelong looks had seemed excessive, tonight. And it sure explained Ted and Jason's weird behavior in the chow line.

"It's not like I fought a duel for her. And anyway, she wouldn't have been expelled."

"Don't be so sure," Zach said. "Your French prof is our anti-bullying official. That'll be one of the big announcements at tonight's all-school assembly. You've heard about the joint coalition and their crusade, right?"

I nodded. Over the summer, Dad and I received the flyer in the mail announcing the anti-bullying effort. After the Arcane Council President's thirteen-year-old son committed suicide, early last year, a CNN investigation revealed that magically inclined teenagers had a suicide rate twelve times that of the national average. So, it wasn't much of a surprise to learn that the major players in the magic community—the Arcane Council, the Paranormal Regulatory Commission, and the North American Rout, to name a few—had formed a coalition to investigate and do something about it. Their biggest initiative, so far, was their program to crack down on bullying within the magic community's private schools and the government's reservations. Not a small task, if you asked me.

Zach continued, "I've heard Professor Trapp has a soft spot for clairvoyants."

Frowning, I speared a green bean with my fork. "Any idea why?"

"His best friend in high school was a clairvoyant."

I nodded. "He mentioned that when we were talking after class." I refrained from adding that she'd died while they were in school. "How'd you hear about it?"

"I know where to listen," Zach said. "Speaking of which, spill it, sister. Did you really stand up to Professor Trapp? What happened? Did you know he's an airmaster?"

"Not until later, and I didn't stand up to him. I *talked* to him. I butted in where I shouldn't have, if you want to get technical about it."

"And everyone and his dog wants to know why, including me." Zach huffed. "Start at the beginning. You showed up for class and then what happened?"

"What are you, the class detective?"

"Worse," Cal said dryly. "He's the king of gossip."

"What can I say? It's in my genetic makeup," Zach retorted. "Come on, Lire. You're killing me."

I smirked, making him wait while I ate a bite of my soufflé. "There's not much to tell," I said, but while I continued to eat, I described everything that happened—minus my after-class discussion with Professor Trapp. The whole school would know about my swan dive soon enough anyway. After all, there'd been something like eighteen other kids in that room.

"So Jason wasn't exaggerating," Zach said. "You're a ringer in French class, aren't you? Nobody knows what you said and the whole school is buzzing about it."

"Jason?" I leaned forward. "You mean Jason Vandermeir?"

"Yep. He was sitting behind Amanda. Like everyone else, he couldn't understand a word of what you were saying. According to him, you sounded like a French exchange student. He thinks you're totally hot, by the way, but wouldn't go near you if someone paid him. The guy's an asshole."

I flinched. Until that moment, I'd never really appreciated the term 'backhanded compliment.'

"Did he see Amanda do it?" Cal asked. "Did he see her trip Lire?"

"Oh, yeah. She did it, all right. What everyone's speculating about, though, is why Lire bothered to get her off the hook. The whole school knows she's had it out for you, Lire, like since *forever.* You wouldn't believe how many people are talking about it. Even a couple of the teachers. Why'd you help her?"

I sighed. "Because I'm an idiot."

"She's had it out for you?" Cal frowned at me. "Why?"

Zach jumped in and relayed the whole girl-detective-discovers-bathroom-vandal backstory while I stared in astonishment.

"Dude, you scare me," I said half-jokingly. "School's been in session for, like, a day, and you know everything."

"It's the family business, princess. It'd be embarrassing if I didn't."

Did that mean the rumors were true? Supposedly, occultums were born into a family whose members were in bed with governments and big businesses, using their skills for spying and espionage. Not that this surprised me in the least, but it was one thing hearing the rumor in terms of an urban legend, quite another to get it direct from the horse's mouth.

"Jesus." Cal practically exhaled the word. "You went up against an airmaster for a stone-cold bitch who's done nothing but call you 'snitch' for the past seven years?" He shook his head. "I'm surprised you didn't sprinkle freaking rose petals on her path out the door."

"I probably should have."

"Then why'd you help her?" Although Zach's gaze was invisible, I felt its sharpness, a prickling sensation along my face and neck that had me shifting in my seat.

"I don't know. I figured it was a way to even the score. It was impulsive. And it looked like she was ready to cry." I groaned. "Like I said, I'm an idiot."

"You won't hear an argument from me," Cal said. "I'd have beaten the shit out of her a long time ago — or stuffed her into a closet or something, since she's a girl."

"And then gotten expelled," Zach put in.

The werewolf blew air over his teeth dismissively. "Been there, done that."

I gaped at him. "You've been expelled?"

"Princess, if I'm the gossip king, then the guy next to you is the detention master. Why'd you think he was home schooled? If it weren't for the Rout's Isangrim and my dad pulling strings, anime-boy wouldn't be here now, scowling at me like a rabid dingo."

"Shut it, Zach," Cal snarled, and, honest-to-goodness, his threatening voice vibrated our shared bench.

"Hey, you're the one who brought it up," Zach said, unfazed. "Besides, everyone knows girls can't resist a bad boy. How 'bout it, princess? Am I right?"

My stomach tried to dip down to my toes, but I ruthlessly got a hold of myself before my inevitable blush.

Don't get worked up, bonehead. He's asking because your magic makes you safe, like asking a nun.

I sipped from my water bottle, hoping to seem casual. "I guess it depends."

"On what? Do tell," Zach drawled, clearly enjoying himself.

"There's bad and then there's no good. A little bad is exciting — nasty and abusive isn't." I shrugged as if, until now, I hadn't given the question any thought, not because I'd read far too many romance novels. "Girls who like that kinda thing want the bad boy with the heart of gold, not an asshole. The problem is that a lot of girls can't tell the difference."

"Girls who like that kinda of thing, huh?" Zach parroted. "Meaning ... you're not one of them? You like the straight-laced, choir-boy type instead?"

For some reason, the whole conversation, not to mention his sardonic tone, had gotten my back up.

"No. *Meaning* — none of it matters because I'm a clairvoyant," I snapped. "You couldn't *pay* guys enough to come near me, remember?"

Skin contact was a no-go, unless I wanted to be overwhelmed by my partner's every stray thought. And it begged the question that had plagued me ever since I started noticing boys. What hot-blooded guy in their right mind would want to wear a full-body skin-suit and face shield every time they wanted to make out with me?

The idea was ridiculous.

If it weren't for my telepathic friend, Daniel, I'd still be waiting for my first kiss. But, let's get real, that peck on the lips behind the library stairwell over three years ago was kid stuff. I still awaited my first *real* kiss — one with the slide of tongues, like those described so captivatingly in my romance novels. God knew how long I'd be waiting for *that* to happen, especially since Daniel wasn't around anymore. His parents had pulled him out of school, without warning or giving him a chance to say goodbye, not long after we'd shared that kiss. The day I learned he was gone for good had been the worst day of my life. I still missed him.

Turning my mind from the dark memories, I pushed food around on my plate while trying not to cringe at the growing silence.

Idiot. You couldn't have kept your mouth shut?

"Guys are dicks," Cal announced.

"You won't hear an argument from me," I shot back, snickering.

"So what the hell is up with Everhart?" he asked a moment later, and I could have hugged him for alleviating any residual awkwardness. "What's with those creepy desks and printing off separate copies of stuff for you?"

"Who knows? The woman's crazy," I said. "I had her last year."

"We should transfer out," Zach said.

I shook my head. "Can't. She's the only English Comp teacher for our level."

Zach cursed.

"Be grateful she doesn't teach Twentieth-Century Lit," I told him. "Otherwise we'd be stuck with her next year, too."

"You dealt with this, all last year?" Cal asked.

I nodded.

"And ... what's his name, the assistant headmaster?" Cal's thick brows dipped down as he tried to think of it. "Gibbs. He saw nothing wrong with it?"

I shrugged.

"You didn't report her, did you?" Zach said, sounding all kinds of disappointed.

"It wouldn't have mattered." I huffed. "Just like this year, she was the only instructor teaching the class. Complaining would have made things worse."

Zach grunted. "You're a boat master."

"A boat master? What—?"

"Don't listen to him," Cal interrupted. "He's being an ass."

"You think, if you don't rock the boat, they'll accept you," Zach said. "But they won't. They'll just walk all over you and expect a fucking 'thank you' for the privilege."

Funny that he used the same analogy as Professor Trapp. I wanted to rant, to argue, to insist that he had it all wrong. I wasn't a doormat, like he assumed. But my bottled emotions—all the frustrations and worries and intense loneliness brought about by my gift's endless trials—surged through me so completely that I couldn't trust myself to open my mouth without screaming or crying, or both.

Body clenched and on the verge of detonation, I rocketed to my feet, turned on my heel, and strode for the exit, realizing later that I'd left my tray, un-bussed, for the first time, ever.

As I stormed away, I heard Cal hiss, "Nice going, dickhead."

I guess that was something, but I couldn't help thinking I'd proved Zach right by running away.

In no mood to sit around and sulk, I stomped back to my dorm room and beelined straight to my bathroom to change into running tights, my favorite sports bra, and Cat Bus t-shirt. My getup looked ridiculous with the elbow-length gloves, but I didn't give a crap.

The all-school assembly was at seven-thirty. Just enough time to fit in a forty-minute run. Who cared if I showed up for the announcements all sweaty? I'd stand at the back of the auditorium, per usual. No one wanted to sit next to me anyway.

"You staying or going, Red?" I called out as I tossed my dirty uniform into my hamper.

Even though Red had never once refused to tag along, I felt better giving him the choice.

"I would accompany you, if it is not too much trouble."

I donned my large fanny pack, leaving the main compartment un-zipped so Red could hop inside while I perched on the bed and smoothed my long hair into a high ponytail.

I avoided picking him up whenever possible. Red was my magically-bound familiar, not a toy. He already rode around in my various packs and purses like a teacup Chihuahua. I didn't need to make it worse by manhandling him.

The sun had dipped below the western hills, the very tops of the trees to the north still painted with orange sunlight, when I barged up to the quarter-mile-long track's entrance and found it chained shut. Apparently, Hugh, the custodian in charge of facilities, hadn't yet unlocked the gate after summer vacation.

Inside the chain-link fence's massive enclosure, the track's new rubberized surface fairly gleamed, its lanes looking crisp with their freshly painted reflective lines and numbers. The sports field inside the oval had been seeded sometime during the summer break. Its lush green carpet begged for a lazy roll followed by sky gazing.

A pristine track with nobody around to give me sour glares? *Yes, please. Sign me up.*

Ignoring the locked gate, I made quick work of toeing myself up and over the five-foot fence. I landed on the soft grass that bordered the entire area.

A few hamstring stretches later, I bounded onto the third lane, starting with an easy-going warmup lap before lengthening my strides, pounding the day's frustrations into the forgiving bounce of the track's innovative surface.

I thought about Zach. Was he right about me? Had I done the wrong thing, deciding to endure Neverhart's repulsive behavior? Because, that's what it was; there was no other word to describe her conduct. With her 'thoughtful' treatment, she singled me out, reminding me and everyone else that I had an alarming gift. It was hurtful and demeaning, and I hated it.

Would she even dare to do the same thing to a student who had dyslexia or some other learning challenge? Put them in a specially labeled desk, print all their schoolwork on brightly colored paper, and make them parade in front of the class because of their difficulties? No way. She'd be reprimanded for doing such insensitive, humiliating things. So why was it okay to do it to me?

I nearly stopped dead on the track.

Duh. It wasn't.

I'd never thought of it like that before, and the comparison reverberated through me, a thunderclap on a clear September night.

After my first mile, I rotated my fanny pack to the front to glance down at Red. He lounged inside the black pouch, like a hammock, and stared up at the twilight sky, his stout little arms folded behind his head.

"Red? Do you think I made a mistake not telling Dad or Mr. Gibbs about Neverhart?"

"Labeling your decision a *mistake*, serves little purpose. It was a decision you made based upon the situation and your feelings at the time," he said in his brisk, formal manner. "Circumstances have changed, therefore it is wise to evaluate and consider your decision anew."

"Circumstances? You mean the busybody, otherwise known as Zach Carter? So far, he's more like a thorn in my side."

"Nevertheless, he and Cal are a source of support—perhaps not a fully trusted one, but a connection nonetheless. You are not alone in this brand of persecution. And do not discount the importance of Professor Trapp's concern for you, nor his apparent role on campus."

"I was stupid, though. Zach's right. I didn't complain because I didn't want to rock the boat, even though I've hated every minute in her class. I'm going to speak with Mr. Gibbs in the morning, whether or not Zach decides to complain too."

"You have my full support and, I am certain, your father's as well. You will never be alone, dearest, no matter what happens."

Jogging down the western length of the unlit track, I finally took more than a passing notice of my shadowed surroundings. The gymnasium, with its small windows and sturdy architecture, loomed off to my right. In the far distance, the windows of MSC—the math, science, and computing building—remained lit as the few night instructors prepared for their vampire dominated classes.

Strigoi, I reminded myself. Dad told me often enough that they didn't like being called vampires, but it was a hard habit to break.

Now that the sun had sunk below the horizon, I wondered if the strigoi were showering and getting ready for their evening classes, just like I did each morning. Would they go to the assembly with the rest of us? This was the first time Mr. Simmons had scheduled an evening start-of-year assembly. Part of me thrilled at the idea of seeing the vampires studded throughout the auditorium like black diamonds sprinkled through a tray of mundane beads. Of course, if the strigoi were anything like my clique-happy classmates, they'd all end up sitting together. Strength in numbers, right?

I wondered what it would be like to be a part of something like that, to know I belonged to a group of powerful friends who'd back me up without question.

No wonder so many teenagers accepted the strigoi curse, I thought bitterly.

Rounding the first turn of my final lap, I glanced up at the northern horizon. The moon hadn't yet risen, and I wondered where it was in its cycle. Not full, otherwise Cal would have started school sequestered at the shifters' compound, safe to roam their secure preserve with the rest of the were-predators.

As I neared the track's far end, a cracking sound and movement inside the forest's edge drew my attention to odd lights twinkling from within the dark undergrowth. One, two … I looked around for more. They might have reminded me of lightning bugs if not for their equidistant, steady appearance.

I almost tripped as fear spiked through me, an icy-sharp jolt stealing my breath.

Those weren't lightning bugs. They were a pair of eyes. Judging by their spacing and distance from the ground, they belonged to something large.

I slowed my pace until I was practically jogging in place. "Red," I croaked. "Something's watching me from the bushes, and it's no rabbit."

All at once, the distance between the track and a populated area loomed large at my back. I hadn't passed anyone on the way here. Nobody in the entire freaking school knew where I was.

The bushes moved, and I didn't need another invitation to get the heck out of Dodge.

"Hang on!" I executed a tight U-turn and sprinted away as fast as my legs would carry me. I rotated my fanny pack to the small of my back as I listened over the sound of my breaths for something big jumping the fence.

"See ... anything?" I forced out.

My legs felt leaden, but adrenaline had me trammeling down the track like a wounded deer evading a ravenous two-hundred-pound mountain lion, which, I knew for absolute fact, inhabited Northern Washington.

"No," Red replied, but as I tore down the lane, a strange cry pierced the air, followed by something that sounded a lot like a frustrated snarl.

Puma P. concolor—cougar, mountain lion, panther, catamount, screamer—it held the Guinness record for the animal with the most number of names, over forty in English alone. They were ambush predators that liked to lurk in dense underbrush, stalking their prey, and had the largest hind legs, proportional to their body, of all the big cats. Perfect for leaping over a measly five-foot-tall chain-link fence and running down ungainly prey in a short sprint on a conveniently rubberized surface.

I'd done a sixth-grade written report on the North American cougar. Right now, more than ever, I could have strangled Professor Rosenberg for assigning it. I would have been much happier not re-membering these things.

I bounded onto the grass at the track entrance, vaulting over the fence in nothing flat, only to plow headlong into a firm, warm body when I dared to glance behind me for signs of pursuit.

A masculine grunt and my own "umph" mingled in my ears as I spun and then sprawled onto the pavement.

"Jesus Christ!" a familiar voice exclaimed. "Lire, what the hell?"

Hands stinging from breaking my fall, I rolled to my butt to find Cal standing over me.

"What the hell is *that*?" he cried, staggering backward, his face twisted into a horrified mask.

I snapped my frightened gaze to my right, expecting to confront a snarling cougar. When I spotted nothing more than Red, I sagged with relief.

"God! You scared the crap out of me!" I exclaimed, panting faster than a frightened rabbit. "That's Red, my familiar. Jeez Louise. First a wild animal and now you," I blurted, pressing my hand over my heart. "All I wanted was a relaxing run. I'll be lucky not to end up dead from a heart attack."

"Th-that's a ... a ... *teddy bear*?" His voice and expression of fright transformed into one of such intense astonishment that I cracked up despite my bruised palms and scraped knee. Fortunately, my skin hadn't been in contact with the ground long enough to glean any unpleasant memories, presumably because not many people went around barefoot.

"Darn it. These were my favorite running tights." I pouted, plucking at the torn spandex. Of course, better a small hole than clawed to shreds by a single-minded carnivore.

Before Cal could sputter anything else, I introduced him to Red, who must have been knocked from my fanny pack when I fell. "Cal, this is my familiar, Red. Don't get too close or you'll run into his repulsion spell again. Zach, you here too?"

"A pleasure to meet you, Cal," Red said as he jumped into my lap and scrambled onto my shoulder. "Lire, how are you? Merely a scrape? Are you okay to stand?"

"Yeah. I'll live." I massaged my aching palms, thankful my gloves had saved them from being a scraped disaster. This was one time when wearing them had come in handy.

'Handy.' Good one, brain.

"You have a stuffed animal for a familiar?" Cal blinked down at me, still standing about six feet away and looking about as perplexed as a person could get. "You're not even a witch."

"You don't have to be. Duh. It's just not very common. And for your information, he's not a toy. He's a three-hundred-year-old necromancer and my best friend, so mind your manners."

His face wrinkled up. "You live in a dorm room with some creepy old dude watching you get naked every day?"

I gasped, my mouth hanging open while I floundered for words. "Gross!" I finally burst out. "What's the matter with you? Don't you know anything? He's not human anymore. And, for your information, I have my own private bathroom. I don't get dressed in front of him, you perv. God!"

Startled by my outburst, he threw up his hands. "Okay. Christ! Give me a break, would you? I haven't met any familiars. And I sure haven't heard of ones that used to be human and are now a frickin' teddy bear."

I glared at him as I wobbled to my feet. "My dad gave him to me before starting kindergarten. I was little. A teddy bear makes perfect sense."

He took a deep breath and blew it out as he paced back and forth a few times. "Okay. I guess I can see that. And you said he has a re-pulsion spell. That's why, a second ago, he looked so—" He shuddered, grimacing at the memory.

"Horrifying. Yes. His body is psi-free. The defensive spells make sure he stays that way."

"That makes sense." He raked his fingers through his hair. "So … Red? You know, sorry about what I said and stuff. Um, no hard feel-ings, I hope."

"Not at all," Red replied. "Your apology is most humbly accepted. I might ask, however, that you keep your knowledge of my existence to yourself. There are those who would cause Lire trouble at learning of me, as your own reaction might illustrate."

"Uh, yeah, sure," Cal said, still looking somewhat bewildered.

"Where's Zach?" I asked.

"Back at the room."

"Oh." I realized this was the first time I'd talked to him without Zach in tow, which was probably a good thing, considering what had just happened. "What are you doing here?"

"I, uh … I heard they re-did the track. I wanted to check it out." He looked me over, raising his eyebrows skeptically. "You usually run without watching where you're going?"

I made a face at him. "There was something in the woods stalking me, something big." I shivered. "I spotted its glowing eyes through the bushes. I kid you not, it was like being in a horror movie." I crossed my arms, absently rubbing away my goosebumps. "I could only think, 'Hello! Mountain lion.' I've never run so darn fast in my life. I think I broke a speed record."

"Did you see it?" He took a step toward the track's entrance, tilting his chin up and scanning the area beyond the gate. I could swear he sniffed the air too.

"No," I admitted. "But I'm sure not going back for a second try. Red, what about you?"

"Something moved inside the tree line, but it never broke cover," he replied. "There was a bark or cry of sorts, a snarl, and then it ventured elsewhere."

"God," I groaned, bending down to rub my knee. "I am never running the track after dinner, ever again."

"Next time, call me and I'll go with you," Cal said.

"Terrific. Then we can both get eaten. I am *so* getting a can of bear spray." I huffed. "That was ridiculous. Not to mention painful."

I checked my watch. "Crud. The assembly starts in ten minutes. No time to change." I unclipped my fanny pack and held it out so Red could jump inside. Since we were going to be around people soon, I asked Red to tuck down and zipped him in. "Do we need to swing by and pick up Zach?"

"Yeah."

As we headed in the direction of the dorms, Cal glanced over at me. "So, uh ... I guess you're not mad at Zach?"

I shook my head and then shrugged. "Not anymore, anyway."

"Zach can be an ass sometimes," Cal said, looking at the ground, his hands in his pockets.

"He wasn't wrong, though. I'm gonna see Mr. Gibbs, tomorrow morning, about Neverhart. What she's doing is wrong. I should have said something a long time ago."

"Yeah?" From the corner of my eye, I saw him look over at me. "You shouldn't let Zach bully you into it, though. Only do it if you want to."

"He wasn't bullying me. He was just ... being brutally honest. Anyway, things are different this year, you know, with Professor Trapp and stuff."

"Neverhart." He snorted. "That's good."

"Yeah. I'm kinda proud of that."

He laughed.

We passed the far side of MSC and turned down the path that led to Stewart House, the men's dormitory.

"I like your shirt," Cal said, breaking our companionable silence.

"Thanks. I have a Cat Bus plushy, too, that's super cute."

Not to mention a *My Neighbor Totoro* pencil pouch, soot sprite key-chain, plus a *Kiki's Delivery Service* wall hanging, but I kept those dorky details to myself.

I stopped at the small path leading up to their dorm. "I guess I'll wait here for you guys."

He frowned, face tilted upward, looking toward the entrance. He drew in several short breaths before turning to me with a strangely unfocused expression.

"No need." Zach's voice came next to my ear.

I jumped a flipping mile.

"Shit, Zach!" I pressed my hand to my chest. "Would you stop doing that? Like I haven't had enough heart attacks for one night. Holy crap."

"Aww," he drawled, not sounding sorry in the least. "Did the big bad wolf scare the princess once already tonight? You look suspiciously rumpled, Lire. What *have* you two been doing?"

"Oh, nothing much, just running from a damn mountain lion," I retorted, probably blushing crimson at his insinuation.

"The both of you?"

"No—only me," I said, wondering at his snap into seriousness. "Actually, I'm not sure what it was. I noticed eyes glinting from the forest. It freaked the hell out of me, so I took off."

"Cal?"

Cal shrugged. "Caught a whiff of something dead, that's about all."

"Damn, princess. What were you thinking, running around after dark near the edge of a nature preserve? That's like waving a juicy steak in front of a hungry wolf. Ask dub-dub. He'll tell you. Sweet little morsel like you? Mountain lion would snap you up in one bite."

I rolled my eyes. "Shut up."

"Don't believe me?" He whispered in my ear, "Then I guess it's a good thing wolf boy went looking for you, huh?" He gave my ponytail a tug.

I gasped and jerked back. I couldn't help it. Nobody, I mean *nobody*, touched me. "You ... you touched my *hair*!" I sputtered. "What's the matter with you? It's not like I can throw away my hair like some old t-shirt, you know!"

Freaking great! Whenever I touched those strands with my bare skin, I'd be stuck with experiencing whatever he'd been thinking the moment he grabbed my ponytail.

I let out an annoyed growl. My hair had finally reached my shoulder blades after a year and a half of growing it out. *Darn it!* I refused to cut it. Of course, part of me (the idiotic part) thrilled at the idea of knowing what he'd been thinking. Had Cal really searched the school for me?

"For shit's sake! Would you relax? I'm wearing gloves," Zach said, his voice rising to quell my freak out. "I'm not an idiot."

He couldn't touch my skin, unless his gloves were psi-free, but my hair or clothes were a different story. Those things weren't alive. Objects couldn't transfer their psychic energy to other objects, so my hair was safe.

"Thank God," I blurted. I massaged my temples and muttered, "Jeez. Way too much excitement for one night."

Zach deepened his voice. "If pulling on your hair gets you that excited, there are *other* things I'd be happy to—"

"Shut it, Zach!" Cal snarled, cutting off what was sure to be a lewd comment.

"Just trying to be helpful." Zach snickered. "Come on. We don't want our princess, here, to miss the assembly."

Our ...

My heart fluttered, and I immediately wanted to kick myself for it. I wasn't a damsel in distress. I could take care of myself.

But, I had to admit, it sure was nice having two guys watching out for me.

When we tiptoed into the auditorium, our headmaster, Mr. Simmons, stood on the wide stage, microphone in hand, introducing the school's newest faculty members. He wore his usual three-piece suit, this one a tan tweed that set off his mahogany skin, complete with suede arm patches, navy tie, and matching pocket hankie.

As he smiled and spoke about our newest history professor, it was hard to imagine Mr. Simmons as anything but cheerful. He had large brown eyes and a kind face that appeared youthful, even with his smattering of gray hair and peek-a-boo laugh lines.

Thankfully, his deep, amplified voice covered the sounds of our late arrival, and I scurried to the shadowed back corner of the theater without attracting any undue attention.

Cal looked puzzled and leaned over to whisper, "There are seats right there."

Sure enough, there were four empty seats in the back row on this side of the main aisle, but they were in the middle, surrounded by students. No matter which side of the row I chose to enter, I'd have to scoot past five people to get there and I knew what would happen if I tried.

"I feel like standing," I whispered back. "Go sit if you want to."

He gave me a funny look, but stayed where he was. Zach must have said something because he turned and whispered to the air at his left.

On stage, Mr. Simmons leaned back on his heels, peering out at the audience, his broad features settling into an authoritative expression. "This year, as many of you know, the joint coalition has resolved to end bullying in our schools. Joining us this year to help Assistant Headmaster Gibbs with implementing that program here at Coventry Academy is our new French instructor, Professor Trapp."

He turned toward the left half of the stage where the instructors sat in three neat rows. While the audience clapped, Professor Trapp stood and issued a cursory wave.

"In addition to teaching French, Professor Trapp will also be coaching our varsity men's soccer team." More than a few rowdy hoots echoed through the theater, no doubt from the team's players, and Mr. Simmons patted the air in the universal 'settle down' motion. "When he isn't teaching or coaching, Professor Trapp will be available in his office alongside our other terrific counselors in the administration building. You'll find his direct line in the faculty directory. I urge you to contact him or Assistant Headmaster Gibbs, if you or anyone you know isn't being treated with the respect that is expected of all our students and staff."

Mr. Simmons tucked his free hand under his opposite arm, clearing his throat before returning the sleek black microphone to his lips. "Now then, a few important announcements and then I'll let you get back to your dormitories. Let me remind you, as I do every year, that Coventry Academy is a closed campus. No student may leave school grounds without express permission. As upperclassmen, juniors and seniors are allowed more latitude and may leave campus for work experience and on Fridays, Saturdays, and Sundays, but all work schedules and weekend excursions must have parental approval and be logged by the main office — no exceptions.

"Now ... curfews. You'll be pleased to hear that Coventry Academy's board of regents has extended the lowerclassmen's curfew by thirty minutes." Several whistles and hoots echoed through the room but Mr. Simmons plowed ahead, his resonant voice overriding them. "This year all seventh through tenth grade students must now be in their dormitories by 9:00 p.m. and lights out no later than 10:00. The curfew for our juniors and seniors remains unchanged at 10:00 p.m. in dorm, 11:00 p.m. lights out. Friday and Saturday night curfews are one hour later. Any student outside of their dormitories after curfew will be issued detention with the usual loss of privileges as outlined in your student handbook.

"Signups for cross country and women's volleyball are open through the fifteenth. All athletic sign-up sheets, in addition to information and signups for the many clubs and extracurricular activities on campus can be found in the student commons.

"On behalf of Coventry Academy's faculty and staff, we look forward to helping each and every one of you make this your most successful school year yet. Thank you all for coming."

I turned to Cal, all set to urge him toward the exit, but he'd already rushed away, presumably to follow Zach. As I stepped into the aisle, a streaming blur whipped past us, flinging open the rear doors until they banged loudly against their wall stops. The backwash of disturbed air billowed around me, accompanied by the peculiar smell of dried flowers and the sounds of diminishing laughter. Clearly, the strigoi students had left the building.

Sure enough, one of them, a dark-haired boy with flawless tawny-skin and cheekbones prominent enough to make a supermodel envious, stopped to regard me.

"Señorita Devon, please excuse us," the vampire said in a sublime, richly accented voice. He paused at the door, long enough for Cal to reach it, before bowing his head in my direction and then disappearing in a blur of motion to rejoin his friends. Behind me, I heard more than a few shocked gasps, followed by a frenzy of whispering that carried over the boisterous chatter of all the exiting students.

"Friend of yours?" Cal asked as we crossed the lobby to the auditorium's front entrance, striding to keep ahead of the stampede.

"Never seen him before."

Apparently, that wasn't the answer he expected because Cal's gait faltered and he looked sharply at me, his thick eyebrows lost somewhere in the fringe of his hair. "The strigoi don't bother showing that kind of respect to just anyone," he said, his skeptical expression illuminated by the auditorium's exterior lights.

I shrugged. Until now, I hadn't thought much about the attention, but I guessed it had to do with Alex — aka 'Hackervamp' — the strigoi senior I'd defended two years ago. By chance, I'd entered the computer lab to find the school bully taunting the well-mannered strigoi, who'd plainly reached his breaking point. Even though I'd been a scrawny freshman at the time, with zero in the way of offensive magic, I hadn't thought twice about defending Alex from Skyler.

Skyler. The cocky ass had graduated last year and, on that score, all I could say was: 'Good riddance.' What an epic jerk. He'd gotten his rocks off giving all the vampires a hard time because he knew they couldn't do anything about it. If a strigoi so much as touched another student, they'd be expelled. A lot of the other kids had more powerful magic than those afflicted with the strigoi curse, but because of their powerful saliva, superhuman strength, and varied gifts, strigoi students were held to a higher standard.

As much as Skyler deserved a solid thrashing, I hadn't wanted Alex to be expelled. Without thinking, I'd jumped between them and threatened Skyler with revealing an embarrassing secret of his if he didn't stop harassing the vampires. It was the first and only time I'd threatened such a thing.

Ever since that incident, whenever a strigoi crossed my path, they often acknowledged me somehow. I guess I'd gotten used to it. Of course, most of the time, they simply gave me an easygoing nod. The strigoi with the delicious accent, knowing my name and going out of his way to speak to me, had come as something of a surprise. Was he friends with Alex?

I wondered what Alex had been doing since graduating. Had he gone to university or was he working his way up the strigoi's corporate ladder? Would I ever see him again?

Alex. I practically went breathless thinking about the good looking, wholly intimidating vampire.

"Ooh," Zach drawled. "Someone has a secret. Do tell."

Jerking out of my reverie, I hoped my expression hadn't been too dopey. "And deprive you of finding out on your own? Where's the fun in that?"

"But that's against the rules. Don't you know there's no secrets between friends?"

"Uh-huh, because, after one day, I'm sure I know everything about *you.*"

"What are you talking about? I'm an open book, here for your *reading pleasure*," he said, dropping his voice a register.

"An open book, huh? Maybe I should return you to the library."

Cal snickered and said, "Oooh, burn!" while Zach feigned injury and complained about being wounded.

"Did your parents give permission for you to leave campus?" Cal asked as we passed the LARTS building.

Inside, I could see several night students entering one of the rooms on the second floor. If I'd been alone, I might have been tempted to stand in the shadows and watch. I couldn't lie, strigoi intrigued me. Scared me, too.

"My dad," I corrected, answering him. "Yeah. What about you guys?"

They answered simultaneously, "Yeah." "Uh-huh."

"You guys get your driver's licenses yet?" I asked.

"Yep," Cal said.

"What about you, Zach?"

"I'm bumming rides from Cal this year." He didn't sound happy about it.

"There are worse things, right? Are you taking Driver's Ed as one of your electives? I would've had to give up one of my art classes and I didn't want to, so my dad signed me up for it over the summer. It totally sucked, but it was worth it."

"Uh, no."

"No? Well, if you live in Seattle, I can give you the name of the place where I took my class. Dad had to search for an instructor who wasn't put off by the gloves, but he managed," I blathered on, oblivious, until Cal elbowed me in the ribs. At least, I hoped it was his sleeve-covered elbow. I loved my Cat Bus shirt. I'd be seriously pissed if I had to throw it away thanks to his skin contact.

I veered to the side. "What the heck — ?" I snapped my mouth shut when I finally took in his exasperated expression.

"It's okay, Cal," Zach said, sounding tired. "Most people don't think about it. I can't get my license, okay? Seeing a car without a driver would freak most people out. Getting a state ID was a problem, too. Hard to have an ID when you don't show up in a photo."

"Oh." I stared at the ground as we walked. "You're right, I didn't think. Sorry."

"S'okay. I've been sneaking into clubs and R-rated movies with my cousins since I was twelve. I figure it evens out. Besides, my family's stinking rich. At home, I have a driver."

I wondered what type of clubs he'd been sneaking into and decided I probably didn't want to know.

"Did Daddy get you a Beemer for your sweet sixteen?" he drawled, his voice so sarcastic it was practically sing-song.

"No. And, even if my dad was the type to spoil me rotten, a BMW is the *last* thing I'd want."

"Yeah?" he challenged.

The rest of the way, we argued in defense of our favorite cars. Zach's dream car was a 1966 Shelby Cobra Mark-something-or-other. I zoned out when he started talking about engines and steering racks. Cal dreamed of having a restored first generation Ford Mustang. Cherry red, of course. I told them I'd be happily driving my top-of-the-line Lexus while their cars were both in the shop.

At the pathway between our dormitories, we slowed to a halt.

"You got a Vespa for your sixteenth birthday?" Zach asked incredulously. "How is it that the two richest kids in school don't have so much as a rusty Volkswagen between them? Where's the justice in that? Jesus. At least Cal has his beater, otherwise we'd be stuck hanging around here every weekend."

"You have a car?" Blue eyes, muscles galore, and he had a car, too? Even the senior girls were going to be all over him as soon as word got around. Maybe some of the boys, too, for that matter.

He shrugged. "Yeah, just a Civic. Nothing special."

"Are you kidding? I'd chew off my left hand for a Honda Civic. At least you can take people places. I'm not allowed to have someone else ride with me. And if it's raining ..." I threw up my hands. That was half the reason Dad allowed me to get the motor scooter, I was sure. He knew most of the time I'd be sidelined by rain.

Cal grinned, and I stuck my tongue out at him.

"Okay ... well, see you guys tomorrow." I gave them an awkward wave before heading down my path.

"See you at breakfast, princess."

I turned, walking backward. "Probably not. I'm gonna try to talk to Mr. Gibbs. I'll see you at lunch, though."

If Zach was surprised to hear it, I didn't hear him say so.

CHAPTER 5

A clever prank

WITH Red's help, I avoided hitting snooze on my alarm more than twice, which gave me enough time to squeeze in a quick shower before hightailing it down to the administration building. I strode into the single-story stone-fronted structure, a few minutes shy of 7:30, hoping to lodge my complaint and still make it to first period by the 8:00 a.m. starting bell.

The front office was student-free when I entered, a good sign, but I almost tripped over my Chucks when I spotted Professor Everhart talking to Mr. Gibbs just inside his office. And, by the look of things, Neverhart was monumentally ticked off.

Of all the darn people ... I was half tempted to turn on my heel and head straight to the refectory for breakfast. Although, if I did that, both Cal and Zach would no doubt ask me how things went with Mr. Gibbs.

Determined to at least make an appointment, I approached the front counter. The office assistants, who normally buzzed with purpose behind the L-shaped waist-level divider, were either in another room or hadn't arrived yet. Mrs. McPherson, the main office secretary, sat at her desk, telephone wedged between her bony shoulder and left ear, tapping the eraser end of her pencil on the open page of her schedule book.

Drat. I'd hoped to make my appointment and get out before I drew Professor Everhart's attention. That wasn't going to happen, though, not with her talking to Mr. Gibbs a mere fifteen feet away.

I caught bits and pieces of Neverhart's hissing rant: " … whoever helped her … won't tolerate … why do you think … patently guilty."

"Miss Devon," Mrs. McPherson declared when she noticed me. She hung up the telephone. "Good. I was trying to reach you."

"You were?" I was only too conscious of the silence now emanating from the direction of Mr. Gibbs' office and could practically feel Neverhart's malicious glare searing the side of my face.

"As if she didn't know," Professor Everhart said in a harsh undertone.

Mrs. McPherson, who'd long ago mastered the look of someone who took her job seriously, turned her unflinching gaze on the Professor. "Since I had *yet* to reach Miss Devon or leave her a message, that would be rather unlikely," she clipped out. "Unless, of course, you believe she has telepathy in addition to clairvoyance."

Whoa. You go, Mrs. McPherson!

I wanted to hug the prim secretary, which was an urge I'd never once entertained. Mrs. McPherson was largely known as Major McFearsome to the student body. Her motto was 'If you expect coddling, go elsewhere.'

Mr. Gibbs cleared his throat. "Thank you, Maggie. Lire, we'd like to have a word with you, please."

"Uh, okay."

This couldn't be good. As I walked toward them, Professor Everhart scowled at me as though she'd just learned I was responsible for single-handedly destroying the school's entire orange paper supply.

What the heck had her granny panties in a twist? I hadn't done anything wrong that I could think of. I mean, seriously — school had been in session for one freaking day.

Uh-oh. Maybe Zach had dropped the note we'd passed back and forth yesterday. But, no, that couldn't be it. Could it? Even if they had the note, though, there was nothing wrong in what I'd written. I'd turned down Zach's proposal. The conversation implicated him in wrongdoing, more than it did me.

I couldn't figure it out. Neverhart obviously thought I was guilty of something, something I'd needed help with, judging by what little of her conversation I'd overheard.

"Please, have a seat," Mr. Gibbs said, gesturing to one of the two chairs that faced his imposing cherry wood desk.

Behind his high-backed executive leather chair, several framed diplomas and certificates decorated the wall. His desk was tidy, with a laptop, telephone, sleek chrome pencil cup, two tiered in/out box, and a photo frame taking a small fraction of its substantial surface area. No doubt the ultra-efficient Mrs. McPherson dusted his desk's orderly contents every morning before he arrived primed for work in his trademark khakis, periwinkle-blue oxford shirt, and silver-gray tie. On casual Fridays, he left the tie at home and wore a pair of dark blue Chucks, instead of his usual black designer loafers.

Mr. Gibbs was a cool guy. He'd always treated me with respect and liked to rib me about our shared good taste in sneakers and whether I'd learned to appreciate listening to the Ramones yet. Today, though, there was no such banter as he took his seat across the desk from me.

"Now, Miss Devon, I won't beat around the bush," he said, considering me with his studious brown eyes. "A ... prank has been played on Professor Everhart that she believes you may be able to shed some light on."

What would I know about a prank? No one ever confided in me, and I'd never so much as edged a toe out of line in all the years I'd attended Coventry.

"Me?" I shook my head. "I've no clue what you're talking about. What prank?"

"Don't play coy, Miss Devon," Professor Everhart sneered from her position to the right of Mr. Gibbs' desk. Apparently, she was feeling too self-righteous to sit. "I know you were plotting, yesterday in class."

"Plotting? What are you — ?"

My question was cut off by Mr. Gibbs smoothing what was once a folded piece of binder paper on his desk where I could see it. It was the cartoon of Professor Everhart that Zach had drawn.

Damn. Zach must have dropped it on our way out the door yesterday.

My cheeks heated.

"Professor Everhart found this under your desk shortly after you left her class, yesterday afternoon."

"Okay."

"This doesn't seem to surprise you."

"No."

"You don't deny drawing it, then?"

I kept my mouth shut and simply stared at him.

Well, it seemed Dad would get his wish, even if I hadn't *done* anything. If drawing an offensive cartoon didn't qualify as 'a little bad,' I didn't know what did.

Mr. Gibbs sighed. "Lire, I have to say, I'd thought better of you."

I fought against the almost mandatory urge to roll my eyes skyward. Clearly, he did think better of me, if he thought I had that kind of talent with a pencil, but saying so would invite questions I didn't relish answering. I hoped he didn't show the drawing to my previous year's art teacher, otherwise the cat would be out of the bag for sure.

"I never thought I'd have to ask you this, but ... where were you, yesterday, between 4:30 and curfew?"

"Where—?" I hesitated, confused. "Huh? The note was found right after class. I don't understand."

"For God's sake, stop play-acting and answer the question," Professor Everhart snapped.

Mr. Gibbs leveled her with a quelling glare. "Professor, I'd appreciate you letting me handle this if you please." He looked at me. "Lire, this disrespectful drawing is only part of the larger issue. Professor Everhart's classroom was vandalized, at some point last night. If you know anything about that, it would behoove you to tell us, now, before considerable manpower is spent to discover the responsible parties."

Vandalized? Okay—this no longer qualified for 'a little bad.' We'd definitely veered into deep shit territory.

"Are you — ?" I sputtered. "You think I'd vandalize a classroom? In my entire history here, have I ever done anything to make you think I'd do something like that?"

"Frankly, no, you haven't," he replied. "But I never expected this drawing to come from you, either."

I stared at him, flabbergasted.

Was he for real? Drawing a cartoon suddenly made me capable of a serious crime?

I gaped for a moment, then took a deep breath, quelling my panic with a reminder that I was not, in fact, a mouse.

"If you're going to question me, I want a Council-ranked truthsayer to verify my answers." I glared at him, my anger making me braver than usual. "And I want to be transferred out of my current English class, immediately, or you can expect a call from my dad." I rolled my eyes. "Actually, scratch that. Once he hears about this accusation, he'll be calling for sure."

"No one is accusing you of anything, Lire," Mr. Gibbs said, sounding annoyed.

Could have fooled me.

I might have laughed, but the door burst open, startling all of us.

The solid bulk of Professor Trapp stalked into the room, suddenly making Mr. Gibbs' spacious office feel cramped.

While I goggled at him, he greeted Mr. Gibbs. "Charles, good morning." He then regarded Professor Everhart and bit out a stern, "Krista," as though her name tasted like an unripe cranberry.

He looked down at me, which was quite a distance since I'd remained seated and he was like a jillion feet tall. "You okay?"

"What is the meaning of this?" Professor Everhart demanded. "In case you haven't noticed, we're conducting a meeting here, *Brandon*, which doesn't concern you."

"A meeting? Funny. It looks more like an interrogation to me."

Mr. Gibbs clenched his jaw, and I swear he grew two additional inches, puffing up in his chair. "Professor Trapp, I take issue with your tone and your insinuation. We are merely asking Miss Devon whether she knows anything about the vandalism — "

"Vandalism!" Professor Trapp laughed. "That's a bit of a stretch, don't you think? Nothing's destroyed. It was a prank. A clever one, if you ask me, because, thanks to the perpetrator, it revealed a deeply troubling issue that is *very much my concern* and one that the joint coalition will no doubt have something to say about." His nostrils flared, all traces of his earlier laughter replaced by a formidable countenance.

"For heaven's sake," Professor Everhart exclaimed. "What does bullying have to do with the misuse of school property and the state of my classroom?"

"A great deal, I should think," he replied coolly. "Lire happened to mention something in conversation, yesterday, that initially got my attention. But it wasn't until I heard complaint from another student that I learned how appalling the situation actually is." He turned his attention on Mr. Gibbs. "Charles, did you happen to examine the classroom for yourself?"

"Yes, of course," he replied impatiently.

"Aside from the disassembled desks, did nothing else strike you as being remotely problematic or unusual?"

Hold the phone! Disassembled?

That was the vandalism? Someone had taken apart the desks in Professor Everhart's classroom? I wondered how many. Had they taken apart hers too? I imagined the room awash in a sea of desk parts. I might have snickered if not for Mr. Gibbs' annoyed expression.

"Nothing comes to mind," he replied shortly, "except for the two intact desks and the fact that there were no signs of forced entry."

"Yes, the two colorfully-intact desks. Interesting that they were left alone," Professor Trapp observed. "And it leads me to ask why assigning clairvoyants and occultums color-coded desks and forcing them to sit at the back of the classroom like second-class citizens is a sanctioned practice here at Coventry Academy."

Mr. Gibbs looked puzzled. "It's to their benefit," he said, as though he was astonished anyone would think of objecting to such a thing. "Miss Devon can be sure her desk won't open her to hundreds, if not thousands, of memories with one wrong move. And Mister Carter won't have a student accidentally sitting on him."

Had I honestly thought Mr. Gibbs was a cool guy? What had I been thinking?

Professor Trapp sighed. "They are both being singled out because of their gifts. And not in a good way. This treatment only highlights the negative aspects of their abilities. In all candor, I'm shocked that you as Assistant Headmaster didn't see it that way. Did anyone bother to ask Miss Devon or Mister Carter whether this was something they needed or, even, wanted?"

Mr. Gibbs seemed shocked by the question. "I've heard no complaint."

"I did complain. Last year, to Professor Everhart," I admitted, finally gathering the courage to speak up, albeit in a scarcely-there voice. "She said she didn't appreciate my ungrateful attitude and then detailed for the entire class all the work she goes through every day to make sure I'm safe to be in her classroom." I looked down at my lap, relaxing my fingers when I noticed I'd been wringing my hands. "After that, I didn't take it further. But I should have."

"There's more to it than the orange desk, isn't there?" Professor Trapp said.

I nodded, wondering how he knew.

"More to it? What are you talking about?" Mr. Gibbs glanced at Professor Everhart who'd stayed remarkably quiet this whole time, fingertips pressed to her throat, doing her best to look persecuted. "Professor?"

"I don't understand," she said, sounding bewildered. "Everything I've done has been with your well-being in mind, Lire. You should be able to come to class and handle your paperwork and studies in the same way as everyone else. I only wanted you to be completely at ease."

"Right," I muttered. "Because walking to the front of the classroom, at least twice a day, to get my bright-orange papers from my bright-orange cubby doesn't make me feel like a freak, not one bit."

"I hardly think that level of sarcasm is warranted, Miss Devon," Mr. Gibbs admonished. "Need I remind you that you're speaking to your professor?"

Professor Trapp made a choking sound. "That's what you have to say? She speaks her mind and you're reprimanding her for it?"

Mr. Gibbs regarded my teacher with a dispassionate eye. "You've only been here one day, but surely, it must be obvious that these things were done with the best of intentions. I see no malice and certainly nothing that would concern the joint coalition. Professor Everhart has treated Lire with nothing but respect. Even if Lire doesn't appreciate those efforts, I expect her complaints to be lodged in a considerate manner." He narrowed his eyes. "To that end, I don't believe your commentary has added anything but a high level of contentiousness to this conversation. Now, if you'd excuse us, I'd like to get back to the matter at hand, which is the vandalism of Professor Everhart's classroom."

"I'm sure Professor Trapp can recommend a Council-ranked truthsayer," I suggested in my most courteous tone.

"A truthsayer?" my French professor all but exploded, making me jump. "You proposed questioning her with a truthsayer?"

"Actually ..." I looked up at him. "I did."

Professor Trapp's brows shot upward.

"They're already half-convinced I'm guilty because of something incriminating Nev—Professor Everhart found under my desk," I explained. "I don't want there to be any doubt about being innocent. I figured a truthsayer would help. Is that bad?"

He blew out a breath. "Not exactly. Not if they stick to relevant questions. And your father is present for the proceedings." He frowned. "What's this incriminating evidence?"

I glanced at Mr. Gibbs who answered, "A drawing, which Miss Devon does not dispute is hers."

"And this drawing is incriminating how? Does it show how to dismantle desks?"

"No, no," Mr. Gibbs replied briskly, and I couldn't help thinking that he sounded disappointed.

"Is that it, there?" Professor Trapp asked, motioning toward the paper on Mr. Gibbs' desk and stepping forward to get a better look.

Mr. Gibbs waved his hand dismissively. "It is, yes."

My mountainous teacher picked up the page and studied it with a barely concealed smile. "This is quite skilled. You drew this?"

"What do you think?" I replied, but there wasn't a lot of heat in it. Professor Trapp wasn't my enemy.

He studied me. "I think you didn't answer the question." He tossed the cartoon back on the desk. "If a truthsayer is what you want, I can make a call."

"It is. Thanks." I stood, gathering my backpack on the way up. "I'm going to see my counselor now, but I'd like to say one final thing."

I turned to address Mr. Gibbs. "In the future, when you or a teacher wants to give a student special treatment, I suggest asking yourselves one question: Would it be okay to do the same thing if the student was dyslexic or disabled or something like that? If the answer's no — that it wouldn't be okay, that it might be considered demeaning — then you shouldn't do it, even for someone who has a gift. Because, as I'm sure you know, not everyone's magic is seen as beneficial."

Holding my head high, I turned and left the room with as much dignity as I could scrape together. I made it to the front counter, heart racing and palms sweating, amazed Mr. Gibbs hadn't scolded me for leaving without permission.

Professor Trapp strode past and said, "Come with me. Owen, pencil Miss Devon in for the next half hour, will you? Thanks. We'll be in with Mrs. Rodriguez."

The blond office assistant, who looked to be around the same age as Professor Trapp, issued a somewhat startled "sure," as he stared at my professor's retreating back.

When his wide baby blues found mine, we shared a thunderstruck moment before I waved and scurried to follow my teacher down the hall.

My first glance inside Mrs. Rodriguez's office solved the mystery of how Professor Trapp had known about my meeting with Mr. Gibbs. Across from my advisor, Cal sat in one of the padded guest chairs. If I had to guess, Zach sat in the other. Professor Trapp waved me inside the room.

As I walked in, I caught Mrs. Rodriguez mid-sentence, " — scenario will work fine." She turned to me. "Lire, good morning. We were just discussing two options, should you, Mr. Carter, or Mr. Mars decide to transfer out of your current English Composition course."

Not surprisingly, the first was the option I'd already considered — take our senior year's required Twentieth-Century Literature class, now, a year early. The other option was to study the English Comp coursework independently, with Professor Trapp acting as our administrator and the English chair grading our classwork and tests. In that scenario, we'd study in Professor Trapp's classroom during his free period, which meant our schedule wouldn't have to change, since his free hour coincided with our seventh-period class with Professor Everhart.

Because there was no way to guarantee we wouldn't end up with Neverhart for English Composition next year, the three of us were unanimous. We wanted to take the class independently, even though it meant we were on the hook for covering all the required material on our own.

Holy moly. At the start of school, I never would have guessed that, on day two, I'd end up in a three-person English class with the intimidating Professor Trapp acting as my advocate and newly-adopted favorite teacher.

Unsurprisingly, news of Professor Everhart's 'desktastrophy' was all over school by the time I made it to my second-period class. The calculating looks and secretive whispers, however, didn't start in earnest until I strode through the dining room at lunch, tray in hand, to meet Cal and Zach at what had become 'our table.' Once again, Cal chased two girls out of the extra seats.

"Jesus! Took you long enough," Zach complained. "What happened this morning? Did you meet with Mr. Gibbs? Mountainside sure looked PO'd after going to find you."

I laughed. "Mountainside?"

"We can't all be as clever with the nicknames as you, princess," Zach teased. "So? Tell us."

I shrugged. "I went in to make an appointment, like I said I would, but Neverhart was in Mr. Gibbs' office when I got there. I had no idea why they both wanted to talk to me, and it took me a few minutes to realize I was being accused of *vandalizing* her classroom."

"Vandalizing?" Cal frowned. "You don't mean the desk thing?"

I nodded and then stared across the table. "And you'll be thrilled to know, I have you to thank for that, *Zach.*"

"*Me*? What'd I do?"

"You dropped that drawing of Neverhart and it must have fallen under my desk."

"Oh, shit. I was wondering where it went."

"Yeah." I sat back. "And I couldn't blame it on someone else because they could tell I'd seen it before. So, now, Mr. Gibbs and

Neverhart think I have it out for her and I'm totally the type who'd sneak into her classroom and take apart all the desks."

I wagged a finger at them. "And if either of you happen to know who's behind Dismantlegate, don't tell me. I told Mr. Gibbs that I wouldn't answer their questions without a truthsayer in the room."

"Holy shit. You did?" Zach blurted. "What'd they say to that?"

"*Ass Head* denied that I was being accused of anything," I said, bandying our assistant headmaster's derogatory nickname for the first time ever, as I dressed my salad. A small part of me cringed at doing so, but I squelched it. "Then Professor Trapp barged in and went off on them about our special desks. It was freaking awesome. I sure hope he doesn't get fired." I glanced at the clock, my first bite of salad poised at the end of my fork. I had twelve minutes.

"He won't," Zach said confidently.

"How would you know?" I asked between bites. "Because Mr. Gibbs sure wasn't happy. He went out of his way to point out that Professor Trapp has only worked as a teacher for one day. It sounded kind of threatening, actually."

"The coalition made it a requirement that every private academy have one of their representatives on staff. If they don't, they'll lose their accreditation. Trust me — Mountainside can't be fired. Well, I suppose the members of the coalition could agree to replace him, but they're not going to do that. He's a Council-ranked airmaster. Those don't come along every day."

"I hope you're right." I shot an arch look at the two of them. "So ... did Professor Trapp show up in Ass Head's office because of you guys?"

"Someone may have mentioned you were there," Cal replied slyly.

I smiled at them. "Well ... thanks. By the way, I think Professor Trapp knows I didn't draw that cartoon. It probably won't take him long to figure out who did."

"Mountainside has half a brain, unlike Ass Head and Neverhart," Zach said.

"Seriously." We were in complete agreement on that. "God, I wish I could have seen Neverhart's expression when she first saw the desktastrophy." I snickered. "She probably looked a lot like that drawing."

"No doubt," Zach said, laughing. "Desktastrophy and Dismantleg-ate. I'm definitely using those."

Cal chuckled too, and the deep rumble went straight to my head, making me feel giddy.

"What can I say? I try." I smirked. "So? I'm dying to know. Did either of you happen to see her classroom? Did someone really take apart all the desks but ours?"

"No idea. Zach's the one who heard about it, this morning, while we were waiting for Professor Trapp."

"You went to see him before seeing Mrs. Rodriguez?"

"Yeah," Zach said. "I left a message on his voicemail, last night, telling him I wanted to lodge a complaint about a teacher. When we showed up this morning, he grilled us about the sitch. Afterward, he took us to Mrs. Rodriguez and then went to find you." He whistled. "I can't believe you went up against him for Amanda. That dude is scary as fuck."

I jerked in my seat, wishing I could see Zach's face to know whether he was joking or not. "You seriously think that?"

"Hell yes. Haven't you noticed? His eyes glow blue when he's pissed. Makes me wonder how much of a handle he has on his magic."

I remembered how intimidating Professor Trapp had looked after casting his spell, but I shrugged it off. "I dunno. He's always seemed in control to me. But, yeah, I don't think he's the type to tolerate much misbehavior. That's for sure."

"Ya think?"

"And for the last time, I didn't *go up against him*, okay? I talked to him. There's a big difference."

"Whatever you say, princess. Hurry up and eat your rabbit food. Lunch is almost over, and I don't wanna listen to your stomach growling all through next period."

"I'd already be finished if a certain someone wasn't grilling me for information this whole time."

"If you learned to talk with your mouth full, like everyone else, this wouldn't be a problem."

I laughed, almost choking on my salad, but without Zach's de-mands for further gossip, I finished ahead of the bell.

"I wonder if they got the desks put back together yet," I said softly as we made our way down the corridor to Professor Trapp's classroom.

"Maybe," Cal said under his breath. "Zach heard the maintenance guy is on it. They moved Neverhart's classes to the auditorium until he's done."

"Poor Hugh." I grimaced. "That sucks for him."

"I dunno," Zach said. "I'd sure rather assemble desks than clean the guy's bathrooms."

"He'll be doing both, jackass," Cal muttered.

I was fairly sure the school had a separate cleaning crew, but I held my tongue, not wanting to prolong the conversation, now that we'd arrived for class.

To my surprise, Professor Trapp spent his entire free period with us, going over the course plan that he received from the English department's chair. By the final bell, we had our first reading assignment and a five-paragraph essay due by Friday.

Before the guys left for their art class, Cal suggested we go for a run around 4:00. I tried to nod casually.

For God's sake, get real. He's not asking for a date! I chastised myself, stomping on my overexcited butterflies. Going for a run was something you did with a friend. Besides, he'd said 'we,' which didn't necessarily mean Zach wouldn't be coming.

As I berated myself for getting excited over nothing, Professor Trapp reminded me to gather my things and sit at his desk for French. He placed a packet of advanced grammar worksheets in front of me after I'd settled in.

"I spoke with my contact at the Arcane Council," he said. "Turns out there was no need for me to call in a favor because they'd already booked a truthsayer for a meeting between you and Mr. Simmons for this Friday. Do you know if your father can make it?"

"I'll check, but I'm thinking he's the one who set up the meeting. My dad was pretty mad when I talked to him after our meeting."

"Understandable. But if it's a problem, let me know. You shouldn't meet with a truthsayer without an adult on your side. You need someone there to ensure the questions are within the scope of the school's investigation."

My lunch turned to concrete in my stomach. Maybe insisting on a truthsayer had been a mistake. The whole situation now sounded terrifyingly serious.

Calm down. You didn't do anything wrong.

"It's fine. If my dad can't come, my familiar can stand in for him."

"A non-human isn't the same as an adult, Lire."

"Maybe in most cases, but Red was a necromancer three hundred years ago. He can totally stand in for my dad."

Professor Trapp's body stilled. When I looked up, he was staring at me, his brown eyes widened by shock. "Red? Do you—?" He stopped, jerking back as he restored his usual composure, an impressive sight, given his size. "Your familiar ... it couldn't—" He hesitated. "It isn't John Redborn is it?"

It was my turn to be surprised. "Yes. You know Red?"

"Well, I'll be godda—" He closed his jaw on the curse, glancing at the students now entering his classroom. His voice dropped to a severe undertone. "That name is well known to anyone of influence within the Council. He was the previous president's familiar. What happened to him after his master's death is a mystery many would be interested in knowing."

He bent forward, planting his broad hand on the desk and affixing me with a steadfast look. "My advice to you is to keep that information private. There are those who won't be pleased to learn his expertise has been relegated to an outsider. Trust me. These are individuals you do *not* want knowing about you."

His expression, not to mention his tone, was so grim, so formidable, it took several beats before I realized I hadn't taken a breath. When I did finally suck in a tremulous gulp of air, things looked foggy for a second.

Straightening, he tapped the French worksheets, his thick finger driving a solid thump from the desk's surface. "Try these. If they're too easy, I'll find something more challenging for tomorrow." In a softer tone, he added, "And if your father can't make Friday, I can serve in his stead. I'm here to help you, Lire."

As he turned away, I remembered what Zach had said about Professor Trapp. My teacher's eyes did, at times, glow blue, but it didn't just happen when he was angry. It also happened when he was alarmed. And if a powerful sorcerer was concerned, I'd be stupid not to take note.

After class, I hurried back to my dorm room, unzipping my backpack's special pocket in record time.

"What the heck, Red? Is it true what Professor Trapp said about your previous ... master?" I scowled saying the final word, mostly because it implied something I refused to consider.

Red wasn't, and would never be, my servant. He was my best friend, my companion. At most, if I was forced to qualify the magical nature of our binding, I'd probably say I was his caretaker. In my whole life, I didn't think I'd ever given Red an order. Not intentionally, anyway.

As I sat down hard on the edge of my bed, Red jumped from the top of my backpack to my desk.

"He was, veritably, a most esteemed member of the Arcane Council," he replied once he'd settled into his customary position, perched next to my laptop. "This was years ago, before the title of president. At the time, I inhabited a markedly different vessel. Still, I suppose there are some who may remember my existence. Mages have ways of prolonging their lives beyond those of most humans."

"Just how many years ago are we talking?"

"Two hundred thirteen. My previous master died more than ninety years ago."

"Jeez. How is it I didn't know this stuff?"

"You knew I previously served a magus. As to the rest, the details were hardly a concern for a young girl without arcane power. I suppose if you were in the habit of speaking my name in conversation or flaunting my existence to every passerby, I might have made issue of it, but over the years, you followed your father's orders to conceal me from the greater public."

"I thought it was to keep people from touching you, not because some powerful mage might try to steal you away from me!"

"I am not without defenses, as you well know, although I doubt it would come to such a thing."

"You let Giselle push you into a plastic treasure chest with a stick and bury you in the backyard." My sister had been eleven at the time, but I didn't need to point that out. His memory was impeccable. I shot him an arch look. "Your defenses are hardly foolproof."

"She was family," he replied sullenly, folding his arms over his stuffed belly. "She took me by surprise."

My heart melted. I couldn't help it. He was just so adorable.

"I know. You had every reason to think you were safe because we *are* family," I said. "And no one is ever going to take you away from me. I swear it."

"I have no intention of allowing such a thing, but your zeal is heartening to hear," he said stoutly. "Speaking of family, you should call your father regarding Friday's meeting, as Professor Trapp advised."

Later, after I'd left a message for Dad, I sat at my desk, contemplating what Red had told me. "You said your previous master died ninety years ago. Why did it take so long for you to be assigned to a new caretaker?"

"After my master's death, I was held in trust by a coven of witches. The terms of his will required that I approve their candidate."

"It took them that long? Were they deliberately proposing horrible people? Did they not want to give you up or something?" I imagined a fleet of nefarious crones who kept him locked up in some dark attic, extorting his knowledge of high necromancy spells and pumping him for the true names of influential demons.

"No. Quite the opposite. The leader of their coven was a dear friend of my previous master. She took her job seriously and, I believe, cared about how I would fare in my future servitude."

"*Servitude.* You're not my servant. God, I hate that word."

"I know." He said this with such fondness and clear amusement that I frowned at him.

"What? Why'd you say it like that?"

He chuckled. "Your attitude simply illustrates why, after waiting ninety years, I chose you. Even when you were but a small child, your strength of character was easy to see. I knew you would grow to become an honorable woman."

I blew a raspberry. "How you saw that, in the three whole minutes we had before our binding ceremony, is a mystery, but I'm glad you decided to go through with it."

"Indeed. However, I observed you on two separate occasions prior to our binding."

"You did?" I straightened in my chair. "When? How?"

"The first time was at a company picnic that you attended with your father. The second was at your sister's eighth birthday party."

My sister Giselle was four years older than me. I always hated going to her birthday parties, especially when they weren't celebrated at home. Her friends all treated me like I had a contagious disease, and I spent most of the time hiding in a corner where I wouldn't be noticed. As to the company picnic, I vaguely remembered longing to bounce in the dinosaur themed bouncy-house. Instead, I'd claimed it didn't interest me, knowing if I dared to enter the crowded inflatable enclosure, all the kids would have left in droves, most of them dragged out by their alarmed parents.

"Do you recall meeting a bespectacled older woman who was presented as a friend of your father's?" Red asked. "She was the coven's matriarch and the longtime friend of my previous master. You spoke with her for quite some time."

"*Maybe ... ?*" I said, trying to dredge up anything at all. Surely, if I'd seen something as unusual as Red, I'd have remembered. "Did she have you in her shoulder bag or something?"

"No. At that time, my soul was bound to an amulet. She wore it around her neck."

I jerked in my chair, and it wasn't until I went to speak that I realized I'd slapped my hand over my mouth. "A necklace. Oh, Red."

For over two hundred years, he'd been confined to a vessel that hadn't allowed independent movement. Naïvely, I'd always pictured him inside something like his current teddy bear body, something soft, huggable, and roughly humanoid. Obviously, a powerful magus would have demanded something less conspicuous and more mature. How stupid of me to think otherwise.

Red rose from his perch to rub my forearm. "Dearest, do not fret. My master was a good man. All in all, I have been incredibly fortunate."

"I wish I could make you human again," I blurted, my voice warbling. "You know that, right? I'd do anything for you, Red. You're my best friend."

"Then I made a good choice, did I not? For, after all my days on this earth, you are, and have been, my fondest companion."

With emotion burning my eyes, I swept him into my arms and hugged him tight.

CHAPTER 6

8

Me and my big mouth

SCHOOL settled into a familiar rhythm. To my astonishment, this included spending a lot of my free time with Zach and Cal, either doing homework in the library, jogging the track, or hanging out in the student commons, and they always saved a spot for me in the dining room. By the time Friday morning rolled around, I'd started to think of them as my two best friends, which was good because, if I was honest, I needed friends a lot more than romance.

Cal was sure cute though.

Shoving that thought aside, I trudged toward the sports courts, on time for first period gym, clad in my psi-free track pants and moisture-wicking full coverage tee. I'd also donned my specially made gloves, the ones with the texturized finger pads that helped with gripping sports equipment, like today's badminton racket. Although, when everyone else turned out for class, wearing their shorts and tees, it was hard not to feel like the bashful kid who goes swimming wearing an oversized undershirt.

Shannon Lutz, the blonde geomancer who sometimes sat next to Cal before I showed up for lunch, voluntarily paired up with me for badminton. It took a few minutes of conversation to figure out why.

"I heard you're in a private English class with Cal and Zach now, ever since Dismantlegate," she said, tucking her short hair behind each ear in quick succession.

"Um, yeah, sort of." I readied the birdie while trying to hold the racket for a short serve, like Coach Rickett had demonstrated earlier. "It's not really a private class, though. We're learning the course material on our own."

Trina and her partner, Jessica, waited on the other side of the net. Knees bent and rackets raised, they looked like an ad for *Badminton Monthly*, if there was such a thing. Each girl sported a healthy tan, athletic physique, and perfectly styled ponytail. With my own pale, freckled coloring, it was hard not to be envious, especially of Jessica's tawny skin and shining black hair, which I assumed came courtesy of her heritage. Although, with a last name like Dawson, I wasn't sure what that nationality might be.

"But Professor Trapp is helping you guys, right?" Shannon asked.

"He's mentoring us." I swung the racket, managing a decent serve that Trina returned.

"Lucky," Shannon gushed, running to hit the birdie but driving it into the net. She didn't seem to care. "Oh, man. A Council-ranked sorcerer. And Cal ... he's so cute." She sighed wistfully.

I tried not to smirk.

While Jessica ran to scoop up the birdie for her turn serving, Shannon pitched her voice to a confidential level. "So is it true that you guys are the ones who took apart the desks?"

I jerked back a step. "No. Jeez. Is that what everyone's saying?"

"Some." She pouted. "Bummer. I was hoping you had, 'cuz that would have been cool."

"Told you it wasn't her," Trina said from the other side of the net.

"Well, someone sure thinks so. I heard a truthsayer is coming." Shannon turned her hazel eyes on me. "Is that part true, at least? Are they coming to interview you?"

"I think Mr. Simmons will ask the questions, but, yeah, later to-day." I considered telling them I'd been the one to demand the interview, but decided against it. Let them think what they wanted.

"She's still not Daredevil material," Jessica said, smacking the birdie in my direction.

I lunged forward, hitting it in a high arc over the net, which Trina rallied back to Shannon's side. This time, Shannon succeeded in sending the birdie back to Trina, who biffed her backhanded swing, hitting the projectile out of bounds.

"I thought that's what the initiations are for," Shannon said on her way to the fallen birdie.

Trina's blue eyes narrowed with contempt. "As if. She's the biggest goody-goody in the whole school. There's no way she'll do it, so it doesn't matter."

I stood taller, my muscles tightening at the insult.

Shannon shrugged as she ambled back to her position, the birdie's frayed feathers pinched between her manicured fingers.

"Do I even want to know what you guys are talking about?" I asked.

Jessica laughed. "Hello. That should tell you everything. She's clueless."

I ground my teeth against the angry response that flirted with my tongue. The 'goody-goody' comment had wired me up for detonation. And being discussed in the third person? That was burning my fuse at warp speed.

"I dunno," Shannon replied. "The vamps talk to her for a reason. And Zach thinks she's cool."

"Whatever," Trina said, as if the whole thing was pointless. "Tell her, if you want, just don't forget the part about *proof*."

Coach Rickett scolded us from her vantage on the bleachers, four courts away. "Let's see some rallies going over there, Shannon, Trina. I'm seeing a lot of talking, not enough moving, girls."

Ten minutes later, after a show of dedicated projectile-smacking, the best rally we'd managed was six hits.

While Trina tapped her foot at the sideline, waiting until it was safe to rescue our birdie from the neighboring court, Shannon turned to me. "You've seriously not heard about the Daredevils or the Grim Reapers?"

"Nope."

"They're secret clubs."

She ignored my noncommittal shrug and continued to babble, glancing away every so often to check on Trina's progress. "Basically, the way it works is: If you do the club's initiation, you're in. So, like, to be a member of the Daredevils, you have to get a picture of yourself in front of the shifter compound's famous dead tree —*at night*." She frowned at me. "You've heard of that tree, right? The one that was struck by lightning?"

When I nodded, she went on, "Okay, so you can go even further. If you prove you were there on the night of a full moon, you'll be a *triple-dee*." Eyes wide, she explained in a stage whisper, "That's double dog daredevil — part of the club's inner circle."

I stared at her, incredulous. "You did that?"

"No." She sulked. "I just got a picture next to the tree. Me and Darla did it together last year."

Had someone really risked doing that during a full moon with all the shifters prowling around? I marveled at the level of insanity.

"Scared her off already?" Trina looked smug as she approached the net, rogue birdie in hand. She tossed it to Shannon since it was now our serve.

"Hardly." I looked at Shannon. "What about the Grim Reapers? What do they have to do?"

"Hoping it'll be easier?" Trina asked.

I ignored her.

Shannon lined up for her serve while we waited for Trina to get into position. "You have to take at least one night class and then get a strigoi to kiss you for two minutes so that at least three different people see it, and none of the witnesses can be your friends. Plus, someone has to take a picture for proof."

On the face of it, that did seem less risky, especially if you could persuade one of the strigoi to help you. Of course, they were a cliquish group and many of them bordered on being snooty. Not necessarily toward me, especially in recent years, but still. I wouldn't want to push my luck. No doubt they'd be insulted by such a tacky proposal. And feigning interest in one of them to win entry to a club seemed awfully skeevy, never mind that they probably all knew about the club and would see anyone coming from a mile away.

It seemed to me, the people who'd likely make it into the Grim Reapers would be the ones who got in by accident because they truly wanted to date a strigoi. Honestly, the whole idea freaked me out. Once injected into the blood stream, vampire saliva acted as a powerful hypnotic. Backed by magic, it was a roofie on steroids. It gave the strigoi total control over their victims, which was why an unsolicited vampire bite was a felony in most states. Most, though, went unreported since strigoi saliva could alter a person's memories.

As far as I was concerned, anyone who dated a vampire had a death wish.

After another three-hit rally, Jessica's swing went awry and I had a moment to ask, "Who's made it into the Grim Reapers?"

"Becky Abbott," Shannon told me. "She's dating that vamp from Estonia. They went to prom together, last year."

Trina wandered near the net. "Don't forget Jennie Huffington."

"Right," Shannon said, nodding. "She went out with that one guy, the one with the spiky blond hair. What was his name?"

"Aaron," Jessica put in, trotting up to toss the feathered projectile over the net, which landed at my feet.

"Yes!" Shannon exclaimed. "Oh, my God. He was so cute. Too bad he graduated. He used to hang out in the commons before his night classes started. He had a thing for peppermint tea."

Strigoi drank tea?

"You planning to go out with that vamp?" Trina asked, eyeing me through the net. "The one who spoke to you after the assembly? I hear he's got some special connection to the Domn. Is that true?"

I shrugged. "How would I know? I don't even know his name."

"He obviously knew yours," Jessica said.

I bent down to scoop up the birdie. "So?"

"So," she drawled, arching a condescending eyebrow. "You might have an in, getting into the Reapers, but your dad can't give you an edge with the Daredevils."

"What does my dad have to do with anything?"

"*Please.* He's the vamp's chief financial guy, not to mention the Arcane Council's. Everyone knows that's why Professor Trapp is on your side and why the vamps pay any attention to you."

I recoiled, too shocked at the accusation to snap anything back at her. "That's a lie," I finally hissed. "Professor Trapp is doing what's *right*. It has nothing to do with my dad. And the strigoi don't 'pay attention' to me—whatever *that* means. I've never even had a conversation with a strigoi, except for one time when I was a freshman. Not like it matters—because I'd never string someone along just to get into a club. At least with the Daredevils, you don't have to do that. It's only about snapping a measly picture."

"Measly!" Jessica flicked her head so her sleek, dark ponytail whipped over her left shoulder. "As if. You couldn't do it, not in a million years."

"Give me a break. It's a picture of a tree."

"If it's so easy, then you shouldn't have any trouble doing it for the full moon," Trina sneered. "The extra light will make taking the picture *so* much easier, right?"

"I've been shooting since I was five," I retorted. "I mastered nighttime photography a long time ago. I could do it with my freaking eyes closed, full moon or not."

It wasn't until afterward, as I stomped back to the locker room, not five minutes later, that I contemplated the mammoth hole I'd managed to dig for myself. Me and my big mouth. Either I'd have to take the photo or live with being the butt of everyone's joke for the next two years.

Dad was a photography buff whose enthusiasm had rubbed off on me. I'd gotten my first camera at five. I developed my own photos in our basement darkroom. My Leica rangefinder, which Dad had given me for my thirteenth birthday, was every street photographer's dream camera. I knew exactly how to take a nighttime photo of a darn tree and have it turn out brilliantly.

But if I knew those girls, they'd tell the whole school I'd accepted their stupid dare. The gossip would spread through the student body faster than a stench spell gone wrong—which was to say, well before lunchtime.

I was so screwed.

Sure enough, when I arrived in the dining room for sixth period lunch, Shannon sat in my usual seat, leaning forward in eager discussion, her forearms braced where her tray would normally be if she hadn't left it at her regular table. Zach or Cal must have alerted her to my impending arrival because she turned before I reached them, a look of sheepish satisfaction on her pug-nosed face.

Here we go.

"I have a map to the compound if you need it," Shannon said in passing as she sauntered back to her friends.

One resigned breath later, I plunked my tray next to Cal's, trying to act casual.

"For someone who doesn't like rocking the boat, you're sure finding a lot of ways to try to sink like the Titanic," Zach said as I'd slid onto the bench. "Did you seriously say that sneaking into the shifters' compound on the night of the full moon was so easy you could do it with your eyes closed?"

"I said I could take the photo of the *tree* with my eyes closed. I've been into photography since I was five. I have a darkroom at home."

"That's not what's going around the entire school. Everyone's saying you said you could do the triple-d challenge, easy as pie. Jessica, Trina, and Amanda are telling everyone you're full of it. Jason and Brad are betting all takers that you'll chicken out. They're going to shave their heads if you do it. They've even convinced their dumbass teammates to do the same." He kicked at my foot. "You're rowing up shit creek without a life vest, princess."

I rolled my eyes, taking a bite of my veggie wrap, ignoring the fact that my stomach wanted no part of it.

Ignoring my obvious disdain, Zach went on, "But since I'm all for anything that proves those idiots are dumber than a bag of broken dildos, we are *definitely* doing this thing."

I choked, trying to swallow and laugh at the same time, and ended up coughing for fifteen seconds. I sputtered, "We?"

He laughed at my reaction. "Why should you have all the fun? Besides, dub-dub wants to see you come out on top." Behind a series of fake coughs, he forced out in a rushed undertone, "Inmorewaysthanone."

"You seriously need to *piss off*," Cal growled, jerking in his seat on the final two words.

Judging by Zach's pained grunt, Cal had nailed his roommate's unprotected shins with a solid kick.

"Dude! What the hell? She knows I'm kidding."

Cal grumbled under his breath, but since all I heard were swears, I didn't try to decipher it. I continued eating, hoping my burning ears weren't noticeably red.

"Okay, so … *Operation: Full Moon*," Zach said in a secretive voice. "What's the plan, princess?"

I huffed, which translated to 'how the hell should I know?' "I'm thinking we throttle Jessica and Trina behind the library until they puke. Or, better yet, sneak hair dye into their shampoo bottles."

Zach chuckled. "Nice. But since we don't have anything incriminating to keep them from tattling, the first is a no-go. The second, though … that one has possibilities," he said, over a bite of something, probably his pizza. "The thing is, you're forgetting the absolute best type of revenge."

"Yeah? What's that?"

"Success," Cal put in. "You prove the assholes wrong. There's nothing better, trust me."

A story lurked behind that statement, but I didn't wonder about it until later, when I replayed our conversation in my head. Now, I simply groaned at the idea of being forced into this ridiculous dare.

"When's the next full moon?" Zach asked.

"Middle of September." Cal glanced around, I assumed for anyone taking an interest in our conversation. "Our first night at the compound is the twelfth. Full is on the thirteenth."

"Please tell me that's a Friday or Saturday." I examined my wrap for green bell peppers. I always forgot to tell Mrs. Godfrey that I hated those.

Cal shook his head. "If you mean full moon, this next one's on a Wednesday."

"Figures," I muttered. "Darn. On the weekend, I might have been able to do it without breaking curfew. Now, not only do I have to get in and out of the compound, I also have to sneak out of my dorm and off campus. Plus, sneak back in when I get back."

"Not if you stick with me," Zach said. "You just need to be spot on with your camera. The rest is easy cheesy lemon squeezy."

"Oh, sure," I drawled. "Never mind the other details, like getting there, scaling the ginormous fence, and not getting attacked by all the little twerps who haven't mastered their alter-egos. Did you know, last year, more than half of the kindergarten class were shifters? They're all first graders now. Maybe not all of them are predators, but still. We'll be lucky not to come out of this in pieces."

"You're underestimating the Hidden, princess," Zach said darkly. "Cal can only track me because I let him."

When I looked at Cal, he nodded.

"Okay. *Fine.*" After a petulant sigh, I leaned forward to ensure no one could hear our conversation above the room's boisterous chatter. "How are you planning for us to get there? It's too far to walk. I could take my Vespa, I guess, but I've never ridden with a double. And if it rains, it would be miserable." I didn't mention it would also mean breaking two of my promises to Dad, which bothered me way more than disobeying any of the school's stupid rules.

"You could take my car," Cal offered.

I stopped eating and widened my eyes at him. "You'd do that? But you hardly know me."

"I figure your dad's good for it if you wreck it." His expression hardened to a scowl. "But definitely don't, okay?"

"Crashing a car isn't on my to do list, so I think we're good."

"Then we've got our plan," Zach murmured. "We'll figure out the details, later."

I nodded, sagging a little. "Thanks. I can't believe you guys are up for this. It's so stupid. If I hadn't opened my big mouth — " I uttered a sound of frustration. "But, jeez, Trina and Jessica are so annoying."

"Annoying doesn't even cover it," Zach said. "You haven't heard what they're saying."

I froze, my wrap midway to my mouth, and narrowed my eyes at his empty seat. "Yeah? What?"

He blew air over his teeth, by the sound of it. "The usual snotty, know-it-all bullshit, not worth repeating. Just keep thinking about how awesome it'll be to see them eat every bitchy word when you shove that glossy eight-by-ten in their faces." He snickered. "Eight-by-fuck-ing-ten, princess. It'll be our catch phrase, you know, our motto. Damn! Am I good, or *am I good*? Repeat it with me: 'Eight-by-fuck-ing-ten.' Am I right?"

I tried not to laugh. "You're a goof."

CHAPTER 7

Truthsayer

AFTER class ended at three, I rushed back to my dorm to dump off my backpack. I took a moment to freshen up, but still managed to get my butt to the administration building a few minutes early.

Dad sat in a guest chair outside Mr. Simmons' office when I arrived. He sipped from a disposable coffee cup, most likely a cappuccino purchased from the espresso cart in the student commons. A magazine was open in his lap. As soon as he spotted me, he tossed the magazine onto the glass-topped accent table and stood.

"Hey, kiddo. How was your first week?" He smiled, eyeing me over the top of his reading glasses before removing the slim wire frames and sliding them into the breast pocket of his sport coat.

"Hi, Dad. First week was good." I ducked my head. "I, uh, made a couple new friends."

"*Ah bon?*" He regarded me fondly. "Was there ever any doubt?"

I shrugged.

"And how is your English Composition class going?"

"It's going fine. I like doing it this way. Turned in my first essay, today."

"Glad to hear it. Keep up the good work. Mr. Simmons assured me they're keeping a close eye on things. My main concern is that you're happy and you learn the required material without your grades suffering."

"It'll be fine, Dad. Don't worry. Professor Trapp is really great."

He nodded. "So I hear. I'm looking forward to meeting this teacher of yours."

At the sound of approaching footsteps, I glanced behind me to find that very teacher heading toward us, looming large next to a petite woman whose shoulder-length black hair and dark olive coloring looked striking against the vibrant pink-and-yellow pattern of her flowing sari. Entranced, I eyed the exotic garment's various pleats as she walked closer, wondering how the fabric attached and draped so perfectly around her trim figure.

How long does it take for her to get dressed in the morning? I wondered, envying her elegance.

"*Bonjour, Mademoiselle Lire.*" Professor Trapp extended his hand to Dad. "You must be Monsieur Devon. I'm Brandon Trapp, your daughter's French teacher."

Dad nodded, taking my professor's hand in a firm shake. "*Bonjour.* It's good to meet you, *Monsieur.*"

Professor Trapp focused on me. "Lire, this is Councilwoman Chopra. She's the Arcane Council's highest-ranked truthsayer. She rarely takes cases outside the Council, but for you, she made an exception."

The councilwoman threw Professor Trapp an annoyed scowl. "I thought you wanted to put her at ease," she said in a voice colored by a slight British accent. She turned to me, her full lips parted by a broad smile. A deep dimple on her left cheek gave her expression a playful bent. "Hello, Lire. I'm Isha." She jerked a thumb at my professor. "The big oaf and I went to school here."

"Oaf? You couldn't possibly be talking about *me*," Professor Trapp announced.

I giggled, somewhat nonplussed, but Isha's easy smile and relaxed demeanor were contagious. "It's nice to meet you."

Isha extended her hand to Dad. "Mr. Devon, it's a pleasure to see you again."

Again?

"Please, call me Lucien," he replied, shaking her hand. "Thank you for coming."

"I was happy to," she assured him. "I've been hoping for an excuse to come back. I'm curious to see how much things have changed since Bran and I were students." She leaned toward me and whispered, "Does Professor Arkin's classroom still smell like there are dead skunks buried under the floor?"

"Yes! That's it. That's exactly how it smells." Wrinkling my nose, I shook my head. "All those weird specimens."

"And the eyes follow you," she added.

"They totally do!" I exclaimed.

Dad smiled amusedly, while Professor Trapp pressed his lips together and gazed down at the floor, clearly holding back a laugh.

The door to Mr. Simmons' office opened, drawing our attention to the head of our school, who smiled cordially at the four of us. Behind him, Mr. Gibbs and Professor Everhart stood side by side, their arms folded, both serious. As Neverhart looked in Professor Trapp's direction, she started, her expression turning to one of utter surprise for a scant second before settling down to a pinched frown. If I'd more than blinked, I might have missed it.

Mr. Simmons' assistant, a gray-haired woman with a stout figure and a thing for pantsuits, slipped from the room carrying a glass carafe in one hand and an empty plate in another. She rushed away, her mind on whatever task required her attention.

Mr. Simmons strode to Dad, his hand extended. "Lucien, good to see you. Good afternoon, Mistress Devon," he said, nodding at each of us. "Hello, Brandon. And you must be Councilwoman Chopra?"

I gazed at Isha, whose expression had turned professional, noting that she hadn't offered any of them her first name.

I couldn't see Dad's face as he shook Mr. Gibbs' hand, followed by Neverhart's, but I didn't imagine that he looked gracious.

"Come in, please," Mr. Simmons said, gesturing the rest of us inside his opulently appointed corner office, which, it seemed to me, had been styled after some wealthy English lord's study.

Polished wood seemed to cover every inch of the L-shaped room, from Mr. Simmons' solid cherry desk to the walnut paneled walls. Across from the door, two leather club chairs sat on either side of a modest, stacked-rock fireplace, which effectively divided the office space from the conference area. Left of the fireplace, Mr. Simmons' desk and the room's corner windows dominated the shorter side of the 'L.'

As I paused, steps from the doorway, allowing Isha to enter in front of me, someone tugged my ponytail. Gasping, I turned to find the waiting area empty.

Zach?

"Miss Devon, is something amiss?" Mr. Simmons asked from his station at the door.

Mind spinning, I quickly mumbled something about mistaking a shadow for a spider.

Is Zach coming inside?

To the right of the door, floor-to-ceiling bookcases lined the walls of the adjoining conference room. A built-in ladder, which could be wheeled along an iron track, allowed access to the books on the higher shelves. The volumes were all tastefully bound in burgundy, brown, or dark green leather, some accented with gold trim, and I wondered whether any of them had been cracked open, even once, by the schools' various headmasters.

After offering everyone coffee and refreshments, which were set out on the nearby sideboard, Mr. Simmons directed us toward his oval mahogany conference table. As instructed, I took the far end and allowed Dad to take the seat at my right, Professor Trapp at my left. Isha sat in the chair on Professor Trapp's left. Mr. Simmons took his place at the opposite end of the table, with Mr. Gibbs and Professor Everhart flanking him.

The table sat ten, leaving the three center-most chairs empty, which had the unintentional effect of drawing a dividing line between 'them' and 'us.' I wondered whether the adults in the room viewed it the same way.

Mr. Simmons' personal assistant sat apart from all of us, choosing a chair near the window, her pencil poised over her steno pad.

Mr. Simmons cleared his throat. "Now then, as you know, we're here today because Mistress Devon declined to answer Assistant Headmaster Gibb's questions regarding a harmless school prank until a truthsayer could verify her responses. Normally, we wouldn't seek such a drastic measure as a part of our investigation into this type of wrongdoing, but it's my understanding that there are extenuating circumstances, which led Miss Devon to believe she was being unfairly judged — namely, a disrespectful cartoon depiction of Professor Everhart that Miss Devon does not refute authoring.

"Merely penciling a cartoon cannot and should not be construed as evidence that Miss Devon had anything to do with the vandalism of Professor Everhart's classroom. However, since both infractions came to light during the same meeting, I understand why Miss Devon might have felt wrongly accused. Mr. Gibbs and Professor Everhart came to no such conclusions and remain impartial."

"That's interesting to hear," Dad said, looking relaxed in his chair. "Especially since my daughter overheard Professor Everhart declare to Mr. Gibbs her steadfast belief of an individual's guilt, moments prior to the meeting you've described. Professor, were you, or were you not, speaking about my daughter when you declared this individual to be *patently guilty*?"

Neverhart blinked for a moment. "This interview isn't about me, Mr. Devon, it's about your daughter and her unwillingness to answer questions regarding what she may or may not know about the vandalism in my classroom."

Dad's smile didn't reach his eyes. "Instead of an answer, I get evasion, which tells me all I need to know about your impartiality. Excuse the interruption, Jerod. Ask your questions, if you will."

Mr. Simmons, looking flustered by Dad's comment, hesitated briefly before considering me. "Miss Devon, did you participate in or have any prior knowledge of the desk dismantling that took place in Professor Everhart's classroom earlier this week?"

"No. The first I heard about it was when Mr. Gibbs brought it up in our meeting on Tuesday morning."

Isha nodded. "True."

Mr. Simmons frowned. "You had no prior knowledge? Nothing mentioned in passing? Nothing that, in light of what happened, you now find suspect?"

"No," I said earnestly. "And I don't understand why anyone would think I did."

Isha, again, nodded.

"Then what brought you to the administration building on Tuesday morning?" Professor Everhart asked.

"I wanted to talk to Mr. Gibbs."

Her eyes narrowed suspiciously. "About what?"

"That would be between my daughter and the assistant headmaster," Dad interrupted. "But since the requisite parties are all here, I'll allow her to answer the question if she wishes."

Hands clasped tightly in my lap, I straightened in my chair and directed my response to Mr. Simmons. "I, uh, wanted to lodge a formal complaint about the way I'm treated in Professor Everhart's class."

"True," Isha said. "And I should add, it's for this reason that the Arcane Council requested my presence here today. President Kessburg has personally tasked me with learning the details and verity of Miss Devon's complaint. It's also come to my attention that another student, Mr. Zachary Carter, has issued a similar grievance. Depending upon how things progress, I may want to speak to him, with his parents' permission, obviously."

"I don't understand," Mr. Gibbs said. "I thought it was clear from our earlier meeting that Professor Everhart's conduct wasn't motivated by malicious intent. Her actions were driven by her sincere effort to make both Ms. Devon and Mr. Carter more comfortable in her class, nothing more."

"With all due respect, this matter is not one that can be dismissed with a simple assurance that everyone involved *meant well*," Isha said. "President Kessburg and the joint coalition have demanded a thorough investigation. As their representative, I have been charged with ascertaining that this alleged treatment isn't the result of a deeper issue or a methodology widely endorsed by your staff."

Mr. Gibbs looked affronted, but Mr. Simmons jumped in, his right hand splayed over his suit's left-hand breast pocket, partially covering his ever-present pocket hankie. "Since the school's inception, Coventry Academy's teachers and staff have taken great pride in their ability to provide a safe and nurturing learning environment for every one of our students. This is a key tenet of our school's charter, and I can assure you we take any threat to our students' peace of mind seriously. The joint coalition has Coventry Academy's earnest cooperation in this matter, Councilor Chopra."

"Excellent. Thank you, Mr. Simmons," Isha replied brightly. She turned to me. "Now, Lire, if you wouldn't mind, I'd like to know about your experiences in Professor Everhart's class. I understand you had her last year, but to start with, perhaps you could describe Monday's class for me. What happened?"

Haltingly, I described my first day of class, starting with why I'd been a minute late. I hadn't anticipated how difficult it would be to detail this stuff while Neverhart stared daggers at me. I tried to avoid looking at her, but it wasn't easy with her sitting almost directly across the table.

I shivered, despite the warmth of the room, and worried that my teeth might start chattering. More than once, I had to repeat myself because Mr. Simmons couldn't hear me. Whenever my account faltered, Isha's questions spurred me along. I volunteered everything, including how I passed 'silly notes to a friend' while avoiding any specifics about their content.

"Would one of those notes be the drawing Professor Everhart found beneath your desk?" Isha asked.

I bit my lip. "Uh, yeah."

"Thank you. Please, continue."

"Aren't you going to ask who she was passing notes to?" Professor Everhart asked.

"No. It hasn't any bearing on the matter at hand."

"No bearing?" Neverhart's voice rose with such incredulity that she all but shrieked the final syllable. "*Of course* it has bearing. Who she chooses to collude with speaks to her character."

Dad leaned forward, but before he could voice his own objection, I blurted, "I wasn't colluding with anyone! And, even if I was, I sure wouldn't give you their name. I barely have any friends as it is. I'm not about to throw one them under the bus for passing stupid notes in class."

"No, that's not your style, is it?" Professor Everhart snapped. "You'd rather threaten them in secret to make them do your bidding. *That's* why you don't have any friends. Admit it, so we can have done with this farce. This has nothing to do with loyalty and everything to do with your little black book of secrets and your penchant for blackmail."

I stared at her with such utter disbelief, my mouth frozen in an astonished oval, that I'm sure I looked like a goggling anime character.

"You're accusing my daughter of blackmail?" I'd never heard Dad's voice become so thunderous in all my life, except, maybe, that one time when I was seven. I'd almost gotten myself run over by a car after recklessly sledding down our driveway into the icy street.

Mouth clacking shut, I turned to Dad, whose glare at Professor Everhart was nothing short of incendiary. *Hoo, boy.* Even without any magical ability, I'd have laid odds on my dad against everyone in the room combined.

Mr. Simmons attempted to intervene, but Neverhart overrode him. "Yes. I have it on good authority, from numerous students, including my nephew," she declared, her posture ramrod straight, chin raised. "Ask her, you'll see."

She has a nephew who goes to school here?

"I don't blackmail," I bit out. "I learned a long time ago to keep my gloves on and any personal details I might accidentally learn to myself."

"My nephew doesn't lie."

"Neither do I." I shot a nervous glance at Isha and added, "Unless you count white ones, or keeping something a secret because you don't want to tattle on someone."

"Who is this nephew of yours?" Dad asked before I could dig my hole any deeper.

"Skyler Martin. He graduated last year. If asked, I'm sure he would come in to be interviewed." Her tone was so gratingly superior, I wanted to punch her, except I was too busy freaking out.

She was talking about Skyler, the school bully! The *one* person in my whole existence who I'd threatened.

Jeez Louise. Why me?

"Lire, is there something you'd like to tell us?" Mr. Gibbs asked.

Grumbling inarticulately, I dropped my hand from my face and sat up straight. "Skyler was a bully. Ask anyone. He liked teasing the strigoi, calling them names, just generally being a jerk to them, because he knew they couldn't fight back."

I scowled across the table. "I don't blackmail … but once, when he was getting into this one strigoi's face, I jumped between them before things got out of hand. I, uh, might have threatened Skyler with telling a secret of his if he didn't stop bullying them."

I clenched my fists. "I couldn't help it. When I saw him picking on that strigoi, who always kept to himself, I sort of lost it." Though Alex had graduated, I avoided mentioning his name. The last thing I wanted was for him to get dragged into this mess.

"What did I tell you? She admits it!" Neverhart exclaimed. "And I resent your accusation, young lady. Skyler doesn't have an aggressive bone in his body. That strigoi boy pushed his buttons and he was merely defending himself."

I snorted.

"You dare to impugn his character?" she accused. "You? A liar and an admitted blackmailer?"

"That's enough!" Dad's bellow echoed through the spacious office, startling everyone, including a pinch-faced Mr. Simmons.

Isha filled the shocked silence. "Is this why you issued Lire a special desk and attempted to keep her from contact with anything that may have been touched by you or her fellow classmates?"

"Yes. I go the extra mile to protect my students. Unfortunately, outside of my class, the most I've been able to do is convince some of her other teachers to keep her at the back of their classrooms." She clicked her tongue disdainfully. "None of them are willing to invest their time like I have. They're not as in touch with their students. They haven't earned their trust, so they don't hear them talk candidly about what Lire's been up to."

"You know of other incidents? Other kids who have been blackmailed or threatened?" Isha asked.

"Yes," Neverhart replied stoutly. "They told me about her black book."

"Then they're lying," I protested. "Councilor, I swear, Skyler's the only person I've ever threatened. I did it because he was pushing that vampire to the breaking point. If I hadn't ..." I shook my head. "I didn't want to see him get expelled just because Skyler was being a big fat jerk."

"Of all the—" Neverhart blustered, but Isha's upraised palm silenced her outburst.

"Miss Devon, regardless of your intent, have you ever gathered details about another student's private life and then revealed those secrets to another individual?"

I wanted to rant. Would my girl-detective mistake ever stop haunting me?

"Once, when I was in third grade, but Mr. Simmons knows all about it. I tattled on Amanda Olander for carving graffiti on the library bathroom wall. After that disaster, I learned telling secrets doesn't earn me any friends. Ever since then, I've gone out of my way to keep what I know to myself. I don't tattle and I don't blackmail. Although, you'd never know it with the way everyone treats me."

Professor Everhart exhaled scornfully.

"True," Isha said, shooting a silencing glare Professor Everhart's way. "This is what comes from taking an individual's word for fact and acting on it without seeking proper validation. The story Professor Everhart has been fed by her students is highly suspect, but I won't know the truth of it until I speak with them directly. For her part, Miss Devon is telling the truth. I'm sure you'll agree that, in light of this, there is ample reason to doubt Professor Everhart's assertion that Lire is an unrepentant blackmailer."

"I should have known," Professor Neverhart said.

"Known what?" Professor Trapp asked, his deep voice laced with warning.

"That you'd take her side. Both of you! All these years and you haven't learned at all. Simply because someone *believes* what they're saying, doesn't make it the truth. It's just like before." She crossed her arms. "It won't bring her back, you know. I know that's why you're doing this. And, you can bet, *unlike last time*, I have no intention of taking it lying down. I have my own contacts at the Council and they're going to expose you for what you are—two zealots backing the story of every purportedly downtrodden psychic in the country, refusing to see how self-serving and duplicitous they might actually be."

"If Councilor Chopra and Professor Trapp are zealots, then they're the most unlikely zealots I've ever met," Mr. Simmons interrupted calmly. "When she called to set up this meeting, Councilor Chopra informed me of your shared history. She insisted that I employ my own truthsayer for the express purpose of verifying her findings, in case her motives were called into question."

He gestured at his assistant, who'd been unobtrusively taking shorthand from her seat near the window. "Not many people know that my executive assistant, Mrs. Franklin, is a PRC-certified truthsayer." He peered at his assistant. "Clarissa, if you please. Does your assessment diverge in any way from Councilor Chopra's?"

"No. Miss Devon has consistently told the truth."

"You didn't ask about her black book," Professor Everhart protested, and I had to wonder what the heck was wrong with her that made her cling to the belief that I blackmailed people.

"Very well," Isha said. Although she looked exasperated, it didn't come through in her tone. "Lire, what about this black book? Do you keep a book that documents whatever secrets you learn?"

"No. I keep a journal, like a lot of girls, but it's for my own private stuff, poems ... you know, things like that. And, anyway, it's not black. It's blue with flowers." I ducked my shoulders. "Besides, anyone who has a clue about clairvoyance would know I don't need a book to keep track of secrets."

"Why's that?" Isha asked.

"Because that's part of it — part of my magic. When I touch something that's been touched by someone else, the memories become my own. They're all up here," I said, tapping the side of my head. "I don't need to write them down."

"So, you deny threatening a certain group of students with your black book?" Professor Everhart asked. She waved her clenched fist as though holding something for everyone to see. "Saying you were keeping track of things, just like Santa?"

"Yeah, like, eight years ago, after Amanda called me a snitch for the *gazillionth* time. Even third graders know about sarcasm. If I did wave something, it was a fake. I've never kept a black book of secrets.

Like I said, if I wanted to blackmail someone, I wouldn't need to write it down in a stupid book."

"Truth," Isha said.

A gentle tug at my ponytail broadcasted Zach's presence before he whispered at my ear, his voice as soft as a humming bee, "That's what Amanda's been telling everyone for years. The whole school thinks you've got this little black book with everyone's secrets."

Without thinking, I gaped at Neverhart and blurted, "Is that true? Amanda's been telling everyone that I keep a black book? This whole time, she's been telling everyone that I'm a blackmailer?" My voice rose with my realization. "*That's* why no one wants to be friends with me, why no one wants to be teamed up with me in gym or for school projects. All because of some stupid thing I said back when I was freaking eight years old?"

"Lire, I can assure you, we'll get to the bottom of this," Mr. Simmons said, his voice gentle.

"Right." I laughed bitterly. "But it doesn't matter. The damage is done. Even my *teachers* believe her!"

Ignoring their stunned expressions, I pushed my chair away from the table and beelined to the door. I had to get out before I screamed. Or lunged across the table to strangle a certain someone.

"Lire, where are you going?"

"Are you okay?"

I might have ignored their questions, except Dad and Professor Trapp both sounded worried.

"I ... need to blow off some steam," I growled, throwing open the door.

I stormed out of the building, ignoring anyone and everyone. After my murderous walk brought me to the front of the school still wanting to kick something, I launched into a run. I ran until my thighs burned, pounding out my anger and frustration on the warm asphalt with every knee jolting stride.

When I finally slowed to a walk, my legs felt like a couple of rubber Slinkys and I was too exhausted to be pissed off. I stopped where the academy's meandering, tree-lined private drive met the two-lane county highway, a mile and a half from the main office. The echo of shoes turned me in my tracks.

Cal staggered to a halt, gasping for breath, and wagged a hand at me, as if to say 'no.' He bent over to brace his hands on his knees. "Holy ... crap," he gushed out. "I ... thought ... you'd ... never ... stop."

Another thirty seconds of panting went by before he stood upright and ran his fingers through his hair. "Jesus H. Christ. You've been holding out on us at the track." He wiped his forehead and flung any accumulated sweat into the dirt on the side of the drive. "I've been yelling at you to hold up. Didn't you hear me? What happened? Why'd you run?"

Just thinking about the meeting made me want to start running again. I clenched my hands into fists and stomped to the school's granite sign. "Why don't you ask Zach. He was there."

With a small jump, I hoisted myself onto the thick rectangular marker, pulling up my legs and hugging my folded knees.

"In your meeting with Simmons and the truthsayer?" He sounded genuinely shocked.

"If you weren't waiting for him, why were you there?"

"I was waiting for *you*," he said, stressing the difference. "I'm not Zach's babysitter, you know."

I pressed my lips together, not completely convinced, but I let it go. "Did you know Amanda's been telling everyone I'm a blackmailer? That I keep everyone's dirty secrets in a little black book?"

His nervous downward glance told me everything. "Yeah. Got that on the first day, after she saw you sitting with me at lunch."

"Boy. Guess you like to live dangerously."

"Not really." He crossed his arms, giving me a stern look. "I just don't believe everything I'm told, especially by some stuck-up know-it-all. Besides, it's easy to see you're not the type."

"It is?"

"Duh."

I sighed. "Too bad not everyone's as smart as you. Even Neverhart believed it. That's why she's been treating me like I've got Ebola."

"Figures. The woman's dumb as a post."

Caught off guard, I burst out laughing. "It's not really funny, though," I said after winding down. I banged my forehead against my folded knees and closed my eyes. "The entire school hates me. This whole time, I assumed it was because of my magic, but it wasn't. Well, not completely."

"The entire school doesn't hate you." He must have walked closer because he nudged my leg—I hoped with his shirt-covered elbow and not his bare skin, but if I had to throw out these pants, I decided it'd be worth it. "*I* don't hate you," he said and then added wryly, "Because I'm smart, remember?"

"Oh, totally." Looking up, I mirrored his smirk. "Smarter than a post, for sure."

He groaned, throwing his head back to glare up at the sky. "No respect. I chase you for three miles and this is what I get?"

"More like one and a half, you big baby." I grinned. "And, what was with all that wheezing? You're a werewolf. You're supposed to be able to run practically forever."

"Not all of us are built like Wile E. Coyote. Some of us have actual muscles, in case you haven't noticed." He puffed himself up. "I'm what you'd call a short distance sprinter."

"Right, right. Next time we go to the track, I'll remind you to bring your walker, Grandpa."

He lunged toward me, maybe to push me over or tickle me, but he veered away at the last moment, stumbling to the side. "Whoa, there," he said, laughing sheepishly while he regained his balance. He wagged his finger at me. "That smart mouth is going to get you into trouble, unless you want to know what I'm thinking, which you probably don't."

"That bad, huh?" As soon as it slipped out of my mouth, I wanted to take it back. It came out sounding way more serious than I'd intended.

"Nah," he said, sticking his hands in his front pockets. "Well, *yeah*, but not in the way you might think."

He cleared his throat, but if he intended to explain, the opportunity was lost when a car came into view from the school's direction, snagging both of our attentions.

"It's my dad," I said, recognizing the black Lexus.

"Nice wheels."

The front passenger window rolled down as the sleek sedan came to a stop next to us. "Hey, princess. Daddy-o says get your butts in here, the both of you."

"Jeez Louise," I grumbled. "Is there no place you can't infiltrate?"

"What can I say? It's my charm."

"Or something." I marched around the car to take the seat behind Dad.

As I buckled in, I noticed Zach's seatbelt shimmering in and out of visibility where it stretched over his hidden form. Apparently, the barrier of his shirt was enough to interfere with his magic, but I knew he could force the strap to be totally invisible if he set his mind to it. After all, he did it all the time with his backpack.

Not for the first time, I wondered at the extent of Zach's power. Could he make the whole car invisible if he chose to?

"Cal, this is my dad, Lucien," I said, once Cal had settled in the seat behind Zach and closed the door. "Dad, this is Cal. I guess you've already met Zach McSneaky Pants."

"That's *Mister* McSneaky Pants," Zach retorted.

I snickered. "Right. *Pardonnez-moi.*"

The car rocked as Dad executed a three-point U-turn.

"How'd you even know where to look for us?" I asked.

"Your dad saw where you went, and Professor Trapp spotted Cal going after you. Boy, oh, boy, princess. I gotta say, you know how to make an exit, but you sure missed the fireworks. After Mountainside and Daddy-o came back to the table, the gloves came *off.* You should've seen them reaming the shi — I mean the crap out of those idiots. It was awesome. And Neverhart's face ... Oh, man. I wish you could've seen her — it was frickin' priceless."

I cringed. "Sorry, Dad. I shouldn't have stormed out, but I — " I blew out a frustrated breath. "I was ready to murder someone."

"You have nothing to be sorry about, *mon coeur.* They are the ones who should be sorry, and will be if they don't make amends. I gave them a week to investigate and issue appropriate restitution. But if you want me to make inquiries at Rotterdam or Cambrian, *tout de suite,* I will."

"No, no. Don't do that," I said, grimacing. The thought of starting all over at a new school made my stomach turn. "Besides, Zach says Rotterdam sucks."

"Word," Zach declared.

I rolled my eyes, unsuccessful in my bid to cover my growing smirk. When I caught Dad's glance in the rearview mirror, I noticed his eyes were crinkled with amusement. Despite the horrible meeting and its revelations, I laughed.

Dad dropped us off at the front of the school after assuring me that Professor Trapp and Isha had things well in hand. Maybe he was right, but unless Amanda stood up on stage and announced at an all-school assembly that she was a liar-liar-pants-on-fire, with Isha on hand to confirm the truth of it, I couldn't see what difference it would make. On the positive side, though, I'd come away from today's disaster with Zach and Cal standing firmly in my corner, which meant a lot.

"Your dad's pretty cool," Zach said as we ambled up the front walkway. "And here I thought *Mountainside* was intimidating. The two of them together … holy shit. Gibbs just about crapped his pants. I kid you not."

I couldn't imagine Dad scaring anyone, much less someone like Mr. Gibbs. "Jeez. What the heck did they say?"

"What didn't they say? Your dad demanded to know why Gibbs and Neverhart still had jobs, for one. By the way, did you know Devon Consulting, the Domn, and the Arcane Council are the largest contributors to Coventry's general fund? If he wanted to, your dad could make the headmaster's life plenty difficult. But Mountainside …" Zach hooted. "He's the one with the big hammer … well, he and Isha. If they tell President Kessburg that discrimination is rampant here, Coventry could lose its accreditation, which means a lot of parents will send their kids to other academies. It could tank the whole school."

I couldn't speak. I stopped and stared in his direction, probably looking like a complete moron.

"You're surprised?"

I shook my head, thought better of it, and then shrugged. "Well, yeah. All *this* because of Skyler and Amanda and Neverhart? Hard to believe it could go all the way to the top of the Arcane Council."

"You don't know the best part," Zach said. "When Neverhart tried bringing up the whole Skyler vampire incident again, Simmons said that if she'd only spoken to him about it, he would have told her that the Domn had alerted him to the incident, two years ago, on the night it happened. Their discussion confirmed your version of the story, not Skyler's."

I jolted. Mr. Simmons had talked to the Domn?

Holy crap. The secrecy surrounding the strigoi leader's identity was legendary. Most people suspected the powerful chieftain was a guy, which ticked me off on principal. *Hello!* Women could totally kick butt too!

To my disgust, though, even *I* couldn't seem to stop myself from picturing a dude whenever I heard the name. *Domn* just sounded masculine to me. As much as I tried to picture a woman in the role, my mind conjured the image of a tall, imposing man shrouded by a black cape, instead. I blamed Hollywood. I couldn't think of a single vampire movie with a woman playing Dracula. At least, not any good ones.

"The Domn? Seriously?" I pressed my lips together. "How would Mr. Simmons know for sure?"

"The Domn has ways of proving it. Trust me." The way he said this, so flatly but with an underlying tremor of apprehension, broke me out in goosebumps. "This Skyler guy sounds like a major piece of shit. Neverhart's an idiot for believing him. She's *so* getting fired."

I wasn't sure how I felt about that. A big part of me lit up with glee, shouting, 'Serves her right, the wench!' I despised her, yet … I kind of felt sorry for her, too. She'd been bamboozled by Skyler and Amanda. If it hadn't been for their lies, I wondered how Neverhart would have treated me. Based on what little I'd heard about Neverhart's history with Professor Trapp and Isha, probably not much better. It sounded like something in her past may have predisposed her to distrusting clairvoyants. Zach, too, seemed to fall within her circle of suspicion.

"I wonder what the deal is with Isha and Professor Trapp and Neverhart," I said. "I think they all went to school here."

"Is Isha the truthsayer?" Cal asked.

I nodded.

"They were all in the same graduating class, but I haven't been able to find out what happened between them," Zach said sourly. "I think it has something to do with their friend Abby, the clairvoyant. They see *disturbing parallels* between Amanda's behavior and what happened to Abby, and they want to know whether Neverhart had any part in it. Whatever *that* means."

Abby. Her name was Abby.

I shrugged but my mind whirled. Did Neverhart have something to do with Abby's death?

"Look. There's Mountainside," Cal said, his gaze locked directly ahead of us. "Is that her, the truthsayer?"

Sure enough, Professor Trapp and Isha strolled through the main quad toward the student commons, occasionally glancing at each other as they talked. Isha's pink and yellow sari provided the sole spot of color amid the earthen tones of the concrete pavers.

"Yeah—Isha," I replied. "She's pretty cool."

"Well, kids, this is where we part ways," Zach announced, his voice vibrating with exertion and growing distant as he hurried away from us. "Don't wait up."

"Zach, what—?" I took a few tentative steps in the direction of his voice, straight toward the quad. "Wait! You're not—?"

"Don't bother," Cal said, interrupting my admonition. "He's too far to hear, unless you want to start yelling. Besides, there's no stopping him when he gets like this. He's like a terrier spotting a squirrel if there's a secret he wants to know."

I watched as Isha and Professor Trapp walked up the steps to the student commons, knowing any minute Zach would be on their heels, listening to their private conversations. "No wonder Neverhart lumped him with me."

When Cal grunted ambiguously, I turned to frown at him. "He's going to spy on them. Doesn't that bother you at all?"

"I guess it might if he was blackmailing or extorting people or telling the world, but he's not."

"How would you even know?"

"I'd know. We've been best friends since first grade."

"If he's not using the information for his benefit, then why's he doing it?"

"He can't stand not knowing. He kind of wasn't kidding when he said it was genetic." With a sigh, he started down the path that led to the dormitories. "Come on."

After a minute of walking in silence, he glanced over at me. "So, uh, you wanna hang out or something?"

I shrugged, trying to play it cool while my heart leapt into a higher gear. "Sure. What do you want to do?"

"We could go to the rec center, sign up for air hockey or ping pong."

"Air hockey." I made a face. "I suck at ping pong."

He smirked. "Fine. If it's too crowded, we could try for a library media room, watch a Miyazaki movie, maybe."

I lit up. "Sure."

"Should we just do that? Stick with the movie?" He examined me. "Maybe do a marathon?"

I grinned at him. "That'd be awesome. But we can play some air hockey, first, if you want."

"Another time. I'll get the movies. You can sign us up for a room. I'll meet you there."

"Okay." I smiled, toning it down so I didn't look like an infatuated sixth grader.

You have no other friends, I sternly reminded myself. *Don't ruin it by going all gaga.*

CHAPTER 8

One measly veep

TWENTY minutes later, Cal and I settled into Media Room B on the second floor of the library. After a good-natured debate, we decided to watch Cal's movies in chronological order by their Japanese release date.

Cal must have left a note for Zach in their room because *Castle in the Sky* was more than halfway through when the media room's door inexplicably burst open.

"Well, well. Isn't this cozy?" Zach crooned, no doubt eyeing the rearranged furniture and gigantic bean bags Cal had dragged in from the upperclassmen's hangout area.

Cal fumbled with the remote to pause the movie. "Dude, go get another one if you want to hang out and watch."

"We're doing a marathon of your favorites, Zach," I piped up. "You've missed most of *Castle in the Sky*, though. I'm sure you're heartbroken."

"Gutted. Totally. You two planning on breaking for dinner or is this a hard-core snacks-only marathon?"

I shrugged. "I don't know. We didn't get that far."

"Yeah. I can see that from here. Too bad."

"*Zach*," Cal growled.

I rolled my eyes. "I hadn't planned that far ahead. If we're doing snacks, I'll have to run back to my room."

"Might as well break for dinner," Cal said. "But we've got another half hour yet. Go grab a bag, Zach."

"Fine."

Roughly a minute later, a lime-green beanbag chair slid through the door to nestle to the left of mine.

"Something amuse you, there, princess?"

"Hard not to be," I said, grinning up at his voice. "What can I say? I'm easily entertained."

I heard him snort before his body hit the rotund bag, a solid *thwack* followed by the pleasant scrunching sound that's synonymous with giant beanbags. "That much is obvious. What're we watching, again?"

"Try to contain your excitement," I said dryly. "*Castle in the Sky.* We're at the part where they go through the storm and find Laputa."

He groaned. "You do know it's Friday night, right?"

"No one's forcing you to be here," Cal snapped.

"Dude, chill out. I was just saying. I thought we were going to check out that pizza place in town."

"You lost your vote when you wandered off," Cal replied. "Anyway, we can do that tomorrow."

"Hey, you know, if you guys already had plans for pizza, that's fine," I said. "We can watch movies another time."

"Nah. It's cool," Zach assured me. "Tomorrow night's fine. But first, don't you want to know what I found out?"

"No," I lied. "If I want to know, I'll ask Professor Trapp myself." I refrained from being an old scold, but I was sorely tempted to chime in about how spying on people was wrong.

"Bor-*ing*. Besides, I bet you a zillion bucks, he won't tell you everything. And, trust me, you want to know *everything*."

"No, I really don't." *God help me.* I really, really did.

"Has anyone told you that you suck at lying?"

Cal leaned away from the wall to glare at the empty space to my left. "Dude, shut it. She said no."

Zach's huff came out in a petulant rush. "You guys are no fun."

As Cal pressed the PLAY button, he muttered under his breath — something about Zach going elsewhere to have his fun, but there were a lot of F-bombs involved, so I could have been wrong on that.

Apparently, playing the movie wasn't about to discourage Zach.

As we got to the part where Sheeta and Pazu exit the massive thunderstorm to land their glider on Laputa, he whispered into my ear, "Mountainside's friend in high school, you know ... the clairvoyant, Abby? She shot herself, their junior year, during Thanksgiving break."

I gasped, turning my horrified gaze in Zach's direction.

"I know. Awful, right? But it gets worse. Neverhart was in love with Professor Trapp, like, big-time. She was insanely jealous of Abby — hated her guts. Did a lot of the same shit that Amanda's been doing to you, except she was more subtle about it. Mountainside had no clue how bad it was until after Abby died. She left a note for him and she kept a journal. It's why he feels responsible for her suicide. I guess, at one point, he believed Neverhart about something and that's what drove Abby to do it."

Oh, no! Poor Abby. Poor Professor Trapp!

Like me, Cal had gone rigid. Clearly, his hearing was good enough to discern Zach's furtive whisper over the movie's soundtrack. Either that, or he was reacting to my earlier gasp. I half worried that I'd end up sandwiched between them if Cal tackled his persistent roommate.

Why couldn't Zach have done something else tonight?

I instantly felt bad for thinking it. Yes, Zach was a blunt-talking wise-ass, but he was also a lot of fun to be around. On top of that, he seemed to be looking out for me. And — let's get real — with two friends to my name, that kind of support would never go under-appreciated.

"Cal, could you pause it? Sorry." I turned back to Zach. "I guess that's why Professor Trapp involved himself in my mess. Except for the love angle, Abby's and my situation aren't that different." Thinking about it, I cursed. "Please tell me he's not worried I'm going to *off* myself."

"Uh, yeah. He is — said as much to the truthsayer chick."

"Isha."

"Right, Isha," Zach agreed. "But she doesn't think you're likely to do something like that. She thinks you're much more confident than Abby ever was. You impressed her. But then Mountainside said something crazy about why he thinks you're so confident. Well, *one* of the reasons ..."

I frowned at him. "Yeah? And that is?"

"He thinks you have a bound familiar that used to belong to the Arcane Council's previous president." He laughed. "You should have seen Isha. You'd have thought Mountainside had called up the ghost of her dead grandma. He immediately swore her to secrecy and told her to keep an ear out to make sure the Council never finds out. Sounds like this familiar is super powerful and more than a few council members would do anything to get it."

"*Him*, not it," Cal said.

For once Zach seemed tongue-tied. He sputtered, "So this ... it's true? And you knew about it? When? Where was I?"

I wanted to throttle Professor Trapp. Why couldn't he have kept his mouth shut? Now, no thanks to him, the biggest gossip in the entire school knew the one secret in my life I absolutely needed to protect. What if Zach told someone who then told someone who then told Amanda? Or worse, what if Zach told his parents, or aunt, or whatever big kahuna ran the Hidden? Then what?

If it was true that more than one council member wanted Red, I could imagine they'd pay or do whatever it took to get him. In the right hands, a secret like this would be worth a crap-ton of money or power—likely both. I didn't know how much Dad had paid for Red, but it was a good bet my beloved familiar hadn't come cheap.

I covered my face.

This was bad. Like, life-changingly bad.

"Please don't tell anyone, Zach," I begged, staring at the empty bean bag next to me through my splayed fingers before letting my arms go slack. "Please. He's my best friend. I can't— I won't let anyone take him away from me. If it weren't for him ..." I shook my head. "Ple—"

"Jesus. Calm down. You think I'd do that? I'm not a complete blabbermouth, you know. I don't sell out my friends and I sure as hell wouldn't do something to get them killed."

I froze, staring in his direction. "*Killed?*"

"You're blood-bound to this familiar, aren't you?"

I nodded.

"Someone can't just take the creature away and start using it, princess. Bound familiars don't work that way. It's your express servant for life. *Your* life. Didn't anyone tell you that?"

"Well ... yeah. I mean, I guess so. I know he's mine until I die. I'm responsible for taking care of him."

"That's all? Didn't anyone tell you about the nature of a blood bond? How it works, what a familiar can do for you? What it means?"

Apparently, Zach didn't like what he saw in my expression.

"Jesus Christ. This critter, he's your servant, obligated to do your bidding without question, defend you, stuff like that, but depending on the creature, it can amplify your magic in different ways, even extend your life. You knew that, right? Until you die, your blood pact seals your familiar's potential from anyone else. So, if someone wants access to its power, they'll have to kill you to break the compact. Then they can take the creature and its potential for themselves."

"I wouldn't call him a creature," Cal said.

"No? Then what *would* you call it? I mean, *him.*"

Terrific. Now what?

Did I clamp down to protect Red's full identity or confide in them and hope they'd always be on my side? If I refused, would that spur Zach to do anything to find out more—like a terrier going after a squirrel—like Cal said? Would Zach start asking questions where he shouldn't, possibly eliciting the attention of the wrong people? Or would he resort to spying, like he spied on Professor Trapp and Isha?

All these thoughts wound me up so tight, I had the insane urge to take off running.

I turned to Cal. Maybe I looked frantic, or maybe he smelled my desperation and fear, because his expression softened. "Lire, it's okay. We grew up together. Zach's parents took me in when I was six. He's not just my best friend; we're brothers. You can trust him." He tipped his head downward, angling his azure gaze to peer directly into my eyes. "But if you don't want to tell him, then don't. I'll keep him off your back. I promise."

"*Hey!*" Zach protested.

"I'll tell you, but you guys have to tell me something in return. Each of you. Something just as important that you don't want other people to know." Leaning back against the wall, I folded my arms. "It's only fair. And it can't be something dumb, like, I jerked off in the shower this morning."

Zach gasped. "Princess! I'm shocked! Such language from someone so sweet." He deepened his voice to drawl, "And totally hot. Say it again. *I jerked off.*"

I shot him an annoyed look.

"Asshole." Cal glared at him. "You seriously need to shut up."

Between the stress, Zach's incessant crudeness, and Cal's disgruntled expression, I giggled until I could barely breathe and tears formed at the corners of my eyes. When I finally wound down, I flopped back against the wall and dabbed my eyes, still chuckling.

"Easy for you to laugh," Cal said. "I have to live with him."

"Fuck you, asswipe. Like you're some model citizen with your dirty boxers and hairballs everywh — "

Cal lurched forward, exploding, "So help me, Zach, if you don't shut your — !"

"Stop!" I shouted. "Holy crap, just cut it out. You want to know about my familiar? Stop acting like five-year-olds and figure out what you're going to pony up for that secret. And it better be good because I'm about ready to go back to my room and watch movies on my own. And when I say good, I mean freaking major, something that will affect your life in the future if certain people found out, because that's what we're talking about, here, with my familiar. This isn't kid stuff. This isn't some lame-ass tidbit about who I have a crush on or what stupid school rule I broke last night. It's a secret you're damn well going to take to your grave and if you can't come up with something significant, then you don't deserve to know mine. Got it?"

Breathing fast, I stared into Cal's wide blue eyes and wondered what the hell I'd gotten myself into. Did I really want to know their deepest, most significant secret? I half hoped they wouldn't be able to come up with anything.

Cal squared his chin. "My biological father is the Isangrim."

Next to me, I heard Zach's shocked intake of breath, but if he objected to Cal's candor, he didn't interrupt when Cal continued, "He traded me to Zach's parents as part of a pact between the North American Rout and the Hidden. In my place, Zach's twin brother is being raised by the Isangrim and his mate. No one knows, except the Hidden's highest echelon and the Isangrim and his second. Everyone else thinks I was killed in a car accident. Same goes for Zach's brother."

"Jesus, Cal," Zach muttered. "If Pop finds out ..."

"He's not going to find out," Cal growled, glaring past me, toward Zach. "She's the only one at this stupid school who has any integrity. You said so yourself."

"Fuck." He blew out a breath. "*Fine*. My father is the head honcho, princess, the Hidden's kingpin. And if you don't know the value of that secret, then you're — " He grunted and I imagined him shaking his head at me.

"Dumber than a post?" I offered.

Cal snorted and Zach said, "Exactly."

"If you're brothers, why don't you guys have the same last name?"

"Zach's parents didn't adopt me, they're my legal guardians," Cal explained. "Mars belongs to my aunt. She died around the time I was born. I needed an alias, so my identity couldn't be traced back to the Isangrim. They did something similar for Zach's brother."

Satisfied, I climbed out of my bean bag and trudged to the nearest table, which had been pushed against the wall to clear space for our more comfortable setup. "If you guys stay where you are, you'll be safe from Red's defensive spells."

"Trust me, bro," Cal murmured. "You wanna listen to what she says on that."

After scooting onto the table to sit cross-legged, I opened my purse. "Red ... you okay with this?"

He climbed out to stand on my right knee, the pressure of his fuzzy paws muted by the fabric of my chinos. "Indeed. Good evening, gentlemen."

"Zach, this is Red. His full name is John Redborn. He's a former necromancer whose soul was captured when he was executed during the Salem witch trials. When I was almost five, my father arranged for him to be my familiar. I've known he had previous owners. He's over three hundred years old, so, *duh*. But I had no idea he was the last A.C. president's familiar until a few days ago. Professor Trapp's the one who figured it out when I happened to mention Red in passing. You could say he was ..." I recalled his glowing eyes. "Yeah ... he was pretty serious when he warned me about keeping Red a secret."

"Gee, ya think?" Zach retorted, following up with a drawn-out whistle. "Most mages have to settle for a magically enhanced toad or snake. Maybe a jackulus or a kitsune, or even one of those specially bred Maine Coons— *if* they have the money. But a soul-bound human familiar is the ultimate. How the hell did your dad manage it?"

I shrugged. "No clue. It took almost a year to find him, though. And you're being rude. Try saying hello."

"Oh, right. Sorry. Nice to meet you, Red."

"The pleasure is mine, Zach. I assure you." Red sat, dangling his stout legs over my knee. "To answer your question, 'twas not Lucien who managed to secure my compact, but, rather, Lire herself, as the decision was mine to make. My previous master saw to it that I had autonomy in my choice of master. However, it would not surprise me to learn that a substantial sum was exchanged as part of the transaction."

"No shit."

"*Dude*," Cal scolded under his breath. "Watch your damned mouth."

"Be at ease, gentlemen. I am not one easily offended by words, lest their intent is to injure Lire."

"And a good thing too," I said wryly. "Otherwise Zach would hardly be able to open his mouth."

"What's this? Are you ... *dissing* me?" Zach asked.

"Would I do that?"

"Never, because you obviously appreciate my magnificence."

I laughed. "Or something."

"Just where is the love?" He huffed. "So, uh, Red, if you don't mind me asking ... why'd you pick a psychic for a master? I mean, with a magus, you'd have gotten to share your expertise. Just as a focus, I know, but still, you would have kept your hand in." He stammered, "Er, I mean ... sorry, bad word choice. What I meant to say was ... um—"

"I take your meaning. I chose Lire for the very simple reason that, even in her youth, her personality captivated me, and, frankly, I could see she needed me. After serving warlocks for three centuries, Lire's brand of magic proved to be a welcome change, indeed."

"Okay ... yeah. I could see how that would be," Zach said.

Cal cleared his throat. "I hate to break this up, but if we want to make it to the refectory for dinner, we should pack up. It's almost six."

"Too bad we can't lock the door. Then we could leave our stuff." I examined Cal. "We are coming back, right? Or were you guys going to do something else?"

"Giving up so soon?" Zach said, tut-tutting. "What a shame. And here I thought you were a hardcore marathoner."

"Shut up," I said, unsuccessfully smothering my smile.

"We're coming back," Cal declared as he pushed to his feet. He grabbed his backpack and strode to the DVD player. "We've got the room signed out until the library closes. I figure we can get through the next two in the rotation if we jet through dinner."

"Got that, princess? No dawdling over dessert. This is serious business."

"Whatever," Cal grumbled, zipping up his backpack with all his DVDs stowed inside. "Come on."

Inside the refectory, the thick smell of grilling hamburgers practically coated the back of my tongue. Even though it'd been twelve-and-a-half years since I'd been able to eat one, my mouth watered and my stomach growled loud enough for Zach to hear.

He laughed. "You hungry, tiger?"

Tiger? Really?

Secretly, the nickname warmed me straight through. It was better than 'princess'—although, with Zach's playful tone, I didn't mind either one. Zach was a sweet talker, all right.

The line moved fast. Sadly, my veggie patty didn't look half as appetizing as Cal's juicy cheeseburger, but at least the tater-tots were psi-free, crispy, and delicious. I popped one into my mouth before my plate had hit my tray.

When we entered the dining room, I noted a distinct lull in the clamor as dozens of students glanced in our direction and turned to whisper to their friends.

"Looks like the word's gotten out about the truthsayer meeting," I muttered as we slid into our usual seats. "I can't see how anyone could know any details, though."

"Sit tight. I'll check around," Zach said.

His hamburger disappeared from his plate, so I assumed he took it with him. Actually, for all I knew, he hadn't left his seat at all. I strained my ears for any hint of movement across from me, but I couldn't hear anything over the steady din of the room's many conversations.

I turned to Cal who hadn't wasted time before devouring his burger. "Is he ... you know ... ?" I subtly tipped my head toward the room.

"Probably," he mumbled. "He's not across from us."

"That you know of."

Nabbing a tot from his plate, he shrugged. "True. But we're brothers. Working that hard to spy on me would be dumb."

I took that to mean they told each other everything. I was jealous. I'd have given almost anything to have grown up with a sister who loved and confided in me.

"You're lucky," I told him. "My sister hates my guts."

I stopped short of volunteering anything else since I wasn't sure whether talking about personal stuff interested him.

"That sucks. How come?" He took an enormous bite of his burger, whittling it down by another third. One thing I'd noticed about Cal, he didn't stand on ceremony when it came to his meals. If he had to say a few words while chewing, so be it.

I shrugged, even though it was hardly a mystery. "My gift scares the crap out of my mom, and Giselle's always taken advantage, milking it for all it's worth. When my parents divorced, she told me it was my fault, that life would have been better for all of them if I'd never been born."

"What a fu—" He cleared his throat. "I mean, *Jesus*. What a wench."

I smirked, wondering what he'd censored. "Yeah. Won't argue with you, there." I pressed a tater-tot into the extra salt on my plate. "She wasn't wrong though. My parents would still be together if they hadn't had me. The whole reason Dad left was because my mom treated me like I was something that should have been buried out back—keeping me inside and stuff. You know, just generally acting like Giselle was her only child. It was bad."

"Doesn't mean your parents would have stayed together. Your dad's solid. Sooner or later he'd have figured out that he married an intolerant asshole." He grimaced and then shook his head. "Sorry. Calling it like I see it."

"Yeah, well … anything's possible, I suppose."

"Trust me. So … your parents divorced and now you live with your dad, yeah?"

I nodded. "Since I was seven."

"Where do you guys live?"

"Seattle. What about you and Zach?"

"It depends. The family … we have homes all over the place. In the states, we live north of Chicago, but Pop's looking into buying a house out here, maybe on the coast."

"That'd be nice."

He grunted noncommittally. "That any good?" He gestured at my half-eaten veggie burger.

"Probably not as good as yours."

"You can't eat meat, can you?"

"I could, but I'd regret it."

I shivered, remembering the one time I'd tried beef when I was little, before I had a clue what *not* to do. Fortunately, I'd only taken a tiny bite of steak and immediately spat it back on my plate. Since I hadn't yet been schooled in how to utilize my psychic shield, the steer's memories had poured into my mind in an unrestrained torrent. Mother had scolded me for my 'disgusting display,' but Dad had come to my rescue, carrying me upstairs and comforting me with his loving words and a cup of honey-sweetened chamomile tea. Honey had always soothed me, which was strange considering its intimate contact with the single-minded determination of thousands of busy bees.

There were few animal related foods I could tolerate. Dairy. Honey. Eggs. I shuddered to think what eating ground beef would be like. God knew how many individual animals went into a single patty. But I kept those thoughts to myself.

"Livestock ... they, uh, don't die in the best way," I said diplomatically. "The only meat I can handle eating is fish. Eggs. That's about it."

"Bummer."

"Deep thought from a wolf."

Grinning, he chomped his teeth together, ending with an exaggerated *clack*. "What'd you expect? Carnivores love their meat. Can't imagine what it'd be like to not be able to eat it. I'd die, probably."

"You can't be serious. You're human too, you know."

"True, but I'm not about to give it up to find out just *how* human." He wolfed down the last bite of his burger and then stood. "Gonna see if I can get seconds."

I laughed. "Okay."

As I finished my sandwich, I scanned the room, wondering where (and on who) Zach might be spying ... until I stopped short, mentally smacking myself.

Jumping to the conclusion that Zach had gone off to spy wasn't any different than Neverhart assuming I'd use my clairvoyance to learn everyone's darkest secrets at the first opportunity.

It wasn't hard to imagine that Zach was chatting up his many admirers. Whenever we were out and about, there seemed to be no shortage of girls who greeted the empty air next to Cal with a hopeful, "Hey, Zach," not only snubbing me but, more recently, ignoring the brooding werewolf too.

Apparently, a week of irritable growls and annoyed glares from Cal were enough to discourage even the most ardent of interested girls. I can't say I was broken up about it, but I'll admit, his universally grumpy responses struck me as unusual. I might have wondered if he preferred guys, except I'd never once caught him scoping anyone out. And, believe me, I went out of my way to pay attention.

I glanced toward the serving area, expecting, any moment now, to see that very werewolf returning with his second burger. Instead, my gaze ran smack into a looming figure whose shadow blotted out the dining room's overhead canned lighting. I reared back, following the svelte yet masculine form upward. I took in a superbly fitted suit and knotted silver-blue tie before coming face to face with a sharp-eyed man with ebony hair and a squared chin so rigidly set it could only belong to someone accustomed to being obeyed.

He examined me, arching one of his thin, perfectly-groomed eyebrows.

"You must be the psychic who's causing so much trouble," he said. His voice was almost as deep as Professor Trapp's, but it resonated with an unpleasant twang that battered the air around me.

"This is Arcane Council Vice President Jacoby," Amanda said, sounding way too smug. I'd been so stunned by this man's censure and imposing stature that I hadn't noticed her standing next to him. She looked down at me, snotty smile firmly in place, and announced: "My *godfather*."

Everything skidded to a stop as I struggled to process this startling tidbit.

Amanda's godfather was the flipping *A.C. Vice President?*

My inner voice woke me up. *Get a grip. Dad's a billionaire CEO. You can deal with one measly veep.*

I stood to face him, ignoring Amanda. "My name is Lire Devon. If you're referring to the *trouble* of Professor Everhart's classroom prank, Councilor Chopra can tell you I had nothing to do with it."

He smiled, but instead of putting me at ease, his toothy grin pricked the hairs along the back of my scalp. Several of his front teeth overlapped, yielding a serrated smile that wouldn't have seemed out of place on a shark. "Ah, yes. Third-year Councilor Chopra. Now that this triviality is over, I've returned her to her post."

"Godfather is a fifty-eight-year legate," Amanda said.

Too bad I didn't have a pin handy. I could have popped her, she was so puffed up.

She calls him 'Godfather?'

I did some quick mental math. Unless he'd joined the Council as a toddler, he was pushing eighty. I remembered what Zach had said about how some familiars prolonged their master's lives. Was that how he managed to look younger than Dad?

Since Amanda hadn't said anything else and the veep continued to examine me with a hint of a knowing smile, I guessed they were waiting for me to say something.

"Uh, okay. Congratulations, I guess?"

Amanda sneered, "God, you're clueless."

Jacoby flicked his fingers dismissively, giving me the distinct impression that he found her irritating, like a bothersome fly. "To be expected."

He folded his arms, raking me from head to toe with his penetrating gaze. "For a simple clairvoyant, you have an interesting aura. Has anyone mentioned it?" Examining my face, his feral smile broadened as though he knew something I didn't. "No. I can see they haven't. Well, Miss Devon, I've little doubt we will meet again. Do enjoy your meal." He glanced down at my plate. "Or what's left of it."

With that, he strolled away, leaving in his wake the scent of sandalwood and something else, something cloying. Amanda shot me a haughty glare before scurrying to his side like a forgotten puppy. It was then that I realized the entire room had gone unusually quiet, the various tables only now resuming their hushed conversations.

"Holy shit, princess. For someone so sweet, trouble sure seems to follow you."

I jumped, slapping a palm over my heart. "Jesus, Zach! Are you *trying* to give me a heart attack?"

"Can I help it if you're jumpy?" His voice now came from the bench across from me.

I returned to my seat, finally catching sight of Cal, his plate in hand, standing outside the serving area's entrance. Amanda appeared to be introducing him to her godfather. My eyes nearly popped out of my head when, instead of shaking the veep's extended hand, Cal stuck his right fist into the pocket of his khakis, blatantly snubbing him.

Zach chuckled. "Cal's smarter than he looks. Never touch a sorcerer, tiger, especially one who's a master in auras. You'll live longer that way. Just sayin'."

"You don't actually think he'd do something to a student?" I whipped my attention back to Cal and Jacoby.

"I'm guessing he's not that stupid, but who knows? I haven't heard good things about that guy, that's for sure. People who disagree with him tend to disappear ... or die unexpectedly."

To my relief, Cal ambled toward us. Jacoby, who remained alongside a sour-faced Amanda, met my gaze. Smiling, he tipped his head subtly in my direction.

When he and Amanda had finally vacated, I all but collapsed in my seat. "Holy crap," I breathed out. "Was that guy freaky, or what?"

"You think?"

How Zach could sound so cheerful about it, I couldn't imagine.

Cal breezed up, climbing over the bench as he plunked down his plate. "Jesus. Did you see that guy? Amanda's godfather, the A.C. Vice President? That dude is creepier than hell, wanted to shake my hand." His blue eyes flashed. "Even if I had a raging head cold with my nose packed full of green snot, I'd smell his business from outer space."

I made a face. "Gross, Cal. Thanks for that."

"Anytime," he told me through a mouthful of his hamburger.

"Bro, spill. What'd you sniff out?"

Cal shrugged and swallowed. "Magic up the wazoo, and not all of it's sweet. He's an ethermancer, a powerful one."

"What'd I tell you? Nothing gets past a dub-dub's nose. I've heard Jacoby can strip a person's aura without touching them, like some fucked-up magic-sucking vampire. Don't know how true that is, and I sure as hell don't want to know," Zach said. "If Amanda has him in her corner …" He sighed. "Dang. I was looking forward to watching her bitchy little ass get kicked to the curb."

"But I thought President Kessburg and Chancellor Evans were behind the coalition, like big-time, and they back Professor Trapp." I frowned. "The Veep Creep might be a big cheese in the Arcane Council, but he's got nothing to do with the Paranormal Regulatory Commission, or the North American Rout for that matter."

"You and your nicknames," Zach said, cracking up. "The Veep Creep. Priceless. But seriously … you'd be surprised how much political B.S. goes on behind the scenes. Trust me. That dude's influence goes way beyond the Arcane Council. Sorry to break it to you, tiger, but I don't see any of the big hitters going up against the Veep Creep for something like this, even if every truthsayer on the planet says Amanda's a lying sack of shit. Besides, you know they're going to say it was all a misunderstanding, right? They'll say you're the one who started it by telling Amanda you kept a naughty list like Santa."

"For real?" Cal snickered. "Do you check it twice?"

"*Please.* I said it in third frickin' grade. You'd have to be denser than a golem to think I was serious."

"We are talking about Amanda," Zach said.

I snorted, but what I really wanted to do was punch something, or, rather, some*one*.

"Did you know about Amanda's godfather?" Cal asked me. "Are they related? Usually godparents are, aren't they?"

"Not necessarily, and I wouldn't know. Amanda doesn't go out of her way to talk to me, unless it's to say something horrible."

"Shannon told me that the Veepster's an old friend of the Olander family," Zach said. "Supposedly, he and Amanda's great-grandfather grew up together. No idea whether that's true or not."

"Pop would know," Cal said.

Zach blew out a raspberry. "Not like it matters. Amanda'll be off the hook by morning."

"Your dad wouldn't really send you to a different school over this, would he?" Cal asked me.

My boiling rage over the injustice nearly evaporated at hearing Cal's concern. Was he worried because he knew starting at a new school sucked or because he didn't want me to go?

Don't be an idiot. He's known you for a week.

"He'll probably make some calls, but it'll be my choice," I replied. "No way am I going to let her win. I'm not going anywhere."

"Fuckin'-A," Zach said. "Now let's get moving, people. We've got movies to watch."

CHAPTER 9

Study your Shakespeare

SITTING in Mr. Simmons' office the next morning, I couldn't help thinking that Zach had a gift for prophecy.

Here it was Saturday, and, instead of sleeping in, I sat at the conference table in the same seat as yesterday, facing a headmaster who looked about as grim-faced as I'd ever seen. Amanda "Snooty-Is-My-Middle-Name" Olander lounged in the chair to his left, twirling a lock of her wavy blonde hair that I personally wanted to yank hard enough to rattle her insensible. Not that anyone would notice a difference, mind you.

Facing my archnemesis this early on a Saturday without the benefit of my morning cup of coffee might have been bad enough, but dealing with Vice President Jacoby, on top of it, escalated this to worst-morning-ever territory. Jacoby, who stood with his hands clasped behind his back, peered out the large picture window to my right. He hadn't bothered to greet me.

Evidently, there was no such thing as weekend casual for the Veep-ster. I'd seen enough of my dad's impeccable bespoke suits to know Arcane Council Vice President Jacoby didn't buy his charcoal single-breasted off the rack. I couldn't see his tie, but I was willing to bet it was knotted precisely enough to make a professional valet envious.

Me, on the other hand ... I barely looked presentable. I'd received my summons at 7:30 a.m. from Mr. Simmons' assistant, giving me twenty piddly minutes to get ready before scurrying to the main office in time for this delightful 8:00 a.m. meeting. My hair was still damp from my fastest shower on record, but I'd managed to fit in a call to Dad on my way out the door. Honestly, though ... part of me wished I hadn't. There was something to be said for ignorance in the face of danger.

Dad's initial silence, when I'd mentioned the vice president, had been less than reassuring, and his terse, "I'll do what I can," had sounded dubious at best. But it was his dead serious warning—"*Mon coeur*, whatever you do, do not antagonize him. *Tu m'entends?*"—that chilled me to the core.

Uh, yeah. Message received, Papa. If I'd thought Jacoby seemed creepy in the dining room where I'd been surrounded by dozens of eyewitnesses, he was downright sinister in Mr. Simmons' quiet office, no thanks to Dad's ominous warning.

Faced with the vice president's forbidding presence, it struck me that I sat at the end of the table, very much alone and unsupported. I might have made a stink about it, requesting a delay so that Dad or, at the very least, Professor Trapp could be present, but Dad's warning rang in my ear, so I kept my mouth shut.

"Thank you for coming, Mistress Devon, and, of course, Mistress Olander and Vice President Jacoby," Mr. Simmons said, tipping his head to each of us in turn. "As you all know, during a meeting con-vened yesterday to investigate a case of school vandalism, unsettling rumors of unrelated wrongdoing were levied against Mistress Devon. With the aid of Councilor Chopra and Vice President Jacoby, we have concluded our investigation into the verity of these rumors, which Professor Everhart attributed to Mistress Olander."

Maybe it was fallout from skipping my morning coffee, but I found myself wanting to shout at him, 'Dude! Spit it out!'

Shifting in his seat, Mr. Simmons cleared his throat. "It is my conclusion that the parties involved acted on knowledge that ultimately stemmed from a misunderstanding. Specifically, the belief—based upon your own declaration, Mistress Devon—that you maintained a black book for the purposes of blackmail. Because you admitted this freely, as witnessed by Mistress Olander, I cannot in good conscience reprimand any of the parties involved for taking your assertion as truth, regardless of how long ago or how you intended your declaration to be taken. Additionally, it is clear from your testimony, Mistress Devon, that you coerced the behavior of another student by threatening him with the revelation of illicitly obtained information. This, young lady, is a casebook definition of blackmail, whether or not it was done for the protection of another student. Considering these factors, we believe Professor Everhart's actions were understandable, though, perhaps, misguided."

In other words, 'This was all your fault, Lire, so Amanda and Neverhart are off the hook.'

Jeez. Zach had been right.

Mr. Simmons sighed. "As to the offense of blackmail against a former student ... normally, this would be grounds for expulsion."

I jolted in my seat. Even Amanda regarded Mr. Simmons with wide eyes.

"In this case, however, the student in question, who is now over the age of consent, has allowed for extenuating circumstances and left it to the school's board of regents to decide Mistress Devon's requital."

Jacoby finally turned from the window, breaking his forbidding silence. "I believe, at the very least, a public apology is in order, for accusing my goddaughter of lying."

Not only would I be punished for defending a classmate but I'd also be forced to apologize to Amanda? In *public?*

The whole thing was so preposterous, so incredibly unfair, I could hardly fathom it much less form coherent thought.

"Not feeling so high and mighty, are we, Miss Devon?"

Faced with the vice president's implacable gaze, anger spiked through me, temporarily unsticking my tongue. "I think you're mistaking me for your goddaughter."

Judging by Amanda's gasp and the veep's narrowed eyes, it wasn't the wisest thing I could have said. I couldn't seem to get worked up about it, though. Truthfully, I felt … numb.

This is a nightmare. I'm dreaming. That must be it.

I turned back to Mr. Simmons, but simply moving my head proved more difficult than usual, as though the surrounding air had turned to syrup, making everything feel fuzzy and surreal. I stared at the far wall, my eyes refusing to focus on anything. I vaguely wondered what the hell was wrong with me.

Before Jacoby could call for my head on a plate, Mrs. Franklin knocked and entered. I watched her through a slow-motion lens. "Excuse me, Jerod. Pardon the interruption, but I have an urgent call for you."

"The headmaster is busy," Jacoby snapped.

To my surprise, Mrs. Franklin didn't back down. She stepped closer and folded her arms. "Yes, sir, I'm aware of that. If the call wasn't of the utmost importance, I wouldn't be interrupting."

"No doubt her fool of a father," Jacoby muttered.

Mr. Simmons pushed back his chair to stand. "Send it through. Thank you, Clarissa."

I blinked long as my thoughts churned sluggishly. The whole thing boggled my mind. How could I go from being the victim of Amanda's rumormongering to facing the charge of blackmail? How did something like this happen?

I'd stood up to a bully. I made sure Skyler would never harass that strigoi boy again. How could that be bad?

Because you used your gift to threaten someone and that scares the crap out of people.

No one enjoyed knowing their dirty laundry might be up for grabs and possibly used against them. It didn't matter that I'd used the information to prevent a bad person from preying on a good one.

Slowly, I became aware of Mr. Simmons' one-sided conversation. I'd been so deep within myself, I hadn't been paying attention.

"I see. Yes. One moment." Mr. Simmons turned toward the conference area. "Vice President, you have a call."

"Indeed," Jacoby said, sounding unimpressed. "Let me guess." He strode across the room, snatching the receiver from Mr. Simmons' outstretched fingers. "Yes. What is it?"

Jacoby stilled, and, even though his expression didn't stray from neutral, his body seemed to grow more rigid the longer he listened to the caller on the other end. Finally, after a good thirty seconds, he bit out, "Yes. I understand," and then slammed the receiver into its cradle without so much as a goodbye.

After a tense moment, in which I imagined Jacoby exploding into a shower of fire and brimstone, he turned to me, eyes narrowed. "It seems you have acquired a highly-placed admirer. Enjoy your victory, Miss Devon. No doubt your father will pay dearly for it."

I stood so quickly, the chair behind me skidded and then fell over backward. "You leave my father alone!" I snarled, clenching my fists. "Or, I swear, I'll ... I'll—"

"Lire!"

Mr. Simmons' sharp admonishment stopped me cold.

"Yes, do be careful," Jacoby advised, his voice an unsavory purr. "No doubt your father's already bartered his pound of flesh in securing your patron savior. You wouldn't want to necessitate further debts by issuing mindless threats."

He clicked his tongue at my expression and glanced at Mr. Simmons. "Don't you teach these students the classics, Jerod? For shame." He sighed. "Study your Shakespeare, Miss Devon. Perhaps your father was as crafty as the Venice merchant when he bargained for your protection, but I do fear he risked his jot of blood, instead. And far more than a mere drop." He smiled at the thought, a wicked show of teeth. "It would have been vastly cheaper for him if he'd left you to your punishments."

He strode to the door. "Come along, Goddaughter. We are adjourned."

"B-but ... what about her public apology?" Amanda stammered. "She's telling everyone I'm a liar!"

His mouth curled reprovingly. "Your ignorance is intolerable. Clearly, the education at this school is a shambles. Take my word, the payment has been most agreeably wrought"—he stared at me meaningfully—"in blood."

He returned his glare to Amanda. "Now, stop quibbling," he ordered, stalking out.

Amanda scowled at me as if she hadn't gotten the pony she was promised. "Godfather is on the school's board of regents. Just try stepping out of line. I'll make sure they catch you, and when they do—"

"That's enough, Miss Olander," Mr. Simmons commanded. "There will be no threats. Please attend to your godfather."

Shooting me a furious glare as her parting gift, she turned on her heel and left.

Mr. Simmons trailed behind, but halted at the threshold, peering out. "Clarissa, a word, please."

When his assistant appeared at the door, he lowered his voice to a conversational undertone. "Now that we've gotten past that bit of unpleasantness, please be so kind as to call Lucien. Let him know his efforts were successful and his daughter will no doubt call him when she gets back to her room, once she and I've had a chance to talk."

"Certainly." Leaning in, she eyed me. "How are you, dear? Can I get you anything to drink?"

"No, thank you, ma'am. I'm fine."

This wasn't a complete fib. For the last ten minutes, I'd felt squashed, as if I'd been weighed down by one of those lead blankets dentists used to protect your body when you got your teeth x-rayed, and, now, the heavy thing had been cast off. The room felt brighter and the air lighter, even though I didn't understand what Jacoby's departure meant in the grand scheme of things.

Looking satisfied, Mrs. Franklin nodded and smiled at me. She closed the door softly behind her.

"Come on over, Lire." Loosening his tie, Mr. Simmons jerked his chin at one of his guest chairs before ambling to his side of the desk. "Make yourself comfortable."

I did as he asked, feeling almost as stunned by his disheveled tie and unbuttoned collar as Jacoby's sudden exit. "Sir ... I don't get it. What just happened?"

He exhaled tiredly as he sat. "That, my young mistress, is what happens when the powerful use a student disagreement to further their political ambitions." He relaxed in his chair, lacing his fingers together over the buttons of his tweed vest, and gave me an arch look. "When that happens, certain fathers and headmasters are forced to think outside the box." He tucked his chin to spear me with his direct glare. "My advice to you is to keep a low profile from now on, especially where Miss Olander is concerned."

"Yes, sir, but—"

"No buts. Your patron's consideration has limits. Do not expect another bail out. Is that clear?"

"Yes, sir. I won't." I hesitated. "Could you please tell me who was on the phone just now? Vice President Jacoby thought it was my dad, but it wasn't. Was it?"

"No, it was not, and I'm not at liberty to reveal their identity. Suffice to say, at some point in the past, your conduct elicited their regard. In fact, I've been informed that you are, I quote — *the only student at that academy with any integrity* — unquote. This is all you need know."

I jolted at the familiar words. Hadn't Cal said something like that? Or had it been Zach? Maybe their father had been the one to call. I didn't know why he'd bother, though. I'd met Cal and Zach five days ago. What could I have possibly done in that time to impress the leader of the Hidden? Unless … maybe he and my father were associates?

Eyeing Mr. Simmons' steadfast expression, I knew I wouldn't get any additional hints from him, but that was okay. I'd get the scoop from Dad, later.

"All right, but what does it all mean?" I asked. "Amanda's off the hook for spreading those rumors about me and, in return, I don't get expelled for threatening Skyler? We basically pretend none of it happened?"

He nodded curtly. "Indeed. I'm afraid, in the real world, ofttimes you'll find winning and being right aren't always the same thing. I advise you to make peace with the stalemate and move on. Let karma take care of the rest."

"And when I get mad, I should keep my darn mouth shut," I muttered.

"Or, at least, think before speaking," he agreed, stressing the word 'think.' "Yes, a wise tenet. One that will keep you out of trouble, more often than not."

For the first time since the beginning of our meeting, he smiled, his white teeth a cheerful contrast against his rosy-brown lips. He waved me out of my chair, his round eyes sparkling kindly. "Go on, now. It's a beautiful Saturday. Take advantage of the warm weather while it lasts."

As I opened his office door, he called out, "And don't forget to call your father."

As if! I practically ran the whole way back to my room.

"I'm sorry, *mon coeur*," Dad said when I called, not fifteen minutes later. "I can't tell you. I've been sworn to secrecy."

To my intense frustration, it seemed I wouldn't be getting any further with him than I'd gotten with Mr. Simmons. I was doomed to ignorance when it came to the identity of my patron. Even my most strategic complaints yielded a firm refusal.

"Fine," I huffed. "At least tell me what Jacoby meant about the Shakespeare reference and paying in flesh and blood. You didn't promise something that'll hurt you somehow, did you?"

"No, no," he said, chuckling as though the mere idea was ludicrous. "You needn't worry about that. But Mr. Simmons is right. You're lucky to have the favor of such a powerful advocate, but you can't count on their intervention again. Stay away from this Olander girl and no gossiping about any of it. Let sleeping dogs lie. *Tu m'entends?*"

"Yes, I get it," I said, sounding more sullen than I intended. "But how did I get this *advocate* in the first place? What amazing thing did I do that someone so powerful would notice? I mean, it's not like I go anywhere. I spend most of my time at school."

I wondered whether this person had spotted me doing readings for Gibson Antiques but quickly discounted the idea. Using my gift wasn't earth-shattering magic.

He chuckled. "I think it's quite clear. It was something you didn't think twice about. You were simply being yourself."

"Right, but that doesn't tell me anything, Dad."

"*Au contraire*, I think it tells a great deal, but I'll say no more. Now, go enjoy your Saturday. I have a tee time to make."

"That was no help," I grumbled after Dad and I had said our goodbyes. I fell back against my pillows on my bed. "Red, you know more about Shakespeare's plays than I do. Why'd Jacoby bring that stuff up? Was he rubbing in the fact that Dad had to spend a lot of money and favors to get that person to help me, or what?"

"Perhaps," Red replied, toddling to sit on the edge of my desk nearest my bed. "Certainly, the phrase about paying a pound of flesh would imply a debt that is contractually owed yet ruthless or unreasonable in its demand. It comes from *The Merchant of Venice*—one of Shakespeare's more interesting plays, in my opinion."

"Yes!" I launched upright to sit cross-legged and leaned forward eagerly. Now, maybe I'd get some answers. "Jacoby said something about a Venice merchant. I assume the merchant is the character who barters a pound of flesh for something important?"

"Technically, he offers it as collateral. And, yes, the borrower is Antonio, the aforementioned merchant. To help a dear friend, Antonio secures a significant sum of money from a much-maligned Jewish moneylender named Shylock. In their contract, Antonio agrees that if he forfeits, he will pay an equal pound of flesh to be cut off and taken, in whatever part of his body pleases the moneylender."

I grimaced. "Ouch."

"Indeed."

"I take it things don't go well for Antonio."

"That is the fear, especially when Antonio is forced to default on the loan," Red agreed. "In the play's climactic scene, Shylock and Antonio appear in court where the moneylender demands the pound of flesh promised him. After much discourse—this is Shakespeare after all—Antonio's lawyer declares that Shylock may have his pound of flesh but without a jot of blood, since blood was not promised in the contract. It is this clever argument that ultimately saves Antonio since there is no way for Shylock to extract his payment without drawing blood." Red waved his paw dismissively. "There are other subplots, but this is the pivotal scene that pertains to the pound of flesh expression."

"I remember Jacoby saying something about Dad risking his jot of blood, too. That means he thinks Dad has no loophole, that Dad will have to pay his pound of flesh, blood included."

I hoped Jacoby had chosen this coined phrase to make a clever point, not because Dad had bartered body parts in return for my protection.

When it came to arcane magic, and dealing with those who controlled it, flesh and blood weren't things you bandied about. And not only flesh and blood, but anything of the body, including hair, fingernails, skin, or — as we learned in fifth-grade puberty-ed — reproductive fluids, which was why consensual sex with a magic user was a potentially dangerous undertaking. With a freely-given donation, a black magus could do any number of horrible things to the donor, anything from complete control to outright torture, even a life-long curse.

Of course, rules against using magic to harm someone or to subvert their will weren't limited to the magic community. There were similar laws at the federal level, too, just like the ones prohibiting unsolicited vampire bites, but that —

I froze.

Vampire ...

"Red, you don't think — " I shook my head, mentally backing up a step. "Jacoby mentioned the pound of flesh thing, like, one time. But he really stressed the part about blood. Do you think that's because the guy Dad bargained with is a strigoi?"

Red, who sat with his legs dangling over the edge of my desk, swung them to and fro as he contemplated the idea. "It is not inconceivable," he replied. "We know the Domn is aware that you stood up to Skyler to help one of his kin. I imagine this would predispose the leader to extol your natural integrity."

I frowned. "About that ... don't you think it's weird that Cal said almost the exact same thing, yesterday, about me being the one person at this school with any integrity?"

"If memory serves, I believe Cal accused Zach of saying it first."

"Exactly. You can't tell me that's not a bizarre coincidence. I mean, not many students go around talking about other kids having *integrity*. It makes me think Zach convinced their father to stand up for me. And maybe Dad and Mr. Simmons were in on it somehow, too. Or maybe Zach knows the Domn." I scoffed at the ridiculousness of that, of all these powerful people coming to my rescue at Zach's behest. "Okay, maybe not. I just hope Dad was telling me the truth, that he really didn't barter anything significant for the help."

Before Red could weigh in with his opinion, my telephone rang.

"Morning, tiger. We're about to leave for breakfast. You wanna come?"

Speak of the devil.

I glanced at the clock. 9:10. If we hurried, we could squeak in prior to the 9:30 cut-off. "Sounds good. I'll meet you over there."

"Hold on. Not the refectory. Sunnyside Café. It's a place in town. Supposed to be good. Cal's driving. Meet us at the main office. We'll sign out and then take off."

"Okay, sure. I'll head back over."

Not many restaurants bothered to put psi-free offerings on their menus (and fewer still had bothered to become licensed by the PRC), but I'd sacrifice eating to have a chance to grill him about his dad. Besides, I was thrilled to be included.

"What do you mean, *back*?" His voice perked up.

"Oh, um, yeah. I was there for a meeting, earlier."

"Dang it. Why didn't you call me? I'd have gone with you."

"Be glad you didn't. The Veep Creep was there."

"You're shitting me."

"Nope. Amanda too." I sighed. "Yeah. Not my best morning ever."

"No doubt. So? Is her royal bitchiness off the hook?"

"You should go into fortune telling."

"Fuck," he declared. "But I called it. Told you, didn't I? I totally called it."

I heard someone grumble in the background, interrupting his fervent boast.

"Shuddup," Zach said, sounding faint, the receiver most likely against his chest. "Okay. Jesus! Keep your shirt on." No longer muffled, he said, "Cal's hungry. See you in the office, okay? And then I want the full story." The line disconnected.

"Bye to you too," I muttered, hanging up. "We're going out, Red. Grab your stuff while I change real fast."

I grabbed my favorite pair of jeans and the first graphic tee I could find and trotted to the bathroom.

Why did everything have to happen so last minute, this morning?

I itched to put on some makeup, something that enhanced my green eyes and camouflaged my freckles, but I only had time to slap on sunblock and pull my hair into a ponytail before speeding out the door, Red in tow.

The main office was quiet when I entered. Behind the front desk, I glimpsed the crown of the blond administrator's bowed head. He jerked upright, sliding a paperback book beneath the counter.

"Hey," he said. "Lire, yeah?"

I smiled at him. "Hi. Yep, that's me. Owen, right?"

When he nodded his head, strands of his white-blond hair escaped his liberally applied styling gel. I might have pegged him as a scroll-sniffing mage nerd—with his gap-toothed smile and lanky physique—but his square-shouldered stance and deep voice projected a cool confidence that surprised me.

Most of the time, the office administrators were high school or college grads who worked here while advancing their chosen arcana, apprenticing under one of our professors. Owen appeared older than a recent college grad, so maybe he was here doing research.

He glanced at my chest and smirked. "Nice shirt."

I looked down. *T-rex hates pushups.* The silly cartoon of a face-down dinosaur with its arms too short to reach the ground, always made me smile. I grinned back. "Thanks."

Since we were on the subject of clothes, I gestured at his intricately woven belt, the leather distressed and made supple by lots of wear. It had a Native American vibe with its knotted, fringe-like decorations on either side of the hammered silver buckle. Personally, I wouldn't have paired it with khaki slacks. It would have looked better with distressed jeans, but to each his own. "Cool belt. That buckle is awesome."

"Thanks." He smiled. "What do you need? The sign out sheet?"

"Yeah."

He pecked away at the nearby computer's keyboard and scrutinized the screen. "Good. You've got parental permission."

He slid the clipboard and pen to me. At the sound of the door, we both looked up to see Cal and Zach stroll inside.

"Hey," Cal said, jerking his chin in greeting when he sidled up to me at the counter. His gaze tracked down to my boobs, and he chuckled. "Good one," he said, gesturing to my shirt.

"Thanks." Apparently, I needed to wear humorous graphic tees more often. Although, there were some guys I'd just as soon not have staring at my chest. Ted and Jason, for starters. Not that I had a ton to gawk at in that department. Still, I didn't think my B-cups were insignificant either. The t-shirt bra helped.

"Hey, princess." Zach gently yanked my ponytail. "You hungry?"

"I could eat," I said, standing aside so they could sign out too.

Interestingly, the pen and clipboard disappeared when Zach signed out, but the ink showed up fine on the form once the items reappeared.

"Don't forget to check in when you get back to campus," Owen said after both Cal and Zach had signed. "Fair warning—Mr. Gibbs has made it clear that getting held up checking in is no excuse for being out of your dorm after curfew, so make sure you plan ahead." He pointed to the sign adhered to the counter with that exact warning written in bold text. "And if you forget to sign back in, it's automatic kitchen duty, so ... yeah, not fun."

"Okay, cool. Appreciate the heads-up," Cal said, turning to the door.

Owen returned my wave before I followed them out.

Cal's silver four-door Honda Civic wasn't exactly clean, but it smelled like pine thanks to the tree-shaped air freshener dangling from the rearview mirror. A burrito wrapper from Taco Bell crinkled under my feet in the front seat footwell.

Behind me, Zach cursed, and I heard an empty cup banging around as his door closed. "Dude, clean out your car once in a while, would you?"

"Half that stuff is yours, asshole," Cal growled. His bulky key ring, complete with Leatherman multi-tool, jingled as he jabbed the proper key into the ignition.

The engine started without a hitch, instantaneously blaring Blink-182's "What's My Age Again" from the car's speakers loud enough to goose my ass two feet out of my seat and give me a heart attack. Cal dove for the volume while I slapped a hand to my chest, dying.

"Jeez!" I wheezed out.

"Sorry," Cal muttered.

"What's the matter?" Zach quipped. "Not a fan of Blink?"

I sucked in a huge breath, restoring my calm. "They're fine, I guess, just not blasting in my ear at six thousand decibels when I don't expect it." I fumbled for the switch to roll down my window, desperate for some cooler air until the a/c kicked in.

"Fine?" Zach gasped. "You guess? I don't know, tiger. Not sure we can be friends."

Looking over his shoulder to back out of his parking spot, Cal caught my eye roll and smirked.

"So, what *do* you like?" Zach asked. "If you say pop, I might puke."

"I think you're safe," I said dryly. "But I don't absolutely hate pop either. I dunno. If I had to pick one style as my favorite, I guess I'd say alternative." I shrugged. "I like a variety, though, movie soundtracks, classic rock, maybe some country. Depends on what I'm in the mood for."

"I can respect that," Zach said magnanimously after a thoughtful pause. "Okay, I suppose we can be friends after all."

"I feel so much better, now," I retorted. "What about you? Blink-182 is what you get when hardcore punk and pop have a baby, right? So, which side do you fall on, the Black Flag side or the alternative side?"

Zach extolled the virtues of various hardcore punk bands and his undying love for the Ramones, The Damned, and The Sex Pistols while, as usual, Cal issued the occasional grunt in agreement or ambivalence. Sometimes it was hard to tell one sound from the other.

"Mr. Gibbs likes the Ramones," I said. "I can't believe I used to think he was a cool guy."

"Gibbs is a tool," Zach announced. "How much you wanna bet half the shit he says is to make himself sound cool. He probably heard "Blitzkrieg Bop" twice on the radio and figured that made him a diehard fan. Was he in your meeting this morning?"

"No. Just Mr. Simmons, Amanda, and the Veep Creep. Lucky me."

"That's it? No one to back you up? Not even Mountainside?" At my head shake, he cursed. "Jesus. Next time, call me. I'll be your invisible wingman, anytime you want. So, it happened like I said, didn't it? They blamed it all on a misunderstanding."

"Of course they did, but what I did to Skyler was different. That was way more serious. That was *blackmail*." I bit off the words, the venom so thick I was lucky to force them out at all.

"You have to be kidding," Zach exclaimed. "Who said that? Jacoby?"

"Mr. Simmons said it, but it was because of Jacoby, I'm sure." My voice trembled as I remembered the sinking terror that had blanketed me from brow to toenail when I realized the power Jacoby possessed—power that had nothing to do with magic. Clutching my hands together, I stared out the passenger window, past the stately maples and the landscape grasses that lined the school's private drive, not really seeing any of it. "By any chance, did either of you guys mention me, or any of this stuff, to your dad?"

I turned to Cal, catching him as he shot meaningful eye daggers at the backseat via his rearview mirror.

"Yeah, I think I might have," Zach replied, as though he couldn't quite remember for sure. "Why?"

"Because right after Jacoby demanded that I publicly apologize to Amanda as part of my punishment, Mrs. Franklin interrupted our meeting with a phone call for Mr. Simmons."

I told them what had happened afterward, including Jacoby's parting comments.

"Not just anyone could shut Jacoby down like that," I said. "It made me wonder whether it was your dad."

"I guess it's possible, but if he knew about your meeting this morning, I'm not the one who told him," Zach said. "A certain *someone* didn't call to tell me about it.

"With all that stuff about blood, sounds more like Jacoby was talking about a strigoi, maybe even the Domn," Cal said.

"That's what I was afraid of," I muttered.

"You're worried your dad got himself in over his head, like Jacoby said?" Cal asked.

"He said no, that he didn't." I sounded doubtful.

"Your dad didn't get where he is without knowing the power of a favor—when it's worth spending it and when it's not," Zach said. "Trust me. Your pop's connected and he's discrete, plus he's got a rep for being an honorable guy. There's a reason most of the big kahunas use him for their financial stuff."

"Big kahunas like your dad?"

"Maybe," Zach drawled, sounding coy.

Cal turned right onto the old county highway, heading toward town. High puffy clouds, sun, and lots of blue sky lifted my spirits. And the company didn't hurt.

"Thanks, you guys. I'm sure you're right about my dad. It's just … you know, the Veepster was convincing." I shivered. "The guy gives me the creeping willies, like, big time. Did you know that he's on the school's board of regents? Amanda couldn't resist throwing that in my face on her way out the door. She said she's waiting for me to screw up so she can make sure they find out."

"Then I guess it's a good thing you're sticking with me for your eight-by-ten, huh?" Zach said.

"Crap." I groaned, slumping in my seat and smacking my palm to my forehead. "With all this stuff, I totally forgot about that. I am so screwed."

"You obviously don't know who you're dealing with," Zach said. "No one can sniff me out if I don't want them to. Plus, dub-dub there isn't about to let anyone get the drop on you in the compound. We haven't started yet and it's practically in the bag."

"It's the 'practically' part that I'm worried about."

Zach clucked his tongue at me. "Your glass is half empty, isn't it?"

"Maybe," I replied, shooting an arch look over my shoulder. "But I'm sure your magnificence is more than enough to make up for it."

"Eight-by-fucking-ten, princess. Now you're talking. Mark my words, the football and basketball teams are two weeks from being totally bald."

Cal chuckled as my laughter filled the car.

For a tiny city bordered by farms and private hunting parcels, Coventry's downtown was unexpectedly picturesque with a surprising number of art galleries and gift shops in addition to its rustic general store. As little as five years ago, it might have gone down as just another dwindling, scruffy farm town if not for some famous chef I'd never heard of opening his farm-to-table restaurant here and the two interior designers who turned the town's Victorian mansion into an upscale B&B. Now, Coventry Village was known as a prime weekend tourist destination for Seattle's well-to-do.

Sunnyside Café appeared to be banking on a rustic, farm-fresh appeal, housed in what was probably a converted ninety-year-old bungalow with a brand-new greenhouse out back. In the main entry, a framed *Seattle Times* newspaper article informed me that Sunnyside Café was one of nine PRC certified psi-free restaurants in Washington State. They'd opened their doors three weeks ago, which explained why I hadn't heard about them until now.

The hostess, a Birkenstock-wearing woman with a brunette pixie cut, hazel eyes, and a petite diamond stud in the crease of her left nostril, didn't even flinch when I'd explained there were three of us, not two. She smiled, looking pleased as punch, and shouted to her "sweetie" through the kitchen opening that he'd finally get his chance to break out the special equipment.

"He's been complaining the psi-free designated pans aren't getting their proper seasoning." She lowered her voice to add, "He'll be thrilled his extra efforts aren't being wasted on just the granola crowd, for once." She winked.

The place was about three-quarters full, but to my relief, I didn't see any kids from Ponderosa High.

The locals generally ignored us, but some, especially the kids from long-standing farming families who resented that our school had gobbled up two of the county's largest land parcels, went out of their way to pick fights. Four years ago, after a particularly bad incident that landed two warlocks and five locals in the hospital, Coventry Academy's board of regents restricted all students to campus for the year.

A lengthy police investigation eventually revealed that the locals had been the aggressors and the warlocks had simply defended themselves. Tensions between 'us' and 'them' hadn't gotten much better since then. Because my gloves were a beacon for whispers and dirty looks at the best of times, I tended to avoid trips into town.

Today wasn't so bad. I endured some wide-eyed stares and a few startled gasps before the three of us settled into a circular booth at the far corner of the cheerful, brightly-lit restaurant.

"How'd you hear about this place, Zach?" I asked as I opened my menu.

"Mountainside and the truthsayer. They talked about it. The owner went to Coventry Academy way back when. She's a dowser. Her husband's a pyro. Not a surprise there, I guess."

I assumed he meant it wasn't a surprise because more than a few pyrokinetics had gone on to become famous chefs. Or maybe he was referring to the fact that psychics tended to marry other psychics.

"Ohmygod," I blurted in a gush, gaping at my menu. "I've died and gone to heaven. There are at least twelve things in the psi-free section! And they're not boring or from a box. Look ... eggs Benedict with spinach and smoked salmon. Holy cow. Even their macaroni and cheese is deluxe."

Normally, if a restaurant had any psi-free offerings at all, my choices were limited to a veggie omelette or grilled cheese, sometimes tuna salad.

Cal returned my smile as I chortled like I'd won a million-dollar jackpot.

"Whoever says 'the way to a guy's heart is through his stomach' clearly hasn't met princess, here," Zach teased.

After giving our orders to a frazzled waitress who dual-wielded glass coffee carafes, Zach announced, "Let's get our plan straight for Wednesday. Cal looked it up last night; moonrise is right around 8:00 p.m. and it sets at 6:22 a.m. So, the midpoint is about one in the morning. That'll be the best time for your eight-by-ten, right?"

My stomach clenched at 'moonrise,' and my thoughts immediately spiraled to Amanda's parting comment and what would happen if things went wrong. How had I gone from such giddiness to complete terror in the span of five minutes?

Shut him down. You're stupid if you don't.

I wished I still had my menu to clutch in front of me. "After what happened with Jacoby, if we get caught—"

"We're not going to get caught," Zach said.

"You might not *plan* for us to get caught, but—"

"*Lire*," Zach cut in, and, honest to goodness, it gave me a start. It was the first time I could remember hearing him utter my name, my *actual* name, let alone in such a disdainful way. "I'm not some brainless snoop with a camouflage charm. You think I'm just another sixteen-year-old trying to get through school with passing grades? Well, I'm not. I've been pulling jobs, solo, since I was thirteen. I don't get *caught*."

I stared at his side of the table, my eyes probably as round as the full moon we'd been discussing. To my intense dismay, I had a hard time breathing past the lump that came out of nowhere to take up residence in my throat. I bit the inside of my cheek in a desperate bid to keep my stupid emotions under wraps. Because, evidently, my day wouldn't be complete without bursting into tears in public.

Grow a backbone, you big baby.

"Dude, chill out," Cal scolded, glancing at the closest tables to be sure our conversation remained unobserved. "She's known you — *us* — for barely a week. And after what happened with Jacoby ..." He blew out a breath. "Jesus Christ. Cut her some slack."

"Dammit," Zach ground out. "I know. I *know*." I heard him shifting on the bench seat and the table wobbled before his tight voice came from above my head, to my right. "Look, I'm sorry. I ... need some air."

I frowned in his direction. Was he sorry for chomping on my ass or for needing some air?

Presumably Zach stalked away because Cal's concerned gaze tracked toward the restaurant's entrance where I saw the door swing open without explanation.

I levered my coffee to my face, but the psi-free disposable cup didn't do much to disguise my trembling. I held it with both hands, the plastic cover firmly against my lips, elbows braced against my abdomen, hoping Cal didn't notice.

He sighed. "Sorry. With Zach, sometimes — " He paused and then cursed. "Who am I kidding? Not sometimes, *most* of the time, it's not easy being the Doyen's son. 'Getting caught' ... it's like an insult for us — for him. When you're an occultum, you don't get caught. Getting caught is for amateurs and idiots. Getting caught can get you killed or tortured, not to mention bring unwanted attention to the family. So, if you screw up, even once ..." He shrugged and looked out the window. "It, uh, leaves a mark."

"Is that what happened?" Lowering my cup to the table, I dropped my voice to whisper, "He was caught doing a job or something for his dad? Er, I mean your dad, um, both your dad?" I wanted to roll my eyes. Could I sound lamer?

"Not my story to tell. But he's not exaggerating when he says stuff about being undetectable. Only Pop's considered better, mostly because he's way more experienced and if he's ever made a mistake, nobody knows about it."

I wondered what Zach had done and who'd caught him doing it. What did it mean that his mistake had left a mark?

"Anyway, you used the 'C' word," Cal continued. "You know— *caught*," he quickly added when he noticed my startled reaction. "Sometimes it sets him off. Don't take it personally, okay?"

Easier said than done.

"I didn't mean to come off like I think he's no good at what he does." Looking away from his penetrating gaze, I took another sip of my coffee. "I don't know much of anything about the occultum curse. We didn't cover it in last year's Curses and Afflictions section ... at least, not that I remember. All I've heard is that most of the world's big shots keep certain types of weres on staff for a reason. I know the security team at my dad's company are all shifters who've passed multiple sensory tests, and he's not alone in doing that. But, for all I know, Zach can turn into smoke and go through keyholes and all their efforts to prevent spying are a waste of time."

Cal gave me a funny look. "Sometimes I wonder if he can't."

"But ... he can't though." I peered at him, half serious. "Right?"

"I don't think he's a vampire. But you might want to start wearing a scarf to be safe."

"As if I'm not covered up enough already." I deliberately eyed his long-sleeve oxford, undershirt, and jeans. He hadn't bothered to roll up the cuffs of his shirt and today was cranking up to be another hot day. "Is that your excuse for the long sleeves: My roommate's a closet vampire?"

I couldn't lie. I'd been dying to see him in shorts and a snug t-shirt and was disappointed when he showed up with Levi's as his sole concession to the weekend's casual dress code. Not that I was complaining. The jeans hugged his hips and thighs a darn sight better than our uniform's requisite chinos. It'd been an effort to stop myself from ogling how well they fit him.

He started at my teasing, his expression shuttering for half a tick before he returned my crooked smile. "You can't be too careful," he said, but something felt off, like his jest had been forced.

It made me wonder whether there was a reason he never showed any more skin than absolutely necessary. Even when we went running, he'd always worn loose-fitting track pants and a black, long-sleeve running shirt with the thumb holes to keep the sleeves from catching the wind. And, now that I considered it, all his t-shirts were black crew-necks. Was this an obsessive fashion preference, or did he dress this way to hide something?

Our waitress showed up with our breakfast, blowing my chance to poke at the mystery.

"Oh, yum." I'd ordered the salmon eggs Benedict. I clapped my hands together. The cook had done the poached eggs right, I could tell. Not too hard, not too watery.

Cal snickered. "Someone's easy to please."

"Do you know how hard it is to get a decent poached egg? Seriously."

"Whatever you say. Runny eggs are disgusting."

I eyed his plate. Steak and scrambled eggs. I thought it was amusing that he'd eat a rare steak with its red juices flowing everywhere, but runny eggs were gross. "The carnivore is a strictly scrambled kind of guy, is he?"

"Got that right," he said, carving into his rare T-bone with all the relish of a starving man.

"Careful, tiger. When steak is involved, you don't want to get too close. You might lose a limb," Zach said as the sound of him sliding into the booth met my ears. "Mmm, this looks good."

Cal rolled his eyes.

The silence lengthened, and I focused on my food so I wouldn't be tempted to break it with a reflexive apology that I had no reason to make.

You didn't say anything wrong, I reminded myself.

I studiously ignored the awkward lack of conversation in favor of savoring every smoky, salty, delicious bite of my breakfast. As I cut into my second egg covered English muffin, the entire booth jolted.

Our plates and silverware jumped, raising a sharp clatter, and Cal's newly refilled coffee splashed out of its mug.

"Ouch!" Zach exclaimed. "Jesus! I get it, okay? You don't have to take out my frickin' shins."

Instead of answering, Cal glared at him like, 'That's what you think, dumbass.'

I heard Zach take a fortifying breath. "Look ... Lire, I'm sorry, all right? I was a dick. I ... I get a little worked up when people assume I'm no better than an amateur."

I put down my fork, narrowing my eyes in his direction. "There's a difference between not understanding someone's magic and thinking they suck. But so what if you can ... I don't know, walk on rainbows and slay dragons in your spare time? I'm *still* going to think about the worst-case scenario, no matter how 'in the bag' you think this picture-taking thing might be. It's how I figure stuff out and head off problems. Because shit happens. That's life. If you go around thinking you can do no wrong, then you're going to be really unprepared when something finally does."

Considering the tangled thoughts in my head, my little speech had come out way better than I'd expected. I folded my arms and gave him a glare that dared him to argue with me.

"Whoa, down, girl."

I ground my teeth at Zach's placating drawl, squaring my shoulders. Cal totally should have kicked him harder.

"Okay, yes! I got the message," he added hastily, probably after assessing my thunderous expression. I imagined him waving his hands at me in surrender. "You weren't assuming I suck. You're trying to figure stuff out. Don't get your panties in a twist. *Jesus.*"

"Pretty sure Jesus didn't wear panties," I pointed out, still sounding peeved but relaxing against the cushioned booth.

"Ha, ha," he said. "Very funny, wiseass."

"At least I have *something* that's wise."

"What're you trying to say there, princess? You wouldn't be *dissing* me, would you?"

I snickered at his deadpan tone. "Would I do that?"

"Definitely not, since you totally acknowledged my magnificence half an hour ago."

"Sure about that, are you?"

"You know ... I think there's only one way to refresh your memory."

"Oh yeah?" I said haughtily. "How're you going to manage that?"

"Like this—"

Cal disappeared without warning, leaving me, by all appearances, alone in our semi-circular booth. I knew they were still there, of course. Occultums were capable of invisibility, not turning to vapor, like the rare vampire supposedly could. To leave, they'd have to slide out Zach's side of the booth. Since the bench was continuous all the way around and squeaked in protest any time one of us moved, there'd be no tricking me on that. I'd hear the seat groaning like a rusted-out wrought iron bed and feel the vibration of their movements from a mile away.

I didn't know what Zach hoped to achieve with this display, other than proving he could indeed pull a person into his sphere of invisibility, which I hadn't really doubted.

"Miss us?" they said in unison, directly into my right ear, as Cal popped into existence crouched next to me in the aisle, his lips two inches from my right cheek.

I shrieked, jerking away and drawing the startled stares of everyone around us. I pressed a hand to my chest in a desperate attempt to keep my heart from pounding its way out.

"Holy crap! What are you guys doing? Trying to surprise me to death? Jeez Louise, how many times do you think I can take this abuse? Seriously."

Leaning on the heels of my hands away from them, it took all my willpower to keep from collapsing into a puddle on the bench seat. Instead, I struggled to sit upright and gather some semblance of poise.

"You tease an occultum, you take the consequences, tiger." Zach chuckled and tugged my ponytail. "Oh, man. That was priceless."

I scowled at Cal, who looked distinctly amused, the traitor. He scooted back to his central spot in our booth, the squeaks and groans of the seat apparent now that he wasn't cloaked by Zach's magic.

"Your magic affects sound? And vibration?"

"I'm cocky for a reason. When I say this is in the bag, I mean it," Zach said, once again sitting in his place across the table from me.

I lowered my voice. "What about the school's perimeter enchantments? Or our dorm's security system? You still have to use doors. You can't walk through walls ... right?" I couldn't believe I was asking that question.

"Let's just say, I don't need to walk through walls. I'm very good with my hands." Somehow, he managed to sound both suggestive and professional at the same time.

I twirled my index finger in the air. "More information, less bragging, *s'il vous plaît.*"

"There isn't a security system I can't breach, and the school's setup is so old it's practically useless. The boundary enchantment is easy to evade if you know what you're doing. I've already done it. More than once. I'll take you along for a test drive, tonight, to prove it to you, if you want."

I didn't see what purpose that would serve. If we got caught during the test run (not that I thought this was likely), I wouldn't be stupid enough to hazard getting caught again for the actual dare. Might as well risk it all on the night of the full moon.

I shook my head. "I believe you." I nibbled on the piece of cantaloupe that came with my breakfast. "So, how's this going to work? Walk me through it. Will you come knock on my door when it's time to leave?"

"I won't knock. You'll open your door at the time I tell you. I'll have to touch you, but I'll be wearing a skin-suit, including the hood but without the face mask. You'll need to do the same. You have one, right?"

I blushed and barely resisted ducking my head like the bashful virgin that I was. "Yeah."

Most of the time, a skin-suit was used for making out or having sex, or sleeping in a place where there were no psi-free sheets. I'd never had occasion to use mine, but I didn't mention that part. "What time did you say the moon's at its highest point? One in the morning?"

"Right around there, yeah," Zach said, and Cal nodded his agreement.

"We'll need to leave plenty of time to drive over and figure out how to get past the compound's security fence," I said. "Any ideas on that?"

"Shannon told us there's a big tree on the neighboring property that overhangs the fence, on the northeast side of the compound," Zach replied. "There's a large branch that helps to bypass the razor wire. That's how she and Darla did it."

"They did it at sunset, though, right?"

"Yeah, on a Saturday when no shifters were there," he acknowledged. "But as long as it's not cloudy, we'll have the full moon, which is almost as good."

The moonlight would make it harder to hide our movements, but I remembered Zach would be with me and bit my tongue. "What time do you think we should leave?"

"Figure half an hour to get out of our dorms and off school grounds, the rest depends on how long it takes to walk to where we'll leave Cal's car."

I blinked, puzzled. "I think I missed something. Why won't his car be in the parking lot?"

"I can get us through the perimeter wards, no problem, but Cal's car is more difficult," Zach said. "It'll be easier if we find a place to park it outside the school's boundaries and walk that far."

"Leaving it on the side of the highway is a bad idea," I said. "It could get ticketed or towed. There's a Les Schwab a couple miles down the highway from the school. It's across from the 7-Eleven, in that strip mall with the Ace Hardware and that paint store. Maybe we could park it there."

Cal nodded. "Yeah, okay, I remember seeing it. Doesn't seem that far to walk, I guess, and it probably won't seem weird for a car to stay at a tire place overnight."

"How long to hoof it there?" Zach asked.

I shrugged. "If we walk, I dunno … maybe forty-five minutes?"

We worked out the rest of the timing, fifteen minutes to get out of the dorms, forty-five to get to Cal's car, another twenty to drive to the compound, if that.

"We're getting close to ninety minutes, right there," Zach said.

"Yeah. It's going to be a long night." I nibbled my bottom lip. "We should do a test drive to the compound, so I know where it is and to be sure of the timing. And we need to figure out where to leave the car while we're taking the picture."

"No time like the present," Cal said.

If only my sinking stomach agreed.

CHAPTER 10

8

This isn't 21 Jump Street

"DIDN'T you tour the compound the weekend before school started?" I asked as we sauntered down the sidewalk toward Cal's car.

Cal shook his head. The action, along with the late-morning breeze, swished his disorderly hair into his eyes. "Our flight didn't get in until after," he replied, tossing his head and then shoving his hand through his hair when that didn't help. "I could have gone on Sunday with the few who missed it, but I didn't care that much."

"Do you know where to go?" I asked, pausing on the sidewalk as Cal circled his car to the driver's side.

"Yep. I have the map that Shannon gave us at dinner, last night."

"Shannon sure is being helpful," I observed, once we'd settled inside the car. "She's hardly said 'boo' to me in all the years we've been in school, but yesterday, she volunteered to be my badminton partner so she could grill me about you guys." Okay, maybe that was a *slight* exaggeration. She'd mostly wanted to know about the desk thing, but I suspected she was crushing on Cal too. Not that I could blame her.

"Whatever." Cal started the car so we could roll down our windows.

"I told you, bro," Zach said. "You should ask her out. She's totally into you."

Cal shot Zach a reproachful glare in his rearview mirror as if that was the last thing on earth he'd want to do. My insides promptly did a fist pump, even though I had no business having feelings one way or another on the matter of who Cal chose to date.

He's a friend. Period.

I hoped this was the last time I'd need to have this conversation with myself.

As far as girls went, Cal could do far worse. While Shannon didn't typically go out of her way to talk to me, she'd never been one to bad mouth or ignore me, either. She and her BFF Darla were two of the few people who said 'hi' when we passed in the halls.

Again, I wondered about Cal. Shannon was far from ugly. She had golden blonde hair and a delicately upturned nose, although, her hazel eyes were spaced kind of close together, which tended to give her a vacant look. On the whole, she wasn't so much pretty as she was cute and her petite figure, along with her short hairstyle, contributed to a pixieish image. But maybe Cal didn't prefer perky blondes. Or maybe he was only interested in werewolves, something I hadn't considered until now.

Cal shifted in his seat, pulling a folded slip of paper from his back pocket. He held it out for me to take. I unfolded it to find a map that looked as though it had been copied from a handbook, probably for the teachers and staff, because I knew for a fact that the compound's location wasn't advertised far and wide.

"I know it's off Duncan Hill Road, but I'll need help getting there," Cal said.

I examined the map, tracing the intersections and pinning each landmark in my mind until I had a sense of the compound's location. "Ah, so that's where it is. It's east of Sorcerer Treblow's property."

As the bird flew, the compound was probably four miles from school, to the west, close to Camas Reservoir, but with the neighboring parcels in between, taking public roads turned it into a much longer trek.

I pointed to the intersection coming up. "Turn left here and then take the next left. That'll get us to Main."

He nodded.

"Treblow's that *ubhnati* that helped found the school," Zach said. "The one that's a total shut-in. I've heard he's nuttier than a pile of squirrel turds. The academy's been keeping him in groceries for years."

"Zach!" I shot him a reproving glare. "Not cool."

Most of the time I appreciated Zach's flair for snicker-worthy wisecracks, but I couldn't bring myself to joke about something like that. It hit too close to home.

More than once, my mother had sneered that my Grandpa Giordano had 'lost his marbles' and drunk himself to death. For some reason, her caustic remarks had always seemed to single me out, as though she thought her father's insanity was somehow my fault, even though he'd died years before I was born.

"What?" he drawled innocently.

Zach, the lovable rascal.

"Ubhnati ... that's a magic weaver, right?" I asked. "They use knots to store their spells."

"Yeah. Pretty rare stuff," he replied. "Plus, the guy's older than God. Pop says he was on the Varangian Council."

I snapped a glance toward the backseat. "That's like ... over nine hundred years!"

The Varangian Council was the progenitor of the Arcane Council, formed back in the tenth century around the time of the Norman Conquest. I remembered because we'd studied the subject at the end of last year.

"At least," Zach agreed. "He has some connection to the sidhe, too. He must be crazy powerful if that's the case."

"Elves?" Cal said, frowning into the rearview mirror. "I thought they were extinct."

"They're not extinct," Zach said. "Didn't you pay attention in Paranormal History? The sidhe can't come here anymore. Big difference."

"Stay on Main until you hit the light at Washington," I interjected when Cal turned onto the town's main drag. "Then you'll turn right."

Picking up the conversation where Zach left off, I glanced at the backseat. "I've never heard of a mage living so long. I mean ... I know they can live longer than normals, like, to well over a hundred. But they're still human, unlike elves. Older than nine hundred is crazy. That's farther back than vampires. Their curse originated at the end of the middle ages, right? So the oldest strigoi can only be ... what? Six hundred at the most?"

I waited, breath suspended, for Zach's announcement that his Pop knew vampires had been around since the beginning of time.

"When it comes to the strigoi, I don't speculate," Zach said flatly.

His tone practically painted a neon sign over his invisible head. 'SUPER SECRET SQUIRREL STUFF. FOR ME TO KNOW AND YOU TO NEVER FIND OUT.'

"You guys don't dare spy on them," I blurted, breaking the silence with something I'd been speculating about for a while. "Some of them can see you, can't they?"

"No one can *see* us. We're cursed. Forever invisible, remember?" He bit out that last part so scathingly that I just about resolved to stop asking him questions, ever again. But then, he sighed his apology and gently tugged my ponytail, taking away the sting of his bite. "Some of them can sense us, though," he admitted in a softer tone. "But without any friendlies, we've not found ways to compensate, like we have with shifters."

"Friendlies? You mean ... ?" I glanced at Cal.

"Yes," Zach replied. "Friendly shifters who work with us to perfect our skills."

"Is that why your and Cal's dad did the, you know ..." I gestured at the two of them. "The switcheroo thing?"

"Partly," Zach replied after a notable pause. "Like Cal told you, it was part of a pact. And this is the last time we're going to talk about it," he said, his voice turning to granite. "Walls have ears. I'd keep that in mind when it comes to Red, too. You feel me, princess?"

I nodded and rubbed my arms, suddenly cold.

"Where do I go from here?" Cal asked, breaking into my thoughts of dark pacts and espionage as he turned right onto Washington Avenue.

"Keep going. Washington eventually curves and turns into Duncan Hill Road." I looked down at the map. "Then it's a little way until you make a left onto Bramble Lane, the compound's private road."

A few blocks outside downtown, the yards of the surrounding homes began to increase in size, until we reached Division Street, where residential neighborhoods finally gave way to cherry orchards and infrequent farmhouses. By the time the road curved north and dumped us onto Duncan Hill, I'd tied myself in knots with worry about Dad's security, both at work and at home, and whether he realized how easily it could be thwarted. I wanted to know how many occultums there were in the world, but I suspected this would be a big fat secret and pressed my lips together before the question could slide off my tongue.

After missing the compound's inconspicuous street and having to backtrack, not once but twice, Cal turned onto a gravel road that more resembled a disused driveway than a named street.

"You sure this is the right private road?" Cal asked after driving at least a mile. He hunched forward, peering ahead nervously, as though a covert army might suddenly surround us and open fire for trespassing. The 'TRESPASSERS WILL BE PROSECUTED TO THE FULLEST EXTENT OF THE LAW' signs every two hundred feet sure didn't help.

On our right, a battered split-rail fence ran the length of the road, delineating fallow field after fallow field, all which looked as though they hadn't seen a plow for decades. To our left, a newer, more robust, four-slat farm fence cordoned off what appeared to be a gentleman's horse ranch. Someone had spent a mint on the pristine fencing, and the barn looked nice enough for people to live in, to say nothing of the sprawling McMansion in the distance, picture-perfect pastures, and horses with coats sleek enough to take part in a tourist ad. If this wasn't a case of the grass being greener on the other side of the fence, I didn't know what was.

"I think so," I replied, which hardly sounded reassuring. I held up the map and then gestured at the shabby field on our right. "I'm almost positive this is Treblow's property. See, here? It's shaped like a backward 'L.' We haven't reached the compound, that's all." I bent my head to scan ahead. "Look. Way up there, past those aspens. Is that a high fence?"

Cal squinted. "Yeah. I think it is."

His tone echoed my relief. However, as we drew closer, the sheer dominance of the black security fencing steadily eroded any consolation I might have felt. Peering up at the twelve-foot metal fence and its wicked topping of razor spirals, I was right back to feeling sick to my stomach.

"Jesus," Zach breathed. "There are prisons that don't have fencing this good."

"No shit," Cal muttered. "That's heavy steel, anti-scale palisade. They're not fooling around." He glanced over his right shoulder, out the passenger window, and gestured toward Treblow's land. "It doesn't run the entire perimeter, though. They switch to welded, anti-climb mesh after two hundred feet or so. Slightly easier to breach, but less expensive than the palisade here at the entrance."

Help me. I've fallen into an episode of "Mission Impossible" *and can't get up.*

I'd just closed my gaping mouth when Cal goosed the accelerator, snapped the wheel to the right, and pulled his little Honda to a stop in front of the compound's security gate.

"They've got clustered sensors every thirty feet, plus spotlights, closed-circuit video, possibly sound, and I'm willing to bet the fencing is wired for intrusion detection."

He rolled down his window, but before he could reach for the green button on the call box, a deep male voice resounded from the black metal speaker, "You are trespassing on private property. Leave immediately or the authorities will be notified."

"We're Coventry Academy students. I'm Caleb Mars. I missed the tour last weekend and was hoping to check things out. My R.A. said he'd talk to Assistant Headmaster Gibbs about stopping by today."

Either Cal was the best bullshitter ever, or he really had spoken with his dorm's resident advisor and not bothered to mention it.

After a brief pause, the cool voice replied, "Who's in the car with you?"

Cal glanced at me, leaning back and gesturing that I speak for myself.

I angled my body so I could see the black box. "Uh, yeah, hi. Lire Devon, here. I'm a junior."

"Zach Carter, junior."

"One moment," the voice said.

Cal turned, took in my expression, and crossed his eyes, making a goofy face at me. Chuckling, he leaned over the center console to whisper, "Relax. You look like you're about to pass out."

I stuck out my tongue at him. "Do not."

"Don't ever play poker, princess." Zach let out an exaggerated groan. "What am I saying? How 'bout we play strip poker, later? You'd be great at it!"

"Shut up." I smirked.

Cal and Zach were snickering when the clang of the gate accompanied the voice's return. "Pull up and park. Have your student IDs ready."

"Someone seriously needs to work on his people skills," I muttered as Cal eased his car forward, impatiently skirting around the sliding gate as soon as there was room.

The smooth asphalt drive pierced the natural landscape, leading us toward a broad cul-de-sac large enough to accommodate the school's minibus several times over. An imposing, black powder-coated steel privacy fence cordoned off a rectangular staging area three times the size of our school's gymnasium, sealing off the circular drive from the private road as well as the rest of the compound. At the end of the fenced cul-de-sac, a locked pedestrian gate provided a pass through to the rest of the facility.

The lush green semi-circular lawn and ornamental plantings did nothing to ease the militaristic feel of the surroundings. I looked up at the wicked spikes topping the fence and shivered.

Cal rounded the circle, passing the pedestrian gate to park in one of three marked parking stalls at the cul-de-sac's edge.

Zach and Cal got out of the car, leaving me alone, while Red helped me dig through my purse for my ID. He found it beneath my wallet.

"Holy crap, Red," I murmured as I slipped my lanyard's black cord around my neck. "This place is crazy intense. The fence looks like something that should be guarding a nuclear missile silo instead of a playground for shifter cubs."

"The school must protect its students as vigilantly as it protects the public from the dangers of untutored shifters."

"You have a point." Not only did they have to prevent unauthorized entry but also escape. If a single shifter predator got loose and attacked someone ... I didn't want to think about what would happen. It was bad enough when a fist fight broke out between Coventry students and the town's bullies outside the local pizza joint. "I guess I imagined it being—I don't know—less high-tech military and more hocus-pocus."

"Permanently warding such a large perimeter would be an insurmountable task, even for the entire Arcane Council."

"Yeah. I knew the place was big, but I didn't realize how big." In the side view mirror, I spied a security guard approaching Cal. I refolded the map and stuck it into my purse. "Tuck down, I'm getting out."

As I exited the car to join Cal, the easy late-morning breeze brushed past me, stirring the loose baby hairs at my temples and ruffling the nearby clusters of aspen trees, making their leaves rustle and shimmer in the sun like paper verdigris coins. I'd always loved aspens, mainly because of their fluttery leaves but also because Dad and I had planted one in our backyard, shortly after moving to Seattle. I'd named it Branchy. The trees bordering the cul-de-sac's fencing appeared to be at least as tall as Branchy, well over fifteen feet.

"Morning," the guard said, assigning the black box's voice to a sternly set face. At least, I think he was a guard. He certainly looked the part, with his black ensemble—cargo pants, utility belt, polo shirt, and combat boots. The only thing missing was a sidearm. He halted five feet away and folded his arms. "I'll need to see your school IDs."

Cal extended his ID while holding out his right hand for Zach's. "Dude, give it up."

When it appeared in Cal's palm, he gave that one over as well.

After the guard inspected the guys' cards and gave them back to Cal, I held up my ID from the lanyard's cord. "Most people don't want to touch it, but if you want me to, I can take it out of its psi-free sleeve for you."

"Hold it up," he commanded, striding closer.

If my gift made him nervous, he sure didn't act like it. He loomed close enough for me to hear his steady breathing, and I had the strongest urge to jerk away from him.

Why didn't you take the stupid lanyard off? I scolded myself while staring anywhere but at the guy's face, which was close enough for me to count the individual hairs of his trimmed goatee.

Just before the guard stepped back, I swear, he leaned a fraction closer and took a deep breath, like he was smelling me.

Goosebumps sprang out on my arms and neck. Even with Cal and Zach standing nearby, I almost shuddered like an anxious Chihuahua. Although, if the guard was a shifter, he probably already knew that he'd completely pegged my freak-o-meter.

Zach, maybe sensing my unease, tugged my ponytail.

The guard grinned. I couldn't see his eyes behind his reflective sunglasses, but I was sure the smile didn't reach that far. "Mr. Mars, please follow me. Mr. Carter and Ms. Devon will wait here. The facility is for shifters only."

Cal shrugged. "Be back in a few, I guess."

Mr. Mercenary hadn't waited for any acknowledgment. His confident stride had already carried him halfway toward the gate.

Cal shot me an arch look and ambled after him. I wondered whether his nonchalant pace was deliberate, just to get on the guard's nerves.

As the guard unlocked the gate with his key, Zach's ultra-bare whisper came at my right ear, "Pretend I'm still here. I'm going in."

I gasped, gaping over my shoulder, my breath suspended, until I realized Mr. Mercenary had finished opening the gate and was examining me with a laser-like stare. It dawned on me what Zach had said. If I didn't do something, the guard would wonder what was up.

I threw up my hands and uttered an inarticulate growl, glaring at the (probably) empty space where Zach had been standing. "Would you stop scaring me like that?" I exclaimed, pouring my very real annoyance into my voice. "Jesus! And, no, I am *not* playing Marco Polo with you. What are you? Five?"

Marco Polo. Served him right, the jackass. I'd be cooling my heels, feeling like an idiot talking to the air as I waited for intruder alarms to sound, while Mr. McSneaky Pants played James Bond inside the shifter-only compound.

I stomped toward the grass at the cul-de-sac's center to sweat it out. Alone.

Jerk!

"Don't talk to me right now. I'm pissed at you," I grumbled, plunking down on the grass, relieved to find it dry. "Scaring me, constantly tugging my ponytail, spying on my meetings with Mr. Simmons. Why do I put up with it?"

You put up with it because I'm charming as heck and you love my nicknames, said my imaginary Zach. *And you don't have any other friends.*

"As if!" I plucked at the grass. "I need to have my head examined, playing this game."

I fell backward onto the springy turf to look up at the blue sky, feet flat on the grass, bent knees pointing skyward. I would *not* think about Zach getting caught. Or that he might be standing above me, right his very minute, listening to me babble like an idiot, simply pretending to be gone in order to make fun of me later.

"Which story are you going to read for our lit assignment?" I asked the air.

I can't believe I'm doing this.

"I think I'm going to read *Frankenstein*. I heard they're reading *The Scarlet Letter* in Neverhart's class. Thank God Mountainside is giving us a choice. Shannon is so jealous. For more than one reason." I smirked. "She has no idea what a pain in the ass the two of you are."

The sun felt deliciously warm and I wished I didn't have to be covered from head to toe so I could feel the heat of its rays directly on my skin. It was probably just as well, though. Without sunblock on my arms and legs, no doubt I'd burn to a crisp in two minutes flat. I closed my eyes, relishing the smell of the grass and the sound of the aspens quaking above me.

I waved my hand lazily. "Dude, chill out. Cal will be done soon and we can go. And stop whispering in my ear. It's getting annoying."

Listening to the birds chirping while the trees and ornamental grasses swished in the breeze, I forced myself to relax. The next thing I knew, something shoved my shoulder.

"Time to wake up, sleepy head."

I shot upright. Blinking back the sun, I squinted up at Cal, who towered over me.

"Yes, *Dad*." From the corner of my eye, I spotted Mr. Mercenary at the gate, watching us.

Was Zach still inside or had he made it out when the guard opened the gate for Cal?

As I got to my feet, I casually looked around until I realized how stupid that was. Just what did I expect to see?

Cal tipped his head toward the car. "Ready?" He raised his chin to smell the air. "Dude, stop messing around. Let's go," he said and sauntered across the lawn.

Relaxing, but on pins and needles with wanting to know what they'd seen inside the compound, I trotted to his side. "So … how was it? Is it nice?"

He shrugged. "Yeah. It's cool. Rooms are a lot like the ones in our dorm, lots of space to run, what's not to like?"

"I don't know. You tell *me*."

He gestured toward the compound. "All this fencing is new. They installed it over the summer. All of it. The entire perimeter." He glanced at me, raising an eyebrow. "We're talking something like twelve miles."

"Holy crap. That must have cost a fortune and a half. It's weird they didn't say anything, though. The school's always bragging whenever they make improvements. They want the parents to know they're getting value for the crazy tuition. I wonder why they didn't say anything."

"Because—" He snapped his mouth shut and looked away. "Uh, I'm sure they had their reasons."

"And those are … ?"

His jaw tightened as he quickened his pace the final few steps to his car, but instead of getting in, he opened the door behind the driver's side and bent down to root around in the backseat.

"Calm down," he carped as he backed out and straightened. "There. All clean. Is that better?" he asked, glaring at the air next to him. He flourished his outstretched hand as though presenting a gift and then closed the door a moment later with a huff.

Catching my eye over the top of his car, he rolled his eyes and then took to the driver's seat.

Inside, I frowned at him as I buckled up. "Zach's not back there, is he?" I whispered.

Instead of answering, Cal slipped me a folded piece of paper. On it, Zach's familiar scrawl said, *Wait for me at the turnout north of the compound.*

"The one on Duncan Hill? The one with the closed produce stand?" I tried to remember whether there was another turnout in that direction, one that was closer.

"Think so."

"Remind me to kill him later, okay?"

"Happy to." He angled his car to the exit side of the circular drive where a call box waited. Cal unrolled his window, but as soon as we pulled up, the gate began to slide open.

"See you in two weeks, Caleb," Mr. Mercenary said through the speaker.

"Yep. See ya, Tom."

I sniffed. Apparently, Mr. Mercenary and Mr. Mars had gotten chummy. I wondered whether 'Tom' sprouted fur at the full moon, too, and what he turned into. Definitely a predator. A big cat of some kind was my guess. I could see a panther, maybe, but for all I knew, his alter ego was a buffalo.

With the gate behind us, I sagged against my seat. "Did you know Zach was going to sneak inside? Or were you as surprised as me?"

"Remember what I told you about Zach and secrets?" he asked, shooting me a wry smile. "As soon as Tom said I was the only one allowed in, I knew."

"He told me to pretend he was still next to me, the asshole. I felt like a complete idiot."

Cal snickered. "Nice touch with the Marco Polo thing."

"Thanks. I try."

Five minutes and several potholes later, Cal pulled his car into the dirt clearing, a quarter mile up the road from the compound's private drive. The shabby wooden produce stand stood shuttered on the northern side of the clearing, its vibrant painting of cherries weathered to pastels. A pristine green metal roof attested to the fact that the stand wasn't an abandoned relic.

"This isn't a bad spot to leave the car when you guys sneak in," Cal said.

"Yeah. There's that turnout the other way, but that one's more like a wide shoulder than anything else. This is better." I released my seatbelt and turned in my seat, partially leaning against the passenger door to converse more easily. "Okay, Mr. Mysterious. What's the deal with the new fencing?"

He eyed me, pressing his lips together, before looking out his side window. "There's no *deal*," he answered. "It means that you and Zach might have a harder time sneaking in than you guys thought. That's all."

Actually, that had been on my mind, ever since he spilled the beans about the new fencing, but I could tell he was hiding something else, something more serious.

"Nice try. There's a juicy reason for the new fencing, and I can tell you know what it is, so spill."

He issued an exasperated grunt, flopping his head back to stare holes through the car's roof.

"Come on. You know I'm not the type to spread secrets," I reasoned. "Who the heck am I gonna blab to, anyway? You guys are my only friends."

About the time I decided he wasn't going to dish, no matter how much I wheedled, he clicked his tongue and blurted, "There have been a couple of suspicious disappearances in the area."

"Disappearances?" I digested this. "They can't be locals, or everyone would know about it. And it can't be a student. The news would be all over the school by now. So ... who?"

When he turned to me, his face was about as grim as I'd ever seen, causing the hairs on the back of my neck to stand and take notice.

"They're both weres," he said. "The first disappeared, the beginning of June, this last summer. The second, about three weeks later—his sister. She came to look for him. Foul play is suspected."

"Weres. You mean werewolves, right?" Technically, the term 'were' could apply to any human suffering from a therianthropic curse, but wolves had become synonymous with the moniker, being the most famous. Or infamous, depending upon how you viewed those things.

He gave me a look: *Duh.* "Yes."

I took in the tightness around his eyes and the subtle downward slant at the corners of his mouth. "You know them, personally. Don't you?"

He turned back to the window, depriving me from reading his expression, but the stiff set of his shoulders spoke volumes. "Yes."

"Are they ... relatives, maybe?"

"Yeah. My older cousins."

"Is that why you and Zach are here, instead of being home-schooled?" As soon as the question left my lips, I wanted to kick myself.

Idiot. He said foul play. What kind of parents sent their teenage sons to investigate a possible kidnapping, maybe even murder? That was a job for law enforcement, not two high school students.

He snapped his gaze from the window to stare at me. "What makes you ask that? I mean ..." He scoffed. "It's not like I've been sniffing the woods around school or anything."

I blinked at him while my eyebrows tried to launch into orbit. I'd expected massive teasing for asking such a dumb question, not a nervous deflection.

His eyes narrowed suspiciously. "What?"

"I wouldn't go playing any strip poker without wearing lots of layers. Just saying."

"*Please.* Somebody's been reading way too much *Nancy Drew.*"

I flinched. I knew I was being sensitive, but the mention of my screw-up back in third grade drew me up short. I turned in my seat to face the front of the car, folding my arms and staring out of the windshield as if my life depended on it.

"Hey. Look ... I didn't mean—" He sighed. "I'm sorry. That was a stupid thing to say."

From the corner of my eye, I noticed him leaning forward to peer at me. "Okay?"

"I don't have to be a girl detective to know you're full of crap. Maybe it's not the only reason you're here, but you're obviously hoping to discover something about their disappearance — or maybe find them."

"Why would you think that?" he asked, this time sounding genuinely curious instead of defensive.

"Gee, I don't know ..." I shot him a withering look. "Maybe because you got all weird about it. And you never *actually* answered my question. When someone answers with another question, it usually means they're hiding something."

The memory of Cal sniffing the air after he'd caught me running from something at the track popped into my head. And Zach had acted all serious about it, too, when it had come up in conversation.

He groaned, glaring up at the ceiling, his shaggy hair crushed against the headrest. "Zach's going to kill me."

"Holy crap. You *are* here to find your cousins. Does your dad know?"

"He's the one who sent us."

I gaped at him. "But ... that's — How ... ? I mean — " I grunted, cutting off my stammering. "You said they disappeared. Foul play means kidnapping or ... or worse. Doesn't he realize this could be, like, you know, *dangerous?*"

Head still pinned to the headrest, he rolled his head in my direction to shoot me a caustic look. "Lire, this is the family business. Zach's not the only one who's been doing contract work since he was thirteen."

I tried to imagine Dad sending Giselle and me to investigate a kidnapping and possible murder. The idea was ludicrous and not simply because Giselle hated my guts. Two people — two *werewolves* — had disappeared! Weres weren't known for being pushovers. Sending a pair of sixteen-year-olds to investigate something so serious seemed beyond reckless.

Of course, Zach wasn't your run-of-the-mill teenager. And Cal wasn't defenseless. He was a werewolf. Then again, his two cousins were weres, too.

The whole thing was so patently nuts, I didn't know what to think.

"It's for sure that they disappeared around here?"

"Yes. Matthew was interviewing for a job at the compound. He disappeared sometime after leaving to drive back home to Montana. Krissy, his sister, went missing, also after her visit to the compound."

My eyes went wide. "You think someone there is responsible?"

"It's possible. We haven't ruled anything out."

"Does Mr. Simmons know why you guys are here?"

"No!"

When I jumped at his outburst, he held up his hand. "Listen, he can't know, okay? Nobody can know. If people find out, parents might panic and pull their kids out of school and the person responsible for my cousins' disappearance will catch wind of it. We want the perp — if he's still in the area — to think he's safe, that not even the Rout realizes my cousins are missing."

Perp? Was he serious?

"Jesus, Cal! This isn't *21 Jump Street*. This is real. People, *students*, could be in danger. What if something bad happens? What if someone else disappears? If people find out that we knew about an axe murderer in the woods but didn't tell anyone — "

"No one's going to find out unless you tell them," Cal broke in. "Besides, notifying the town's sheriff will hardly make things better. The local cops couldn't find their assholes with both hands, GPS, and written instructions in their underwear, much less a kidnapper who can take on two werewolves without leaving any evidence of struggle. And, anyway, do you really think they'll give a damn about two weres who disappeared on their way back to Montana? You know what they'll say. They'll say they must have gone for a run in the woods and turned feral. We're barely human as it is. Right?" He spat out that last bit with so much scorn, his mouth twisted by a snarl, I could nearly see the wolf inside him trying to break free.

He sighed and his gaze softened, spoiling the illusion, but I shivered anyway.

"You know it's true," he said. "Normals might tolerate Glindarians and their feel-good magic, but werewolves are a different story. We're right up there with necromancers and devil worshipers. You, of all people, know what I'm talking about. I saw how the people looked at you at the café this morning. You know I'm right."

I frowned. "Okay ... maybe I get not telling the police, but Mr. Simmons—"

"Doesn't know jack about catching a kidnapper," Cal supplied. "If you think he has more experience than me because he's older, think again. I've been working surveillance, counter-terrorism, extraction, and espionage jobs for five years—ever since I was thirteen. The Hidden trains all its members to be top-notch bodyguards and mercenaries, starting as soon as we're out of diapers. It's a way of life, a different world, Lire. I don't expect you to understand, but at least give Zach and me credit for being more experienced than a Walmart security guard."

He shifted in his seat to lean against his door and folded his arms. "And it's not just Zach and me. You do realize that half the guys at the compound are the Hidden's."

"They are?"

"Yes. They came when the new fence was installed."

"I don't understand. If the school doesn't know about your cousins, why'd they decide to replace it?"

"The Rout demanded the upgrade as part of a deal with the school. The Isangrim picked up the tab and sent Pop's security firm to install and manage it. The Rout wants to send more weres here for school, but the compound wasn't up to snuff. Simmons thinks I'm the guinea pig, here to give everything a test run."

"That's a crapload of moola to spend on a cover story."

"It's not only for cover. The Isangrim cares about keeping Coventry's students safe. And the Rout really does intend for some weres to come here for school."

I wondered how much truth there was in that. Maybe it was the softy in me, but I hoped the real reason the Isangrim invested in the extra security was because he knew Cal, his son, would be a student here.

But the student thing didn't quite jive, did it? Cal's comment about his experience had stuck in my head.

"You're not sixteen. Are you?" I accused. "You're eighteen."

His annoyed grumble said this was yet something else he hadn't intended on telling me. "Not yet. Not until December."

"What about Zach?"

The muscles of his jaw flexed. Pinching the bridge of his nose, he briefly closed his eyes. "It's official. He's totally going to kill me."

"How old?"

"Five months older than me."

I did the mental math. "Then he turned eighteen not that long ago. Is he really your brother? Or was that a lie too?"

He gazed at me sharply. "I didn't lie. You assumed I was sixteen because I'm here as a junior."

I rolled my eyes. "Like you wouldn't have said you were sixteen if I'd asked."

"I'd have said seventeen. Some juniors are seventeen, you know."

"Not usually eighteen, though. Not so early in the year," I pointed out. "Not unless they were held back."

"Why are we even talking about this?"

I shrugged. "So, you're telling me Zach's your brother?"

"Yes. He really is my brother. Well, not by blood." He shook his head, annoyed. "You know what I mean. What we told you, yesterday, was the truth."

"You don't need to be in school at all, do you? You probably already graduated."

"Only because I took the GED, last year. This would've been my senior year."

"Right. And once this is over, you and Zach are out." *Leaving me friendless.* I drooped in my seat. "And here I was starting to think this was going to be a good year." I was being petty and self-centered, but I couldn't help it.

Out of everything he'd told me, their 'student' charade was what upset me the most, which was stupid, I knew. His cousins were missing and a freaking kidnapper was probably at large, for God's sake.

"Come on," he coaxed. "It's still going to be a good year. In a week and a half, you'll have your eight-by-ten and the football and basketball teams will be bald. That's not a bad start, right?"

I didn't answer. Maybe I should shut things down, now. Why get more attached to them, more invested in their friendship, when they were going to up and leave as soon as they caught their bad guy?

Or you could stop being a big baby and enjoy hanging out with them while they're here.

Before I could decide either way, the rear passenger door blew open and Zach hooted victoriously. "That was fucking awesome!" The backseat shifted with his weight. "Finally, something to sink my teeth into." He slammed his door closed, barring the warmer air and insect noises from the car's air conditioned interior. "Why can't all our jobs be that challenging?"

Was I supposed to play dumb, or what?

Dubious about my acting skills at the best of times, I kept my mouth shut and waited to follow Cal's lead. Problem was, Cal didn't say anything either.

"Alright," Zach grumbled after the suspiciously long silence. "What the hell happened?"

I peeked sidelong at Cal, who blew out a resigned sigh and muttered, "She knows."

"What do you mean 'she knows?'" He paused and I imagined him shooting a fiery stare at Cal's head. "Like, *she-knows* knows? Like, *she-knows-because-you-couldn't-keep-your-goddamned-mouth-shut* knows?" With each question, Zach's voice escalated in volume and aggravation. "I knew it. Didn't I tell you? As soon as we met her, I knew you wouldn't be able to keep your goddamned teeth together. You owe me a hundred bucks, asshole. And if this tanks the whole show—"

"It's not going to tank anything," Cal cut in, sounding as angry as his brother. "Calm the hell down. She's not going to tell anyone. She knows what's at stake."

"Yeah? Then why's she looking like she heard the family dog got run over by a tractor trailer?"

"Why do you think, dumbass? She figured out we've been lying to her."

"We're undercover. There's a difference."

"You can believe that if you want to," Cal retorted. "She's not buying it, though."

I issued an annoyed huff. "Would you stop talking like I'm not right here in the car? Jeez."

"Oh, are you here?" Zach asked sweetly. "Good to know. I couldn't tell, with the way you were impersonating an empty seat."

Cal sighed.

"Well, *pardon-moi.*" *Jackass.* "I just found out my only two friends in the whole flipping school aren't even students."

Way to go, moron. Maybe you should *pretend to be an empty seat. At least that way you'd avoid sounding like a friendless loser.*

I ground my molars together. "You know what? Never mind." I opened the car door and got out. "Enjoy the empty seat. I'd rather walk back."

I slammed the door and stormed off, cutting through the dirt parking lot like I'd spotted a roadside espresso cart giving away free iced mochas.

At least the weather was nice, I reasoned, as I squinted up at the blue sky. Although, I'd have preferred my running shoes. Walking the ten miles back to campus in my Chucks was sure to reward me with more than a few blisters.

But if I was lucky, by the time I got back to school, I'd be too tired to be angry, embarrassed, or depressed.

Ha. You wish.

The slam of a car door echoed behind me, but I didn't turn around to see who might be in pursuit. I angled north on Duncan Hill, keeping to the bike lane and lengthening my strides on the paved surface. Weren't pedestrians supposed to walk against traffic? I considered crossing, but I didn't want to turn to look behind me like some pathetic drama queen, hoping one of the guys was back there, chasing after me. I hadn't stormed off, hoping to be pursued.

Honest.

But when a strong hand grasped my shoulder, making me gasp and jerk off kilter, I slowed to a stop, all too aware of the relief that washed through me at hearing Zach's voice.

"Lire ... hold on. You can't walk all the way back to school."

I whirled on him, glaring at the air. "I can do whatever the hell I want, Zach. I'm sixteen, not five. I think I can handle a measly ten-mile walk."

"I'm well aware. Believe me. But you're doing it because you're pissed at us — at me — not because you planned it." He sighed. "Come on. You don't have water ... and you're not dressed for it. Look, I'm sorry. I could have handled that better. It's my fault you're mad." He paused before muttering, "Seems like all I do, lately, is make you mad at me."

He sounded so earnest, so annoyed with himself, it just about drained the anger right out of me.

"If it's any consolation, you've made coming back to school a lot more fun than I thought it would be." His voice had gone quiet and almost hesitant. "I mean, Cal and I weren't exactly jumping for joy when Pop signed us up for this gig. School and I have never gotten along. Been there, done that," he said, biting out the phrase. "I won't lie, I'll be glad when this job is over. But hanging out with you kinda makes me wish I'd done my junior and senior years, here, instead of being home schooled."

I shot a dubious look his way. "Even with Neverhart?"

"Are you kidding? Taking her down a peg's been a high point," he replied, and darned if his enthusiasm didn't seem genuine.

"Yeah ... well, thanks, I guess." I kicked at some stray pieces of gravel that had migrated into the bike lane. "I know I wouldn't want to come back to school if I didn't have to, that's for sure. I can see why you'd be annoyed about it."

I glanced back at the car where Cal stood with his door opened, hand cupped over his eyes against the sun, watching us. "Don't be mad at Cal, okay? It's not like he planned to tell me about stuff. He said a couple things that sounded weird and I ended up figuring most of it out on my own. You don't have to worry. I'm not going to tell anyone."

"I know. I was mad. I bet the dork he wouldn't be able to keep his cover a secret and he *still* told you."

I tucked my fingers into my front pockets to keep myself from making any self-conscious gestures and peered at the source of his voice. "You said, as soon as you met me, you knew he wouldn't be able to keep it a secret. Why? What made you think that?"

"Because you're totally his type."

"*Right.*" As far as teasing went, that sucked big time, but I hid my bruised feelings behind a massive eye roll. "Seriously, though. What's the deal?"

"That wasn't a joke, princess. You do it for him. Why'd you think he didn't want you to sit with us that first day?"

I laughed bitterly. "Oh, gee, I don't know. Maybe the same reason everyone *else* doesn't want to sit with me." I wiggled my gloved fingers at him. "What does that mean, 'his type?' I didn't know I *was* a type, unless you mean the type that makes guys run in the other direction."

He probably thought I was fishing for compliments, but I wasn't. I simply hadn't figured, in a million years, that I'd ever be some guy's type, especially a guy as attractive as Cal.

"Any guy who runs in the other direction after checking you out is an idiot."

I blinked at him.

"Jesus. That look. They've really done a number on you, haven't they?"

They?

Before I could get a handle on what he meant—was he talking about the kids at school?—Zach suggested we head back to the car.

"When you took off, Cal was about two seconds away from beating the crap out of me. If I say anything else, he's going to lose his shit. You with me, princess?"

I could tell from the positional shift in his voice that he'd taken a few steps toward the car.

"Um, yeah … okay."

If there was ever a time I wanted to put the thumb screws to some-one, this was it, but pressing Zach to reveal private details about his brother would definitely veer into compliment seeking territory. Plus, I knew it wasn't a cool thing to do, so I kept my mouth shut and re-traced my steps back to the car, while my little voice cheered, 'I do it for him! That means he likes me, right? Like, more than just a friend?'

It took me a nanosecond to remember that, even if he did like me that way, it didn't matter. Cal wasn't going to be around for long. As soon as the missing-werewolf mystery was solved, he and Zach would be out of here.

All the more reason to keep your feet firmly planted in the friend zone, I scolded myself.

Now, if I could get my stupid daydreams to cooperate, my life would be way less complicated.

CHAPTER 11

As if this wasn't complicated enough

THE second week of school progressed much as the first, minus any classroom pranks, headmaster meetings, threats of expulsion, or ridiculous dares. As far as my weekend meeting with the Veep Creep went, only Professor Trapp made any mention of the standoff. Despite everything ending in a bitter-tasting draw, he assured me that things had changed for the better. I guessed time would tell. For now, I tried to go about my business as though none of it ever happened.

The one break from the regular monotony was the start of MEW, also known as Magic Enrichment Wednesdays. (The school had originally called it Paranormal Enrichment Wednesday, I guess to be inclusive, but that name hadn't lasted long, for obvious reasons.) From here on out, every Wednesday, we skipped our regular schedule in favor of our segregated class where we learned about all things magical.

A lot of students complained about how boring magic enrichment class was, but secretly, MEW was my favorite day of the week. Since I'd been raised by a normal parent, a lot of what we covered was new and interesting for me. It also didn't hurt that we were only in class for half the day on Wednesdays.

There weren't enough third- and fourth-year psychics to fill an entire classroom, much less a quarter of one, so we were lumped in with the cursed students. This meant Cal and Zach were in my class, along with Ted Mason, Jason Vandermeir, Brad Perry, and what seemed like half the varsity sports teams. Shifters tended to be a highly physical bunch. Go figure.

The class wasn't entirely comprised of shifters, though. As I settled into my back-row seat, I spied several psychics — a dowser, telekinetic, pyrokinetic, and the school's one truthsayer. Of all the non-shifter cursed students, Zach had the rarest affliction, but Evelyn came in a close second with the eye-of-the-beholder curse. To me, she was one of the prettiest girls in school, but not everyone saw her that way. People who did ugly things saw her as ugly, which made me wonder how Amanda saw her. As much as I wanted to know the answer to that question, MEW was the one day every week when I didn't have to share a class with the treacherous little rat. Oh, my bad. That was an insult to rodents.

Zach, Cal, and I snagged three seats in a line at the far corner of the classroom. We fell into our familiar formation, me in the very back row, Zach in front of me with Cal in front of him. It was the best way to insulate Zach from anyone who might think the desk was empty, in case they happened to miss Zach's open binder or backpack stashed under his seat. The fact that it allowed Zach to more easily pass notes between us was an added bonus.

I'd just retrieved my notebook from my backpack when Ted Mason folded himself into the desk to my left.

"Hey. How's it going?" he said in that cool, easygoing way that all the jocks seemed to nail.

My echoed "hey" was barely audible above the room's chatter. Belatedly, I remembered his question and quickly added, "Not bad. How 'bout you?"

"I'd be better if it was twelve thirty instead of"—he craned his head to peer at the clock—"seven fifty-six."

"Yeah. But I'll take this over trigonometry, any day of the week."

He smiled. "You have Professor Blackwell?"

I nodded.

"She's not bad. I got an A in there, last year. If you need help, I can tutor you. Just let me know."

It was a good thing he'd chosen that moment to pull his notebook from his backpack because my expression must have been comical.

Ted leaned into the aisle, a sly look on his face. "I hear there might be some excitement at the compound next Wednesday night." He splayed his legs beneath his desk, but even bent, his feet extended far under the chair in front of him.

He watched me, brows raised, a lopsided smile lending him a mischievous air.

I shrugged, feigning indifference. "Did you?"

"Yup." Again, he briefly leaned closer to murmur, "No hard feelings, but you know I'm obligated to put a stop to it." Ted glanced at Cal and then smirked, but when I followed his gaze I didn't see anything out of the ordinary. As far as I could tell, Cal wasn't paying the least bit of attention to our muted discussion.

"Are you? Why's that?" I gave him an arch look. "I mean, not that I have the first clue what you're talking about."

"Some idiot decided to pit the entire basketball and football teams against a certain *someone* taking a photo. If we lose, we're gonna have to shave our heads. With Homecoming in a few weeks, you wouldn't want to see these glorious locks go under the clippers, now would you?" He ran his fingers through his thick blond hair, shaking his head like a shampoo model, before shooting me a disarming grin.

"I dunno," I said, giving him the once-over. "Bald could work for you."

"You think so, huh?"

"Sure. It's all the rage ... if you're an Olympic swimmer." I gave him the side-eye. "Ever think of trying a new sport?"

"We'd need a swimming pool for that."

I snapped my fingers. "Aw, that's too bad." I leaned closer and added, *sotto voce*, "You might want to invest in some hats, then. Wouldn't want you to catch cold."

He chuckled. Leaning in he whispered, "Losing might be more bearable if you went to the dance with me."

To say I was stunned would be a massive understatement.

He glanced at Cal. "Or ... maybe you're already going with some-one?"

"Um ..."

Although he seemed genuine, Stephen King's *Carrie* sprang to mind. How could it not? The horror novel was based on a true story, after all. There wasn't a psychic around who hadn't read it or seen the movie. Ted, here, was a shoo-in for homecoming king. And let's be honest, except for not being a telekinetic, wasn't I just about tailor-made for the role of Carrie White — the least popular girl in the whole school who thinks the cute guy is genuinely interested in her? Hoo, boy. I could see it now, a bucket of pig's blood sloshing over my head during the king and queen's crowning ceremony. I'd better steer clear of white dresses.

I was being ridiculous, of course. There wasn't anything nefarious in Ted's invitation. But even though he was good looking and popular, I had no desire to be his date for the homecoming dance. In fact, the whole idea broke me out in a cold sweat. And that was without con-sidering that, for most of last year, he and Amanda had an on-again-off-again boyfriend-girlfriend thing going. This was one drama I did not want any part in.

"Yeah, uh, I'm ... I've already ... you know ..." I ducked my head and my gaze unerringly tracked to the guy sitting one seat away, the werewolf I hoped would come to my rescue.

Did Cal's shoulders seem higher and more tense than usual?

Scalding heat rushed to my cheeks and my ears felt like they might burst into flames. If Zach had been feeding me a line about Cal being interested in me, I was about to look like a complete idiot. Actually, with all my embarrassed stammering, I'd achieved idiot status five minutes ago.

Where was a geomancer when you needed one? I'd have killed for a hole to fall into.

"I'm too late, huh? Dang." Ted gave me a sheepish, utterly charming smile. "That's cool. Maybe we can get together another time. If you're ever bored and want to hang out, you could give me a call, maybe."

Wowzers. Talk about a smooth recovery. Somehow, he managed to ooze confidence and be totally adorable at the same time. Quite a feat for a guy sporting a broad-shouldered physique, bad-boy stubble, and who towered over practically every teacher in school. Throw in that level of charm and it was no wonder he never seemed to lack for a girlfriend.

Before I could come up with a suitable reply, the bell rang and Professor Petersen called our attention to the start of class. In all honesty, I don't think I've ever been so happy to open a textbook in all my life, but I should have known Zach wouldn't let the discussion pass without comment.

His folded note appeared ten minutes into class when we were supposed to be reading the section in our text books about Vodou. Too bad Vodou families sent their kids to their exclusive school in New Orleans. I could have used a *gris-gris* right about now. Or was it a fetish? An amulet? Even though I'd just read the section on Vodou charms, I hadn't kept straight which ones offered the user protection, good luck, or were used to hex someone.

Whatever the case, as I unfolded the note, I decided a Vodou charm against Zach's teasing could clearly have its uses.

Instead of a snarky comment, though, what I found was another of Zach's perfectly rendered sketches. In this one, he'd drawn a brawny, bare-chested Ted, leaning out the window of a high tower, his hair a lion's mane that morphed into a Rapunzel-long lock cascading all the way to the ground. At the bottom of the tower, my doppelgänger gazed upward, holding a gleaming pair of scissors, a maniacal expression on her face. At my cartoon counterpart's feet, a massive wolf lazed, chin atop its paws, one eye opened to the action, a toothy smirk visible beneath its muzzle.

I slapped a hand over my mouth to prevent any giggles from escaping. Of course, by doing so, I'd left the page more visible to a certain set of prying eyes.

A JOT OF BLOOD

Ted issued what sounded like a muted growl. Before I could slide the cartoon into my lap, he snatched it from my desk, the gesture quick as a lightning spell.

Oh, shit!

I snapped my attention to the werelion, waiting for his reaction.

To my astonishment, Ted chuckled quietly as he examined the drawing. After glancing over at Professor Petersen, who sat at his desk grading papers, Ted leaned toward me. "This. Is. *Awesome,*" he whispered. "Who drew it? Carter?"

I shot him a disapproving glare and pretended to zip my lips. Jason, who'd taken the seat in front of Ted when the bell rang, turned to see what his roommate was whispering about.

Ted's gaze flicked to the empty chair in front of me. "Come on. It has to be him, right? This is so frickin' cool." He glanced at the teacher, making sure we remained unobserved. "Can I keep it?"

Before I could answer, Zach snorted. "Fine. Go ahead."

I pushed out my lower lip, pouting. "But I wanted it."

Zach snickered. "I'll make you another one, later."

I wondered whether he'd laugh at me if I asked him to do it on thick drawing paper so I could frame it.

We made it through the day's instruction without any further mishaps. What's more, I learned a *gris-gris* bag, or mojo bag, gave good luck and warded off evil. A hex bag, on the other hand, seemed to do the opposite — it provoked a specific effect, mostly of a malicious nature but not always. It was the fetish, though, that truly gave me the creeps. A fetish, if created by a Vodou practitioner in possession of someone's bodily donation, had the power to control that person.

How the heck a Vodou priest ever got anyone to have sex with them, I couldn't imagine. Talk about putting your life into someone else's hands. Of course, the same could be said for any magic user, not just Vodou priests. This prompted a lively class discussion about negative stereotypes and why society dubbed some types of magic users as evil when any spellcaster had the ability to cause harm, even Glindarian witches who were known for their healing magic.

Cal, Zach, and I were the last to leave the room after class ended. In the hallway, Ted was leaning against the wall opposite the door, but he straightened when he saw me.

182

"Yo, Lire." He glanced around as if to verify that none of his friends were watching. "Hey, can I, uh, talk to you for a sec?"

The urge to say, 'I don't know, *can* you?' was almost overwhelming.

I shot Cal an arch look and shrugged. "I'll catch you guys at the refectory, I guess?"

"We'll wait for you outside," he said, his voice clipped and threatening. He glared at Ted and then stalked away. I wasn't about to lay odds on whether Zach had elected to stay behind to eavesdrop.

I tried not to frown at Ted while nervous excitement clenched my stomach down to the size of a marble. "What's up?"

"Look ... I'm not enthused about shaving my head, okay? But I don't want you to get into trouble either." He shifted on his feet, hands stuck into his front pockets, and took a half-step closer.

Even though we were alone in the hallway, he leaned down and lowered his already subdued voice until it came out in a raspy murmur. "I don't know if you know it, but Amanda's totally gunning for you. On the full moon, she's going to have one of her friends put a vigilance spell on the door to your room. When you leave in the middle of the night, she'll know." He gazed at me significantly. "She plans to give you time to get off school grounds before setting off the dorm's fire alarm."

I jerked, realizing what that meant. "They'll do a headcount and discover I'm gone."

He nodded. "Just so we're clear, I'm not the one who told you. And ... if you somehow figure out a way to get out, watch your back at the compound, okay? A lot of guys are ready to make sure you don't get the picture." With a final telling look, he turned and walked away.

Watching him disappear around the corner, I massaged my forehead and muttered, "Craptastic. As if this wasn't complicated enough."

"Relax, tiger. All you need to worry about is having your camera ready and getting the money shot. Leave the rest to me."

I snorted, unsurprised by Zach's voice in my ear. Turning toward the other end of the hall, I walked to where Cal waited outside.

"And how, may I ask, do you plan on getting around this latest catastrophe?" I huffed, throwing my arms up in disgust. "Let's say you find a way to disarm the vigilance spell. Amanda can still pull the fire alarm without it. If she's smart, she'll take her chances and pull it around one in the morning when it's safe to assume I'm at the compound."

"Then I guess I'll have to find a way to make sure the alarm doesn't go off, won't I?"

I laughed bitterly. "Good luck with that. If the alarm doesn't go off, she'll try something else. You'd have to tie her to the bed and muzzle her. Her and her roommate, *both*. And, even then, she'd probably find some way to alert everyone. She hates my guts. She'll do anything she can to put a torpedo into me."

"I've overheard enough of her backbiting to figure that out, ten times over," Zach informed me. "I've got this. Trust me, okay? Think you can do that?"

I shoved the crash bar of the door with more force than necessary and strode toward Cal, who leaned against the thick trunk of a nearby tree. "Fine. But don't do anything stupid. I want to get this photo, but not enough for you to risk getting into serious trouble. It's not worth it." I stopped next to Cal. "You got that, Zach?"

"Yes, Mommy."

I aimed my glare in his direction. "Zach, I'm serious."

"What's going on?" Cal demanded. "What'd beanpole want?"

I took in his irritable frown. "You have something against Ted?"

"Yeah. The guy's a dick."

I hadn't realized they knew each other.

"Okay," I drawled, looking at him askance. "Are you talking general dickishness, or did he do something specific to piss you off?"

He folded his arms. "Let's just say, I know the type."

"Huh. Well, you might want to rethink things." I focused on the empty space next to me. "Don't you think, Zach?"

"Telling you about Amanda was cool," Zach conceded. "But he only did it because he wants to get into your pants. Most likely he's still a dick."

"What?" I laughed. "*Please*. That is not the vibe I got. At all."

"That's because you don't have a clue, princess."

I eye-rolled so hard, I was lucky not to break anything. "Whatever. Since I don't plan on hanging out with him, it doesn't matter. What matters is what he said about Amanda." I told Cal the details.

Cal looked grimly in Zach's direction. "You'll have to fix her. And her roommate, too — what's her name? — Shania. Anything else is a risk."

"Fix? What the heck does that mean?" Maybe I hadn't been too far off with my muzzle comment, which was more than a little distressing.

"Transfix — spell or drug them so they sleep through the night," Cal elaborated, checking around to make sure we weren't overheard. "If they're not awake, they can't pull the alarm."

I gaped at him before shaking my head and leaning in to whisper vehemently, "Whoa. No way. Spelling someone against their will is grounds for expulsion. You know that, right? And, with Amanda's godfather, you'd be lucky not to face the Arcane Council's tribunal and sent to Alcatraz."

"You're assuming I'll be caught," Zach replied, even though my disapproval had been aimed at Cal. "But if the spell idea bothers you, then a non-magical sleeping draught can do the trick. I kind of prefer it. It's more foolproof."

"Zach — "

"Lire, I've done this, like a million times," he cut in. "It comes up a lot on ... certain jobs. It's not a big deal. I'll slip it into their drinks at dinner. It's a slow acting sedative. They won't feel impaired, only tired. The effect is so gradual that they'll have no idea anything is different. The Hidden spent years perfecting it. It's safe, subtle, and untraceable. When they go back to their room, they'll get more and more tired until they fall asleep. No weird dreams. No hallucinations. No loss of inhibition. Just the best night's sleep they've ever had."

"But they'll be out cold," I exclaimed. "What if there's a fire? What if someone breaks into their room? They'll be defenseless. You can't think that's okay!"

"No. Jesus Christ! Calm down. This isn't crude, like a frickin' roofie. That's not how this stuff works. You can still be woken up. It might take a little more effort and, yes, they'll want to go back to sleep again, but if someone attacks them, they're not going to lie there, okay? Look, I've taken it myself. All of us have, to know what it's like and recognize the signs. Cal had no trouble waking me up. I was massively tired, like I'd stayed up until three in the morning studying, but I never felt drugged. I just wanted to get some sleep."

I frowned at him. "I don't know, Zach."

"Would it make you feel better to try it yourself? Or, no, you can test it on *me*, this weekend. I'll smuggle you up to our room. We can watch movies and you can see how it works." He lowered his voice seductively. "You can take advantage of me in my massively uninhibited, drugged-out state."

I shot him an exasperated glare.

"No, not you," Cal said, ignoring Zach's comment. "You'll have to be awake to sneak her back out of our dorm in time for curfew. I'll take it."

I examined him. "You'd do that?"

"Sure." Cal shrugged. "Just means I'll sleep like a baby."

I pressed my lips together, unconvinced. Drugging someone was a big freaking deal; I didn't care what Zach said. But I also didn't know any other way to keep Amanda from devoting her entire night to my comeuppance. The way things stood, she'd win either way. If I stayed, she'd label me a chickenshit for not following through on the dare. I'd never live it down. But if I left school grounds to get the photo, she'd get me into trouble for sneaking out.

If I hadn't gotten tangled up with that stupid blackmail mess, I might have elected to do it anyway. Dad told me to be a little bad, right? But there was no way I'd be so reckless, not now, with the Veep Creep on the school's board of regents, itching to make an example out of me.

"What if we set her up, instead?" I asked. "You know, trick Amanda into thinking I've left the dorm, let her get caught triggering the alarm." I smiled at them. "Wouldn't that be awesome? Can't you see the expression on her face when she realizes I'm still in my room?"

Zach chuckled. "Did you know you look like a kid in a candy store when you get all devious like that?"

I snickered. "What can I say? Turning the tables on her would be the absolute best. You can't tell me there's anything that could top that."

"Oh, pretty sure I can, princess," Zach intoned, his voice ripe with innuendo.

"Zach," Cal warned.

"Fine." He sighed petulantly. "Setting off the vigilance spell is easy. We'll leave but then sneak right back inside. The problem is catching her when she sets off the alarm. If she has one of her witchy friends put a transference spell on the lever, she could be anywhere inside the building and set it off with no one the wiser."

I shook my head. "The fire alarms are warded. A couple years ago, they kept going off for *no reason*," I said, miming air quotes. "The school hired a defensive warlock to fix the problem. Now, a stray spell can't *accidentally* set them off. Someone has to pull the lever, and I'd bet any money they're all enchanted to boot. Whoever pulls it will be marked somehow."

"How likely is it that she'll do the deed herself?" Zach asked.

"I doubt anyone would be stupid enough to do it for her, but you never know." I considered it. "If it was me, I'd stage a fire in my microwave to have a believable story to fall back on in case the lever really is enchanted."

"You begin to impress me, tiger. Sure you're not a criminal mastermind?"

I smirked.

"So ... that makes things easier," Zach observed. "We pretend to leave, sneak back into your room, and then wait for the fireworks. Amanda will cool her heels long enough to ensure we're off school grounds, she'll then pretend to have a fire, either she or Shania will pull the lever, and you'll stumble out of your room looking sleepy and concerned when the alarm goes off. Your R.A. will freak out, screaming at everyone to evacuate. She'll do a headcount on the south forty while Gibbs shits a bucketload of bricks and the firetrucks show up. Eventually, everyone will go back to their rooms once the fire department finds a bag of burnt popcorn in Shania and Amanda's microwave. They won't dare to set off the alarm again, so we'll be good to go." He paused for that to sink in. "What do you think? That about cover it?"

"Why do I think it sounds too pat?" I asked.

"Because there's still plenty that could go wrong, like, what if she waits hours before pulling the alarm? Even if she does pull the alarm, with or without a lot of waiting, there's nothing to stop her from telling your R.A., an hour after everyone's back in bed, that she saw you leaving campus through her window. Everyone would call her a snitch, but after the alarm debacle, she might not care. There's also the possibility that she'll cause an anonymous fire in the common area, which is totally whack but would get her out of having to pull the alarm altogether." He sighed. "I'm telling you, fixing her with a visit from the Sandman is more foolproof, but if you feel strongly about it ... I guess your idea is the next best choice. Just prepare to get caught."

Cal gave me a direct stare. "You do realize, if Amanda was in your shoes, she'd tell Zach to drug you in an instant, right?"

"And that wouldn't be all," Zack hastened to add. "She'd demand that I get embarrassing photos of you drooling on your pillow, too. If we do this my way, I won't need to set foot in Amanda's room. The only thing that'll happen is she and Shania will get tired right in time for curfew. They'll go to sleep in their beds and have sweet dreams until morning. End of problem."

"Hey, don't stress," Cal said, probably noticing that the more they pressed the issue, the quieter I became. He tipped his head to the side and peered at me. "You don't need to make a decision right this minute." He shot a glare to the empty air to my left and growled, "And Zach won't pressure you to do something you're not comfortable with." He looked back at me, his expression softening. "We'll show you the fix in action, Friday or Saturday night, in our room. I'll take a nap and then you can decide. We'll go with whatever you say, no pressure. Okay?"

"I guess we could do that," I said.

Considering this meant I'd get to hang out with Cal, in his bedroom of all places, you'd think I'd have been more enthusiastic. Seeing him cuddled in his blankets (with permission to watch him while he slept, no less) wouldn't be a hardship, right? Besides, I knew Cal was right. If our places had been reversed, I had zero doubt that Amanda would have jumped on the let's-slip-Lire-a-roofie idea without sparing any thought to my health or safety. Honestly, given that thought alone, I was mad at myself for being so uptight about it. But no matter how much I argued with my inner voice, drugging Amanda and Shania just felt ... *wrong*.

I didn't think anything would change my mind, but I was tired of talking about it.

And, yeah, call me shallow, but I wasn't about to turn down a chance to ogle Cal in his bedroom — especially when Zach wouldn't leave me alone until I agreed.

CHAPTER 12

He's only mostly dead

SATURDAY night, after eating dinner with Cal and Zach, I left the dining hall, alone. Instead of heading back to my dorm, though, I took the path that circled toward LARTS. With the refectory's windows out of sight and a quick check to ensure I was unobserved, I slipped through the refectory's landscaping and ducked around the corner to the far side of the building.

Safely in the shadows, I stopped near the kitchen's dumpster to wait.

"Those were some killer stealth moves," Zach said, his voice emanating from the corner of the building where I'd just come. "I'm totally putting in a word for you with my dad. He'll be all over recruiting you after graduation."

"Shut up."

His snicker came at my shoulder. "I'm kinda not joking, though. Dad would cut off a limb to have a clairvoyant on the payroll, willing to read and tell, at his beck and call. You should think about it. Seriously. You'd make a killing. Clairvoyants don't come cheap."

I shivered at the thought of spying and reading people's belongings to learn all their dark secrets. I wasn't sure why, but reading antiques felt different. Maybe because the people whose privacy I invaded weren't alive anymore.

"Not in the plan. But thanks for the offer." I grimaced. "Can we get going. This dumpster stinks."

"Gimme your hand."

I hesitated. "You're wearing gloves, right?" I didn't want to have to throw mine away if he wasn't.

"Yes, princess," he said in an overly patient sing-song. "I wear a skin-suit and gloves, every day. You and your clothes won't learn any of my thoughts, no matter how wicked and dirty." He lowered his voice to sultry depths. "Unless you say 'please.'"

I served up my left hand, along with my standard eye roll.

At Zach's grasp, my surroundings dimmed and took on a shimmery bent, as though I viewed the world through slightly tinted, antique glass.

"Wow," I breathed, marveling at our surroundings. When I glanced down at our joined hands, I nearly yanked my hand from his grasp. Our linked hands were black—like, light-sucking swallow-the-universe black.

I scanned upward—mapping out his wrist, arm, and shoulder—taking in the full scope of his opaque form. He was so utterly black, he could have been a cardboard cutout.

I gasped. "You! I can see you! I mean, I can't *see-you* see you, but—"

All at once, clutching his fingers wasn't enough. With my other hand, I reached out to verify that this body-shaped projection wasn't some bizarre optical illusion, but I froze, startled by my own inky appendage. I held up my hand for inspection, turning it over and spreading my fingers wide before looking down at myself. "Whoa! I'm all black, too. This is nuts. How do you see anything you touch if it turns black like this?"

"Because I'm an occultum. To me, you look normal."

"This is amazing! I can see your shape. I didn't expect that." I gazed up at the smooth silhouette of his head. Not much contour there. Either he had a supremely short crew cut or his hair was long enough that it appeared flat. "You're taller than I thought."

And broader.

Because of his wry comments about Cal's muscles, I'd always pictured him being on the small side. But after one look at Zach's obsidian shape, it was clear to see genetics hadn't failed him in the height or fitness category. He didn't appear to be as thickly built as Cal, but still, his lean muscular form was a shock to see.

"You thought I was short and fat, didn't you?" he teased, leaning closer to loom over me. "Admit it."

"Did not."

"Uh-huh. Sure."

"I swear." I giggled. "Okay, fine. If you must know, I pictured you being short and skinny."

"I knew it. Zero respect, that's what I get. Girls get a load of Cal's muscles and start drooling, but they hear my voice and think I'm a smart ass with a Napoleon complex."

"Now that you mention it ..." Grinning, I hip checked him, something I'd never done with anyone in my whole life. It made me positively giddy. "You *are* a smart ass, I can't lie. How tall was Napoleon, anyway?"

"Apparently, he was six-three."

I laughed. "Was not."

"Whatever you say, Miss Valedictorian. Come on. Cal's going to wonder where we got to." He yanked my hand and led the way toward the dorms.

As we walked side by side, I relished the novelty of holding a guy's hand, something else I'd never done.

I snuck a glance to my left and realized I could make out Zach's profile. Stunned, I stopped in my tracks, pulling him to a halt beside me.

"Stop right there. No. Look straight ahead," I ordered, examining him. "Jeez, Zach! Why the heck didn't we do this a long time ago? I can see what you look like!"

"Don't you think that's stretching things? You can see my humongous nose when I turn the right way. That's about it."

There was no denying he had a high-bridged, prominent nose, but it was strikingly straight and balanced by a strong chin. There was absolutely nothing wrong with his profile, other than the strangeness of him being a Zach-shaped black hole, which was disconcerting, mostly because it made him appear one-dimensional while the contours of his silhouette said he was most decidedly otherwise. From the beginning, it had made me want to touch him, just to verify he was there, a part of my world.

"Give me a break. Your nose isn't humongous," I scolded. "And I can see all your profile—your forehead, lips, and chin, too, wise guy. I like it, okay? It's a treat to see. So you need to shut up." I tugged on our joined hands. "Okay, you passed inspection. We can go now."

Chuckling, he succumbed to my pull and walked at my side again. "A treat to see, huh?" he said, after a moment of silence. "That's a new one. Most girls freak out and drop my hand in a hot second. Seeing me is like looking into the pit of despair, or so I've been told."

"What?" I stumbled over my own feet when I glanced over at him. "The pit of despair? A girl actually compared you to something out of *The Princess Bride* movie?"

"Yup."

"Jesus. Talk about dumb. The pit of despair is Count Rugen's torture chamber and it isn't black. It isn't even all that dark. Hello! It's a movie. Gotta be able to see what's going on. In the book, the author called it the 'zoo of death,' or something like that." I shook my head. I was such a nerd. "Anyway, whoever this girl was, she's a complete dope. 'Pit of despair' is *not* what I thought when I first saw you. In fact, it was the total opposite. Just saying."

"Yeah?" His features were a mystery, but in that one drawn out word, my mind's eye saw his left eyebrow perk up. "The total opposite, huh?"

Way to go, bonehead. Why didn't you tell him you were stunned by his hot body and make your embarrassment complete?

I shrugged like it was no big thing.

"Come on. You can't go dropping a hint like that and not tell me what you were thinking."

"I hate to break it to you, but, *yeah*, I totally can. And, for your information, I wasn't dropping a hint."

"Princess, princess, princess ..." he chastised. "You do realize, that's like waving a red cape at the bull, right? One way or another, I'll get you to spill. It's only a matter of time, so you might as well tell me and get it over with."

I could have left him hanging but realized, the more I resisted telling him what he wanted to hear, the more blown out of proportion it would get. He'd assume I was too embarrassed to tell him and jump to the conclusion that I was totally into him or that I'd been thinking something massively naughty, when neither was precisely true.

"You're a brat," I groused, though not unkindly. "It's not that I was thinking anything specific, okay? I never thought I'd be able to see you, and, when I did, it was kind of a shock. I went from thinking you were a pipsqueak to seeing" — without breaking stride, I waved my free hand up and down as if to encompass his whole body — "*this magnificence*. It was a surprise, that's all."

I left out describing my inexplicable and overwhelming urge to touch him. That could be misinterpreted. Nor did I want to explain the complicated feelings that churned inside of me at coming face to face with the indisputable fact that Zach wasn't some disembodied voice. I'd known that he had an actual body (*duh* — I wasn't a complete moron), but seeing it, seeing *him*, made me realize that, despite Zach's penchant for lewd comments, I'd managed to overlook his masculinity.

It was exactly like he'd said. I'd gone gaga over Cal and his muscular physique, but hadn't thought twice about Zach. I'd allowed his invisibility to neuter him. Maybe this was why he seemed to go out of his way to make so many risqué comments.

Why hadn't I figured that out sooner?

"Now who's the smart ass?" Zach replied, a smile in his voice. "Somehow, I don't think 'magnificent' was the word you were thinking."

I hadn't realized I'd slowed to a halt until my arm stretched out in front of me to pull on Zach's hand. He stopped and turned to me.

"I'm sorry," I said, peering up at him. "You were right ... what you said. God! I'm like all those other girls. I saw Cal and the way he looks and—" I swallowed hard. "You deserve better. It shouldn't take seeing you like this to realize that. I'm a total jerk."

He puffed out an astonished breath as he stepped closer. "No. You're not. You didn't drop my hand like you touched a man-eating slug. That's a first, okay?"

He reached out with his free hand to give my hair an affable tug. "You're not a jerk. The thing with Cal ... Look, I get it. He's a great guy. And the two of you have a lot in common. You're into a lot of the same things, so I'm not surprised that you'd like him." He paused and tipped his head to the side. "But now that you know why we're here, you realize that we'll be leaving at some point, yeah? And Cal ... well, he's got his own issues. He's not the type to get close to people. I just ..." He sighed. "I don't want you get hurt, and I know that's the last thing Cal wants. So ... be careful, okay?"

"I know. It's not like I haven't thought about that already." I frowned as I considered him. "But what do you mean about Cal? Does this have something to do with him covering himself up all the time? When it's hot and we hit the track, I've noticed he never even wears a short sleeve shirt."

Turning away, he tugged my hand. "Not my place to explain. When he's ready, I'm sure he'll tell you."

We walked the remaining distance in thoughtful silence.

Zach slowed to a stop in front of Stewart House. The modern lodge-style building was a mirror image of the women's dormitory, except its wood siding was stained a dark green instead of brown.

"This is where we need to be careful so we don't get trampled. I'll be using more juice, so the shifters don't sniff you out. It'll feel weird. Don't freak out. Stick to holding my hand and don't resist me, okay?"

"Uh ... okay."

"Right, let's go."

At his words, our surroundings seemed to narrow and darken while at the same time inexplicably staying sharp. When he opened his dorm's front door, I was sure we squeezed through what should have been way too small an opening for me, much less the both of us. Stranger still, I swore our feet weren't touching the floor. I wanted to look down to check, but I didn't dare, for fear that I'd trip, especially since Brad was right there, working the front desk.

I followed Zach as if I were his balloon at the end of a short string. With a gentle tug, he guided me to the stairs. We zipped upward, flowing effortlessly between two guys on their way down, and I found myself inside Zach and Cal's shared room almost before I could process the journey.

Released from Zach's grip, I blinked back the room's sudden brightness and stumbled to the nearest place to sit, which turned out to be someone's bed. I felt as though I'd stepped off a moving conveyor belt, like the kind they had at some airports. It was that bizarre feeling of going super fast, even though I'd taken a few small steps.

"Whoa," I rasped, sitting down hard. "I can see why you told me not to freak out."

I scanned the empty areas around me, on the assumption that Zach hadn't gone far. "That was incredible, though. Did we walk on air? Because that's totally what it felt like. And I don't know how we got past those two dudes on the stairs. There was barely enough room for a mouse to squeeze through." I practically bounced on the bed. "That was so cool!"

As I adjusted to being back in the real world, I took in my surroundings. Their dorm room was generously sized, maybe three times as big as mine. Cal sat on a faded brown couch, which had been placed in the center of their space, creating a small sitting area that separated their two halves. Across from the couch, against the wall, was a television atop a low-lying console.

I waved. "Hey, Cal. How's it going?"

He shook his head, chuckling. "Glad to hear you didn't throw up or something. You guys took long enough, I was beginning to wonder."

"That I'd barf?" I goggled at him. "Are you serious? Who the heck would barf after something like that? It was awesome."

"You'd be surprised," Zach said.

My eyebrows shot up. "Lemme guess, Miss Pit of Despair?"

Cal's eyes went wide. "You told her about that?"

"Yeah." Zach laughed. "Lire's reaction was about as opposite as you could get from Lauren's. Dude, you should've heard her go on about *The Princess Bride* and how the pit of despair isn't black. She sounded just like you, except without all the f-bombs."

"I couldn't help it," I said. "Not to be mean, but the girl kind of sounds like a ditz."

"No 'kind of' about it." Cal stared at me, an odd expression on his face, but it disappeared so quickly I couldn't decide whether he'd been bewildered or what. "We should totally watch that, don't you think?"

"*The Princess Bride*? You have it?" I beamed at him. "Sure. I love that movie. That okay, Zach?"

"Sure. I'm down with a little Buttercup. I'll fix it so it's lights out for Cal, right in time for Westley's life-sucking in the pit of despair."

"Oh, yeah," I drawled. "When Westley dies. Perfect." I shot a nasty look in Zach's direction. "Nice way to put me at ease, bonehead."

Cal snickered. "I'll be fine." He strode to the bookcase on other side of the room. "Make some popcorn, bro. The psi-free stuff. I'll set up the movie. Lire, drag that weird chair of Zach's over to the couch."

I spotted a squat stuffed rocking chair, not far from where I was sitting. "This blue one, you mean?"

"Yeah."

It was heavier than I expected, but I did what he asked while he turned on the TV and popped the movie into the DVD player. Fortunately, I didn't need to slide the odd chair very far.

Armed with the remote, Cal sat on the left half of the couch. He glanced up at me and then jerked his chin at the other end. "Go ahead and sit. Zach likes that stupid chair."

"I know you're not dissing the rock-and-roll chair," Zach said from behind us as the artificial-butter smell of his microwave popcorn suffused the room. "That chair is the shit. It has frickin' speakers, bro."

I laughed at Cal's arch look.

Zach served up the popcorn in red plastic Solo cups and we watched the movie, none of us shy about hooting at our favorite scenes or parroting the more memorable lines. 'Inconceivable!' was shouted more than once.

While we watched the scene where Westley faces off with Fezzik, Cal grabbed everyone a soda and then slumped into the crook of the couch, his sprawl ending with his socked feet in my lap along with an adorable demand for a foot massage as payment for my movie admission. I think I did a credible job of hiding my inner glee behind a gulp of my psi-free Diet Coke and my best exasperated glare.

This sure seemed to be the night for firsts—my first hip check, first hand holding, and, now, giving a guy a foot rub. It was hard to keep all of it from going to my head, especially with all the electrically-charged zings darting through my body at touching Cal, even if it was through his crew socks. His occasional groans of pleasure didn't help. I barely noticed the movie.

When we got to the part where Miracle Max examines Westley's 'mostly dead' body, Zach's voice came at my right ear, startling me. "Well, I guess my timing was a little off. Not by much, though, right?"

In the, now, dark room, lit by the glow of the television, it took me a moment to figure out what he was talking about.

Curled at the opposite end of the couch, Cal slept on his side, his left arm crooked with his hand beneath his ear.

I gasped. I'd gotten so caught up in touching him and trying to watch the movie that I'd forgotten about the drugging.

"Don't worry. He's only *mostly* dead."

My disapproval must have been plain to see in the flickering light because he snickered at me. "Go ahead. Have your way with him, tiger. See how easy it is to wake him up."

The shock of being presented with such a bizarre and thrilling opportunity temporarily paralyzed me. I froze, my hands hovering indecisively above Cal's ankles.

"These are my favorite gloves," I rasped. More accurately, they were my expensive gloves, the ones I used for eating because of their moisture repelling fabric. If I touched Cal's skin while wearing them, they'd absorb his psychic essence and then I'd have to throw them away since I often touched my lips when I ate finger foods like popcorn.

I cleared my throat, casting a glance at Cal to be sure I hadn't inadvertently woken him. "Do you have any disposable ones I could have?"

"Sure." His chair rocked forward and thirty seconds later a package of flesh-toned gloves dropped onto my stomach.

I thanked him, quickly trading out my black pair for the disposable ones. These were drastically thinner. I marveled at the silky fabric, holding them up for examination and rubbing my fingers together. I scrambled to locate the psi-free wrapper I'd discarded and found it wedged between my right thigh and the arm of the couch. I snatched it up to read the understated label.

Stunned, I searched the room, unsure where Zach was now standing. "Holy crap! These are PsiShield gloves!"

"Yeah?" His voice, coming from the direction of his bed, held a note of puzzlement, as if he didn't understand why I'd freaked, which was nuts.

"Zach! I asked you for disposable gloves, not your freaking two-hundred-dollar state-of-the-art ones. Jesus!"

Cal stirred at the end of the couch, muttering at us to 'keep it down.'

"Would you relax?" Zach murmured. "Those *are* my disposable ones. Pop owns the company. I get them for free. Here—" I heard him rummaging around in his closet before another, notably larger, cellophane-wrapped package slapped onto the right arm of the couch. "That's our newest skin-suit. The best there is. You can wear it on Wednesday. You'll have to roll up the legs and the sleeves, but if you like it, I'll have Pop send you a case of them in the right size, along with a box of gloves. You prefer black?"

Nodding numbly, I glanced down at the package. The lowest priced PsiShield skin-suit started at five hundred bucks. I couldn't imagine what their latest and greatest ones went for. Frankly, I'd always wanted one, but I'd been too bashful to mention it to Dad, and I'd never bothered asking for their gloves since I'd be forced to throw them away if they got contaminated. It seemed like a frivolous expenditure for some extra comfort, but now that I had a pair on, I wanted to kick myself.

"Dammit, Zach." I groaned as I experimented with running my fingers over the arm of the couch. "Now, I'm spoiled for life. I can practically feel every stitch of the upholstery. This is insane."

"Yep. Thinnest on the market, and their breathable moisture barrier make them impossible to beat." He laughed. "Jesus. I sound like a goddamned infomercial. Anyway, wearing gloves every day, I'm surprised you've never tried them."

"Too expensive. I knew I'd want to cry every time I screwed up and had to throw them away."

"Right, I forget sometimes. Don't worry about those. I'll get you extras. So, go ahead. Touch away. See what'll wake him up. That's why we're here, yeah?"

Facing such an open-ended task, I didn't know where to start. I gazed down at Cal's feet in my lap and followed the line of his body upward to his face. His eyes remained closed, the dark fan of his eyelashes visible against his cheeks, even in the flickering light. His chest rose and fell steadily and he wore a serene expression that came from sound sleep.

I imagined what it might be like to trace my fingers across the fullness of his bottom lip or smooth them over each of his unruly eyebrows. Would he wake up? What if I ran the flat of my hands over his shoulders and down to his chest? As heat blossomed through me, I promptly stowed my escalating thoughts.

This is an experiment, dummy, not an excuse to feel him up.

Turning my attention back to his legs, I decided to go with small, light touches and methodically work my way from there. Beginning at his bent knee, I stroked my left hand down his calf, ending at his ankle. I repeated the process, increasing the pressure each time until he finally stirred when I gave his calf a few massaging squeezes on the way down.

Blinking sleepily, he took in a deep, lazy breath. "Hey." His eyes sagged shut, but he smiled and murmured, "Feels nice. Do that some more."

He didn't have to ask twice.

After a few more tests, it became clear that anything that approached massage-like pressure had the potential to wake him up and, when he did stir, he tended to fall back to sleep in seconds.

"As riveting as this is, I'm gonna take off for a few," Zach said from behind me.

I jolted. "What? No ... you can't." I twisted my body, trying to look over my shoulder as though I might see him, which was stupid. "What if ... um ..." I nibbled my lip.

"I think it safe to say he's not going to bite you. Not until you ask him to, that is."

It wasn't Cal's behavior that worried me, but I was too embarrassed to admit it. "It seems, I don't know, wrong to be doing this when he can't tell me 'no.'"

He blew out an exasperated breath. "That's the whole point of this exercise — to prove to you that it's not possible to do something like that. Cal knew the score going in. If the thought of you touching him was a turn off, he wouldn't have volunteered. You get my drift?"

I frowned, turning back to regard Cal's peaceful face. "I don't know ..."

Cal's eyes flew open and he knifed upright, pushing his feet from my lap onto the couch arm as though something had bit him. Zach's skin-suit went flying and I heard the package hit the floor somewhere to my right. Rubbing his chest, Cal examined me with an odd combination of surprise and wonderment.

"Jesus," I exclaimed, pressing my hand to the base of my throat. "You scared the heck out of me."

He snorted, the amused sound accompanied by a slow upward curve at the corners of his mouth. "What did you expect?"

"Huh? What do you — ?" I cast an accusing glare over my left shoulder. "Zach, what the heck did you do?"

He snickered. "Just proving my point. No matter what you do, he's not going to mind."

The couch jostled as Cal flailed his hand above his head. I heard the smack of him batting something away. "Knock it off," he growled.

"He minds."

"That's 'cuz I'm messing with his precious hair." In my ear, Zach whispered, "But when I gave his left nipple a twist, he assumed it was you. Did it look like he minded?"

"Dude, you really need to fuck off," Cal mumbled sluggishly as he flopped to his back instead of his side. His feet returned to my lap, toes pointing upward, the bottoms pressing into the arm of the couch.

"So I've been told," Zach retorted. "I'll be back in time to take you to your dorm, tiger." Before I could argue, their door opened and shut, leaving Cal and I alone.

"Sorry," I mumbled. "If I'd known he was going to do that, I would have stopped him."

"It's fine." As his eyes closed, he donned a sleepy smirk. "Do what you want. I trust you."

As I watched him slip back into sleep, I muttered, "If you only knew."

When it came down to it, though, Cal wasn't wrong to trust me. Regardless of what Zach had proved with his little nipple-twist stunt, I'd never dream of going that far. Heck, if Cal was awake and begging me for it, I'd struggle. (Although, I'd be lying if I said the thought didn't shoot a jolt of heat straight through to my panties.)

Safe from Zach's teasing, I took a long moment to admire Cal. He'd again positioned his left hand beneath the back of his head, his muscular arm forming an enticing triangle that partially jutted over the edge of the couch. His lips were parted, and, over the sound of the movie, I heard his quiet snores. So cute.

I shook myself.

Okay, what next?

So far, everything I'd seen agreed with what the guys had told me. Cal wasn't so sedated that he didn't wake when firmly jostled. Even loud voices caused him to stir, which probably meant that a fire alarm would roust him, too. But what about gentle things? Could I get away with running my hands over his upper body without waking him? What about his clothes? If I took it slow, could I remove his shirt or open his pants without his knowledge? Could I take a photo of him in a compromised state? I suspected the answer might be 'D' — yes to all the above — but I wouldn't know for sure until I tried. The problem was that some of those things crossed the line, which meant I'd have to find other ways to prove my suspicions.

With his feet in my lap, the only place I could reach was his fly, but there was no way in hell I'd be brazen enough to unzip his pants. Unbuttoning his shirt, on the other hand, I could handle, especially since, like usual, he wore a crew-neck tee beneath his long-sleeved oxford.

First, though, I'd try something less drastic.

After tentatively stroking the top of Cal's right foot without him so much as twitching, I pinched his sock at the tip of his big toe and pulled, ever so slowly, until the garment slid all the way off.

A quick examination of Cal's face revealed that my move hadn't disturbed him. I guess that's why it took me a few seconds to notice something strange about his foot. The top was darker than the underside. For a puzzling moment, I thought he had on a second pair of socks. It wasn't until the television lit up the room with a brighter scene that I discovered why.

The top of his foot was covered by brown fur. Although, it might have been more precise to describe it as a dense layer of hair since it appeared to be a lot like what was on his head. Certainly, in the lambent light, it looked about as silky. The main difference seemed to be that the individual hairs were shorter and, overall, it appeared smoother and not as thick.

I stroked my fingers along his foot, in the same direction as his hair growth, and about fell out of my seat. Thanks to Zach's snazzy, hi-tech gloves, I could feel the hairs sliding beneath my fingertips, something that would have been imperceptible if I'd been wearing my much thicker, less expensive gloves. Still, I wished I could feel more. Was his hair as soft as it looked? I would have given almost anything to know.

Eyeing the leg opening of his jeans, I wondered how far this glossy layer extended. Did it go up past his knees? Did it coat his entire body? Strangely, I felt all weird and tingly just thinking about that. I wasn't so innocent that I'd never fantasized about guys, but this felt different. Naughtier. Probably because I was touching him while imagining him naked.

Down, girl.

"Are you seriously petting me?"

I jumped at Cal's accusatory tone, snatching my hand away.

He pushed himself up until he reclined on his elbows to glare at me.

"That depends," I blurted, resisting an intense desire to shrink until I slipped between the cushions like loose change.

"Yeah? On what?"

"I guess ... on whether you liked it?"

His left eyebrow went up. "You have a fur fetish or something?"

"The school's fresh out of Vodou priests," I replied with an incredulous laugh. "Anyway, what would be the point?"

204

After giving me a look of utter astonishment, he collapsed back against the arm of the couch and cracked up. "Not that kind of fetish." He shook his head, rolling it side to side against the upholstery as he continued to chuckle. "How is it possible for a clairvoyant to be so innocent? Don't you learn things when you touch stuff? Or watch internet porn like everyone else?"

I jolted at the questions, the light finally dawning. He was talking about a sexual fetish, not a magical one. He thought I was one of those people who exclusively pursued weres, hoping to have sex with them while they were in their animal forms. I'd not watched any were porn, but I wasn't so clueless that I hadn't heard about it.

"Shut up, perv." I shoved at his legs, almost spilling them off my lap. If my cheeks weren't on fire before, now they were volcanic. "I'm not that naïve. I was thinking about our last MEW class. Can I help it if you have a dirty mind?"

"Hey, you started it." He eyed me archly. "You weren't thinking about Vodou while you were petting me. That's for damn sure."

My body heated at the memory, but lying about it would be useless. Mr. Pheromone Sniffer would see right through it.

"You're right," I admitted. "But that doesn't mean I was thinking about furry porn sex, either. Jeez. Why would you even think that?"

"You're kidding, right?" He took one look at my expression and sneered, "Hairballs aren't a turn-on for most girls, Lire. I've had enough experience to know that much."

I opened my mouth to argue, but what the hell was I going to say? Admit that I'd got all hot and bothered picturing him naked? Or that, ever since seeing the silky hair on his foot, I wondered what it might feel like sliding against my touch-starved skin? He'd think I was a pervert for sure.

I glared at him. "I think it's safe to say that there's a big difference between that kind of thing and ..." I searched for something that wasn't too telling. "I don't know. Normal interest."

He gave me a disbelieving look. "Normal interest?"

"Yes." I huffed. "Why can't you go back to sleep?"

"I could, but this conversation is making it easy to fight the urge." He inched backward so he could sit more upright against the arm of the couch. "The fix isn't like a roofie, remember?"

I was starting to regret that it wasn't.

He nudged me with his naked foot, and I realized I'd allowed it to drop down onto my lap. Too bad his fur didn't extend to the bottom of his foot. Hair, being dead, couldn't impart a psychic imprint to other objects. Now, I'd have to toss my jeans. Thank God all my favorites had been in the hamper when I'd gotten dressed this morning.

"You were about to tell me about your *normal interest* in guys with fur," he reminded me. "I'm sure it's one of your top five things you want in a guy. Right up there with crooked teeth, bad breath, a microscopic dick, and a beer gut."

His mocking tone brought Zach's earlier words to mind.

Cal … well, he's got his own issues. He's not the type to get close to people.

I guessed this was why. He'd been teased about his hairy body. And, judging by his comments, at some point in his past, an idiot girl had freaked out about it.

I flicked his big toe with my middle finger. "Keeping a wish list would be pointless since most guys stay as far away from me as humanly possible."

"Nice dodge." He folded his arms. "Because the gross guy with fur would never make anyone's list. I'm not an idiot, you know."

Something between a gasp and an annoyed grunt slipped out of my mouth. "Are you sure? Because only an absolute idiot would say you're gross. And it's not a dodge. Jeez, Cal. Might as well call me a liar."

I pushed his legs off my lap and stood, stalking away to glare at him from across the room, but his scowl remained impervious.

"What do I have to do to get you to believe me?" I asked. "Spill my guts?"

His belligerent frown was answer enough.

"Fine." I squared my shoulders defiantly. "I don't need some stupid list to tell me that you're the hottest guy I've ever met, with or without fur."

Cheeks blazing, I stared at the ceiling. "I can't believe I'm telling you this." I glared back at him, annoyed with myself for avoiding his penetrating gaze, even for a second. "Was I surprised to find hair on top of your foot? *Yes.* Does it make me wonder a lot of things? *Yes* — it does. So sue me. Is it a turn off? That would be a big fat *no.* I guess that means I'm a pervert, but whatever."

Folding my arms, I took in his expression, which had slowly morphed from churlish to something caught between disbelief and chagrin.

"You happy now?" I snapped. "Anything else you want to know before I go back to my room and hide in my closet for a year?"

He shook his head dazedly as a sheepish smile tugged at the corners of his mouth.

I rolled my eyes. At least *one* of us felt better.

Okay, Zach. You can come back any time now ...

"You planning to stand there for the rest of the night?" He watched me, blinking slowly. "Come on. Don't be that way. Come back and sit. Look ... thanks for, you know, setting me straight. I'm sorry for being a jerk. I'm just—" He sighed. "I'm used to people freaking out or getting that pitying look on their faces that makes me want to punch them."

Relenting, I trudged back to the couch, but instead of sitting in my previous spot, I plunked down on the floor, using the couch for a back rest. The movie had run through to the credits. Its ending song, so romantic, spilled through the room.

Cal chuckled and then struggled to turn around so his head rested where his feet used to be.

"Hey," he said from behind my right shoulder, once he'd gotten comfortable. He'd propped his head on his hand and regarded me with a lazy smile when I turned to look at him. "If it makes you feel better, I think you're cute as hell. Love it when you bite your lip when you're nervous. For some reason, that gets me, every time. So many things about you, really." He shifted to rest his head on his folded arms. His eyes drifted shut. "Babe ... don't be mad at me, okay?"

Apparently, it was harder for him to fight the drug, now that our conversation had calmed down. After melting into a pile of goo, I swiveled on my butt so I could see him without putting a crick in my neck.

Babe. It sounded so ... grown up. It gave me the shivers.

Emboldened by what he'd said, I reached out and did the one thing I'd wanted to do since our first meeting. I traced the tips of my fingers over his eyebrow.

His mouth curved upward. "Can't ... resist me ... can you?" he mumbled thickly.

"Sorry. I'll stop."

"No ... I like it. Wish I could ... stay awake ... though."

Thank God he'd closed his eyes because I couldn't have masked my ginormous grin if I'd tried. As I combed my fingers through his thick hair, I must have replayed his sleepy encouragement about a million times in my head. Cutest. Thing. Ever. Almost as endearing as the sounds of contentment he made whenever he stirred from my gentle touches. Surely, I'd died and gone to heaven.

I'd moved on to drawing on his back when their door opened and closed, sometime later. The looping music for the DVD's main menu played behind me, long forgotten.

"So ... what do you say, tiger? You done feeling up my brother?"

You will not smile like a dork. You will not smile like a dork ...

"What time is it?" I sounded normal, casual, even.

"Ten thirty. We could push it another fifteen. You want me to come back?"

"No. You didn't have to leave in the first place, you know."

He made a 'pfft' sound. "Yeah. I did."

What does he think we were going to get up to?

I shot a dubious glare in his direction as I stood, but I kept the thought to myself. "Should we cover him? Do you have a blanket?"

"He doesn't need it, but snag the comforter from his bed if it makes you feel better."

I longed to give Cal's cheek one final caress after tucking him in, but I was too embarrassed with Zach watching. I'd probably never hear the end of it as it was.

Under the cover of Zach's magic, the two of us swept through the hallways and down the stairs, hand in hand. After squeezing through the dorm's barely opened front door, I felt the pavement restored beneath my feet. The world resolved to a more normal (if not somewhat shimmery) intensity. The cool night air drew out my shiver and I rubbed my free hand over my opposite arm.

"Walking with you is so freaking cool," I gushed. "How small a crack can you squeeze through, anyway?"

Even though it wasn't necessary now that we were out of his dorm, Zach kept me within his sphere of invisibility, holding my hand as we walked to the women's dormitory. "I could tell you that, but then I'd have to kill you."

"Right. I'm starting to think my keyhole idea wasn't too far off."

"That might be pushing it, but it's fine with me if you want to think that."

"Right, Mr. Mysterious, be that way."

He chuckled.

We slowed to a halt at the short pathway that branched toward Spencer Hall's front door.

I gazed up at his silhouette. "Um, well, thanks for tonight. It was ... an interesting night."

"Interesting, huh? Poor Cal. That's like saying, 'But he has a great personality.'"

"Shut up. Is not. For your information, Mr. Noseypants, tonight was a lot more than interesting. I'm just not up for spilling my guts, okay? Once was enough for one night." I had to stop myself from cringing at the memory. "Trust me, Cal knows what I think."

"Really," he drawled, giving the word a dozen more vowels. "So, you're saying tomorrow I won't be dealing with a grumpy werewolf, two days before the full moon?"

"You mean because of me?" I thought about my discovery. "I hope not. I mean, I saw ... you know, why he covers up. He's fine about it, though. At least, that's how he seemed once I convinced him that it doesn't make any difference to me. Whether he still believes that, when tomorrow morning rolls around, I can't tell you. He darn-well better, though, since it's the truth."

"Interesting."

"Isn't that what *I* said?" I teased. "But, um, you should know ... seeing that drug in action, it didn't change my mind about doing that to Amanda. I know she'd jump at doing it to me if she had the chance and all that, but—" I sighed. "I can't do it. It's wrong." I wished I could see his features. "You're not mad at me. Are you?"

"No, I'm not mad." He squeezed my hand. "A little frustrated, I guess. I don't want you to get into trouble when I can easily fix it. But I promised Cal not to give you a hard time. We'll do what you want."

He didn't sound happy about it. "I'll have to figure something else out. Maybe I can catch her in the act, get a photo of her pulling the alarm or something. It's chancy, but better than not doing anything at all."

"I'm sorry," I mumbled.

"Stop. It's fine. We already figured you weren't going to change your mind." He lowered his voice. "You know Cal only wanted an excuse so you'd have to touch him."

Blushing, I gave him an exasperated glare. "*Please.*"

"Like you weren't dying for the chance. I saw your expression, princess. You've got it bad."

"Shut up." I shoved at his shoulder. Not like I could push him far while he still held on to my other hand. "God. Please don't tell him that. I'm embarrassed enough as it is."

"Don't know why. I'd be — " He shook his head. "That's not something he's going to be upset about. Trust me." He released my hand and his black form instantly disappeared from my view. "Okay. Get going. It's getting close to curfew."

I squinted against the brilliant overhead pathway light. "Okay. Talk to you tomorrow."

"Yep. Don't forget to make sure you have everything you need for Wednesday, you know, camera-wise or whatever. Tomorrow's the last day we can run into town for any last-minute supplies."

My stomach plunged at the dwindling timeline, but I nodded. If only I could stock up on some courage.

Tiger? More like cowardly lion.

CHAPTER 13

Operation Full Moon

ON the night of the full moon, I crept out of my room exactly twenty minutes after lights-out.

To be absolutely sure I tripped the vigilance spell, Zach waited to grab my hand until I'd stepped all the way into the hallway and closed my door as if I'd really left for a night out.

If my door was enchanted, the spell didn't so much as twitch a single hair on the back of my neck when I crossed over the threshold.

"Darn. I didn't feel anything." I kept my voice down, even though his magic probably masked our voices.

"That's the whole point of a vigilance spell, yeah?"

"I know." I stuck out my bottom lip. "Poop. I guess I was hoping she'd gotten some first-year to do it. It'd be nice to know whether we're waiting around for nothing, or not."

"Trust me, it's not going to be a mystery for long. That's why you have me around." He tugged my hand until we both faced my closed dorm room door. "You ready? The squeeze might make you sick to your stomach. Fair warning."

We'd gone back and forth about this in our planning, but there was no way around it. In case the fire alarm went off, I had to wait in my room while Zach pursued Amanda. Unfortunately, because of the vigilance spell, we couldn't go back inside the normal way, not without triggering the spell and alerting Amanda.

I took a deep breath and nodded. "Go for it."

The world stretched and compressed as the narrow slice of darkness between the carpet and the bottom of my door rushed at me in a psychotropic surge, swallowing me whole. Darkness stole my vision and I lost all sense of my body, but before I could panic, I felt the inexplicable tug of Zach's magic, pulling at my core. All at once, my dimly lit room exploded into gigantic proportion and then, just as quickly, shrank down to its normal size. I seemed to grow into my feet as the carpeted floor solidified beneath me.

Swallowing thickly, I stumbled to my bed and sat down hard. "Now I know how Alice felt after her whole eat-me-drink-me thing."

Zach chuckled. "You gonna be okay?"

I gave him two thumbs up, since anything but a grim smile was beyond me.

"Rock on. By the way, nice jammies." I could hear the smirk in his voice. "Okay. Sit tight. Take a nap. I'll be back."

My door didn't quaver one nanometer, even though I knew Zach had passed beneath it. After thirty seconds of listening intently, I fell backwards on my bed, pressing a hand to the base of my throat, and groaned. "Good thing I didn't eat much at dinner. That was horrible."

Red regarded me from his perch on my desk. "I believe you already know how I feel about this ridiculous undertaking, therefore I will withhold comment."

I laughed, rolling my head sideways to see him. "Come on, Red. You already admitted that this is exactly what Dad was talking about when he told me to be a little bit bad. It's harmless. The worst that'll happen is I'll get caught and assigned kitchen duty for the rest of the semester. Honestly, if I get that photo, it'll be worth it. And if Amanda gets caught pulling the fire alarm ..." I sat up, marveling at the wondrous thought. "I swear, that'd be worth an entire *year* of garbage patrol."

"If you recall, your father also told you to let sleeping dogs lie."

"That's right. Wow. Who knew the sleeping dog thing would turn out to be so spot on?" I sniffed. "I probably should have let Zach fix her. Then I wouldn't have to wait here for God-knows-how-long, wondering what the heck is happening."

Zach had been gone a grand total of three minutes and I'd already started grumbling and pacing the length of my room. I could be waiting for as long as an hour, maybe more, which is why, in our planning, I'd lobbied to stick with Zach. But both he and Cal had vetoed the idea. They'd reasoned (rightly, as much as I hated to admit it) that I'd only get in Zach's way and increase my chance of getting caught out of my room if I went with him.

I needed a distraction. I'd make some coffee and, since I'd taken a nap earlier, I'd check over my camera equipment for the zillionth time, maybe take some long exposure stills to pass the time and get me into the low-light-photography zone.

I jumped several inches when the fire alarm blared through my room, about forty minutes later. I'd already messed up my bed to make it look like I'd been sleeping, in the off chance someone decided to peek into my room. All I had to do was throw on my robe and slippers. Red jumped into my purse, which I looped over my body, and then I stumbled into the hallway, squinting at the emergency lights and covering my ears against the shrill alarm.

Ms. Hopkins, our floor's R.A. ran from one end of the hall to the other with her clipboard, ordering us to file outside to the designated evacuation area and stopping to scold the girls who tried to return to their rooms for any forgotten items. When the vaguest whiff of smoke hit us, she completely freaked out, yelling, "Move your butts, this isn't a drill!"

I filed out with the rest of the bleary-eyed students, keeping a surreptitious eye peeled for Amanda and Shania.

Outside, the cool night air swirled lazily around me, hitting the exposed skin of my ankles. Looking up at the sky, I was relieved to see the weather report had been right on. A smattering of wispy clouds moved overhead, but nothing that would interfere with tonight's photo. In fact, as long as they didn't obscure the moon completely, a few clouds in front of it could be a good thing. I'd be dealing with long exposures to bring out detail in the tree, which would turn the moon into a blown-out mess if I wasn't careful.

Huddling inside my terrycloth robe, I scuffed along the path to our building's assigned picnic area. In the distance, the obnoxious din of sirens pierced the night. I shook my head. Clearly, Amanda's stupidity knew no bounds.

I stopped near Shannon and Darla, on the eastern side of the rectangular grass field, where it was less crowded.

"Lire!" Shannon exclaimed before leaning closer to whisper excitedly, "Gosh! It's so lucky you're still here." Her face fell. "Or — oh no. Did you and Zach change your minds about getting the photo tonight?"

"Shh." I glanced around for anyone standing close enough to overhear.

"No one's listening," Darla murmured. "Everyone's freaking out with their usual homies and waiting for the fire trucks."

True enough, everyone had fallen into loose groups, chattering, staring at our dorm, and probably speculating about what had happened. I spied Amanda as she headed toward the main picnic area with Shania. Ironically, the full moon was visible above the roofline of our dormitory.

Was it my imagination or did Amanda and Shania look agitated? I had to stop myself from bouncing up and down on the balls of my feet in anticipation of what might have happened. Although, to my immense disappointment, Amanda didn't have soot all over her face or clothes. Nothing screamed, 'I'm an idiot pyromaniac! Come arrest me!' Although, when she finally spotted me, she jolted with surprise and then leveled the vilest look imaginable in my direction.

"Jesus. Why is Amanda staring at you like she caught you taking a dump on her Chanel two fifty-five?" Darla asked.

Her acerbic tone caught me off guard, and I laughed. "Her what?"

"You mean you haven't heard about her prized handbag? Where have you been?" Darla pressed a hand over her heart and affected a solemn tone. "Her vintage Coco Chanel handbag. Highly collectible and worth a mint." She rolled her eyes. "The way she goes on, you'd think the darn thing does her homework and wipes her bony ass, too."

I blinked at her. I'd never traded more than a passing 'hello' with Darla. I'd no idea she was so sarcastic. Or that she didn't care for Amanda.

"I'm the last person she'd go out of her way to brag to about some stupid purse."

"Stupid?" Darla gasped and held up her hands, banging together her index fingers to form a cross. "Back, non-believer! Get back!"

We all snickered as Shannon peered across the grassy area at Amanda. "Now that you mention it ..." Shannon turned to us. "Where is it? You'd think she'd have grabbed it for sure before coming out here."

"The girl probably keeps it in a fireproof safe in her room."

Darla's crack earned another giggle from Shannon. "Really, though. That's weird, don't you think?" Shannon frowned. "I mean, the three of us grabbed our bags. Look around. Most of us did. Nancy and Trina even have their backpacks. And we don't have some famous designer thing like Amanda's. Right?" Shannon waved a dismissive hand at my faux-leather bag.

"She probably figured this is a drill," Darla said.

"At midnight on a school night?" Shannon gave her a disbelieving look. "And I heard the smoke smelled stronger, upstairs. The same floor as Amanda."

"What are you saying? That Amanda somehow knows for a fact there's no fire?" Darla's eyebrows shot up. "All because she doesn't have her purse?"

"I don't know. Maybe." Shannon canted her head slightly as she examined me. "It would also explain why she gave Lire the nuclear-death stink-eye. She's pissed that Lire didn't get caught. She hoped she'd be gone, doing the photo thing."

"So, now you're saying she arranged for the fire alarm to go off, just to get Lire into trouble?" As Darla leaned closer, the beads in her hair clicked together in a strangely satisfying way. "I know Amanda's on our list of people we want to see eaten by a land shark, but don't you think that's stupid, even for her? Besides, if she wanted Lire to get caught, she could have shoved an anonymous note under Ms. Hopkins' door."

"That would hardly be anonymous. Everyone in the whole school knows she has it out for Lire," Shannon replied. "Whatever. All I'm saying is that I wouldn't put it past her."

I knew better than to add to this conversation, as much as I wanted to, so I kept my mouth shut and mirrored Shannon's shrug. Fortunately, Ms. Hopkins and the second-floor R.A. chose that moment to blow their whistles. As half-a-dozen firefighters descended on our dormitory, I lined up for headcount with all the other girls from the first floor and listened for Ms. Hopkins to call my name.

Thirty-five minutes (and a truckload of Amanda's dirty looks) later, a grim-faced Mr. Gibbs stalked up to our building's resident advisors. They had what appeared to be a heated conversation before Mr. Gibbs' two-fingered whistle pierced the air.

"After a thorough search, firefighters have found clear evidence that Spencer Hall's fire alarm was deliberately triggered." His angry voice boomed across the picnic area, easily heard over the rumble of the three firetrucks at the front of the school. "Whoever perpetrated this reckless prank would do well to report to my office first thing tomorrow morning. If you come clean, if you take responsibility for your actions, I personally guarantee my pledge for leniency with our board of regents."

He folded his arms and scanned our faces. "Because, I am here to tell you, our board will not look favorably upon the guilty party, or parties, when they are found. And, make no mistake, *you will be found*. I'm sure I don't need to tell you that the penalties will be severe. In addition to expulsion, there's also the possibly of criminal charges and a fine to recoup the cost of the emergency response. However ... if you report to my office by lunchtime tomorrow, such drastic punishment is not a foregone conclusion."

He paused for dramatic effect before waving a dismissive hand toward our dorm. "You're dismissed to return *quietly* to your rooms. Anyone lingering to gossip with friends will receive detention. It's lights out."

Back inside, I sniffed the air as I trudged down the hall, not detecting anything out of the ordinary—just the usual combination of stale popcorn, Top Ramen, and air freshener. As I neared my room, though, in addition to the odors of detergent and dryer sheets from the nearby laundry area, I caught the lingering scent of smoke. Curious, I passed up my room and, instead, cracked open the metal door leading to the eastern stairwell.

I wrinkled my nose as soon as I poked my head inside. Peering up the flight of stairs that led to the first landing, I didn't see anything out of the ordinary, but the acrid smell of smoke was unmistakable.

Inside my room, I plunked my purse on top of my desk and opened the flap to make it easier for Red to hop out.

"Zach, you here?" I waited for his reply, listening for any sound of movement.

I sighed, turning to Red. "Well, poop. I'm dying to know what happened. You should have seen the dirty looks Amanda was shooting me the entire time we were outside. And the stairwell reeks of smoke." I shook my head. "I never thought she'd be so stupid as to start an actual fire. I figured she'd try to find a way to pull the lever."

"Pulling the lever would have marked her. Apparently, she decided a fire was worth the risk to remain anonymous."

"If that's the case, it would have been a lot less risky to slip a note under Ms. Hopkins' door, telling her about my plans for tonight, like Shannon said." I glanced at the clock. "Shoot. It's after 12:30." I snatched the skin-suit package out of my wardrobe and hurried to the bathroom. "I'm going to change real quick."

"Very well."

Red had trotted out his *resigned* voice, the one that said, 'What you're doing is stupid, but you're old enough to make your own decisions.' I knew he meant well, but there were times when having Red for my bunkmate felt a lot like rooming with my grandpa.

I frowned, immediately regretting the ungrateful thought. When it came down to it, Red's attitudes were downright progressive for a guy who lived in the late 1600s, even if his speech patterns often sounded stilted and formal. Besides, he wasn't wrong about this endeavor. Sneaking out to get the photo ranked pretty high on the list of dumb things I could be doing on a school night.

So was wearing this skin-suit.

"Crapadoodle." I peered at my reflection in my bathroom's full-length mirror as I folded up the sleeves to a reasonable length.

I'd discovered the downside of Zach's gifted skin-suit, aside from the fact that the legs and sleeves were too long. It was crafted from such thin, high-tech fabric that it left nothing to the imagination. While you couldn't see the precise color of my bra and panties, their outline and lacy texture were both obvious. Thank God the skin-suit was black, instead of nude, otherwise, I'd have looked naked.

I was definitely putting on a tank-top and running shorts over this getup.

"Hey, tiger," Zach chirped as soon as I threw open the bathroom door, so intent on my cover-up mission that I hadn't considered his arrival while I'd been changing.

I squinted, blinking as my eyes adjusted from the bright bathroom lights to the darkness of my room. Not that it really mattered when it came to Zach, though, since I couldn't see him anyway.

"You're here."

Call me Sherlock.

"Nothing gets past you." He whistled low. "Wow. Cal's eyeballs are going to fall out of his head when he sees you tonight."

"Since that sounds especially painful, I guess it's a good thing I'm putting on something else."

"No. I need you in the suit," Zach said. "Hood up, covering your hair. With what we're doing tonight, I can't worry about accidentally touching your skin or your hair hitting my face."

"Okay—whoa. Cool your jets, Mr. Bossypants. I'm not taking it off. I'm putting running shorts and a tank over it. You're nuts if you think I'm setting one foot outside in nothing but this thin strip of fabric. You can see every freaking bulge and fold."

"Jesus Christ. Are you saying what I think you're saying? All I see are amazing curves, in all the right places, you dip. And I wasn't shitting you about Cal." He sighed. "But, do what you want. It should be fine, as long as you have freedom of movement."

"Oh! Thank God. I was so worried you wouldn't approve. A thousand thanks for giving me your permission, master."

"Smart ass. Although—" He deepened his voice. "I could get used to the master thing ... if you know what I mean."

Making gagging noises, I pretended to stick my finger down my throat. "Give me a break." I searched my wardrobe for my black running shorts. "Just ... tell me what happened with Amanda."

"But teasing you is so much more fun." He chuckled at my murderous look. "Fine. Thanks to me, you don't need to worry about that bitch, ever again. I caught her and her roommate, dead to rights, setting fire to some stuff inside a stairwell garbage can. It's lucky my magic forces me to use that ancient piece-of-shit camera. She had one of her witchy friends set up a discord field to disable the stairwell's closed-circuit video."

"Whoa. Really?" I straightened the elastic of my Nike running shorts before glowering at him. "And shut up. Your vintage Polaroid is totally cool."

"It's a lame-ass antique. I'd trade it for your cool digital one if my magic didn't turn those into doorstops. My behemoth got the job done, though, so I'm not going to complain." He snickered. "Let's just say, Amanda and Shania were a little upset when I slipped my envelope beneath their door after you guys got back from the fire drill. Oh, man. I wish you could have heard it."

I giggled. "Me too. What was in the envelope?"

"An incriminating picture, plus a note saying that if they, or any of their friends, so much as twitches in your direction ever again, or anyone gets it into their head to tell your R.A. to check on you later tonight, the rest of the photos will go to Gibbs, Amanda's godfather, and the head of the school newspaper, along with a detailed anonymous letter. Here, wanna see?"

An old-fashioned Polaroid appeared in the air in front of me. In it, Amanda held a burning piece of paper over a garbage can. Shania stood next to her.

"I still can't believe they were so stupid," I said. "Do you think they know you're the one who took this?"

"It was one of Amanda's guesses. But then she decided it must have been *that totally hot Latino vampire*, the one who said something to you after the start-of-school assembly. Or, any vampire because, apparently, you have an in with them. *It's just so disgusting*," he sneered, mimicking Amanda's high-pitched voice.

"What a wench."

"Tiger, you have no idea. She planned to frame you for setting the fire in the stairwell."

"She ... *what*? How?"

"The stuff she burned in the garbage can ... it was a pile of the orange papers from Neverhart's classroom."

My stomach attempted to punch a hole through my heels. "Oh, shit." I paced the length of my room, my hand in a death grip on the tank top I'd pulled from my drawer. "Zach ... if she really did that ... Oh, my God! The fire might not have burned everything and even if it did, there are investigators, experts, who can test stuff. As soon as they figure out what's in the garbage, Mr. Gibbs will—"

"I took care of it."

"—immediately jump to the—" I stopped to gape in his direction. "You what? How? How could you possibly—"

"Jesus, lower your voice, would you? And calm down. Did you know a person's IQ drops fifteen points when they freak out?" He added dryly, "In your case, maybe more."

I narrowed my eyes at him.

"Look, it's not like it was hard to deal with, okay? As soon as Amanda and Shania scurried away, like the rodents they are, I wedged the door shut so no one could use the stairwell. After the smoke set off the fire alarm and you guys were busy evacuating, I put out the flames before they triggered the sprinklers. Then, I hid the incriminating trashcan, along with the papers Amanda scattered all over the stairs."

He snorted. "As if you'd actually be stupid enough to leave an orange trail to the downstairs landing. Anyway, I substituted the trashcan from the other stairwell, lit up a scrap inside, and left it for the firefighters to find. End of story and job well done. You're welcome."

"Jesus, Zach! You could have gotten seriously hurt. And what about all that smoke? Please tell me you weren't breathing it the whole time."

"I wasn't breathing it the whole time," he parroted.

"I'm serious." I approached the left side of my room where I knew he was standing. "If you got hurt—" I frowned, shivering at the sudden thought. "What if you'd passed out from the smoke? Nobody would have known you were there." It was an effort not to yell at him.

"Aw, princess. I didn't know you cared."

"You're such a brat."

"Yeah, but you love me anyway. Admit it."

Smirking, I stalked to my photography backpack, which I'd left on my desk chair. While Red settled into his specially made pocket, I snugged the skin-suit's fitted hood over my head and tucked my hair inside.

Voilà—my land scuba suit.

Trying not to grumble about how utterly ridiculous I looked, I donned my black tank top and slung my backpack over my shoulders.

"Check you out, all stealthy like a ninja princess going for her nightly run."

I glared at him. "I will cut you. Cal's key chain has a pocket knife on it, right?"

He laughed. "The weapon of ninjas everywhere. Come on. Gimme your hand."

"Can't we leave my room the normal way?" I tried not to whine.

"Why give Amanda something to stew on? This way, if the vigilance spell is still active, she won't know for sure whether we've gone out or not."

"Fine." I held out my right hand.

"Don't get too excited. You might stroke out on me."

I scowled at his dark form, which I could now see, thanks to his cloaking magic. "Remind me to turn in your direction when I puke."

Chuckling, he gave my hand an affectionate jostle. "I could try doing this slower, but I don't think it'll help."

"No. Probably not." I sighed. "Go ahead. I'll live."

Maybe I was getting used to it. This time, after the dizzying squeeze, I only had to swallow five times to stop feeling queasy. But, if I'd thought going under my threshold was bad, slipping through the thin crack between my dormitory's front doors was about ten times worse. After that fun ride, where, I swear, my body stretched into a spaghettified line of disjointed molecules, I staggered to the front flower beds and bent over, all while taking deep breaths and studiously thinking about things that smelled good — laundry detergent, peppermint, jasmine flowers. Zach, wisely, remained silent, squeezing my hand and rubbing my shoulder with his free one.

I avoided barfing on my shoes, but it was a near thing.

"Yay," I rasped, straightening and wiping my sweaty forehead. "Can't wait to do that again, later tonight."

"I'm impressed. Cal threw up the first few times. And he still can't eat beforehand."

"Can't imagine why." I tugged his hand. "Thank you for what you did. You know, with Amanda and the fire and stuff."

"Anytime, princess."

"I forgot to ask. What did you do with the garbage can?"

"Took it into the woods, dumped it out, and then left the can in Amanda's room. She and Shania were freaking out over it when I slipped the envelope under their door."

I cracked up, this time doubling over with trying not to laugh too loudly. "Oh. My. God. That is classic." I imagined Amanda's expression, eyes bugged out at spotting the incriminating room decor. "You're my hero, Zach. I'll never forget this as long as I live."

"I do have a certain *je ne sais quoi*, don't I?"

"*Tu m'étonnes.*" *Tell me something I don't know.*

"You said I'm awesome, right?"

I grinned. "Duh."

He snickered and then yanked on my hand. "Let's make some tracks. The night's not getting any younger."

At first, trying to jog while holding hands proved to be as awkward as I'd imagined, but once we synchronized our stride, pumping our arms in unison, the going got easier. I think it helped that we'd been running together practically every day for three weeks.

We ran most of the way to Les Schwab, stopping briefly to slip undetected past the school's border enchantment, which felt a lot like squeezing through the crack under the door to my dorm room. To my surprise, the school's magical perimeter didn't align with the school's fence line. If Zach hadn't been with me, I would have plowed through the enchantment, totally clueless, setting off God knew how many phantom alarms.

When I asked how he knew about the border's location, Zach gave me his canned response about having to kill me if he revealed his source. Truthfully, I didn't care enough to pursue it. I was just grateful for his help.

By the time we arrived at Cal's car, a little after 1:00 a.m., my tank top and skin-suit were soaked through with sweat, my scalp itched like crazy beneath my tight fitting hood, and I hated my camera bag with a burning passion. Early on, Zach had offered to trade my backpack for his, but stubborn me, I'd refused. Instead, I spent most of our run dreaming about that Gitzo carbon fiber tripod I'd had my eye on over the summer. My aluminum one was nice, but the Gitzo was nicer and, more importantly, lighter.

Since I'd taken Cal's car for a test spin on Sunday, I wasn't as stressed out about driving it as I might have been. Still, I drove the precise speed limit the entire way to the fruit stand, relieved that we encountered only one car in passing before I turned into the dirt clearing. I coasted to the farthest end of the turnout and parked, silently praying that Cal's Honda went unnoticed by any passing police patrols.

"*Vámonos, chica!*" Zach exclaimed.

"Someone's excited," I muttered as I plucked my backpack from the footwell behind the passenger seat. I was excited too, but my enthusiasm had a side helping of dread, which my nervous stomach readily attested.

Taking me in hand, Zach led the way toward the so-called *B&E* tree — the tree that overhung the section of fence where we'd break and enter — a location which, after ten minutes of dodging weeds and random shrubs, he assured me he knew exactly how to find. In the distance, two of the curtained windows in Sorcerer Treblow's small cottage glowed with a warm yellow light.

"Look, there. What'd I tell you?" Zach said when the tree in question came into view. "Am I good or am I good?"

Under the full moon's silver light, the tree's broad trunk and thick limbs stood out like a line art drawing, the silhouette easily rendered by its lack of foliage.

My shiver wasn't entirely due to the dampness of my tank top and the cool night air. "Uh. It's not quite what I imagined."

"It isn't?"

"No. You left out he part about it being mostly dead. There're no leaves to camouflage me when I'm climbing."

"Less stuff to catch on your clothes and get into your face."

"Okay. But that doesn't make me feel any better, Zach. You're not the one who's gonna have their ass hanging out, fourteen-or-what-ever-feet up, for everyone to see. Can't you use your magic to squeeze us in somewhere else?"

"Where's the fun in that? The ass-hanging thing sounds way better." He laughed as he dodged the full force of my back-handed smack. "Stop worrying. Your ass won't be hanging out. Not for long, at least. Anyway, the holes in the fencing are too small for me to squeeze through. Sorry to break it to you, princess: I'm good, but not that good. There are other ways inside, but this is the quickest way to the lightning tree."

He tugged my hand. "Come on. I need to deal with the sensors. Then you can take your practice pictures."

I followed him to a section of fence several yards to the left of the tree.

"Okay, tiger, the moment you've been waiting for. Time to grab my hot bod."

I considered flicking him on the ear, but instead, did what we'd practiced on Sunday. To maintain my invisibility, I grabbed his waist with my left hand before he released his grip on my right, careful to maintain constant contact.

"Tuck in. Arms around me like you're riding behind me on a motorcycle. I need most my concentration for this. Wouldn't want your ass to hang out."

The bulk of his backpack hit my stomach and chest, but I wrapped my arms loosely around his waist without too much trouble. "Fine. How's this?"

"That'll work. Okay ..." He adjusted my arms, pushing them up for a moment, as he unzipped something at his belt. Some muted clicks preceded the subtle echo of metal sliding against metal.

Rising to the balls of my feet, I tried to peek over his shoulder to see what he was doing, but he was too tall. All I could see was the black pit of his body. I leaned to the side, instead, shifting my stance to peer past his left arm. With his backpack in the way, it wasn't easy to do without jostling him, so I eased a step sideways, slipping my right foot between his feet so I could get a better view.

Zach's head fell forward as he issued an annoyed, growly sort of grunt. "Jesus," he croaked. "You keep wiggling against me like that and I can't promise I won't set this thing off. Have mercy, okay?"

Mortified, I loosened my hold, making sure there was a definitive gap between our bodies. If we'd been anywhere else, I probably would have jumped backwards by a mile. Maybe he worried I was going to do that, because he pinned my hands against his abdomen, which tensed beneath my palms.

"There. You're good. Stay, like that," he said, and, to my relief, he sounded more like himself. "I'll be done in just a sec."

As he worked his security mojo, using whatever tools he'd pulled from his belt, I took a deep breath and focused on the dead tree, wondering how the hell I was going to climb it without breaking my neck. Between thoughts of 'foot goes there, pull up on that, shimmy around this' and alerting on every animal cry and leafy rustle emanating from inside the compound, I stopped noticing the heat of Zach's body or the way his muscles moved beneath my linked hands.

After Zach had dragged me to the other nearby sensor, mumbling something about parallel systems, priority-switching, and a slew of other mysterious buzz-words, he fist-pumped, declared himself a security-breach god, and told me to hurry up and get my test shots done, so we could finally get the show on the road.

I pulled him toward a spot clear of weeds, about ten yards from the B&E tree. "Now it's your turn. Put your hands here." I patted my sides.

It wasn't easy to avoid bumping into him, but I managed to position my tripod and camera while Zach kept me invisible.

Since my Canon was a fully digital camera, Zach's magic not only messed with its shutter release but also its interface. This meant he had to let go of me whenever I needed to change any of my camera's settings—precisely why it was important to have everything ready to go ahead of time.

For the next ten minutes, I took about a dozen test photos with different filters, adjusting for the difficult lighting conditions. Seeing my body pop in and out of Zach's sphere of influence demonstrated how visible I'd be when it came time for the shot, but I shoved the worry aside to concentrate on getting a proper exposure. Using my remote to trigger the shutter release while I posed in front of the B&E tree, we practiced nailing the timing so me and my ass weren't visible for any longer than necessary.

"You forgot," I told him after our initial attempt. "Don't grab me until the camera has taken all three pictures. These are long exposures, about thirty seconds each."

"And that's because ... ?"

"It's dark and I'm not using a flash, so the camera's sensor needs more time to gather the light."

"Is that why you're taking three pictures at a time like that?"

"Because of the low light? Yeah, sort of. It's called bracketing. I use it when the lighting is tricky. I press the shutter release once and it takes three photos, each in a different exposure, one right after the other. Later, I'll combine them or pick the one I like the best. I'm basically hedging my bets, so I get the best possible picture."

Nine successful photos later, I figured we had the timing down. I switched out my DSLR for my Leica rangefinder and set that one up, too. With such a risky enterprise, having my film camera for backup seemed like a smart idea.

"What's with the cheesy point and shoot?" Zach asked. "I thought you were the photography nut with the top-of-the-line camera and zoom lenses out to here." He threw his arm wide.

"I hate to break it to you, Zach, but bigger isn't always better." I didn't mention the fact that this modest-looking camera was probably worth more than Cal's car. Frankly, it was embarrassing.

"Oh, princess." Zach tsked at me. "If you only knew."

I laughed at his pitying tone. "Yeah, yeah. For your information, Leica makes some of the best cameras in the world, especially for film."

"Film is so ten years ago."

"Film is awesome. It sure got Amanda out of our hair, remember?"

He blew out a raspberry. "Whatever. You done? Because I'm ready to see that ass hanging out."

"You're climbing into the compound first, dummy. If anyone's going to have their ass hanging out, it's you."

"Why do you think I suggested we do this? It's about time you had a chance to appreciate my magnificent butt."

Rolling my eyes, I snickered. "Shut up."

CHAPTER 14

Did you even smile?

CLIMBING the tree turned out to be much easier than I'd imagined, especially with Zach giving me a leg up before he sprang to my side like a freaking gymnast. How he did that, while constantly maintaining contact with me, I didn't know.

"Holy crap. What are you, part monkey?"

Zach made a choking sound. "Oh, man. I could make *such* a dirty joke right now. But I won't."

"I don't even want to know."

"My point. Plus, I don't want Cal to kick my ass." He turned to pat the closest branch above us. "Upsy-daisy, tiger. You're in luck. This half-dead tree is better than a frickin' ladder."

I had to admit, he was right. The bark was reasonably smooth, there weren't a ton of leaves or twigs to get in the way, and its wide growth pattern provided sturdy, almost horizontal branches that were easy to balance upon but also spaced close enough to offer plenty of hand-holds.

"This branch is thicker than I thought," Zach said, once we stood side by side on the gently sloping bough that overhung the fence. He bounced up and down, while I clung for dear life to the smaller branch above me and waited for our narrow foothold to crack and give way. Thankfully, the limb beneath our feet hardly moved.

"Looks like we can stay together, at least as far as the fence." He turned to me and laughed. "You can stop strangling that branch, now."

Positioning his feet crosswise on the thick limb, he lightly gripped the higher branch and urged me to copy his stance. "Okay, good, like you'd hold a stair railing. Keep that hand on my wrist like you've been doing. We'll work our way down the branch sideways. Easy as pie. You okay with that?"

I nodded. "I think so."

Considering we were inching along, my heels fourteen feet above the ground, our combined weight on a single branch, I wasn't as nervous as I thought I'd be. Zach had been right. Even dead, the limb hardly shifted beneath us as we shuffled along. It also helped that the fence wasn't more than six feet from the trunk of the tree, which meant we didn't have far to go.

In the distance, an animal cry, which might have been a coyote, sliced through the air.

"Relax, princess. Cal's down there. He'll keep the area clear."

As we approached the point where the fence ran beneath the limb at our feet, I no longer worried about the compound's inhabitants. Instead, I wondered how the heck I was going to climb down without plummeting to my death or, more likely, earning a trip to the E.R. with a slew of broken bones.

The black metal fence, which plunged into the shadows and met the dirt about a mile beneath my feet, was unlike any fence I'd ever seen. Instead of the usual diamond pattern of chain link, this one was comprised of narrow metal rectangles. Cal had called it 'anti-climb welded mesh,' and I could see why.

"As much as I've enjoyed watching you trying not to look terrified, I have a surprise for you," Zach said, once we stopped in our final position above the fence. He transferred my hand to his waist. "Here, grab ahold of me while I get it out of my pack."

After some struggling, Zach pulled a large, twisted black shape from his backpack. When part of the silhouetted mass slithered from his grip to hang in a coil, I realized he held a pile of rope. "Okay, do what you can to keep your hands on me while I get this set up."

Turned out, he'd gotten his hands on an eight-foot rope ladder. Zach unfurled and tied it off in a matter of minutes. "Obviously, it doesn't reach the ground, but I'll be there to help you at the bottom. I'll signal you when I'm down, so listen for my hoot. Be careful and take your time." He leaned toward me. "You okay with this?"

"Yeah, I'm good." I breathed out a steadying breath. "Thanks. This'll make it a lot easier. Go ahead."

He didn't need to remind me that this was the point where my ass, along with everything else, would be hanging out, visible for anyone to see. We'd discussed this several times during our planning. The quicker we both climbed down, the sooner I'd be back inside his sphere of invisibility. The assorted animal noises that randomly emanated from inside the compound didn't help ease my mind.

Zach's black silhouette disappeared as soon as he let go of me. I jerked at the reappearance of my nose, plain on my face and radiating moonlight like a freaking beacon. My nose wasn't large by most standards, yet until this escapade, I'd never realized how much the darn thing protruded into my vision.

Not more than two short minutes later, the distinctive hoot of an owl echoed below me. It sounded so authentic, I wondered whether it was Zach's signal before I chided myself. Of course it was Zach! How likely was it that an owl would be down there hooting away?

As I looked for the easiest way to lower myself onto the first rung, I was particularly thankful the ladder had been secured where several neighboring branches intersected, providing me with some convenient handholds.

Centered above the ladder, I squatted on the branch and extended my leg over the edge in search of the rung closest to my dangling foot. After some indecorous flailing, I found purchase and managed to follow suit with my other leg, while clinging desperately to the main branch. The tree's bark dug into my stomach and forearms as the entire ladder wavered and then steadied under the added weight of my body.

I imagined Zach on the ground beneath me, struggling to pull the ladder taut. And then, because my mind was a total bitch, I pictured the entire thing cutting loose from the limb and my body crashing to the ground, squishing Zach flat. Why have only one person in traction when we could share a hospital room?

Idiot brain, just shut the hell up!

I slowly relinquished my death hold on the branch and worked my way down the ladder. With every flailing step, I chanted: *Don't think. Slow and steady.* My thighs burned, my arms shook, and if I gripped the rope any harder, singularities would form beneath my palms and the resulting black holes would destroy the Earth.

Finally, after I didn't know how many steps, Zach said, "Almost there," and I felt his hands on my calves. As his magic camouflaged me, my nose again merged with the darkness.

Trembling with exertion, I looked over my shoulder. My feet were at the level of his chest.

"Here, squat down. That's it. I've got you." Both hands at my hips, he pulled me from the ladder and set me on the ground. "Well, what do you know? Nobody died."

With my hands frozen into claw-like appendages, humor was beyond me. I staggered and bumped into him, but instead of reflexively bouncing away, I sagged against his body, breathing hard.

His arm went around my shoulders to steady me. "Jesus. You're shaking like crazy. You okay?"

I shook my head as I tried moving my fingers. "Owie … my hands," I croaked out.

"You didn't do much tree or rope climbing as a kid, huh?" He gave me a comforting squeeze. "Maybe we should take the long way back."

The idea had major appeal.

As I experimented with straightening my fingers, movement from the bushes caught my eye. Crouched mid-stride, not more than two body-lengths away, and staring in our direction with a singularly penetrating gaze was the first wolf I'd seen outside of a photograph or documentary.

Since Zach remained relaxed, instead of invoking the highest level of his invisibility, I knew this compelling creature had to be Cal. Even so, I found myself struggling to swallow my terrified scream, take off running, or both. Those blue eyes, which were so dreamy on Cal the human, seemed to pierce right through me.

"For fuck's sake, Cal," Zach snapped, making me jump, to which he responded by squeezing my shoulders tighter. "Stop staring at us like we're a couple of injured deer. Are you *trying* to scare the crap out of her? What the hell's the matter with you?"

Cal sneezed, his snout jerking down with the action, sending dirt and leaves skittering across the ground. With a plaintive whine, he sat back on his powerful haunches and then eased his front paws forward to lie down. As if he didn't look adorable and harmless enough, he rested his chin on his outstretched front legs, angling his muzzle away from us, avoiding eye contact.

"He's sorry." Zach hip checked me. "Go say hi. He won't bite. That is, unless — "

I elbowed him. "Yeah, yeah. Unless I ask him to. I've heard it all before."

Leaving the safety of Zach's side and approaching the prone wolf was harder than I'd like to admit. As if sensing my trepidation, Cal remained still and relaxed, except his eyes, which he swiveled in my direction every few seconds to keep tabs on my progress. His tactic worked. He looked so dang lovable, with his blue eyes furtively considering me as if he was worried I might cut and run, that I had to stop myself from squealing in a ridiculous baby voice, 'Aw, you're such a cute puppy!'

"Hey," I said, kneeling next to him. "You don't have to stay like that. I won't run away if you sit up."

He eyed me suspiciously, but raised his head. I noticed he was careful to avoid holding my gaze for too long, though. Yep, he'd definitely smelled my fear, earlier.

"It's okay, Cal. I'm sorry. You took me by surprise. I've never seen a wolf in real life." I smiled at him. "It's an experience. You're kind of impressive, you know? Way more impressive than a dog." I studied his fur, which looked nearly black in the darkness, and the way the moonlight made his blue eyes appear more gray than usual. "More beautiful, too."

He sneezed, which I imagined was the wolf version of a snort.

I laughed. "Fine. You're ridiculously handsome. Feel better?"

He issued a quiet bark and rose to all fours before shaking himself.

I admired him. "Could I ... touch you, maybe? Or would that be weird?" Grimacing, I sputtered, "I mean, I know you're not a dog." I ducked my shoulders as the heat of embarrassment blossomed on my cheeks. "You know what? Forget it. Sorry. That was a stupid—"

Tipping his head down, he butted his forehead against my arm.

I released my pent breath and tentatively ran my fingers through his thick fur, wishing I'd worn a pair of Zach's wonder gloves instead of the thicker ones I typically donned for gym class.

"I don't care what you say," I whispered as I stroked his neck and body. "You're gorgeous."

He issued a groan that was so unexpected, I laughed.

"I hate to break this up, but we need to get going," Zach said, coming up behind me.

"Okay. Let me get my camera on the tripod, so it's all ready to go."

"You're going to carry it out like that? The lightning tree is still some ways away."

"I'll leave the tripod closed up. I want the camera attached, though, so all I need to do is extend the legs. Plus, I want to get a picture of Cal."

Cal whined.

"Oh, come on. *Please.*" I wasn't beneath begging. "How can you expect me to pass that up? You're amazing."

He sat and looked away. I took that to mean he'd allow me to do it, but he wasn't thrilled.

Before he could change his mind, I tore into my backpack. I left the tripod in its shortest form, using it to steady my shot. Actually, I liked this better since it gave me a low-angle view, making the photo feel more intimate. The ones where I successfully got the moon into the frame were killer.

"Nailed it," I bragged as I examined the digital photos on my camera's LCD screen, zooming in on the individual images to verify their sharpness. "The split ND filter helps with the moon. No blown highlights. And look at the detail in his fur. So pretty."

Cal sneezed.

"Okay, Miss Paparazza," Zach said. "Can we go now?"

Under the heavy cloak of Zach's magic, we made our way toward the lightning-struck tree, invisible to any prowling weres. Cal loped ahead of us to flush out anyone who might be waiting in ambush.

After tripping over yet another protruding root or exposed rock, I cursed Zach's magic for turning an easy walk into an accident waiting to happen. During the day, the shimmery perspective of his magic wasn't a big deal. At night, though, it made the ground more difficult to discern.

"This isn't a race," Zach chided, giving our clasped hands a firm shake. "This whole thing is moot if you fall and break your camera, yeah? And I really don't want to carry you if you twist an ankle."

I knew he was right, but I stuck my tongue out at him — and resolved to walk slower.

"Do you want me to schlep your camera for a while?" he asked. "I don't mind."

"No. I got it."

I'd already depended on Zach and Cal for practically everything in this reckless venture — dealing with Amanda, getting off campus undetected, lending me the car to get here, bringing the rope ladder ...

Jeez. I could carry my own freaking equipment.

I think I must have grumbled something under my breath because Zach chuckled and tweaked my hand. "Okay, I get it. Forget I asked."

Between the darkness and Zach's magic, it was difficult to know how far we'd walked before the lightning-struck tree finally came into view. It stood majestically in a large clearing, its nearest companions an enormous boulder, a broad cluster of bushes, and a stand of young alders. In its time, the dead tree must have soared over the entire landscape, including the lodgepole pines in the distance. Even now, without foliage and minus a good portion of its height due to the lightning strike, the silvery carcass stood at least forty feet tall.

"Wow." The word gushed out of me, almost of its own accord.

"Yeah. Now you know why everyone talks about it."

"It's way bigger than I thought."

"That's what *she* said."

I puzzled over his reply, wondering who he was talking about for a good five seconds. I shouldered into him, shoving him sideways. "Shuddup."

He laughed. "Took you long enough."

"You're a brat." My snickering took all the heat out of what might have been a waspish reply.

"What do you expect when you give me such obvious openings?"

"Yeah, yeah." As we closed the distance to the singular tree, I pointed to the lower half of the weathered trunk where a vertical wound, etched into the tree's flesh, sliced through the bark toward the ground. "Look at the scar. How cool is that?"

"Wicked."

"I like this distance," I told him. "With my thirty-five millimeter, I'll be able to capture some of the surrounding landscape." I gazed at the sky. "But the moon is that way. We need to circle around to the other side of the clearing to get the right framing." I pointed to a spot about a hundred feet away. "Let's move over there, near those bushes. That should be about right."

"Yeah. If you're looking to get ambushed."

"Oh … right." Feeling stupid, I examined their thick foliage with a more skeptical eye and shrugged. "But that's the deal. I can't exactly move the moon. To get it into the frame, we have to be on that side of the tree."

As if scripted for the sole purpose of demonstrating Zach's foresight, a thunderous crash, accompanied by a cacophony of ear-shattering snarls, reverberated from across the clearing. The bushes I'd pointed out, serene just moments ago, thrashed violently from side to side as the piercing cracks of broken branches announced a large skirmish somewhere behind the tall thicket.

"Whoa!" I flinched backward as a massive bear crashed through the bracken, stumbling before collapsing on its side, practically shaking the ground with the weight of its fall.

Hot on its heels, a wolf darted out of the bushes to nip at the grizzly's exposed stomach, just missing a powerful swipe of the bear's front paw.

"Fucking *Brad Perry*," Zach spat. "I hope Cal rips his balls off."

I shook my head at him, as though the action could stop that from happening. "It's a freaking picture. I don't want anyone to get hurt over it. That's stupid!"

"Calm down. Nobody's going to get hurt. Well ... not much."
Zach waved his hand dismissively. "Weres heal quick, remember? *You*,
on the other hand, are soft and squishy and entirely too breakable.
Cal's just reminding Perry to pick on someone his own size."

With a roar, the bear reared up and lumbered after the elusive wolf,
giving chase as Cal dashed through the clearing. Cal yipped excitedly,
circling back to dive in for the occasional nip at Brad's flanks. With
Cal's bushy tail up and mouth parted by a wolfish grin, he clearly enjoyed the game. Brad, however, growled incessantly, teeth barred by a
seriously pissed-off snarl.

In their wake, a bevy of other animals — several coyotes, foxes,
and ... holy cow, was that a hyena? — raced to keep up, staying well
away from the main conflict, probably to avoid getting trampled by
Brad's ponderous weight or Cal's unpredictable zigs and zags.

"Come on," Zach urged, pulling me in the direction of the trampled bushes. "Let's get this over with while Perry and Cal are
distracting everyone."

I trundled after him, no doubt earning a bruise the size of Montana
where my folded tripod battered my collarbone with each jarring step.
Once we reached the trampled bushes, Zach slowed to a crawl and
insisted we thoroughly search the area for other interlopers.

"Thank God most of the cats are in another enclosure," Zach said
while I followed him around one of the few remaining upright bushes.
"Otherwise, we'd be throwing down catnip and two-day-old fish all
over the place." He made a gagging sound. "Not my favorite thing."

Thankfully, Zach was too busy surveying the area to notice my
stunned expression. Going into this, it hadn't occurred to me to plan
for dealing with the werecats and their ingrained aptitude for stalking
and ambushing prey. I hadn't even known they were kept in a different
section of the compound. It showed what an idiot I'd been about this
whole thing.

"What do you mean *most* of the cats? Some are still in here?"

"Yeah. The lions. They can't jump as high. The enclosure for the
others is like twenty-five feet. Good thing we didn't have to climb that
one, huh?"

"No shit."

He laughed. "Okay, we're all clear. Where do you want to setup?"

I positioned my tripod where I had the moon and tree inside my camera's frame. Since nothing had happened to alter the lighting during the last thirty minutes, I didn't need to make any adjustments to my settings. Snapping my bracketed shots was a simple matter of coordination with Zach.

Thanks to Cal's efforts in keeping Brad-the-pissed-off-bear busy, my sudden appearance in the clearing went unchallenged. One thing was for sure, though — standing stock still with my butt hanging out for the three thirty-second-long shots was, by far, the most nerve-wracking experience of my life. My neck practically twitched with my desire to whip my head around for any signs of danger.

"Badass ninja pose," Zach teased when I scrolled through the photos, quickly checking them for sharpness and exposure. "Did you even smile?"

"I could have." Before Zach took my hand, I yanked my hood up, which I'd pushed down for the photos, and tucked my hair back inside. "But then my mouth would have ended up blurry since I don't think I can smile the same way for three minutes straight. And if I tried, I'd end up with the cheesiest smile ever. Why do you think people in old-time photos are always serious? The daguerreotype needed something like fifteen-minute exposures."

I picked up my kit and towed him through the clearing to the tree.

Zach yelped when my tripod swung wide, whacking him. "Watch it with that thing!"

"Oops. Sorry." I planted it about six feet from the trunk.

"Is there a reason you've dragged us over here?"

"I want some shots of that." I pointed at the lightning scar. "It's way too cool to pass up."

"You're risking your skin so you can be artsy-fartsy?"

"It'll only take a couple minutes." I listened to the distant barks and growls. "It sounds like they're still far off." I switched out my Canon for my Leica.

Zach gave me an earful when I told him I needed a minute to change its settings.

"I'm aware just how much my ass will be hanging out," I said. "Look, if you see anyone coming, you can just grab me, okay?"

"Fine, but I'm telling you, this is a bad idea. Half of the football and basketball teams are in this enclosure and I'd bet serious money not all of them were lured into racing after Brad and Cal."

"I'll work fast."

He sighed but let go of me.

With my nose glaring brighter than a lodestar, I whizzed through my setup and managed to take several shots before Zach's sudden intake of breath and fervent curse shattered my concentration.

One second, I was looking through my viewfinder, and the next, Zach just about folded me in half, heaving me by my waist to drag me to the far side of the tree. If I hadn't left my Leica's camera strap around my neck like I always did, tripod or not, my equipment would have been left in the dust, all eight-thousand-plus dollars of it. As it was, my tripod bounced and skittered over the dirt a few feet past my toes while my camera's leather strap bit into the back of my neck, pulled taut by the combined weight of my kit.

"Jeez! What the—"

A lion snarled, its guttural rumble so nearby it drummed along the ground, pulsing up through my heels and into my teeth.

Scrabbling to my feet, I think I tried to merge with Zach's body as the primitive part of of my brain demanded that I make myself as small as possible.

"Shhh. I've got you," Zach rasped at my ear. "Pull up your tripod. It's at the limit of my range."

I reeled in my dangling tripod, careful to keep its legs from grating along the ground. With Zach's continuous touch and assurance that he had things under control, I calmed down enough to fold my tripod and stow my equipment. Not more than a dozen feet away, what was probably a lion moved in the darkness.

"Is now a good time to say, 'I told you so'?" Zach asked, his voice conveying a broad, self-satisfied grin.

"How about later, when we're not about to be on tonight's menu?" I whispered.

Chuckling, he inched sideways to peer around the wide tree trunk, pulling me along behind him.

Emboldened by his confidence, I squeezed between his body and the tree so I could have my own peek.

A lion, powerfully built and crowned with a luxurious mane, snuffled the ground where I'd been standing with my tripod moments ago. The moonlit night had robbed the predator of his tawny color, instead, painting his sleek coat in a silvery-gray palette.

I couldn't fathom how anyone could confuse a regular animal for a were, or vise-versa. There was no mistaking the human intelligence that lurked behind those pale eyes.

The werelion issued a resonant grunt, which sounded like something between a cough and a subdued roar. Roughly translated, I was betting he'd said, 'I know you're there, meat bag.'

After taking a moment to indulge in a full-body stretch, front paws extended forward, backside in the air, and yawning wide enough to display his alarmingly long canines, the king of beasts vigorously shook his mane and then padded three strides away. Pausing, he looked over his shoulder, lifted his black-tipped tail, and unceremoniously sprayed urine in a wide swath over the dirt. Seemingly satisfied, the lion resumed his casual trek through the clearing.

Thank God Zach and I hadn't been standing any closer. Covering my nose against the combined aroma of urine and eau de lion, I watched as the big cat stopped about fifty feet away to do more sniffing. After a guttural chuff, he moved a few paces and graced the dirt with another impressive urine shower.

"Am I wrong, or did he just pee on both places where I took my photos?" I asked from behind my hand.

"You're not wrong. He's masking your scent. That's gotta be Ted. The guy's totally hoping to score points with you." He cleared his throat. "Among other things."

I made a face. "Pass. I mean, don't get me wrong, it's cool what he's doing to help me, but the fact that he dated Amanda ..." I shuddered. "Yuck."

"And let's not forget what she said about the guy's ding-dong. No girl wants — "

I shoved at him. "Ew, no! Just ... *ugh*. Don't even go there. I don't want to know. Seriously."

Laughing, he pulled me away from the tree. "Fine. Come on. It's time to go. I'd like to get at least a few hours of sleep."

With my mind churning over everything I'd seen tonight, along with worries about the photos I'd taken and what I might have done differently, it took me a while to realize where Zach was leading us.

"I thought you said you'd take us out a different way," I grumbled, too exhausted to keep from sounding anything but petulant.

Adrenaline crash and the late hour had left me light headed and sick to my stomach. Climbing the rope ladder was right up there with juggling knives on my 'Top Ten Ways To Get Maimed Or Killed At Three In The Morning' list.

"I never got a chance to tell Cal, so we need to stick to the plan. We'll meet up with him at the fence and then decide where to go from there, okay?"

Fine. Except, I knew what would happen when we got there. I'd feel obligated to attempt the climb, which annoyed and frustrated the hell out of me. I knew better than to say anything, though. As tired as I was, whatever came out of my mouth would be snippy. Zach was doing his best to be accommodating. Actually, when it came down to it, he'd been a lot more than accommodating. He'd been solidly behind me for this entire adventure, from the planning to the execution. Not only that, but tonight, at every turn, he'd gone out of his way to protect me. Biting his head off was the last thing I wanted to do.

I hadn't realized how quiet the night had become until an alarming roar echoed through the landscape, a roar that had nothing to do with lions or bears.

We both jerked to a stop.

"What the heck was that? It sounded like—" I replayed it in my mind. "Okay, I know it's stupid, but it sounded like a jet engine. Didn't it?"

"Or a train, yeah, which is just as stupid. It lasted for what? A few seconds ... if that?"

In the distance, a wolf howled, piercing the night with its low-pitched lamentable cry.

Next to me, Zach stiffened.

"Was that Cal?"

He shook his head. "Cal's a lone wolf. He never howls. Wolves do that to communicate with their pack. A lone wolf doesn't want that kind of attention."

"Maybe it was a coyote."

"No. It was definitely a wolf."

"But Cal's the only wolf here." I sucked in a breath. "Wait. Do you think it's one of Cal's missing cousins?"

"I don't know. Maybe." He strode forward, tugging my hand. "Come on. We need to meet up with Cal."

Ten minutes later, the B&E tree came into view.

Or what was left of it.

"Son of a—!" Zach's stride hitched as we took in the unexpected scene.

Instead of the upright silhouette of a mostly-bare magnolia, we found a felled carcass, its twisted branches splayed over the ground like the bony tentacles of some otherworldly beast. The fence that seemed so imposing, barely an hour ago, had been smashed by the tree's massive trunk, which now rested, bridge-like, over the crumpled section of fencing. Wood shrapnel littered the ground in a wide swath. Somewhere beneath the combined weight of tree and metal, Zach's rope ladder lay buried.

If the timing had been different, he and I could have been squashed right along with it—a gruesome thought.

"Jesus." I shivered. "It seemed so sturdy."

Zach said nothing as he rocketed forward, towing me along as he scrutinized the scene from several different angles. He seemed almost frantic.

"I don't think you're going to get the rope ladder out," I said.

Turning from the fallen tree, I looked around us, peering into the nearby shadows for the familiar silhouette. "Where's Cal? Do you see him?"

"No. Thank Christ," he croaked emphatically.

I snapped my gaze to the black hole of his face and then to the fallen tree. "Oh, my God. That's why—" I shook my head, horrified. "I'm so stupid. I assumed nobody was around. I didn't think Cal might ... that he might've been ..."

"It's okay," Zach said, his obvious relief gushing out with the words. Lifting our clasped hands, he gestured to our left. "Look."

From between the nearest bushes, the dark shape of a wolf trotted toward us.

I sagged, leaning into Zach. His arm went around me, but I was only there for a moment before I dropped to my knees, popping into the moonlight at Cal's approach.

"Cal. Thank God, you're okay," I whispered as I slipped my fingers into his scruff. I longed to bury my face in the thick fur. "Zach worried that you'd been caught by the tree."

Looking toward the fallen magnolia and crushed fence, he issued a muted growl.

"Uh-oh! Lights in the distance," Zach said. "The guards are coming. Lire, we need to go. *Now.*"

I gave Cal one final stroke. "Thanks for all your help. You were awesome. See you tomorrow night, okay?"

Zach grasped my hand and, once again, my body disappeared inside his identity-stealing magical sphere. He bent down to whisper something hasty into Cal's ear, but we didn't linger for a response. Zach towed me toward the tree, where we started up the natural trellis provided by its spreading branches.

"No — take that one, there." Zach pointed, directing me toward a sturdier limb. "Don't let go of me. Most of the guards are weres. We don't need them getting a fresh whiff."

"Isn't it a little late for that? My scent is all over the place from when I climbed down the ladder."

"Cal's gonna do his best to take care of that."

"You mean like Ted did?"

"Yeah. And then some."

With Zach's magic distorting the surroundings, it was a miracle I scrabbled to the topside of the tree without so much as a stubbed toe. I was beginning to wonder whether Zach had kissed a leprechaun or been blessed by a fleet of pixies prior to leaving on this crazy adventure.

Risking a glance over my shoulder as I clambered around a stout branch, I caught my last hazy image of Cal, who, sure enough, squatted near the far side of the tree. Perhaps more shockingly, though, Ted had poised himself on the opposite side, and it looked like he was doing much the same thing.

Several curses and an emphatic "Jesus Christ!" echoed in the distance as the guards approached the fallen magnolia. Light beams from at least three flashlights danced over the surrounding branches, and I half wished one of them would strike me full and steady, just to see what would happen. Would it pass through my body, like I was made of air?

Zach's hasty, "Get ready," distracted me from my reckless curiosity.

Before I could ask why, my view shrank to a dim pinpoint and Zach's magic pulled me in his wake, stretching me to a thin ribbon. With little sense of time, I wove through the darkness, around obstacles and over the ground, as though I'd somehow transformed into an inky, astral snake. I had the terrifying notion that if I let go of Zach, I'd be lost to the ether, stuck in this form and doomed to slither through the shadows of this dimly lit wormhole, for all eternity.

With that dismal notion still in mind, the world expanded in a burst of silvery moonlight, forcing me back into confines of my body like the filling in an overstuffed sausage. I wobbled two steps and vomited into the bushes.

Zach rubbed my back. "Shit. Sorry. I wanted to get us out of there quick. You okay?"

"I'll live," I rasped. I spat in the dirt and wiped my mouth with the back of my hand. "Yuck. Let's not do that again, okay?"

He chuckled. "Fine by me."

I pulled Zach away from the bush I'd christened, and he waited while I searched my backpack for some gum.

In the distance, at least half-a-football-field away, beams from several flashlights and the headlights from a four-person electric cart illuminated the destruction.

"Do you think the tree falling was the weird sound we heard?" I asked.

"Maybe." He sounded distracted. "Do you smell that?" He tilted his head, sniffing the air.

I slapped my free hand over my mouth. "Sorry. Give my gum a few seconds to work."

"No ..." He turned to scan the ground behind us. "It smells like—" The grip on my hand tightened.

I stepped around him to see what he was looking at.

"Blood," he said. "Fuck me."

With the gum in my mouth and my nose still stuffy from throwing up, I couldn't smell anything besides peppermint, but judging by the distorted shape on the ground not fifteen feet away and the dark stain surrounding it, that was probably a good thing. The smell of death wasn't something I wanted to revisit.

The downside of appraising antiques with my gift was that, occasionally, it exposed me to some rather unpleasant memories. The first time I saw through the eyes of a soldier, after touching an American Civil War saber one sunny afternoon at Ben's shop, I passed out. Poor Ben had panicked and almost called 9-1-1. Fortunately, Red had been on hand to tell him what to do. I'd woken up in the back of Dad's car, halfway home.

Still, memories of nineteenth-century war killings was one thing, a dead body, here, in real life was something else entirely.

"Is that ... ?" My voice warbled as my brain resolved the outline to be that of a human body. "Do you think they're —?" I didn't want to utter the word, as if it might jinx the person lying there.

"Christ." Shifting on his feet, he ran his free hand over the back of his neck. "That's a lot of blood. I guess we should check to see whether, uh ... you know."

I might have sought Red's advice if the nature of Zach's magic didn't require that I stand so close to him. If Zach succumbed to Red's defensive spells, he'd freak for sure and then I'd be left standing in the open for everyone to see. With a potential dead body nearby, that didn't seem like a great idea.

"We could alert them somehow," I said meekly, gesturing at the bouncing lights in the distance.

Standing straighter, Zach cleared his throat. "Let's see if they're alive, first." With a steeling breath, he pulled me toward the body. "Get behind me if you don't want to see."

I didn't hide, but it was more difficult to keep pace with Zach than I wanted to admit.

Our closer look confirmed my guess that the victim was a man. It also revealed several other details that I would have been happier not knowing. He'd been tall and thin with long hair. His face was so bloody and ravaged that it took me several long seconds to sort out what I was looking at. Even in the relative darkness, it was obvious that something large and vicious had taken dozens of bites out of this man. His nose was missing. A ragged hole, where his right cheek used to be, revealed a meager gleam of teeth, and his ripped shirt and slacks were saturated with dark stains that I didn't have to guess about.

Surrounding the body, chunks of soil and uprooted weeds attested to a violent struggle. I wondered whether a trained eye would be able to identify animal tracks amid the clods and blood-soaked soil. Probably they'd notice my and Zach's footprints, too.

This couldn't be Sorcerer Treblow, could it? Didn't old sorcerers wear robes?

As Zach attempted to find a pulse behind the broken man's right ear, an odd buzzing grew loud in my head. Above the noise, I vaguely heard myself say, "They'll have to use dental records."

Time slipped. I didn't see Zach stand from his crouch. Next thing I knew, his silhouette filled my vision as he stared down at me, gripping my shoulders. "You okay?"

"Sure." I nodded numbly.

He led me away.

Sometime later, in the shadow of Sorcerer Treblow's house, Zach pushed my back against a tree and bent down to peer into my eyes. At least, I imagined he was peering into my eyes. Without notable features, it was hard to tell for sure.

He shook me by my shoulders. "Come on, tiger. Snap out of it. You've not said a single word for ten minutes and you're stumbling along like a zombie." He tilted his head. "You weren't bitten by one when I wasn't looking, were you?"

Bitten ...

I sagged and if he hadn't held me against the tree, I might have stumbled. "Oh, Zach. That poor man. Something tried to ..." My voice broke. "It tried ... it ... it ... "

It had tried to eat him.

Not just *tried*—it had succeeded. Parts of his face were missing. Although, I supposed it was possible the chunks had been buried in the dirt.

I covered my mouth, fighting my rising nausea and the sobs that would surely turn me into a snotty disgusting mess. Only my vanity kept me from barfing all over Zack's shoes and then collapsing into a puddle of useless tears.

He pulled me closer and wrapped his arms around me. "Sorry. That was a stupid thing to say after ..." His thready voice tapered to a shaky sigh.

To my surprise, where our bodies touched, I felt Zach's trembling. He might have exuded confidence and a devil-may-care attitude, but what we'd seen had disturbed him too. This, almost as much as his embrace, soothed me like nothing else could have. Relaxing, I hugged him back, resting my cheek against his chest, relieved when I didn't get a psychic reading from the fabric of his skin-suit. He smelled pleasantly spicy, and I wondered whether it was his deodorant or cologne.

We stood that way for at least a minute before distant shouts permeated my temporary slice of comfort.

"They found the body," Zach said as he released me in favor of holding my hand.

We watched in silence as several figures swarmed near the dead man's crumpled form, their flashlights bouncing over the ground, one beam tracking all the way out here, at the lifeless house behind us.

I examined the bungalow's curtained windows and peered into the shadowy confines of the wrap-around porch for any signs of movement. Seeing nothing, I turned to Zach. "Do you think the body ... Do you think it's Sorcerer Treblow?"

Zach shrugged. "Could be. Nobody's coming out of the house to find out what the hoopla's about."

"But I thought Treblow was, like, super old. That guy's hair wasn't gray."

"It wouldn't be. He's got power up the wazoo. Or had. Pop saw him once. He said he hadn't looked older than forty."

I wondered how someone with so much power could get himself murdered like that.

After watching the activity for a while longer, Zach jiggled my hand. "We should go."

I wanted to see the police overrun the place, to see what they'd do, but he was right. It was late—not that I'd be doing much sleeping after what we'd seen. "Yeah. Okay."

For the second time tonight, I heard sirens echoing in the distance.

I'd stopped trembling by the time we reached the produce stand. With all the sirens and pulsating lights to the west of us, I half expected to find the highway cordoned off and Cal's car impounded. Instead, his little Honda waited where we'd left it, parked alone at the back of the dirt lot, no emergency vehicles in sight. I guess that wasn't too surprising, though. The man's death had plainly been an animal kill, not the result of some crazed axe murderer.

Safely ensconced inside Cal's car, I finally voiced the question that had been pinging through my mind for the last half an hour. "What type of animal do you think attacked him? A mountain lion? And when? The blood still looked, you know … wet."

"I don't think he'd been dead long. His body still felt warm to me when I touched him and rigor mortis hadn't set in. That usually takes between four and twelve hours after a person dies. It depends on the temperature."

Stunned, I wondered how the heck he knew that.

"I couldn't see enough in the dark to know what attacked him," he said. "An animal, obviously. Mountain lion's as good a guess as any. I just hope … " His voice trailed off. "We should get going before a cop spots you."

The emergency vehicles must have been coming from the direction of town because we didn't pass a single car on the way back to Les Schwab. Even so, I didn't start to relax until I'd parked Cal's car in their lot and Zach had taken my hand to render me invisible. We staggered back to campus, the both of us too exhausted to run. Besides, now that I'd taken the photos, the pressure was off. As long as we made it back in time for first period, we were golden.

"Hey, Zach? I've been thinking …"

"Don't hurt yourself."

I elbowed him. "Seriously. Listen, I don't think that body was there when we first got to the compound. I'm almost positive we walked right by where he was lying, or at least close enough that we would have noticed."

"Yeah." He didn't sound happy about it.

"That would mean he was killed while we were inside." I glanced at him. "And what's creepier is the animal that killed him might have been nearby when we were taking my test photos."

Zach didn't reply, and I wondered whether he didn't want to admit to being freaked out or if he was too tired to make conversation.

Aside from the few sirens we'd heard after the guards discovered the body, the night had gone eerily quiet. I kicked a fist-sized rock that had crept into the bike lane, returning it to the dirt shoulder. Looking ahead, I noted we were one curve away from the school's private drive.

"I wonder what Treblow was doing walking around his property so late. If that was him, I mean." I sucked in a breath as a terrible thought occurred to me. My gait hitched, briefly forcing Zach to slow down. I looked over at him. "You don't think he heard us or saw me taking pictures and that's why he came outside ... do you?"

"It might not have been Treblow. But even if it was, my magic had us hidden most of the time. And we weren't that close to his house. If he saw us, it's because he was already out walking around. Old people are weird that way. My great-grandpa used to fall asleep in front of the TV, right after dinner, and he'd be up at 3:00 a.m. Half the time, he'd take the dog for a walk."

"Is your great-grandpa still alive?"

"No. He died when I was in second grade." He glanced at me. "What about you? Are your great-grandparents still around?"

"No. My mom and dad were both late children. I never knew my great-grandparents and I barely knew any of my grandparents."

"That sucks."

I shrugged. "I've never known anything different, but I wish I'd gotten to meet my grandpa Giordano. He's where I got my—" I snapped my mouth shut.

"Where you got your what?"

I sighed. "My red hair."

"Red? Wait ..."

"I lighten it."

"You do?" He turned to peer me. "Why?"

"I don't know," I lied. "I wanted something different. And I think strawberry-blonde suits me."

The truth was I'd been teased mercilessly throughout my childhood by my sister and countless others. I was either Raggedy Ann or Anne of Green Gables or Little Orphan Annie. What was the deal with the name Ann? After I'd begged for over a year, Dad had finally relented and let me lighten it to strawberry-blonde, the summer before eighth grade.

Time for a new subject. "Don't you think it's a crazy coincidence that the tree fell down around the time that man was killed?"

"Huh. You think it wasn't?"

"A coincidence?"

"Yeah."

I shrugged. "The tree sure didn't feel rickety to me. It felt rock solid. Did it feel rickety to you?"

"No."

"Do dying trees fall down like that? Without any warning when they were really sturdy just thirty minutes earlier?"

"Our climb could have loosened it up," he said, but I could tell by his tone that he didn't buy it.

"You'd think if it was that close to falling down, we would have heard creaks or cracks or something when we were climbing."

"True." After a moment, he admitted, "I don't think it was a coincidence either."

We turned down the school's driveway, skirting the granite sign. In the moonlight, shadow thickened the elegantly engraved letters to a bold typeface.

"Do you think the animal that killed him knocked down the tree?"

"I'm not sure even an elephant could have done that," he said. "Anyway, why would a mountain lion or wolf or a rabid dog go out of their way to do it? And, there was that weird sound, remember? It sounded like ... wind."

"Couldn't have been from the weather. There's hardly been a breeze, all night."

"Then I guess that leaves magic."

I glanced at him. "What? Like, a cyclone spell?"

"Probably not. The force was narrow. The fence was fine on either side of the tree ... the bushes, too."

"Sticks were all over the place, but that could have come from when it hit the ground. An air blast spell has a tighter cone. Not sure it'd be strong enough to knock down such a big tree, though. Could it've been a geomancer spell?"

"Possibly." He cursed. "I wish we'd gotten a closer look." From the corner of my eye, I saw him glance over at me. "You know what the authorities are going to think, don't you?"

I nodded grimly. "They're going to assume one or more weres escaped and killed that guy."

"Sure as hell."

"If it's Treblow, like we're thinking … maybe *he's* the one who knocked down the tree. You know—while fighting off his attacker. What kind of magic does an ubhnati sorcerer practice?"

"From what Pop told me, they're not confined to a single discipline and they don't cast their spells from memory, like most sorcerers. Ubhnati weave their spells into knots for later use. Which means they can conjure all manner of shit off the cuff, stuff that would normally require insane concentration or one or more focal objects. That's what makes them powerful as fuck. I heard this Treblow guy has spent his whole life researching and weaving obscure magic, making him more powerful than all the Council's members combined. If it's really Treblow—the dead body, I mean—then whatever attacked him got ridiculously lucky or somehow discovered a way around his arsenal."

"If that's true, if he's as powerful as you say, how likely is it that a wild animal killed him?"

"About as likely as me scoring with a *Sport's Illustrated* swimsuit model."

I shoved him, snickering. "Dork."

In the distance, the school's landscaping lights popped into view. I imagined myself collapsing into bed and almost groaned at the thought.

"He was super old, right?" I said after some musing, mostly about how exhausted I was. "Maybe he was tired of life."

"Suicide by wild animal?" he asked, clearly amused. "Not exactly a sure-fire way to go. Messy, too."

"That's not what I—" I laughed. "Never mind. You're right. That was a dumb idea."

"We're brainstorming, here. There are no dumb ideas."

We stopped to bypass the school's barrier enchantment. After my barf-inducing scrape fleeing the compound, this easy squeeze hardly fazed me. I didn't have to stop to recover my bearings, we just kept right on walking.

I shook my head. "This is insane. I can't believe we found a dead body."

"Yeah."

"I've never seen one in real life," I admitted, my voice sounding small. "I mean, I've seen them in other people's memories when I've touched antiques and stuff, but seeing one for real was ..." I grimaced. "It was way freakier." I pressed my fist against my breastbone where unease had knitted into a tight ball. "And I get scared thinking about it, even though I know I don't have any reason to be."

I peered at his black silhouette when he didn't say anything. Not for the first time, I wished like hell I could see his expression. "Have you ever seen a dead body before?" I asked hesitantly. "I mean, you seem to know about it, like an investigator or something."

"Once or twice." He shrugged, but it was a jerky movement, as though his shoulders resisted a force that pulled on them. "I'm no expert. I watch *CSI*, and I guess I've looked a few things up."

Once or twice? Jeez. What kind of missions does your father send you on?

The mile-wide 'OFF LIMITS' sign posted by his body language silenced my question.

"Yeah, well ... once was enough for me," I said. "I'll be lucky to sleep at all tonight."

"I know I won't."

I glanced over at him, nibbling my lower lip. "Zach ... you don't think ..." I frowned. "We might know stuff the police should know. Shouldn't we — "

"We don't know more than anyone else," he interrupted. "Not really. The guards found the body thirty seconds after we did. And anyone in the compound would have heard that weird sound, way better than us. Weres, remember? Their senses are off the charts."

"Exactly. They'll find your rope ladder and sniff me out, even with Cal and Ted helping to mask my scent. And if the police talk to anyone who might have seen me, they'll find out I was there. I could get into more trouble by not saying anything."

"Remember what I told you? My dad has guards at the compound. They'll deal with the rope ladder. Cal will make sure of it. And, if one of the weres rats you out, which I doubt they would, nobody knows we saw the body. The worst that'll happen is we'll get in trouble for breaking curfew and going off campus."

"You say 'we,' but nobody will know you were there."

"You think I'd lurk in the shadows while you take all the blame?" His affronted tone took me aback. I jerked him to a stop and glared at him. "You think I'd let you get in trouble when there's no reason?"

"I'd like to see you stop me. But it's not going to come to that, okay? If you'd relax, you'd figure that out. Jesus."

"Yeah?" I retorted, bristling at his condescension. "And what am I supposed to figure out?"

"That there's no reason to go to the police. *Duh.* The compound was full of weres who heard and saw the same stuff we did, including Cal and the guards. We don't know anything that they don't. So, what will running to the police accomplish, other than getting us into trouble *for no reason?*"

Ready to rumble, I opened my mouth to tell him we had to go to the police, that it was the right thing to do, the responsible thing, but shut it after not being able to come up with a compelling reason. And it had to be compelling—because it wouldn't only be *me* getting into trouble. If I turned myself in, Zach would join me. He'd already said as much.

"Fine," I said, yanking him into resuming our walk. I didn't huff but it was a struggle. "You have a point. As soon as the police talk to the kids in the compound, they'll hear about everything we saw. And heard."

"Boom, baby. Told you you'd figure it out."

I rolled my eyes.

By the time we reached campus, I'd gone from exhausted to downright punchy.

Staring at my dorm's front doors, I leaned my head on Zach's shoulder and pouted. "I'm not up for this. Maybe I should sleep in the locker with my Vespa."

"Don't be a baby. Just two more squeezes and you're home free." He waggled my hand. "Come on. Ready?"

I heaved out a titanic sigh. "Yes."

The nauseating experience of Zach's magic yanking me through the crack wasn't improved by fatigue. As soon as I'd grown back into my shoes, Zach towed me to the nearest trash can.

Swallowing thickly, I croaked, "I'm okay," and pulled him toward my room.

For the past hour, I'd been daydreaming about falling into bed, snuggling under the covers, and sleeping for a week. Now that I was almost there, I altered my fantasy to include a quick detour to the bathroom to pee. Forget brushing my teeth, I'd be lucky to strip off my skin-suit before face-planting into my pillow.

I groaned with relief after Zach slipped us beneath my door. The readout on my digital clock told me it was 4:03 a.m. *Good Lord.* My alarm would go off in just three hours.

I turned and threw my arms around Zach, hugging him tight enough to feel his belt pack pressing into my stomach. "Thank you," I murmured sleepily. "I couldn't have done that without you."

His chuckle rumbled through his chest beneath my ear. "Anytime, princess."

I released him before things got weird and dropped my backpack onto my chair. "God, I'm so glad to be home." I pushed back my hood, exposing my sweaty scalp and ears to the cool air of my room. "Ugh. My hair feels gross."

"Get some sleep. I'm skipping breakfast, but I'll see you for lunch."

I smiled in his direction. "Okay. Sleep well, Zach."

"You too. See ya."

While Red climbed to his perch on my desk, I staggered to my bathroom. It wasn't until I'd slid between my sheets that I wondered whether Zach had remained in my room, maybe hoping to catch me in my panties.

With that absurd thought, I drifted off to sleep, sure I could smell Zach's scent still lingering on the air.

CHAPTER 15

Don't say I didn't warn you

SKIPPING breakfast would've shaved thirty minutes from my morning routine, but instead of hitting the snooze button, I pitched out of bed and stumbled to my coffee pot, bleary-eyed but determined to review last night's photos.

Bolstered by caffeine, I tweaked my favorite composition in Photoshop, deftly combining all three exposures into one masterpiece, before printing the final snapshot on premium photo paper. Despite Zach's motto, I didn't print an eight-by-ten. After last night's deadly turn, waving around a poster-sized photo of the compound seemed like a monumentally bad idea, so I went with a more discrete four-by-six.

My absolute favorite photo, on the other hand—the one I'd taken of Cal in his wolf form—was a different story. I printed that one as an eight-by-ten and taped it to the side of my wardrobe cabinet where

I could see it from my desk and bed. For anyone standing in my doorway, though, it would remain safely out of view.

Hair still wet from my lightning-fast shower, I shambled into the women's locker room for first period gym, unenthusiastic about anything more strenuous than holding down the nearest bench. My eyes felt like the inside of a witch's cauldron.

"Lire!" Shannon exclaimed, trotting over to me. "We missed you and Zach at breakfast." She lowered her voice to an excited whisper. "So ... ? Did you guys do it?"

I reached into my gym locker and pulled the photo from my backpack.

"Holy crap! I can't believe you guys did it." She shook her head, her hazel eyes going wide. "You and Zach are triple Ds. This is so cool. You're the only ones. Did you know that? I mean besides that shadow-mage, five years ago."

"Wait. I thought Trina and Jessica were triple Ds."

"They wish. They did what Darla and I did. Didn't even break curfew, 'cuz they waited to do it on the weekend." She chortled and then pitched her voice low. "I can't wait to see their faces when they get a look at this." She waved the photo. "Oh! There they are."

Before I could get a word in edgewise, she beckoned the two girls over. "Hey, you guys!" Shoving her short blonde hair behind her ear, she glanced around, I assumed for Coach Rickett. "You gotta come check this out."

Jessica frowned as she crowded in to look over Trina's shoulder at my photo. "No way."

"You went, after the fire alarm thing?" Trina asked, her eyes narrowed suspiciously.

I gave her an arch look. *Duh.* "What do you think?"

She snatched the photo from Shannon's hand to examine it more closely. "Photos can be doctored."

"As *if.* The photos are still on my camera's memory card. And I have others on film."

"Face it," Shannon said. "She did it. But if you want to be a big poop about it, go ask Zach. He went with her. And I bet some of the weres saw or smelled her there, too. You can ask Ted or Brad when they get back." She laughed. "Supercuts is going to be busy this week-end."

"Brad is going to be so pissed." Trina shot me an accusatory glare.

"What are you looking at me for?" I asked. "I had nothing to do with their stupid bet. They did that all on their own."

"After you guys encouraged them," Shannon reminded her, eagerly piling on. "If anyone's to blame, it's you and Amanda for going on and on about how Lire would chicken out."

Trina tossed the photo back at Shannon. "Yeah, well … whatever." She eyed me. "Since Lire never accepted the bet, they don't have to do it."

"It was an open bet," Shannon retorted, bending to retrieve the photo, which had twirled to the floor. "They announced to everyone who'd listen that they'd shave their heads if Lire got the photo. They're a bunch of chickenshit liars if they don't do it."

I blinked at Shannon, stunned by her fervent support, but the first period bell rang before I could add to the conversation. Although, to be honest, if they'd asked me, I probably would have let Ted, Brad, and the rest of them off the hook. I had fun giggling with Zach about the fantasy, but in real life, being known as 'the girl who forced the football and basketball teams to shave their heads' might not be all that funny.

"Can I keep this?" Shannon asked, holding my photo. "I want to show it to the rest of the daredevils."

"If a teacher sees this, I'll be majorly busted." With the dead body, I'd be beyond busted.

"I'll be careful." She regarded me earnestly. "I promise."

After eyeing her, I reluctantly nodded. What was I going to say? 'I can't allow that because I stumbled across a dead body last night?'

Yeah, right.

"Thanks." Her smile was blinding. "Darla's going to freak." She leaned closer to murmur, "She's wanted to stick it to Amanda and her clique of princess wanabees, for ages. Having someone else do it is almost as good."

"Why? What does Darla have against Amanda?"

Her eyes widened even as she frowned. "Didn't you know? Darla and Ted were totally together, until Amanda waved her boobs in his face and sucked his dick after the homecoming dance, beginning of last year."

I winced. "Wow. Uh, no. I had no idea."

"You're not the only one who'd love to see that bitch trip face-first into a bubbling lake of diarrhea. Trust me."

I cracked up. "Good to know."

For the rest of the day, every time I thought of Shannon's quip, I had to stop myself from snickering. With three hours of sleep under my belt, it was the one thing that kept me from going narcoleptic, especially in trigonometry.

At lunch, I aimed for my usual table, relieved when I spotted Zach's tray.

"Hey. How's it going?" I asked as I sank into my spot.

"I've had better days." His voice sounded rough, like he'd sung himself hoarse with too much karaoke. "Pop called me, early. They've got the compound in lockdown. Parents are being called, the school's getting releases so the police can interview all the students. I'm betting the weres won't be allowed back to school today."

"Whoa. When do you think they'll be back?"

"Dunno. Tomorrow, maybe. They'll probably release the non-predators first, though."

I leaned closer, lowering my voice to match his. "That's routine, though, right? You don't really think they'll suspect a student ... do you?"

"The local police? Hell, yes. It's way easier than trying to find the actual culprit. Just blame it on the compound's out-of-control were-wolf."

"Werewolf!" I clamped my teeth together, too late to cover my near shout. Leaning forward, I murmured, "There are other predators in the compound besides Cal, you know."

"I bet you dollars to doughnuts Treblow was killed by a wolf."

"Why? Because we heard that animal howling?" I shot him a dubious look. "It could have been a Siberian husky."

Zach snorted. "It wasn't a husky."

"You speak fluent wolf or something?"

"Let's just say I've spent a lot of time around the Rout."

"We know for a fact that Cal didn't do it. Look ... I hate to say it, but—"

Before I could finish telling him this was exactly why we needed to go to the police with our story, Shannon and Darla swept in and, to my surprise, planted their trays on the table and settled into the two extra seats. Shannon sat next to Zach and Darla took the left side of my bench where Cal normally sat.

"Hey, you two," Shannon chirped.

Someone was sure in a good mood.

"Shannon showed me the photo," Darla said, flicking her braids behind her shoulder. "You guys are my heroes."

"Photo?" Zach asked, sounding livelier. "Would that be a gorgeous eight-by-ten?"

"I thought a postcard size would be less ... in-your-face," I said. "I'll print you an eight-by-ten, later, if you really want it."

"You disappoint me, princess. In-your-face is my middle name."

I laughed.

"Congratulations on the triple-D thing, Zach," Shannon said after sipping her chocolate milk.

Zach grunted indifferently. "Can't prove it. Not that I care. I did it to help Lire."

"Yeah," Shannon said, sulking. "The bitch triplets are going to be all poopy about the photo evidence thing, even though everyone will know you're the one who helped Lire sneak out." Scowling, she tossed her head to get her blonde bangs out of her eyes. "They're idiots."

"That goes without saying," Darla said.

"So ... did either of you guys happen to see anything weird at the compound last night?" Shannon peered at me.

I shook my head, midway into a bite of my grilled cheese, which gave me a few seconds to think of something to say. "I got to see Cal flush Brad out of the bushes and then take him on a chase through the compound. Which was frickin' awesome. I wouldn't call it weird, though."

Trying not to squirm, I glanced at Darla before looking back to Shannon. "Why?"

"I heard the weres are in lockdown," Shannon replied. "The whole compound. No one's allowed to leave or go outside."

"Really? I wonder why." I think I did a credible job of acting surprised. "How'd you find out?"

"Nancy told me," she said, finally turning her attention to her food instead of scrutinizing me. "Brad texted her after they locked the doors. He thought they might confiscate cell phones, too."

"During second period, I *overheard*" — Darla cocked her fingers to form air quotes — "Amanda say that Ted had texted her about it. They've been confined to their rooms."

"Please. I can't believe she still does that," Shannon said. "As if you give a crap that Ted texts her."

"Um ..." Ignoring the underlying drama about Amanda, I pretended to be worried, which wasn't much of a stretch. "You don't think it's because we broke in, do you?"

"Why? Did you do something to the fence?" Shannon frowned at me. "I thought you climbed that tree we told you about."

I nodded. "We did. The tree worked great. Thanks for telling Zach."

"If you didn't cut a hole in the fence or something like that, then I don't see why the lockdown would have anything to do with you. Unless ..." Shannon tilted her head slightly. "Do you think a guard saw you?"

I pondered that, but Zach jumped in. "Lire was invisible most of the time. But if they happened to spot her, I can see why they'd lock everything down. If someone ever got attacked, even while trespassing, it wouldn't look good for the school."

Boy, oh boy. Zach sure knew how to sound convincing. Although, when you got down to it, he hadn't said anything that wasn't true.

"If that's the case, I sure hope word doesn't get back to the school," Darla said. "Mr. Gibbs is already in a bad mood because of the fire thing last night."

"Oh!" Shannon clamped a hand over her mouth. She leaned toward me, lowering her voice to murmur, "If Mr. Gibbs finds out you broke into the compound, he might think you set the fire for a diversion, so you could sneak out without anyone noticing."

I didn't have to pretend to be horrified. "That's stupid. Why would I need a diversion if Zach was helping me?"

"How's Mr. Gibbs gonna know?" she asked, her thin blonde brows furrowing together. "It's not like anyone could see Zach."

"No way is Lire taking all the blame," Zach said gruffly. "If she gets caught, I'll be right there with her."

"Zach—"

"Sorry, tiger. You can't stop me, so how 'bout we make sure we don't get caught?"

I sighed. "Shannon, how many people did you show the photo to?"

She cringed. "A few."

"A few, huh?" I arched a brow. "Like who?"

Her gaze shifted to the side as she thought about it. "Well ... you know about Trina and Jessica. In second period, there was Nancy, Eric, and Shania. Jennie and Cyprian in third—oh, and Emily. Becky in fourth."

"Only a few," I said dryly.

Shannon shrugged, looking sheepish. "I couldn't help it. It's just so cool."

"Can I see it?" Zach asked.

"The photo? Sure." She rummaged through the outside pocket of her backpack before holding it out for him.

When the photo disappeared from her hand, her eyes widened. "Whoa. Wicked."

"Totally," Darla murmured.

"The thing is ... this photo could have been taken over the summer," Zach said. "It's not like Lire's holding a newspaper with yesterday's headline on it, right?"

"That's true," Shannon conceded. "But if any of the weres say that they saw her inside the compound ..."

"Then I'm screwed." I jabbed a fork into my salad.

"You were visible for a total of five minutes, tops," Zach pointed out.

"But if someone saw me, that part doesn't really matter, does it?" I shot his empty seat a pointed stare.

"Let's just hope nobody tattles." He didn't sound optimistic.

Forcing myself to eat my grilled cheese, I bounced my heel against the polished concrete floor and debated with myself about confessing everything to Mr. Simmons. Why did Darla and Shannon have to be around, right when I needed to talk things over with Zach? I already knew what Zach would say, though. He'd tell me to calm down and use my head, which was insulting when I considered it. It wasn't as if I ran around like a freshly sacrificed chicken whenever anything stressful came up.

"Did you see us evacuating, last night, Zach?" Shannon asked.

"Yup. Was on my way to get Lire."

"Thank God you guys hadn't left yet," Darla said.

"So ... ?" Shannon ogled Zach's side of the table expectantly. "What've you heard? Did Amanda have something to do with the fire?"

Darla groaned. "Not this again."

"She totally did, didn't she?" Shannon practically bounced on the bench. "Darla thinks Amanda values her own skin too much to do something so stupid, but I don't know ... If it meant getting Lire into big trouble and maybe expelled, I think she'd go for it."

"Sorry, homies. I'm not going anywhere near this one," Zach replied.

Shannon brightened, her spine going straight. "Oh, my God. I knew it."

Darla blinked before her expression folded down to a dubious scowl. "Shannon, he didn't say she did it."

"But he didn't say she didn't, either."

Darla rolled her eyes.

"You're totally hoping that she did it and gets caught, too. Don't bother denying it." Shannon pointed her fork at her roommate and then at me. "That goes for you, too, sister."

I grinned.

"Come *on*, you guys," Shannon drawled, after eating some of her pizza. "If you won't dish about the fire, you at least have to tell us about last night. When did you end up leaving? And how did you get there? Did you take your bikes? That's what Darla and I did, until we had to go off road."

I flicked my gaze to Zach's empty bench. When he didn't say anything, I shrugged. "I'm not saying it was last night ..." I shot them a knowing look. "But on the *particular* night that I got the photo, I left around twelve-forty-five. Ran part of the way. Drove some and then walked the off-road part."

"You drove?" Darla's eyes went wide. "You have a car this term?"

I shook my head. "Borrowed one."

"Cal lent you his, didn't he?" Shannon said.

"How'd you get past the border enchantment?" Darla asked. "That's why we had to go on the weekend, before curfew, like everyone else. Nobody knew how to get past it or where it is."

"I could tell you, but then I'd have to kill you," I replied.

"Come on. Help us out, here, you guys," Shannon whined. "That's the best part."

I made a zipping motion across the seam of my lips.

Darla looked disappointed, but Shannon full-on pouted, folding her arms. "Man. That's what everyone wants to know, too."

I compressed my lips even tighter. Admitting to knowing the location of the border enchantment, not to mention how we got past it, would seal our doom if Mr. Gibbs ever got wind of it.

"That's my girl," Zach whispered in my right ear, startling the crap out of me.

"Dammit, Zach!" I pressed my hand to my chest and glared at the space next to my bench. "Stop scaring the bejeezus out of me!" I shoved my hair behind my ear as several students at the nearest tables stared at me.

He laughed, the butthead. "Gonna go see if I can sweet talk Mrs. Godfrey into another brownie. You homies want anything?"

Both girls declined.

"Tiger, you good?"

"Yes," I grumbled.

"Okay. Back in a few," he called, his voice growing distant as he moved away.

"I hate it when he does that." I had to stop myself from pressing my hands to my flushed cheeks.

"Oh, my God," Shannon gushed. "He's so into you."

I jolted. "What? No. We're good friends. He just thinks it's freaking hilarious to scare the crap out of me."

"He doesn't do that to anyone else," Shannon said. "And all the pet names for you ..." She shook her head, her expression a combination of delight and envy. "It's the cutest thing ever."

Pet names? I tried not to make a face. "He has nicknames for everyone."

There was homie, bro, and dude, right off the bat. Although, those didn't seem to be exclusive nicknames. He used them interchangeably, with lots of different people. Of course, it wasn't like I took part in all his private conversations. I had little doubt, there were plenty of other girls who had cute nicknames, too.

"Not that I've ever heard," Darla said, contradicting my thought. "He calls everyone else homie, except the guys. He calls guys dude."

"Or bro," Shannon added.

"You're the only one who has a cute nickname," Darla reiterated.

"Did Cal really ask you to Homecoming?" Shannon asked.

"Where'd you hear that?" Wheeling from the change of subject, I sounded like a caffeinated chipmunk.

"From Jason," she replied. "He was teasing Ted about how you turned him down in favor of a furball."

Jeez. If Zach was the gossip king, then Shannon deserved to be his queen.

"Jason's a werefox," I said. "That's like the pot calling the caldron black."

Shannon looked puzzled and whispered, "You mean you don't know?"

"Know what?"

Forearms flanking her tray, she leaned toward me. "Cal is *covered* with hair. Like, *a lot* of hair ... like, *all over*. Remember that stupid movie *Wolfboy*, from way back?" She widened her eyes and nodded. "Yeah. Like that—full-on fur."

I wondered how she expected me to react. Did she think I'd run for the hills? "And you know this, how?" If she said she'd seen him naked, I prepared to throttle her.

"Practically everyone knows," Shannon replied. "I can't remember who told me first. A lot of the guys are in his gym class."

"Someone took a locker room photo," Darla said quietly, looking uncomfortable as she shifted in her seat.

"They *what?*"

She held up her hands as if to fend me off. "We haven't seen it. That's just what we've heard."

"From who?" I almost didn't recognize my voice. It had dropped to such a threatening level that it was almost a bear-like snarl, which wasn't too far off, since I was about ready to rip whoever took that photo limb from limb.

Darla's anxious gaze shifted in Shannon's direction.

"Lire, chill. Everyone's watching," Shannon hissed. Frowning at me, she shook her head. "I thought you knew." She leaned over the table again. "I told Zach, like two weeks ago. He said it was handled."

My hands throbbed and I realized I'd clenched them into tight fists without realizing it.

"I can't believe someone would do something so totally ... totally— God! I'm so freaking mad right now, I can't think of a word for how bad that is, how low and ... and slimy, not to mention illegal. Taking a photo of him in the locker room ..." I ground my teeth. "People are such sleezebag jerks."

"I'm guessing it was either Brad or Jason," Darla murmured.

"Zach didn't say?" I looked at each of them in turn.

"I asked, but he wouldn't tell me." Shannon slumped back to her side of the table.

After pausing a beat, Darla peered at me. "Did Ted really ask you to Homecoming?"

This again?

Taking a deep breath to calm down, I pinched the bridge of my nose before shaking my head indecisively. "Uh, yeah. I guess. During MEW, last week." I fought against ducking my head. Did she still like Ted? "But I, uh, you know, sort of let Ted think that Cal had asked me. I mean ... Ted seems like a nice guy and everything, but with Amanda in the picture ..." I made a face. "I seriously don't need that drama."

Shannon's head shot up. "So, you're not actually going to the dance with Cal?"

"I, um—" I bit my lip as heat sprang out on my cheeks and neck. "The two of us, we're ..." I shrugged. I wasn't entirely sure what Cal and I were. Friends, mostly.

"Poor Zach," Darla said solemnly, as if she'd heard Zach's dog had died in a lawnmower accident. "Does he know you're crushing on his roommate?"

"Darla, I already told you. He doesn't like me like that." With Zach due back any second, I leaned toward her and pitched my voice low. "With all the time we've spent together lately, I'd know if he did, okay? Besides, he's known about Cal for a while. If you haven't figured it out by now, Zach's got a thing about secrets and he's annoyingly good at noticing stuff." Sitting up straight, I rolled my eyes. "So, yeah, we've talked about it. Well—he's teased me about it, more like."

"Teased you about what?" Zach asked, startling all of us as he returned to his seat.

"Nothing." I glared at both girls while I prayed Zach hadn't overheard me fending off Darla's mistaken assumption. "That's the point."

"You're sounding kinda worked up over *nothing*, tiger. Just saying."

I had to stop myself from issuing an inarticulate growl. Thanks to the line of questioning, sweat trickled down my sides and my blouse probably had damp circles beneath both of my armpits. *Lovely.*

The bell rang before Zach could interrogate us, but since he and I had class together, I braced myself for his inevitable cross-examination.

"I need your help after school," he murmured, surprising me, as we strode down the breezeway toward LARTS. "We might not get done until dinnertime, so do as much of your homework in class as you can."

"Uh ... okay."

Was he trying to distract me, hoping to catch me off guard when he started in on his twenty questions, or what?

I shot a dubious look to my right where he walked invisibly at my side. "What am I helping you with?"

"I want to check out the fallen tree and Treblow's property during the day."

"What!" My voice echoed along the breezeway. Snapping my mouth shut, I made sure no one was near enough to overhear. "You want to go back there? Why?"

"Because the police will have no clue what to look for."

"And you and I do?" I struggled to keep my voice down. "I don't know the first thing about animal attacks."

"No, but you do have a gift that will tell us exactly what happened, if we go back to the spot where that guy was killed."

I gaped at him. He wanted me to touch something that would put me into the sorcerer's head as he was dying? Or, worse, to relive the animal's experience as it attacked and ate its victim?

"My pop thinks they're going to arrest Cal. We have to be ready if that happens. Not only that, but if Cal's cousins had anything to do with this attack, the Isangrim needs to know, like, *yesterday*. If word gets out that two werewolves have gone feral, whether it's true or not ..." He blew out an agitated breath. "You know what'll happen. Normals barely tolerate weres as it is. Every time there's even a hint of a were attack, some asshole in Congress proposes tagging and bagging and reopening the Tracts."

I shivered. The Alaskan Tracts, a wide swath of inhospitable land in central Alaska, was where the Fed interned the country's registered weres until the paranormal identification program was overturned by the Supreme Court.

Wringing my hands, I absently rubbed my thumbs. Lunch hadn't done me any favors. My stomach clenched around what little I'd eaten of my grilled cheese, making me feel ill.

"You know what I mean," he said. "You have the tattoos, there, on your thumbs, right? Or did you have them removed?"

I shoved my hands into my pants pockets to stop my tell-tale fidgeting. "Since I wear gloves anyway, I didn't see the point."

Never mind that I'd heard laser tattoo removal hurt like crazy.

"So, you get what I'm saying," he said impatiently.

Magic users and psychics had never been forced into internment camps, unlike the shifters, but we were similarly registered and tracked before the practice was declared unconstitutional. The unlucky ones, like telepaths and clairvoyants, were tattooed, to make it impossible to hide our gifts from the paranoid public.

"Yes. I get it. I'm not an idiot." I pressed my lips together. "But using my power for something like this isn't as easy as you make it sound. This last summer, I face-planted when I got a mind full of a Civil War soldier's memories. I was unconscious for more than an hour and woke up with a gigantic fat lip. It scared the crap out of Ben, the shop owner I told you about, remember?"

"Yes. You also told me your summer job helped, that it made you stronger."

"True, but that doesn't mean I won't lose it, especially if the memories are bad." I grimaced at the thought of last night's discovery. "Zach, you saw the body. What you're asking me to do is *guaranteed* to be horrible. Processing the memories of a murderer or a victim, on top of handling my own response to reliving it—" I huffed, shaking my head. "My mind can only handle so much until it shuts down. When that happens, there's nothing I can do about it. Ninety-nine percent of the time, I don't know I'm going to overload until it's too late. And when I do overload, there's no telling how long I'll be out. I've woken up in Swedish Medical's psi-ward twice in the last five years. Both times, I'd been unconscious for more than three days."

"All right. I hear you," he said, sounding downright gloomy. "Will you at least come with me? You might spot something that I don't. I promise I won't give you a hard time if you decide not to touch anything."

The starting bell rang, jolting me.

Even though I knew I'd end up touching something nasty at the murder site, I gave in. How could I refuse? Zach had done so much for me. Besides, who was I kidding? This was Cal we were talking about. When it came down to it, I'd do anything in my power to help him.

"Fine." I resumed my stride to the building's double doors, hoping Zach would follow. "This has disaster written all over it, though. Don't say I didn't warn you."

"I won't," he said, sounding relieved. "And thanks."

The fact that he didn't respond with a clever comeback, told me how worried he was.

After rushing through the day's reading and then writing a half-assed answer to our assigned essay question, I pulled out my math notebook and finished all my homework before the bell rang. I hoped I'd have time to improve my essay, later, after we got back from our ill-advised caper.

As we packed up, Professor Trapp wandered over. "It was awfully quiet in here, today." He mostly eyed me, since I was the only one visible. "You both doing okay?"

"Yep," Zach and I answered at once.

Laughing, I stood and hefted my backpack over my shoulder. "Trying to get as much done as we can." I turned to where Zach had been sitting. "Hey, Zach? Where'd you want to meet for our run? Let's do the school loop, today. I'm getting sick of the track."

"Sure. That'll work out great. Cal wants us to pick up his car from the shop since it's ready. We'll jog there and drive back. Meet me at the office, so we can get permission to go off campus."

"Okay. I guess we could do that."

"Great," he replied. "Later, Professor."

"See you tomorrow, Zach."

"So, you like to run?" Professor Trapp asked as I lugged my backpack to his desk.

"Not sure if 'like' is the right word," I replied honestly, dropping my load next to his chair and sitting down. "I feel better when I do it, though, so I've stuck with it."

"You ever thought about going out for track and field?"

"Sports and I have never gotten along. Anyway, I'm not that good. I just do it for the exercise." *And to pound out my frustrations.*

"You run every day?"

"When it's nice out. During the winter, it gets harder." I shot him a sour look. "Maybe you could tell Mr. Simmons that one treadmill, a rowing machine, and some puny free weights doesn't cut it when it's raining and there are fifty girls fighting for time on them."

He chuckled. "I'll be sure to pass that on. But instead of duking it out for the treadmill, why not consider track? Zach and Caleb, too. Cross country has already started, but indoor track doesn't start until November."

"Not really my thing." I forced myself to smile, regretting that I'd used the jogging gambit to get my plan straight with Zach. "But I'll pass it along to the guys."

"All right. I'll put away my coach hat," he grumbled amiably. "But if you change your mind, let me know. Coach Rickett talked me into being her assistant coach."

I nodded, grateful, for once, to start working on the French grammar packet he slid in front of me.

After class, I hustled back to my room, pondering my clothing options for this afternoon's covert outing. I figured I could wear last night's outfit without looking too ridiculous. After all, it wasn't uncommon to see runners wearing exercise tights beneath their shorts, especially on a day like today, which had dawned clear with a crispness in the air that hinted of the coming fall weather.

My photography backpack, however, was a different story. I had no desire to repeat last night's misery, running with that dead weight bouncing on my back. I donned my fanny pack, instead. With Red taking much of the space, though, I scarcely had room for my license and cell phone.

As Red and I discussed the likelihood that I'd read something at the murder scene, I remembered to wedge Cal's bulky key ring between his feet. I considered removing his car key from the fob and leaving the bulk of it behind, but with my luck, I'd end up losing the darn thing. Besides, you never knew when that multi-tool of his might come in handy.

Without Cal around, meeting Zach was more complicated than usual. After lingering outside for a moment, I ventured into the main office to see if he'd beaten me to the sign-out sheet.

"There she is," I heard Zach say when I approached the counter.

Owen extended one of the office's silly flower pens my way. This one had a giant plastic daisy duct taped to the end. As he handed it to me, the cuff of his long sleeve oxford pulled back to reveal a killer woven bracelet that reminded me of his belt. It was on my mind to ask where he'd gotten it when he interrupted my thoughts.

"I was just telling Zach that even though you guys are meeting his dad for dinner, Mr. Gibbs expects you both to be back before curfew. Be sure you leave enough time to sign in, okay? I don't want you guys to get into trouble."

My mouth nearly fell open. *Dinner with Papa Carter, the Hidden's head honcho?*

I mumbled a feeble acknowledgment. My handwriting was a mess. I could only hope neither of them noticed my trembling.

I left the pen atop the clipboard and barely remembered to say thank you to Owen.

"You set the pace," Zach told me, once we landed on the sidewalk out front. "I'll be on your right. Leave room for me."

I took off, aiming toward the front of the school.

"I'm not exactly dressed for dinner," I finally ground out when we'd rounded the main office building. It took most of my willpower to avoid strangling him.

"So that's what has your panties in a twist." He laughed at my murderous expression. "Calm down. Pop told Gibbs we were going to meet for dinner so we'd have more time off-campus."

My gait faltered as I cut a path through the school's brick paved cul-de-sac. I hadn't realized how tensely I'd been holding my shoulders until I found myself deflating at Zach's admission.

"Besides, if we do meet up with him, it'll be in his limo, not a restaurant," he informed me. "Pop's totally old school. He travels with his chef. He doesn't do restaurants."

"What do you mean 'old school?'" Did his dad worry about being poisoned or something? Did he have food testers too, like some medieval monarch?

"Haven't you heard that saying before? It means — "

"I know what the saying means," I interrupted, slowing my pace to a leisurely jog so we could talk more easily. "Old fashioned or traditional. So why doesn't he eat at restaurants? Why is that old school?"

"The less interaction we have with the public, the less we draw attention to ourselves and the less normals know about us. Pop thinks it's important to keep it that way, you know, for the safety of the family." He bit out that last part.

I sent an arch look his way. "And you think that's overkill, nowadays?"

"Yes." He paused and then sighed. "Well, sort of. I mean ... I know we need to be careful. But it's not like I'm going to post our address on the internet or something. Me and my cousins ... we want to be a part of the frickin' world, right? We want to do the stuff that everyone else gets to do. But he doesn't get it. He won't listen."

"He? You mean your dad?"

"Yes." He bit out the word so harshly it had teeth marks.

"And I thought *I* had it bad," I said after several strides. I threw him a sympathetic smile. "Normals get weird around me and treat me like I have an infectious disease, but at least I can mostly do the stuff I want to do without anyone grabbing the pitchforks or throwing bricks through my windows."

"That's exactly what I mean. I'm not going to be lynched for being invisible. Mobs aren't going to follow me home. But he refuses to listen." Between his strenuous breaths, he deepened his voice to a theatrical baritone. "'This isn't a game, Zachary. The sooner you realize that, the better. You put all of us in danger with your reckless behavior. Entire families have gone missing.'"

He huffed his annoyance. "That was ages ago, like, during the cold war and stuff. Besides, if only family knows about us, how would anyone figure out if we all went missing. Seems to me, it's worse to remain completely hidden."

"Yeah. I guess so ..." I thought about everything I'd heard about the Hidden and the type of work they did — spying for super powerful organizations and stuff. "But, uh, doesn't that depend on who you guys work for and the secrets you know?" I glanced inquisitively to my right where I knew he kept pace with me. "Maybe there's a reason your dad is being super careful."

"Please tell me you don't think we're all assassins and government spies." Clearly, he'd heard this accusation one too many times.

When I didn't immediately answer, he sneered, "You shouldn't believe everything you hear, princess."

Chastised, I almost stumbled and over-corrected too far to my left. I swerved back on course, holding steady where I'd placed an imaginary bike lane at the right edge of the school's private road. Reluctant to slow to a walk, I focused on taking steady breaths, which was a good thing since it forced me to consider his comment instead of getting all heated up about it.

"In a way, what you're talking about is kind of an issue for both of us." Even though I knew there was nothing to see, I couldn't stop myself from glancing in his direction. "Our magic is so rare that people end up speculating and assuming the worst. Red said something about that, the other day. He said that when it comes to magic, it's rarity, not familiarity, that breeds contempt. I don't know about you, but for me, that's definitely true. Most people don't know any clairvoyants, so they believe the worst things they've been told by Hollywood or in books or online. Most of the time, what they *know*"—I made air quotes—"is either overblown or completely wrong." I shook my head. "You'd think the magic community would be different, but they're not. And I guess I'm not, either, since—you're right—I assumed that the Hidden was mainly into spying and stuff because that's what I've always heard."

As the slap of our shoes on the asphalt echoed in my ears for a full minute without his reply, I began racking my brain, trying to figure out what I'd said that might have pissed him off. I was about to apologize for making him mad when his clipped voice startled me.

"What you've heard—" He let out a disgruntled sigh and then snapped, "Some of it's not totally wrong, okay? That's part of the problem."

Again, the silence stretched between us, but I was reluctant to break it since he was notably testy about the subject. I tried to think of something else to say. Something not about the Hidden and spying, but all I could seem to dwell on was the fact that people in his family had gone missing.

Had they been murdered to silence them? Or had they been kidnapped?

One of the more disturbing rumors I'd heard was that the KGB had abducted dozens of occultums to be bred like cats for their spy program. Of course, it wasn't always the Russians. Depending on who you talked to, it was the Chinese or the Iranians or the North Koreans. Some people said our own government had done it and was still doing it—whisking away baby occultums to raise them in top secret facilities, brainwashing them into doing their bidding without question. To me, that sounded ridiculously over the top, but given how often Congress discussed reinstating their registration program, sometimes I wondered.

Again, it occurred to me that maybe Zach's dad wasn't wrong to worry.

"Well ... whatever." I sniffed. "I base my opinions on a person's actions and what they say, and you and Cal have been nothing but totally cool to me. You were friends with me even though everyone told you I was a blackmailer. I'll never forget that. So ... yeah. There's no way in hell I wouldn't notice if you suddenly went missing. That can't be a bad thing, right?"

He grunted, but it sounded more pleased than angry. "Thanks. By the way, you know that being friends with you isn't a hardship. You get that, right? Anyone who thinks otherwise is a dumbass."

I marveled at how I lucky I'd gotten, picking their table to sit at on our first day of school. "Back atcha, wonder boy."

"Wonder boy? This is punishment for pushing you down a well in a previous life, isn't it?"

I snickered. "You prefer Mr. McSneaky Pants?"

He groaned. "That's almost as bad, but anything's better than *wonder boy*. You got that from a manga, didn't you?"

"No." If I told him I'd gotten it from a Disney movie, he'd never stop harping about it. "But if it makes you feel any better—to me, you'll always be TDM."

"What the hell is tee dee—? Oh. Wait. Don't tell me. Um ..." He drew out the sound while considering it. "I know—totally damned macho. No? Okay. How about ... tremendously ... darn ... muscular? Or, no. Hold on, I've got it. Talented ... dominant ... master!" He deepened his voice. "I knew it. You want me to be your master. Admit it."

Making gagging sounds, I puffed out my cheeks like I was about to vomit. "Now I totally regret telling you anything."

"What? Are you serious with that?" He tsked at me. "Come on, princess. When will you learn? BFFs don't keep secrets."

"That's a rule, huh?" I tried to hide my smile. We were BFFs? If we weren't jogging, I might have hugged him.

"Duh."

I laughed. "Fine. Since you can't stand not knowing ... TDM—tall, dark, and magnificent."

He blew out a raspberry. "No shit, Sherlock. Everyone knows that. With mad detecting skills like those, you'll have us swimming in clues in no time."

"Yeah." My stomach constricted at the reminder. "For sure."

If my nervous response grated on his ears as much as it did mine, he pretended not to notice.

Twenty minutes later, we rescued Cal's Civic from the deserted end of the Les Schwab parking lot. As I pulled onto the highway, I sternly told my butterflies to take five. We had permission to be out and about. There was no reason to be nervous ... right?

Right.

Except for the part where we'd be trespassing on private property and potentially tramping all over a murder scene.

I avoided thinking about that part.

CHAPTER 16

Here goes nothing

I pulled Cal's car into the produce stand's empty dirt lot and eased to a stop where we parked last night.

"*Déjà vu,*" I said, returning Cal's key ring to my fanny pack and throwing open my door. I groaned as I got out. "Except this time, my legs feel like overused rubber bands."

"You're a machine."

"I wish I felt like one."

He laughed. "Come on. Gimme your hand. I'm tired, too. We'll go easy."

Zach's gloved hand was warm in mine as we crossed the two-lane highway, invisible to the flock of sparrows that chortled from the power lines overhead. As we navigated the gravel slope leading down to Treblow's property, an eighteen-wheeler rumbled past, its wind wake sluicing through the dirt and spindly shrubs on the side of the road, kicking dust into our eyes. The smell of diesel invaded my nose and coated the back of my throat.

Coughing, I followed Zach over the split rail fence where it had partially collapsed, retracing last night's steps. As we dodged the cracked furrows and lumps of vegetation, I wondered how many years of disuse it took for a farm to become as overgrown as this one. If the rusted-out forties-vintage pickup truck we found abandoned in the middle of this clod-ridden field was anything to go by, I guessed several decades, at least.

Years of obvious neglect aside, Treblow's property had a certain rustic charm. Even the dilapidated truck would have made a stunning photograph with its original paint color lost to rust, its bonnet, headlights, and tires missing, and golden-yellow grass obscuring its apron. I couldn't help but wonder what memories I'd glean if I touched its steering wheel.

Squinting at the brightness of the afternoon sun, I gazed up at the clear sky and promptly tripped over an exposed tree root. Stumbling, I would have gone down on my knees if Zach hadn't tightened his grip on my hand and hauled me upright.

"I think I tripped on that, last night, too," I grumbled. "Stupid tree root."

As we rounded the nearby row of closely spaced trees, Sorcerer Treblow's small farmhouse slid into view. Interestingly, it looked nothing like the looming structure I remembered from last night. The house wasn't sinister in the least, nor was it as run down as the rest of his property. It was, in a word, charming, boasting everything someone might expect to see in a traditional farmhouse — wrap around porch, dormers, and cheery yellow paint.

The landscaping that surrounded his house was lush and well-kept, with rosebushes and purple lobelia bordering the driveway, a weeping crabapple at the corner of the flagstone walk, and trimmed boxwoods lining the front porch. The only things that marred the quaint farmhouse's scenic perfection were the Coventry County Sheriff cars parked along the circular front drive.

I scanned the area to the left of the house, in the direction of the compound, and spotted the fallen tree, at least three football-field-lengths away. Last night, the tree and house hadn't seemed so far apart — probably because Zach had whisked me off the fallen trunk using his magic for part of the distance and I'd walked the rest in a shocked stupor after finding the body.

Speaking of which ... even from here, it wasn't hard to figure out where the victim had been discovered. Yellow 'DO NOT CROSS' tape cordoned off a rectangular area about halfway between the house and the fallen tree. I breathed a sigh of relief when I didn't see a blanket-draped lump.

Two figures moved in the distance, detectives looking for evidence, most likely.

As we neared the house, a slammed car door drew my attention to a woman marching up the driveway as though her deputy sheriff's uniform granted her super powers and darned if she wasn't going to use them. Her straight brown hair had been pulled into a tight ponytail, emphasizing her broad forehead and blade-straight eyebrows.

Near the porch, another uniformed deputy, this one a clean-shaven, muscular man with close-cropped black hair and a complexion a few shades lighter, stood with his thumbs hooked over his utility belt, his eyes focused on his approaching colleague.

"Come on," Zach said, pulling me into a jog toward the porch.

The increased shimmery aspect of the air around us told me that Zach was expending more of his magic to keep us fully hidden.

" — sticking together like you'd expect," the female deputy said as we drew near enough to overhear their conversation. She folded her arms and rocked back on her heels. "The guards claim they made it to the smashed fence within minutes of the breach and that all their students were accounted for after they'd cordoned it off, finding none of them outside. They have video surveillance that backs up some of the timing." She arched her left eyebrow. "Coincidentally, the two cameras closest to the tree malfunctioned about ninety minutes prior to the incident."

"Imagine that."

She snorted. "Baxter interviewed their head of security and reviewed their tapes. The logs show the first camera malfunctioning at 1:33 a.m. and the next going dark five minutes later. The fence shorted out at 2:56 a.m., but without those two cameras, there's no video of the tree coming down."

"Does Baxter think the data's been doctored?"

"He says no, but we won't know for sure until the forensic analysis. Their closest functional camera shows the guards passing in their electric cart twelve minutes after the fence went down."

The male deputy scoffed. "More than enough time for that werewolf to have his morning snack."

I shot an anxious glare at Zach. Without sparing me a glance, he squeezed my hand tightly as if to say, 'Not now.'

"Sure doesn't rule it out, like they're claiming." The woman jerked her chin toward the deputy. "What's the word here?"

He shrugged. "Final survey's done. You're free to look. Higgs and Mortensen are in the field. The caretaker left the house open. He asked us to lock up and drop the key at the school when we're finished."

"He can't be a student?" Her nose wrinkled like she'd whiffed a warm dog turd.

"No. Employee. Dude gave me the creeps."

"You're not alone. I heard Dasko saying the same thing after he interviewed him, early this morning." She tipped her head toward the house. "Anyone checked inside since then?"

"Nobody while I've been on duty. You'll have to ask Higgs about anyone before that."

She nodded. "When Higgs comes around, tell him I'm inside."

"Will do."

Zach trailed behind the female deputy, pulling me along behind him, as she strode up the stairs.

Strangely, though, instead of throwing open the door and barreling into the house, she froze on the door mat, as if someone had pressed her 'OFF' switch.

I peeked around Zach's right arm. "What's she doing?"

"No idea." He skirted around to her right.

I scooted sideways, craning my neck to get a better view. "She looks stunned. And — check out her hand. She's not turning the knob."

No sooner had I said the words than she blinked rapidly several times and released her grip, her arm drifting back to her side. With a satisfied huff, she squared her shoulders and headed back down the steps. Thank God, Zach had moved us out of the way.

"Back so soon?" the male deputy asked, humor in his voice.

"Absolutely nothing of relevance in there."

The man's head jolted. "You didn't even open the door."

Her thin lips pressed together. "Go see for yourself." She folded her arms, chin stiffly inclined. "Dinner and the first round of beer is on me if you find anything." She didn't have to say, 'I dare you.'

His brows dove toward the bridge of his nose as he turned to regard the front door with narrow-eyed suspicion. Throwing her a smug look, he said, "Ruth's Chris. I like my steak medium rare," and then ambled up the steps. His arch expression said he figured this was a joke.

Zach and I watched in fascination as the guy proceeded to behave in the same manner as his female counterpart. He froze with his thick fingers wrapped around the knob, gazing down vacantly, before coming back to his senses about ten seconds later. Looking satisfied if not sheepish, he rejoined the woman on the walkway.

Zach inched us to the edge of the porch where we had a better view of the two deputies.

"Well?"

Shaking his head, he grinned. "Guess your wallet's safe. This time."

"Whatever you say, deputy." She gazed toward the shifter compound. "I'm gonna look around. You need anything?"

"No, ma'am. I'm good." He cleared his throat. "Watch out for wolf landmines. I hear he left more than a few turds out there."

"Unbelievable," she muttered as she stalked away.

I turned to Zach. "Oh, God. You were right. They're assuming Cal did it. Zach, we need to go to Mr. Simmons. We have to tell him that we were with Cal, last night, that we know there's no way he could have done it."

"Told you, didn't I?" he said, giving my hand a reassuring squeeze. "But we'll have to debate the witness stuff, later. Right now, we're here to get clues." With half an eye on the remaining deputy, he yanked me toward the front door.

I hauled back on his hand, wrenching him to a stop before he could step onto the woven coir doormat.

His pained grunt was followed by a curse. "Jesus! What — ?"

"Watch out," I snapped. It was all I could do to not shout at him. "Something spelled them. Or hexed them. Look where you're about to step." I pointed at the doormat.

"Crap." Rubbing his shoulder, he blew out a breath. "I'm an idiot. I was thinking it was the knob, but you're right. It could be the mat."

We both hunched over, inspecting the woven rectangle as though it was a bomb wired to go off if we so much as breathed on it.

"There." I pointed to the right side of the mat where a section at the upper corner had been rewoven with a slightly darker fiber. To an unassuming observer it would look innocuous, like the homeowner had repaired a section that had started to unravel.

Zach nodded. "I think the knob's spelled too. See that?"

He pointed between the knob and the door, where the rounded brass handle tapered to form the stem. There, invisible to anything but a studious examination, a thin strand of intricately braided material wrapped around the doorknob's shaft, its brassy color blending with the metal.

"How much you wanna bet that's an ubhnati enchantment?" Zach said. "And the mat's a no brainer, right? It's already woven."

"Holy pixie puke," I breathed.

He stepped back, turning his attention to the window to the right of the door. "Any bets on whether there's something like that on all the windows, too?"

Sure enough, at the bottom edge of each of the porch's four casement windows, we discovered a hair-thin braided loop, pinched beneath the window and the sill. The spell probably wouldn't activate unless we touched the window, but we kept our distance just in case.

"Gee," I drawled. "Somebody's not uptight about their privacy or anything."

"Then I guess it's a good thing we don't have to touch the windows or doors to get inside, isn't it?"

I started, jerking a half-step back. "No way. With magic like this, who knows what nastiness the guy's left inside for trespassers."

"I'm betting, not much, if any." He shook his head at my dubious expression. "I'm serious. Think about it. Even the most talented sensitive won't detect this type of woven enchantment. Most people will get hung up outside, like those deputies. I see this happen with security all the time. It's like a rule or something. Powerful magic users get overconfident. And, the more powerful they are, the cockier they get.

I bet you a million bucks that this guy's put his most effective deterrents at each entry point and, inside, he'll have a single spell guarding his highest value items."

Now who's cocky? I wanted to ask.

No doubt Zach had a ton of experience to back up his hunch, like he'd said, but I didn't care. It seemed to me that this guy Treblow, being older than the Varangian Council, was in a league of his own. No way was I going anywhere near the inside of his house, much less his high value items.

"We're not here to snoop through Treblow's stuff." I squared my chin and stared at his black form, round about where I figured his eyes were. "We're here to check the tree and where we found that dead body. But if we don't get on with it, the sun will disappear behind the hills and we won't be able to see anything, which was the whole darn point to this trip."

"You're no fun. Where's your sense of adventure?"

"I left it back at school." I tugged his hand. Thankfully, he didn't resist. "Come on. Let's get this over with."

It occurred to me that I stood a higher chance of going to the hospital by sticking to our plan. Maybe I should have let Zach pull me into the house after all.

As we trudged across the field toward the cordoned-off plot, I noticed the female deputy had beaten us there. She paced slowly, her sharp-eyed gaze focused on the ground. At that rate, she wouldn't make it outside the staked boundary for some time. Although, I couldn't imagine what she expected to find that hadn't already been tagged by one of those plastic flags that landscapers used to mark irrigation lines. From here, I could see at least a dozen brightly-colored plastic pennants fluttering listlessly in the breeze.

"I guess the yellow ones mark scat," Zach said after we veered to inspect one of the many outlying flags. He nudged the plastic rectangle with his foot, pointing at the black lettering that had been printed on the plastic. "They're all geo-tagged. If they're smart, they've collected samples for DNA testing."

I goggled at him. "They DNA test *poop*?"

"Yup."

"Wow. Do you think they're actually going to do that?"

"If they don't, I'm sure Pop will be all up in their business. A good sample could help clear Cal."

"Seriously?" Maybe I'd been worrying for nothing.

He nodded. "Even an incomplete DNA strand could tell them whether it's from a dub-dub or not and whether it came from a male or female."

I thought about the body. "They'll test the saliva samples from the bite wounds, too, won't they?"

"Yup. That's why the Rout is calling in so many favors. The Isangrim's throwing everything he can into finding Cal's cousins before the public gets wind of this."

"I'm surprised it hasn't turned into a circus already. A wolf attack, on its own, is sensational enough. A *were*wolf attack is off the freaking charts, especially one that ended up with someone getting killed. You'd think, at the very least, the local news would be here."

"That's because Pop and the Isangrim have gone to the mat," he said darkly, tugging me into resuming our trek. "There're a lot of powerful people in charge of organizations that don't want Treblow's death to make the news. The Hidden and the Rout have rallied all of them."

I could see why. A werewolf attack would give the anti-magic types exactly what they needed to spin the entire country into a major freak out. The fact that the victim wasn't a normal, like them, wouldn't matter. A registration bill would be in front of Congress faster than you could say 'abracadabra.' And it wouldn't draw the line at identifying and registering werewolves — they'd want to register anyone capable of magic or affected by magic, just to be safe. After that, it would be a matter of time before the paranoid masses started calling for segregation. I still bore the government's marks from the last go-round, so it wasn't a huge leap to think that it could happen again.

Zach pulled me into resuming our walk. "Since Deputy Do-Right is in our way, let's go check out the tree. Nobody's over there."

As we approached the fallen magnolia, it became clear that an extraordinarily powerful force had knocked it over. The massive tree, most of which now rested atop the crumpled fencing, had been snapped in two, like a twig in the hands of a cyclops with anger issues.

A jagged stump that protruded two feet above the ground was all that remained of the once stately tree.

"It's bigger around than I thought." I rolled my eyes as soon as the ill-chosen words left my mouth and wagged my finger at him. "Don't even *think* about saying it."

He snickered. "Too late."

Trying not to smirk, I gestured to the serrated surface of the four-foot-diameter stump. "Not a clean break. And it wasn't totally dead. All that spiky stuff, that's green wood, isn't it?"

"Yeah. It would take a lot to snap it off like that. But we knew that already." He shook his head. "Definitely wasn't a geo spell. Whatever happened was above ground."

I gave the undisturbed soil around the tree a glance before examining the nearby fence. "The fence is only damaged where the tree and those biggest branches fell on it. The bushes, there, are fine." I pointed to the healthy shrubs that were planted both inside and outside of the fence line. "If wind was involved, it was tightly focused, but I can't think of a narrow enough *aenai* spell with the force to snap the tree like that. Can you?"

"No. But even if there is one, a pinpoint spell like that would blow the bark clean off the trunk, like a sandblaster, and probably break all the nearby branches."

For a better view, we climbed up on the stump, using it like a step stool.

"I don't see any damage like that," he said. "Do you?"

"Not that I can see. The bark looks normal and some of the branches still have leaves on them."

"I think that rules out an air blast." He steadied me as we jumped back down to the ground. "A hydro spell could do it, but we'd have noticed water all over the tree, last night, and there wasn't any. Besides, a water blast would break branches and leave a mark on the bark, too." He huffed. "It's like an invisible hand reached out and pushed the tree over."

"A telekinetic couldn't do this. Could one?"

"It would take a few telekinetics, at least. If not more." He shrugged and gestured at the tree. "Maybe ubhnati have a way of weaving a kinetic spell of some kind. Maybe one that stores energy and releases it all at once."

"Who knows? What I don't know about ubhnati sorcerers could fill a library."

"Yeah." Zach turned toward Treblow's house. "And that library's right over there."

I snapped my wrist, jerking our linked hands. "I told you. We're not breaking into his house, so forget about it."

He echoed my words, mimicking me in a high-pitched voice, but before I could smack him, he hip checked me. "Fine. Have it your way. We won't break in." He sighed and added nonchalantly, "I'll just have to come back later."

"Zach!" I shoved him for good measure. "You will not."

He chuckled. "Fine. I'll tell you what — if we find some solid evidence on who did this thing, I won't need to break into his house, will I?"

"Gee, no pressure." I shoved him again, but it was a token effort. I returned my attention to the felled tree. "Okay. What about a strigoi? Do you think one is strong enough to snap a tree?"

"Definitely, but they don't take chunks out of their victims. And there was blood all over the place. A vamp wouldn't waste it like that."

I grimaced at the too-fresh memory. "What if this wasn't an illegal feeding gone wrong? What if they wanted to murder him and make it look like an animal kill?"

He shrugged. "I suppose a strigoi could do it. Their teeth are sharp enough and their strength is off the charts. But why bother with the tree? Why make it look like someone in the compound escaped? The strigoi have just as much to lose when news of this goes public. Plus, their saliva would be a major giveaway, so it's not as though the ploy would throw off the authorities for long."

I scowled at him. "I don't know why you thought I'd be any help figuring things out. This is useless."

"No, it isn't. Look. The deputies are on their way out."

Sure enough, in the distance, four people walked in a loose cluster toward the driveway.

Zach pulled me in the direction of the taped-off area.

As we walked, I examined the ground.

"It's strange. If Treblow knocked down the tree with a stored kinetic spell, while fighting off his attacker ... you'd think there'd be claw marks in the dirt or signs of a scuffle, but I don't see any. Do you?"

Zach slowed to a stop, turning to survey the ground around us. "No. But maybe the creature didn't catch up to him until he got over there." He motioned to the place where we'd found the body.

We resumed walking. With every reluctant step, I practically heard the drum beat of doom counting down in my ears.

By the time we slipped beneath the police tape, my jaw ached from gritting my teeth and a blossoming headache stirred behind my eyes. Any minute I'd hear Zach utter the dreaded words, the ones compelling me to touch something that would reveal, definitively, what or who had brutally killed the man we assumed was Sorcerer Treblow.

Standing on the periphery, it was easy to see where the body had been found. Even discounting the high concentration of flags at the plot's center, the excessively churned, noticeably darker earth would have been a dead giveaway.

Heh. Dead giveaway. Good one.

I pinched the bridge of my nose. My little voice really needed to shut up.

"Do you think it's safe to walk around in here?" I asked. "Should we worry about footprints?"

I wondered how long they'd leave the area cordoned off and the flags in place. Who'd be responsible for clearing them all away? The caretaker? One of the deputies? Or did they hire a cleanup crew to do it?

"The crime scene investigators finished hours ago. Besides, our prints are already in here, from last night, remember? I wouldn't be surprised if there are flags marking all of them." He pointed. "See that gray stuff? They took a plaster cast of that one."

He snickered at my bug eyes. "Relax, tiger. Until the school asks everyone to turn in their shoes, you're safe. And if they do, don't be surprised when your sneakers suddenly go missing." He nudged me. "I've got you covered, okay? You don't have to worry."

I frowned down at my favorite running shoes. As soon as we got back to school, I'd ask Zach how to destroy and dispose of them.

That's the kind of thing a criminal would do.

"What's with that face?" Zach asked.

Cheeks heating, I shook my head. "What are we looking for?"

He stepped into the field of flags, pulling me along with him. "Anything that would exonerate my brother."

The nearest flag marked an oblong divot into the packed soil that could have been gouged out by an animal. The leading edge had a few narrow grooves that might have been from claws or nails. From what I could see, more than a few of the nearby flags marked similar tracks.

"I think these red flags mark spots where an animal left a print."

"Yeah." Zach looked around. "Let's work the edge, first, and then we can move our way in."

I shrugged. "Sure."

Several feet away, the next flag marked a shallow indentation that might have been a footprint. If it was, then maybe it'd been left by the ball of someone's foot. This flag was orange.

"The orange, blue, and green flags seem to mark human footprints," Zach said several minutes later, after we'd patrolled most of the outer perimeter. "I think the orange ones are Treblow's. They're smooth, like from a leather loafer. The blue and green ones look like they mark sneaker prints and there aren't as many. Those prints have to be ours. The blue flags mark the smallest ones. Any guesses on who those belong to? Green are mine." He traced an imaginary line through the site with his index finger. "See how the green and blue flags go straight to where the body was? And then they go out that way? The orange ones are mostly through here and then they're concentrated near the middle. They don't lead out again, like the others."

With a more calculating eye, I examined the area. "There are a lot of red flags. Twice as many, at least. Do you think that's because there were two animals, or because, being on all fours, one naturally left more prints, or, maybe, because it was more active, running all around, it left a lot more divots?" Making a face, I ducked my head. "Sorry. I'm thinking out loud and not making sense."

"No. I get you. It's hard to tell. I'm trying not to jump to the conclusion that it was Cal's cousins, but ... yeah, there're a lot of red flags. Could be there were two attackers, but probably only an expert tracker would be able to tell for sure."

He gestured to our right. "If we come in from that side, there are fewer flags we'll have to avoid. It'll be easier to get closer to where the body was."

I took a steadying breath. "Okay."

After inspecting the ground, closer in, I didn't know how the investigators could tell rhyme from reason. Flags were all over the place, but, to me, it all looked like a random jumble of matted weeds and dirt clods with blood mixed in. If I'd been a casual observer with no idea a body had been found in this spot, I might have assumed the weeds and dirt had been stained from a chemical spill.

The thought didn't make me feel better, though.

I realized I'd been breathing through my mouth, out of reflex, so I cautiously tested the air. Any scent of blood (or other nasty smells) had dissipated, at least for me. A were could undoubtedly smell a million odors my own nose missed, but I considered my human shortcoming a bonus.

Even though he hadn't said a word, Zach's hope that I'd use my gift to help Cal pressed against me from all sides. My palms felt sweaty beneath my gloves.

Straightening, I turned to him. "You and I both know, I could stare down at this spot, forever, but it's not going to make a difference. Unless there's a signed confession that says, 'This paw print is mine. Sincerely, Joe Werewolf,' I'm not going to come up with anything that helps Cal—not from just *looking*."

Gazing into the distance, I blew out a resigned sigh, but it did nothing to relieve the dread that had settled into the pit of my stomach, weighing me down.

"When I touch the dirt ... be ready to catch me." I glanced at him. "You know, in case I pass out or something. Oh, and watch out where my mouth is pointing. I might throw up."

He tightened his grip on my hand. "You really think you'll pass out?"

"It's his blood, Zach. I won't just be reliving his murder. I'll get all his memories for the past four months. That's about how old red blood cells are before they're replaced. White blood cells live longer, about a year. But there aren't as many of those, so supposedly I'll only get the occasional memory that's older than four months."

He reared back. "For real?"

I nodded. "Skin cells are younger. They're about three weeks to a month old."

"Are you shitting me? That's how it works?" He shook his head. "Then why have I always heard that you get all of someone's memories when you touch them?"

"Because, sometimes, I do. It depends on what part I'm touching, for how long, and whether they're alive or dead when I touch them." I made a face. "Not that I've ever touched a dead person."

I huffed at his puzzled frown. "It's complicated, okay? If the tissue is separated from the person's life force before they die, that's where things can be different. But I've also been told to never touch a dead body, that I could overload and never wake up. Supposedly, a person's soul is a natural shield. When the soul is gone, there's nothing to interfere with me getting every last memory. I don't know how true that is, but I'm not about to test the theory."

"Hold it. *What you've been told? Supposedly?* You don't actually know any of this for sure?" His tone accused me of being a gullible idiot who believed everything I heard, no matter how stupid.

"I didn't learn this stuff from *The National Enquirer*, Zach. I trained with a master clairvoyant from the PRC. You know, the Paranormal Regulatory Commission? Maybe you've heard of them?" I sighed. "If not for my mentor, I'd be in a clean-room right now, or warehoused."

Training or not, I'd always be one bad reading away from a nervous breakdown or, worse, a permanent psi-coma. But I didn't mention that part.

I massaged my forehead, letting go of my annoyance. "Look, I've used my gift enough to know what's a good idea and what isn't." I pointed at the ground. "*This* isn't a good idea, but it's not as bad as some of the things I could read. My summer job helped, so I hope that means I won't overload, but if I do, Red will tell you what to do. He's in my fanny pack. Just don't go unzipping it or his defensive spells will do bad things to you. Hey, Red. You hearing this?"

A muffled "indeed" came from my waist.

I looked over my shoulder, even though I couldn't see the pouch at the small of my back. "Aren't you going to tell me how this is a bad idea?"

"Have the circumstances changed since our discussion in your room?" Red asked.

I shook my head, which was stupid since he couldn't see me. "If anything, things against Cal have gotten worse."

"Then you know my opinion," Red replied. "Remember your training. Use your shield to provide distance. Visualize physical walls to compartmentalize, like you were taught."

"I know." I didn't bother reminding him that if I got overwhelmed, all those things went right out the window. I took a deep breath. "Okay. Let's do this."

I started to crouch down, but Zach pulled me into an awkward hug, my shoulder hitting the center of his chest.

"Wait." He eased up on his hug to look down at me. "Are you sure about this? I swear I won't be mad if you tell me no."

"I'm not doing this because you asked me to." I stared into the blackness of his face. "I want to help Cal. And this absolutely will. It'll tell us who did it. Do you really think I could go back to school without trying?"

He bumped the crown of his forehead against mine, probably where the hood of his skin-suit protected him since my magic remained dormant. "Be careful. Cal wouldn't like it if you got hurt."

And what about you? my little voice asked, although the answer was obvious.

Zach crouched along with me as I knelt beside the large blood stain. If I fell, I hoped he'd have time to pull me away before I tumbled face-first into the middle of the flag-strewn dirt. To be safe, though, I pulled my hood over my head, now wishing I'd brought the face shield with me.

"I need both of my hands for this." I jiggled our linked hands.

He transferred his grip to my right arm. "Is this okay?"

Nodding, I tucked my hair inside my hood and then removed my left glove. "If I do pass out, keep my skin away from stuff, okay? My magic doesn't stop working just because I'm unconscious. Here. Hold on to this." I offered him my glove. "Your skin-suit should be safe as long as you're sure nobody's touched it, but try to put my glove back on if you can."

"I'm starting to think this is a majorly bad idea."

"It'll be fine," I said, exuding a confidence I didn't feel. "But if I'm wrong, whatever you do, don't call 9-1-1. Get me back to school and put me on my bed. Red will take care of calling my dad."

He scoffed. "Like I could call anyway. Cell phones don't work for me, remember?"

"Duh. I'm just saying, don't make anyone else do it. Red can use my cell if he needs to. He could call your dad for a ride if you don't want to involve the school. Otherwise, he'll call my dad who'll no doubt call Mr. Simmons, which will invite all kinds of questions that I'm sure you don't want to answer."

"Yeah, if you put it that way, Pop would be better. Only ... try not to pass out, okay?"

"Gee, you think?"

He elbowed me. "Smart ass."

I looked down at the dirt. "Well ... here goes nothing."

Hunching over my folded knees, I placed my bare hand flat on the ground, right where the soil was darkest.

The familiar burn of my magic flared from my core, forging an instantaneous connection. In a blink, psychic energy blasted into my mind, a brilliant, ethereal torrent. But I was ready for it. I wielded my psychic shield like a medieval knight, deflecting the molten stream into something that resembled a densely packed spiral galaxy, one that would drive thousands of shards into my mind if I didn't keep it spinning.

Even inside your own head, you're a nerd.

Dorky or not, those bizarre mental constructs were my only tools to keep the memories from overwhelming me.

I could do this. I needed to work fast and use my shield to distance myself as much as possible. Unfortunately, the more traumatizing the experience, the harder it was to keep my head and not get lost in the memories.

Examining the swirling disk, it wasn't hard to see where the worst experiences were located. Near the outside, the stream went from a blinding brilliance to something bleaker, like tarnished silver. But I'd worry about that later. I'd learned that it was best ease into the stream at its center and experience the memories one by one, compartmentalizing along the way.

Thinning my shield so I could experience the psychic stream, I dipped in at the spiral's center and fell headfirst into …

… sitting at my desk, I unroll the parchment and place a brass weight at each of the four corners.

Finally. The last scroll from the German emissary's lot. Thank the four winds. Translating these old high Germanic passages is mind-numbing.

Again, my gaze wanders to the shipment that arrived this morning by express courier. From across the room, I feel the prickling of their preserving enchantment, a constant reminder of their presence.

Perhaps these will be the ones — the scrolls that will release me from this interminable duty.

After sparing a moment indulging in the foolish dream, I chide myself. Haven't you learned? This is your cursed life — sworn to uphold a fruitless search for an obsessed king.

With a sigh, I turn my wandering attention back to the parchment …

I was inside Sindre Treblow's mind. The blood on the ground was his. As I worked my way through his memories, one faded into the next. So far, the guy had the most boring life imaginable. Day after day, hour after hour, the ceaseless reading, translating, and searching ran together, until …

… I shift in my seat and curse.

Damn the mage to hell! His writing is atrocious. If only this godforsaken scroll had been crafted by a skilled scribe instead of some arthritic dolt! Maybe then I'd be deciphering it in a timely manner instead of this snail's pace.

I rub my eyes.

This is the one. I know it. The references to ingressus and sidhe in the same passage? It won't be long, now.

Tír na hÓige — how I long to return!

Midsummer's Eve is nearly upon me, but I dare not risk even a brief visit, especially when I am so close to a discovery. Besides, leaving my library unprotected is sure to invite trespassers. There are several on the Council who have grown too curious about the direction of my studies, and I am sure that my apprentice is their spy.

But if I'm correct, soon I'll have the knowledge I promised my king. With the ability to come and go as I please, I'll be able to move my library and my unremitting interment on Earth will be at an end.

I resolve to finish this scroll by day's end and return my focus to the obscure letters beneath my magnifying glass.

Treblow's memories sped through my mind, more reading, more translating, until they blurred and I no longer knew day from night, week from week. I knew the stream careened from my control, but I could do little about it. I'd lost track of my constructs. I had no tools, no walls to keep them contained. The sheer number of memories, dull as they were, overwhelmed me. Before I knew it, I stood in familiar territory ...

I step off my front porch, peering into the darkness at the lone figure near the school's fence. A young woman posing for photos? Damnation! How did she elude my wards until now, halfway across my property?

Foolish girl, here because of that inane school dare. What possessed me to allow it to go on for so long?

Because you remembered what it was like to be a child and deemed it a harmless lark.

As it would be —if not for the wolves.

Curse it! I'll not have her death on my conscience. Besides, the scrutiny of a police investigation would be intolerable.

The ignorant child has no idea of the dangers that lurk in the shadows. But I only have myself to blame. I should have dealt with those wolves weeks ago.

If only that latest scroll had described the gateway magic in more detail! All this would be moot. I'd be in my beloved Tír na hÓige, along with my renowned library, instead of merely shoving my belongings sideways.

This side-travel spell is related, though. I know it!

Stowing my frustrations, I tighten my vest and mark my defensive knots. As I walk, I slide my fingers along the desired leather plait, my spells tingling against my skin.

'Ontígan.' I invest the thought with my will.

The leather knot unravels beneath my fingers, releasing the spell. Shadow engulfs me, but it may be for naught. As I scan the distance, I no longer see or sense the girl.

A shadowmancer?

Perhaps. Although, only a master sorcerer could circumvent both my perimeter wards and encroachment enchantments.

A spark from my ward shoots through me, and I catch sight of the girl as I draw closer to the magnolia. She has reappeared, now, in the tree, on a branch that overhangs the school's property. I watch as she scrabbles down a rope ladder beyond the reach of my enchantments. When she nears the ground, I hear a masculine voice say, "Almost there," just before she disappears.

An accomplice —one who can veil her from view! This must be how they evaded my perimeter ward.

Interesting.

No doubt her partner's veil is enough to hide the two of them from the wolves, too.

I turn away and head toward my house. My latest scroll beckons me home, but after considering the full moon, I stop.

My scroll can wait. It would be wiser to pursue the wolves. They've been running roughshod over my property for far too long. My apprentice is right, even if he is *the Council's spy. The wolves need to be trapped or eliminated. Why they've chosen my property to frequent, I cannot fathom. I have no livestock. Perhaps the scents emanating from the school's compound draws them here.*

As if called by my thoughts, my wards alert me to an incursion on the far side of my property —two trespassers, not far from my apprentice's cottage. I feel my underling's presence, too, trailing in their wake, maintaining a safe distance. I've no need for his help but will make allowances.

I monitor my wards as these intruders, followed by my apprentice, move slowly and erratically through my property. After reaching the southern edge, though, their pace increases as they turn to head in my direction.

Have they scented the girl and her companion?

Well then. It seems I must do little more than wait. The wolves will come to me.

I drop my shadow camouflage and smile as I run my fingers over my vest. I unhook the plaits I want and lay them on the ground, forming a triangle with me at its center. The defensive spells are purely cautionary. I don't plan on either of them getting close enough to invoke such explosive spells, but I've learned to be cautious, especially when dealing with predators.

Now, for the trap ... A snaring vine will do nicely. I finger the knot. This field of desiccated weeds is perfect. Dead will always seek the living.

I wait, eyeing the direction where I feel them coming. They're running now, and my apprentice is struggling to keep up. I shake my head. Apparently, he still hasn't mastered knotting the wind-walking spell.

Several minutes pass before I sight my trespassers. They emerge from the line of trees to the south—Canis lupus occidentalis—*two northwestern wolves. These both have melanistic coats, making them much darker than the normal gray and white. Unusual to see a pack of two. Were they ostracized because of their anomalous coloring?*

Fortunate that I elected to use a trap. It would be a shame to harm them.

I know the moment they spot me. They stop, noses working to sniff the air, and when they resume their approach, their stance is slow and low to the ground. Eyes focused on me, they separate, one staying on its present course, the other stalking to the left.

As they advance on my position, I do my best to affect helplessness.

Easy, now ... a little closer.

Almost there ...

At twenty feet, they're in range. I focus my will on the knot between my thumb and index finger.

'Ontígan.'

As the spell's potential swells inside my core, I crouch and press the flat of my hand to the ground. I invest the enchantment with direction and purpose, willing its power into the soil.

Immediately, the ground is a blur of movement, and the crackling sound of dead foliage echoes through the night's silence.

Excellent.

Before I can stand, the earsplitting report of my two stored kinetic spells rends the air, nearly knocking me over. A sharp crack, followed by an earth-shuddering crash and sounds of twisting metal, reverberates behind me.

Dust is everywhere. Coughing, I pull the collar of my shirt over my nose and mouth and stand up. I turn to find the magnolia felled, its thick trunk now laying across the school's crushed fence. At the base of its jagged stump, movement draws my eye to one of the wolves. I watch as it rolls to its feet and shakes itself as if rising from a light slumber.

Impossible!

My spell unleashed three months of stored kinetic energy. No normal creature could survive such an impact.

Werewolves! They must be.

Except ... how is this possible? There hasn't been a feral lycanthrope for decades — not since the packs united behind the Isangrim and the Sköll Concord.

Nevertheless, the proof of it stares me in the face. The werewolf's intelligence is as unmistakable as its menace.

I must get word to the Isangrim. Now. The longer these two remain feral, the harder it will be to rehabilitate them. God help us if they kill anyone.

I find the desired spell on my vest. 'Ontígan.'

As the werewolf near the stump takes on a threatening stance, a twig snaps behind me.

My cloaking spell's potential erupts in my core, none too soon. I allow it to envelop me and bound toward my house, secure in the knowledge that my chosen path is hidden from the two predators.

In my wake, the wolves snarl at my sudden disappearance.

Searching my vest, I easily find the spell that will propel me home the quickest.

'Ontígan.'

The knot unravels beneath my fingers, unleashing my stored windwalking spell, which I channel with practiced ease. Gusts of air blossom beneath my feet, driving me forward far faster than I can naturally run. One of the werewolves issues a howl.

Halfway to my house, with the safety of my darkened porch in view, the air beneath my feet unexpectedly disintegrates. My right ankle twists as I strike ground instead of the gout of air I'd expected. Helpless to stop it, I fall to the ground and slide painfully across the dirt. My hands, knees, and left hip pulse with the sharp stinging of abraded flesh and the deep ache of what are sure to be bruises.

I roll to my back, but before I can struggle upright, a heavy weight plows into my chest, hurling me back into the dirt. My head strikes the ground and dark spots cloud my vision. Instinctively, I thrust my hands out to protect myself and encounter coarse fur.

The heat of indignant anger roars through me.

'Enough! I am Archmage Treblow, not some bumbling neophyte!'

I focus my will on the knot at my wrist.

'Ontígan.'

The spell coils inside of me and I direct it at the werewolf.

I focus my will upon the creature and think, 'Release me.'

Instead, the creature snarls louder as it scrabbles in the dirt for better purchase.

Ah! Now, I understand.

Lurking to my left is my apprentice. Not just a spy, after all. And, at his side, his other servant, held in reserve.

The werewolf won't answer my command because it is under my traitorous underling's control!

So, this is what it comes to.

I have no choice. I invoke the spell I hammered long ago into the metal knot around my middle finger.

'Ontígan.'

I feel the ring disintegrate as the spell slithers from my core into the raving beast. I lock my elbows and stare into the snarling wolf's murderous eyes. I steel myself for the inevitable guilt that ever accompanies such a ruinous incantation. Soon its eyes will dull as its blood freezes in its veins and life will leave its body, never to return.

My arms tremble with the strain of keeping the wild, snapping wolf from the flesh at my neck. Dread coils in my gut as another realization takes hold.

The spell isn't working!

But that can't be!

My hands slip down the creature's taut, muscular neck, and I encounter the reason — a woven collar radiating a singularly abhorrent form of magic.

My insides recoil at the contact.

Blasphemy!

If only ... I'd sensed it ... earlier.

Too late ...

Intense pressure and excruciating pain rips through me as the wolf's teeth sink into my throat. Warmth bathes my neck and chest as I struggle, flailing helplessly for the breath that cannot come.

The werewolf's snarling follows me as I am sucked into the void.

CHAPTER 17

Never thought I'd see you here

I'D no idea how long the deep voice had been rumbling at the tender edges of my awareness before I noticed. I was too relaxed, too warm and loose, to bother piecing the words together. I floated contentedly in my detached darkness. Unfortunately, once awareness had breached my cozy retreat, there was no going back. It continued to pluck at my cocoon's outer fringes, like a mouse nibbling at holes in an old blanket.

As I came back to my senses, I figured out one thing almost immediately. I was sitting on Zach's lap, curled against his body, his arms holding me close. This explained why his voice sounded so deep. My right ear was pressed tight to his chest.

I must have fallen asleep in Zach and Cal's room. But if that was the case, why did I feel so ... unsettled? And why was I wearing my skin-suit's hood? I could feel it compressing my hair and pinning my ears to my scalp.

Duh, maybe because you're sprawled all over Zach.

Somehow, I knew that wasn't it. There was absolutely nothing lovey-dovey about the way Zach held me. No. Even groggy as I was, I knew something else was wrong, and my inner alarm bells were loud enough that I continued to feign sleep until I could sort it out.

"Are you sure we shouldn't call 9-1-1 instead?" someone asked — someone *not* Cal.

Oddly, the voice settled over me like a message from the Grim Reaper, and I found myself suppressing the urge to run for the hills instead of sticking around to play possum.

Zach is here. Calm down and think!

If we were sitting in Zach's room, why would this guy want to call 9-1-1? And why did his voice activate my creep-o-meter? He sounded familiar, but with my brain feeling fuzzier than a baby chinchilla, I couldn't dredge up the memory. Maybe he was someone from Zach and Cal's floor. Had we been watching movies too loudly in their room? If that was the case, calling 9-1-1 seemed a tad extreme.

I briefly opened my eyes to the barest of slits, but I couldn't see anything besides the black silhouette of Zach's body and a thin slice of generic white ceiling.

"I'm sure," Zach said, his chest rumbling beneath my ear. "She told me that if this ever happened I should take her back to her dorm room and then have — um, you know, someone call her dad. I think they only take her to the hospital if she's unconscious for more than a few hours."

Crap. That meant I hadn't fallen asleep. I'd passed out. Clearly, I'd touched something that had thrown me for a loop.

Were we in my dorm room, then?

No. That didn't make any sense. Zach wouldn't invite a stranger into my room.

I wanted to smack sense into myself. Why did my brain have to take so long restarting whenever I overloaded?

"I hope you're sure on that and not blowing smoke up my ass," the familiar voice said. "Because I'll get into a lot of trouble for helping you if you're wrong. You know?"

"I'm not wrong. And I wouldn't lie. She's my best friend."

"I know — having dinner, later, with you and your dad — I remember. And I wouldn't have thought twice, except your story is fishier than last week's clam chowder."

I'm having dinner, later, with Zach's dad?

In a startling flash, I remembered meeting up with Zach at the front office before our off-campus run.

That's why this guy's voice sounded familiar. It was Owen from the front desk. I remembered, now. The run had been an excuse to go to Sorcerer Treblow's property to look for clues.

Treblow . . .

The name. That was all it took. In an instant, I went from oblivious to overwhelmed as Treblow's memories crashed through my subconscious defenses and rushed into my mind from where they'd been locked away by my gift. It was all I could do to keep my body relaxed.

Zach snorted. "Dunno what's fishy about it. Lire wanted to check out the compound for that stupid dare. She heard that tree was the only way inside."

As I struggled to make sense of all the foreign memories clouding my mind, it took me a tick or two to realize that Zach had just lied. Did that mean he suspected Owen? Or was he making sure we didn't get into trouble in case Owen told Mr. Gibbs?

"And she touched it to see why it had fallen over," Owen parroted. "I heard you the first time. I might have believed you if the guy who lives here hadn't been attacked and killed by a wolf last night."

Gone was the image of Owen, the front office admin. Now, I saw him for what he truly was: Sorcerer Treblow's treacherous apprentice. This was why his voice had me on edge. He was a murderer. He'd killed Treblow by ordering those werewolves to attack him. At least, that's what Treblow had realized at the end. And I'd bet any amount of money that the two werewolves were Cal's missing cousins.

Zach blew out a breath. "Okay, fine. We were curious about the crime scene, too. Two birds, one stone, you know? I mean, can you blame us? The whole school is buzzing about it."

"And I'm sure the fact that your brother's been arrested for it has nothing *at all* to do with why you're here."

Zach's body went rigid. "Arrested? They arrested Cal? Are you sure?"

"I overheard Gibbs talking about it when the cops dropped off the keys. You really didn't know?"

"No." Zach's mumbled reply was barely above a whisper.

Oh, Zach. I wanted to hug him tight and tell him not to worry. I knew who the killer was! Instead, I could only fume in silence as Owen kept up his sleazy charade.

"Christ." He blew out a loud breath. "Sorry, man. I thought you did. I figured that's why you and Lire were out here, why she was unconscious. I assumed it was because she'd tried to get a line on who really did it."

I froze.

Why you're here ...

Out here ...

My stomach bottomed out as the words registered. *Oh, shit!* We weren't safe in Zach and Cal's room, like I'd stupidly imagined, nor anywhere else at school.

We were in serious trouble, because 'out here' could only mean one thing. We were inside Sorcerer Treblow's house.

"Maybe she did. Maybe that's why she's been out of it for longer than she thought." Zach's excited voice rang out with hope. "That's why I really want to get back. I need to get her to her room and call her dad. Maybe he knows some way to wake her up quicker. Look — I swear I won't tell anyone that you gave us a ride back to campus, okay? What do you say?"

I was half-tempted to whisper a dire warning in Zach's ear, but I quickly decided against it. If Owen got wind that Zach or I knew he was the murderer ...

No. It was safer to wait. If Zach tried to sneak us out of here, now, we could end up triggering God knew how many magic snares and the jig would be up. Owen wasn't stupid. We needed to tread carefully. Once we got outside, once I knew for sure that we were clear of any uhbnati booby traps, I'd tell Zach to make us disappear and *run.*

"Okay, sure. But listen, I have a crazy idea." I heard his footsteps as he moved closer. "Why don't we wait a little longer before going back? You said she didn't think she'd be out for very long, right? When she wakes up, maybe she'll want to try touching the place where they found the body. She could end the whole investigation, right there, and get your brother out of jail. I'll drive you straight to the main office. We'll just leave out the part where I let you in here to wait."

No, no. Tell him no!

"Um, well … that's the thing," Zach said sheepishly. "We don't have to wait. She already touched the place you're talking about."

Crap! Not that!

"*Dude*. Seriously? Why didn't you say so? Okay, then. Let's get going."

Shit. Shit! What should I do?

I had no offensive magic. Heck, I didn't even possess any *defensive* magic. I didn't have a weapon. What could I possibly do to disable an ubhnati? Because that's what Owen was. That's why he wore those unusual woven leather items. Those were his stored spells. And the guy had skill because he'd killed Sorcerer Treblow — his own master! A sorcerer who was almost a thousand years old!

If I suddenly launched myself at Owen, trying to knock him senseless, then he'd know for sure that I'd uncovered his secret. And I didn't need Nancy Drew to tell me what a murdering apprentice would do once he figured that out.

I nearly cringed as I remembered the werewolf taking a bite out of my neck.

No — not *mine* … Treblow's. He'd died after trying spell after powerful spell to fend off the werewolf and every single one had failed. The kinetic spell that ultimately knocked down the tree had merely delayed their attack.

Those unstoppable werewolves were somewhere, maybe in this house, lying in wait. And they were under Owen's control.

There was nothing I could do to fend off that kind of magic, so I played dead and prayed that Zach and I would get a better chance to escape, soon.

Zach slipped his arm beneath my bent knees and then grunted as he hefted me higher up in his lap, jolting my body against his torso.

"You need help up?" Owen asked.

"Yeah. Since you have those gloves on, that'd be great," Zach said, sounding embarrassed. "Getting up is the hard part."

"They're not psi-free, though."

"It's fine. I'll make sure you don't touch her skin." My body shifted suddenly as Zach lurched forward, but I managed to stay limp. "Here. Yeah. That's my elbow. If you could reach around for—" Zach's sentence ended with an *oof*, as though he'd been sucker punched.

"You will not speak unless I ask you a question," Owen ordered, sounding anything but friendly. "Now, stand up."

My unease catapulted to DEFCON 1.

Again, my body shifted in Zach's arms, but after a brief jolt or two, everything settled into eerie stillness. I knew Zach must be standing since I no longer felt the warmth and support of his legs beneath me. He held me tight in his arms, silent and seemingly frozen. Only the sound of his fast beating heart beneath my ear told me he hadn't been turned to stone.

"Now then. Let's have a look at your burden. Show me the girl."

Quick as a flash, I burrowed my forehead against Zach's chest to better hide my eyes and then forced my body go slack. I'd already discovered that it was easier to keep my eyelids smooth if I let my eyeballs roll upward behind my lids, like I was trying to go to sleep.

Relaxed. Sleeping. Don't mind me.

Something touched my head, but thankfully, Zach's sudden jolt covered any involuntary flinch I might have made.

Zach's chest rose and fell sharply and then the barest of sounds came from his throat.

"Interesting. Does that bother you, occultum? Me touching your *friend?* You afraid I might cast something nasty on her too? Maybe compel her to do things you won't like?" His blatant threat had my clenched stomach spiraling through to the floor.

Again, Zach's chest tensed. This time, though, instead of a strangled sound, he uttered a tortured "fuck" and "off" that sounded like they'd been slowly yanked from his throat with pliers.

Owen chuckled. "Obviously, it does bother you, quite a bit, if you're trying to fight my compulsion spell. From what I'm told, that hurts like hell." He sniffed. "Keep her restrained, follow my instructions, and I won't need to touch her further. Now, let's get to the bottom of this. When I ask you a question, you will speak only the truth. You will leave no significant detail out of your telling." I heard him move, fabric brushing against fabric. "Tell me—who knows of your plans to investigate the crime scene? Who knows you're out here on Treblow's land?"

Zach's muscles constricted beneath my ear and after a slight hitch, he bit out, "My father." His voice sounded pained and robotic.

I suppressed my shiver.

This was bad. Bad, bad, bad. Bending someone's will with magic was expressly forbidden. The Arcane Council regularly sent magic users to Alcatraz for things like this.

What are you thinking, you big dummy? Like he cares. The guy's a murderer.

"And anyone else your dad might have trusted with that information. Is that right?" Owen probed further.

"Yes."

"What were his exact instructions?"

"Investigate the crime scene for anything that might exonerate my brother and convince Lire to use her magic to discover the murderer's identity."

"And did you get Lire to touch the area where the body was discovered?" I pictured Owen leaning forward breathlessly, his blue-eyes flashing. "Is that why she passed out?"

"Yes."

"What happened after she touched the ground?"

"She stayed there for a few minutes, with her hand on the dirt. Then she fell over. I caught her."

"Since then, has she woken up to tell you anything? Anything at all?" Owen's question was particularly pointed, and I spared a moment to thank God that I'd pretended to be comatose this whole time.

"No."

I practically felt Owen's nefarious gaze on me, like a slobbery lick up the exposed side of my face.

You're relaxed. You're warm and cozy.

Steady breaths.

In ... and ... out.

"What does your father expect you to do after your investigation?"

Again, Zach fought it, his muscles tensing, but his resistance didn't last long. His breath gushed out as though he'd just dropped a heavy weight and he croaked, "Report to him at the compound." After a brief pause, he issued a pained groan and then added, "Or call once I get back to school."

"I see." I heard footsteps, followed by a pause, and then more footsteps. After several turns of this, I guessed that Owen was pacing the room.

"Okay. Follow me. You will continue to keep Lire restrained in your arms and visible."

Zach held me tighter as my lax body jounced against him with each of his steps.

Where are we going?

A door opened somewhere ahead.

"Go on," Owen ordered. "Careful. You wouldn't want to trip and hurt your *friend.*"

Zach's arms tensed around me and I sensed his brief hesitation before my body vibrated with the thud of a heavy step, followed by another. And another. But it wasn't the number of steps that filled me with dread. It was the hollow echo that accompanied each one that froze my blood.

Zach was walking down a set of stairs. Ones that led below ground, if the growing darkness behind my closed lids was any indication, not to mention the musty, cooler air that enveloped us.

"That's it," Owen said. "Keep going. All the way to the bottom. Okay, move further in. That's right. Stop and turn around."

Owen's footsteps on the stairs stopped.

"I'm sorry, but I can't allow you to return to school right now. I have my own investigation to do and I can't have you guys mucking it up. Put her, there, on that bed."

Investigation? What the heck does that mean?

Zach moved to comply with Owen's order. His arms pinned me tightly to his chest as I felt him lowering me to a soft surface. Feigning sleep was more difficult than I realized, especially when I couldn't track and prepare for Zach's movements. It took all my concentration to keep my limbs wholly limp, expression lax, and eyelids still. As he pulled his arms from beneath my knees and upper back, I felt the warmth of his breath on my cheek.

I wondered whether he knew I was awake because he took extra care in arranging my extremities and deliberately tipped my face away when he tucked a pillow beneath my head.

"Now come with me," Owen commanded. "You have a phone call to make."

He quickly squeezed my arm before he withdrew. Their footsteps reverberated loudly as they trooped upstairs.

After the door clicked shut, I waited a full minute, my ears peeled for any sounds. Strangely, once the door had clicked shut, I heard absolutely nothing. No further footsteps as Zach and Owen walked away. No muted voices. Nothing. It was as if the world outside had ceased to exist.

Did I dare move? What if Owen had video surveillance down here? *This is Treblow's house. Why would Treblow have installed video equipment to spy on his own basement?*

After thinking back on Treblow's memories, I couldn't dredge up anything about video surveillance, but I did remember one interesting thing. Treblow had placed a spell on his laundry room. He'd grown tired of being disturbed by his infernal washing machine's constant thumping and buzzing, so he'd done what any intelligent sorcerer would do. He'd sealed it off, sound-wise. Out of hearing, out of mind.

It might have been funny, except … I knew that's where Zach had been forced to carry me. And, when I opened my eyes, I remembered exactly what I would see.

It was dark, but not so dark that I didn't recognize the basic contents of Sorcerer Treblow's basement laundry room. I was lying on a wrought iron daybed, which had been pushed up against a white painted cinderblock wall. Above me, shabby looking acoustic tiles covered the ceiling, some of them stained from various leaks over the decades.

I rose to a sitting position and turned to find the source of the room's illumination, a night-light with an ivory plastic cover plugged into an outlet near the base of the wooden stairs. The basement had no windows and a single-bulb light fixture that was currently switched off. In the far corner, opposite the stairs, was the basement laundry area, complete with the customary white washing machine, matching clothes dryer, and fiberglass deep-well sink. A dull stripe worn into the concrete floor, leading from the stairs to the washer and dryer, bisected the room, and I imagined it had taken many generations of homeowners trudging to and fro with their loaded laundry baskets to chisel that path. But, try as I might, I couldn't remember Sorcerer Treblow ever doing such a domestic chore. Maybe he'd done his laundry with magic.

Or maybe his apprentice had done it.

Duh. Which was why Owen had ordered Zach to bring me down here. Treblow's apprentice-slash-caretaker had known the room was soundproof.

"Wonderful," I muttered. Maybe I should have taken my chances with trying to kick Owen in the nuts. "Red? Can you hear me?"

"Indeed, as I have heard everything else that has transpired. Perhaps, now, you will no longer label my counsel as 'over-protective.'"

"This isn't the time for the 'I told you so' speech, okay? You need to call or text Dad and tell him where we are."

"The thought had occurred," Red said dryly. "Unfortunately, Mr. Carter's magic made such an undertaking impossible."

"And let me guess, my cell phone doesn't work down here, either."

"Correct."

"Crap! What am I going to do? Owen's an ubhnati. I can't fight him. And he's got control of Zach." I wanted to get up and pace the room, but if Owen came back with Zach and caught me awake, I didn't know what might happen. "I could play dumb and pretend I didn't get a reading, but I'm positive he's not that stupid."

Anyone who had half a clue about how clairvoyance worked would know that if I woke up from a reading, it wasn't because I'd failed. Failing was when you *didn't* wake up.

"Continue to play unconscious. When I get the opportunity, I will use my defensive spells to incapacitate him."

"No. You can't risk him touching you. And if he finds out how powerful you are and that you're my familiar ..." I shivered. "That'll give him yet another reason to kill me. Besides, I can't leave Zach. Owen could order him to make them disappear and then —"

I shook my head as the full horror dawned on me. "Oh, my God. He'll never let him go! Zach can help Owen evade capture, even from the Arcane Council. Red, I need to find a way to release him. Quick—what do you know about control spells? How do I break it?"

"That would depend upon the spell. If blood was involved, then a ritual cleansing is required. If it was accomplished by means of a focus object, the object must be found and physically broken. Sometimes the spell is a combination of those two, in which case, cleansing and a shattering will be necessary. If the spell was invoked by a domination of will, then disrupting the spellcaster's focus can shatter that control. But unless Zach is strong enough to keep Owen out of his mind, the effect would only be temporary."

"The control happened fast. Like, super fast. A battle of wills would have taken longer. It must be one of the other two. Could—"

The doorknob rattled.

I flopped back on the bed and quickly arranged my arms, hoping I looked the same as when Zach had done it.

"Go downstairs and sit on the floor, right on top of that drain in the concrete." Owen's command was accompanied by the sound of the door flinging wide and colliding with its wall-stop.

I mentally tracked Zach's footsteps as I listened to him coming down the stairs, except ... something was off. The footsteps were curiously clunky, as if Zach had on heels instead of sneakers.

The rustling of fabric, of someone moving, resonated nearby.

"You'll stay there, in contact with that drain until I say otherwise," Owen said. "Zach, follow me. Maybe you'll prove more useful than that douchebag."

Wait. Isn't Zach, down here, on the floor?

The door slammed shut.

Ears primed, I listened for any indication that Owen hadn't actually left. I would have stayed prone, pretending to be unconscious and thinking this was a trick, if a familiar voice hadn't spoken up.

"I would recognize that aura anywhere. You needn't bother pretending, Miss Devon. I know you're awake."

I jolted. It couldn't be ...

I rolled to a sitting position and regarded the last person I expected to see in Treblow's basement.

"Vice President Jacoby." I tried not to gape at the absurdity of seeing the imposing sorcerer, sitting cross-legged on the cement floor.

His impeccable suit had never looked more out of place, although, at some point, he'd unbuttoned the suit jacket and loosened his tie. "Never thought I'd see you here."

"Quite. I might have said the same about you, if not for the unpleasant greeting I received from your invisible cohort."

I leaned forward, fisting the front edge of the mattress. "Whatever he did, he couldn't help it. Owen is controlling him."

"I'm well aware of that. No need to get your hackles up. However, I will point out that if you and Mr. Carter hadn't ventured into Sorcerer Treblow's territory to begin with, none of us would be in this situation."

"Exactly. You'd be down here by yourself."

"Don't be obtuse." His eyes glinted in his face like two obsidian beads. "A novice, especially one as inept as Sorcerer Treblow's apprentice, poses little threat to a master. Any first-year council member could have fended him off without blinking an eye. Unfortunately, your friend, the occultum, has enabled Owen to strike without warning."

Scowling, he dusted off his jacket before giving up in disgust. He glared at me. "Once that faithless worm gets his hands on his master's library, he will possess more power than you can imagine. With an occultum on his side, few will be able to stand against him."

I figured Jacoby wasn't completely wrong about that. Over his lifetime, Treblow had not only translated hundreds of rare scrolls containing obscure incantations but had also woven each of his spells into every manner of textile imaginable, sometimes dozens of times over. Needlepoints, tapestries, crocheted wall hangings, afghans, leather utility vests, sweaters, belts, necklaces ... you name it, he'd woven spells into it.

Once tied, each incantation could be loosed by any magic user with a basic understanding of spellweaving. A knot, in a sense, became a loaded gun. So, yeah, on that point, Jacoby had reason to be concerned, especially since all those textiles were stored inside Treblow's private library.

On the other hand, only Treblow would remember the feel of the knots he'd tied. Without that knowledge — without knowing the unique resonance of each spell—Owen wouldn't know what a particular knot would do until he unleashed it. It'd be like pulling a gun's trigger without knowing whether it was loaded with blanks or nuclear missiles.

Sure, if Owen got his greedy hands on Treblow's library, he had the potential to become an unstoppable powerhouse—*in theory*—but his rise to power wouldn't happen overnight and it wasn't guaranteed. Really, he'd be lucky to survive the learning curve.

It seemed to me that the greater threat was allowing a master—or worse, a group of masters—access to Treblow's library. With the group's combined experience, they could organize Treblow's textiles and teach each other the nature of each knot without the need for trial and error. And if one of them happened to be the leader of the group, someone like, say, Vice President Jacoby ...

I shivered.

This was why Treblow had discounted the threat of his spying apprentice and been more concerned about certain members of the Arcane Council. In hindsight, he'd been wrong to ignore Owen, but that didn't mean he'd also been wrong about the Arcane Council.

I scrutinized the veep. "Why are you here?"

"For good reason. To secure Sorcerer Treblow's library on behalf of the Arcane Council."

His patronizing demeanor sat at such odds with his position atop the floor's drain that it was almost impossible for me to keep a straight face, especially when he squared his chin and added, "Sorcerer Treblow was a very old, very famous magus. The breadth of his repository is legendary. There are many miscreants, besides his apprentice, who would sacrifice their own children to access such knowledge."

It was all I could do to avoid rolling my eyes, but then I remembered confronting the vice president over this very issue. Last week, we'd argued vehemently about my security measures after he—

Wait ...

I mentally shook myself. Not me. *Treblow.*

Treblow and Jacoby argued several times during the last four months. In fact, there was almost nothing about Treblow's library that hadn't become a source of conflict between them. But what really tore it for Treblow was learning that Jacoby had been behind the Council's majority decision to saddle him with an apprentice.

From day one, Jacoby feigned concern for Owen's welfare as an excuse to trespass on Treblow's property. He even barged into his house uninvited at least twice, which led to a couple of incendiary arguments. It also prompted Treblow to take extraordinary measures in securing his library.

Filing those memories away for later, I focused on the here and now.

"Actually, I've heard a lot about the sorcerer," I said. "If he were alive, I'm sure he'd be one-hundred-percent grateful for your help. You'd never be one to plant a spy in his household or show up unannounced just to sniff out his security, not like those other *miscreants.*"

Treblow visibly tensed before he seemed to remember himself. Straightening his legs, he crossed them at the ankles and then leaned back to support his weight on his hands. "Is this something you learned from your occultum friend, or by other, more direct means, I wonder."

"Does it matter?"

"Oh, yes. I'm afraid it matters a great deal. Because, although I did initiate the proposal that forced Sorcerer Treblow to train an apprentice, the Council rejected my recommended applicant. Instead, they chose to appoint a puppet to the position, one who they mistakenly believed they could control. My frequent visits were aimed at keeping Treblow's library secure, *not* because I'm a power-hungry megalomaniac. If the old fool had listened to reason, instead of blockading me at every turn, his library would be safe under our joint control in the Arcane Council's central vault."

He sighed. "Unfortunately, we are now paying the price for the Council's blunder. With Treblow dead, Owen has limited time to gain access to the library before a contingent is tasked with moving everything to the Council's central vault. He is clearly desperate. If you've reaped Treblow's memories, as I suspect you have, I can only imagine what Owen will do to learn those secrets. It certainly explains why he's risked keeping you here."

He pressed his lips together disapprovingly. "And to think, all this because your werewolf friend has such poor impulse control. What a shame. Your two friends sure haven't done you any favors, have they?"

Was he serious? "You're not as smart as I thought if you actually think Cal killed Sorcerer Treblow."

He pinned me with his sharp gaze. "Is that so?"

I cocked my head as I pondered him. "You know, you sure are relaxed for a guy who's supposedly under the control of a faithless worm."

"Perhaps I'm an easy-going guy."

I almost laughed. "I don't think so. Which makes me think you're not under Owen's control at all. Either that, or you know how to break free and are playing along for some reason." I watched him skeptically. "Or maybe you guys are working together and you're pretending to hate him."

His thin lips curved downward in disgust. "The man is a power-seeking cretin. I would no sooner join forces with such a creature than cut out my own tongue."

But you didn't think twice about urging the Council to force your own chosen spy on someone.

"Then what's the deal? Are you really under Owen's control?"

He extended his right hand, palm up, and tugged down his cuff to reveal a braided band of leather that snugly encircled his wrist. Lowering his arm, he narrowed his eyes at me. "Why hasn't he done the same to you?"

"How do you know he hasn't?"

He shot me a look probably reserved for his dealings with lesser worms. "I'm a master ethermancer. If your will had been compromised, I'd know it."

It was an effort not to squirm under the intensity of his gaze as I studied him.

Was all this an elaborate trick? Act like a prisoner to get as much willing information from me as possible? If so, then it would be foolish to tell him anything. On the other hand, if he was truly under Owen's control, then we'd be stupid not to join forces. He'd be a powerful ally once he got free, even if he was a superior, condescending jerk. Besides, it wasn't like I'd be telling Jacoby anything Owen didn't already know.

"Any time, Miss Devon."

"Fine. If you must know, Owen hasn't tried to spell me because, for a while, I was unconscious. I did a reading, earlier, that was more than I could handle, and Zach ended up having to carry me. He needed to figure out a way to get us both back to school, so I'm guessing that when Zach saw Owen drive up to Treblow's house, he must have asked him for a ride. It was either that or call Mr. Simmons. Zach must have followed Owen inside to wait, or maybe to use the phone."

"You used your magic before going inside?" Jacoby's left eyebrow went up. "Are you sure you didn't read something, here, in the house? Perhaps *after* you and the occultum found a way to sneak in?"

"We didn't break in." I gave him a dirty look. "We came over here to get clues about who *really* killed Sorcerer Treblow. The yellow tape made it obvious where he was killed. Why would we bother with the house?"

"Are you trying to tell me that you used your gift to read something inside the taped-off area?"

"Yes. Like I said, we were looking for clues." *Duh.*

He sat forward, his eyes like lasers. "And you did this on *purpose?*"

His voice was so disbelieving, I wanted to pinch his ear.

"No. That would be *stupid,*" I drawled, imparting it with enough sarcasm to choke a six-headed hydra. "I accidentally hit the bloody dirt with my face and then laid there for ten minutes, just for fun."

He appraised me, ignoring my rudeness. "You purposely touched his blood." He said this flatly, as though he needed to come to terms with such an outrageous idea.

Seriously? What kind of person did he think I was? Cal was my friend. I might not have been thrilled about doing the reading, but Cal was worth a trip to the hospital. Heck, he was worth fifty trips to the hospital. Why was that so hard for Jacoby to believe?

Amanda. That's why.

Folding my arms, I glared at him. "You know what? Screw this. I help my friends, no matter what Amanda's been saying. But if you want to believe whatever crap she's spewing about me, just because she's your precious goddaughter, go right ahead. I couldn't care less."

Jerk.

"Childish drivel does not concern me." Somehow, he managed to peer down his nose at me from his lowly seat on the concrete. "I do, however, take note of extraordinary exploits. Whether you know it or not, there are remarkably few clairvoyants who would volunteer to perform such a reading. And fewer still who do and manage to remain sane. During my fifty-eight-year tenure on the Arcane Council, I have encountered precisely one other. He, too, possessed a similar aura, although he wasn't human." His beady eyes regarded me in a way that made me nervous, like maybe he'd discovered a golden egg and wondered if I was the goose.

Why did I think telling him about the reading had been a huge mistake?

"This makes things rather interesting," he practically chortled. "Come here and tell me what you make of this." Once again, he exposed the leather band around his wrist.

When I regarded his extended arm with about as much enthusiasm as I'd afford a poisonous snake, he scoffed at me. "Come closer, Miss Devon. I don't bite."

I pushed myself to my feet but stopped short of walking over to him. "I've heard that you can strip someone's aura without touching them. Like a moroi. Well ... except for the dead part, I guess." I eyed him. "Is that really true?"

He blinked at me for a moment before throwing his head back and cackling. "No, Miss Devon. I don't feed on human auras to sustain myself. I find a healthy diet rich in vegetables and whole grains to be much more nutritious and far less likely to result in a prison term. As to whether I have the ability to strip a person of their aura ..." He twirled his hand dismissively. "If I wished to leave someone weak as a newborn and vulnerable to any number of enchantments, I could certainly do so, even from a distance."

He looked at me askance, obviously still amused. "Worried, Miss Devon?"

I folded my arms. "I don't know. Should I be?"

His eyes hardened, all traces of his previous humor gone in an instant. "I would normally take offense to such impertinence, but evidently my efforts defending my goddaughter has led you to believe the worst aspersions against my character. One does not rise to a position such as mine without trampling a fair share of egos. Inevitably, those disgruntled council members have painted me as an irredeemable villain. I can only assure you, as a gentleman and distinguished member of the Arcane Council, that stripping someone's aura is not my normal practice."

He bared his wrist at me, displaying the leather manacle. "However, I cannot guarantee that Owen will allow me to continue on that course."

He had a point.

Grumbling to myself, I trudged toward him and knelt as far away as I could get while still being close enough to inspect Owen's handiwork. This put my folded knees about twelve inches from his right thigh.

"Get on with it," he said, thrusting his wrist at me. "We don't have an infinite amount of time."

My eyes went big. "You don't mean — ?"

"No, no. Skin contact isn't necessary, nor wise. Keep your gloves on. Touch it and tell me exactly what goes through your mind."

I frowned down at his hand.

"Do it!"

Jumping at his unexpected bark, I grabbed his wrist, palming the bracelet without thought.

I opened my mouth to give him a piece of my mind, but the familiar resonance vibrating up my arm stopped me cold. I gasped, instead.

That's my spell!

As Treblow's distinctive magic and the unmistakable consonance of his blood sacrifice rang through my body, all his disjointed memories clicked into place. I now realized why all but one of Treblow's powerful spells hadn't worked against his werewolf attackers. Better yet, I finally had Owen's number. That little shit-stain was going *down*. First, though, I needed to get Jacoby and Zach free of these control spells, which had been stolen from Sorcerer Treblow.

I reached around to unzip my fanny pack. "I know Cal's keys are here somewhere."

Ignoring Jacoby's frown when my hand emerged from behind my back with the keys, I fumbled to open Cal's multi-tool key fob.

"Crap. The knife has to be one of these, right?" I wedged my thumbnail into one of the grooves, but with my gloves in the way, I couldn't get enough friction to lever it out.

"This isn't a novice spell," Jacoby sneered. "Any attempt to cut it off is a wasted effort."

"I'm not stupid." *You idiot.* "I need a sacrifice."

Jacoby snatched the keys from my grasp. He deftly located and extracted the tool's small blade and then handed it back. "You have Treblow's memories. Don't you?"

His greedy eyes bored into mine.

Scowling, I removed my left glove. Even though I'd never done this in my life, *déjà vu* seemed to guide my hands. After a brief pause to strengthen my psychic shield, I flicked the knife's sharp tip against the pad of my middle finger like a seasoned magus. I hissed at the pain as my clairvoyance flared to life, but with such a brief touch, corralling the blade's psychic history behind my shield was a snap. I shoved the fleeting memories from my mind before they had a chance to enter my thoughts.

"This sacrifice belongs to no one but me," I said, shooting a pointed glare at Jacoby. I squeezed the wound until blood began oozing from the cut. "This blood is mine and mine alone. You may not have it. It is not a gift. I am using it, in its entirety, for my own purpose."

As I stared at the blood welling from my finger, I realized that smearing my sacrifice over the leather bracelet presented a problem. This wouldn't be a brief touch where I could casually flick the few intruding memories from my mind. I'd be in contact with the bracelet for many long seconds. And I did *not* want to learn the ghastly mix of thoughts left by Owen, never mind the dying cow.

Ah! Instead of using my injured finger to do the drawing, I'd use my pooling blood like an inkwell. Unconventional, but I was sure it would work.

I focused on my sacrifice, imbuing it with my will as I dipped my gloved index finger into my blood and then traced it along the bracelet's surface like some gruesome art project.

When my bloody path connected with the place I'd started, a powerful snap of magical energy reverberated through my body, the unexpected shock jolting my spine straight as a ruler. Goosebumps raced down my arms and up my neck as the answering rush of magic potential blossomed in my core.

It worked! I'd created a conjuring circle, only in miniature.

I'd learned about magic circles way back in first grade, but as a psychic, it wasn't something I ever needed to do. Generally, magic circles were used to confine and collect a spellcaster's energies until they had enough power to invoke their chosen spell.

I swallowed, tasting the sharp tang of electricity as I instinctively directed this harnessed potential into the heart of Treblow's spell.

My spell.

No — *our* spell.

As my pent energy merged with the achingly familiar melody that I recognized as Treblow's essence, a resounding pulse thrummed through my core.

Ontigan!

I flinched as the fierce command to untie tore through my mind, shattering Treblow's incantation. If Jacoby hadn't grabbed me by the shoulder, I might have fallen over.

I blinked quickly, trying to clear my head, which felt fuzzier than my blurred vision. Everything seemed to be shrouded in a thick gray fog. I muttered something to that effect, or, at least, I tried to, but what came out sounded like an unintelligible snarl.

All at once, Jacoby released me. I pitched to the right, but steadied myself at the last second. Thankfully, after a few deep breaths, my vision cleared. I snatched up my discarded glove and put it on.

Jacoby stared at me, wide eyed, his skin the color of bleached driftwood.

He looked so upset, I sagged in defeat. "Crap. Did the spell not break? I could have sworn—"

He held up his arm. The leather band, which had previously been a rich brown and snug against his skin, dangled loosely from his wrist. It had turned an ashy gray.

Heart hammering, I breathed a sigh of relief. "You scared me. I thought it hadn't worked or something."

He spoke, but what came out of his mouth wasn't English. It sounded vaguely German.

"Come again?"

"You didn't understand that?" He peered intently at my face.

"No." I retrieved Cal's keys from where I'd dropped them, careful not to stab myself on the extended knife. "What did you say?"

"It's what you said."

"Huh?" I tried to think. Had I missed something? "I don't understand."

"You just spoke to me in a language that dates to the fifth century."

I waited for the punchline. When he continued to stare at me, dead serious, I shook my head. "You must have misheard. In case you hadn't noticed, I was kinda out of it a minute ago."

"No, Miss Devon. You were abundantly clear."

"That's news to me. What did I say?"

"Those who trespass will know only torment." His tone couldn't have been more daunting, a tall order, since Jacoby tended to be about as friendly as a hungry crocodile.

"Okay. That sounds … uh, not good. And you think I said this in another language? Which one?"

"An Anglian dialect of Old English."

I made a face. "Are you sure it wasn't French? I'm fluent, you know."

"*Je le suis aussi, Mademoiselle,*" he said. "*Et ce n'était pas du français.*" *So am I, young lady. It wasn't French.*

"I don't know any ancient languages," I told him. "I worked in an antiques shop over the summer, appraising stuff, but I've never read anything more than a couple hundred years old."

"Yes, you have."

"Now you know everything about me? Look. I don't know what you think you know about my magic, but it's not possible for me to forget something I've read. I'm telling you—"

"You read Sorcerer Treblow's blood."

"Learn your biology. Red blood cells are four months old, not hundreds of years."

"This has nothing to do with human physiology," he snapped, his eyes flinty. "Treblow was an exceedingly powerful sorcerer. You spoke his language, the language of the Varangian Council, which I know well. And not three minutes ago, you broke his blood-wrought spell with your own blood, after your aura materially transformed, both of which should not have been possible. You have more than just four months of his memories, Miss Devon. Ignore this at your own peril."

I gaped at him. "What do you mean I have more than just his memories? And auras can't *materially* transform. They're like fingerprints. We covered that in MEWs, last year."

"Five minutes ago, I would have agreed with you." A look of unease overshadowed his superior tone.

At this rate, my mouth was going to dry out, given how many times I'd left it hanging open.

I pressed my hand to my chest. "What did my aura do?"

"It—"

I jumped at the basement door being kicked open. Interestingly, instead of Owen standing at the top, an imposing man dominated the threshold, one who immediately began to stomp down the stairs.

CHAPTER 18

An unpleasant discovery

I gaped at the newcomer. In the dim light, I couldn't get a read on his features to judge his age, but his size was another story — six foot four, at least, and lots of muscle. If he'd taken a shower any time in the last month, I'd have been surprised. His dark hair was a tangled mess and his shaggy beard looked like a home for wayward mice. He wore filthy gray sweatpants low on his hips and nothing else, but it took me more than a moment to figure out that last part because his torso was almost as hairy as a bear's. As the man drew closer, I wondered whether he had a skin condition. The skin of his face and neck appeared blotchy and the hair covering his torso and arms was matted and bald in spots, as if he had mange.

Jacoby seemed to be about as nonplussed by this guy's arrival as me.

Dammit! Instead of wasting time talking about my aura and arguing over whether I'd spoken Old English, we should have been planning how to rescue Zach and make our escape.

At least, I'd managed to free Jacoby. That was something. Maybe we could use that to our advantage.

"*Fais semblant d'être toujours sous son contrôle,*" I whispered to Jacoby, sticking with French to make my suggestion that he pretend to be under Owen's control.

Owen's order came from the top of the stairs, "Put him on the floor, next to the bed."

Him?

Oh, crap.

Sure enough, Mr. Tall and Scruffy walked with his arms outstretched, elbows tucked against his abdomen, as though he carried a heavy, invisible weight.

"Or — *hello,*" Owen drawled, finally catching glimpse of me on the floor alongside Jacoby. "It seems Sleeping Beauty has woken from her slumber. Awesome. Matthew, put him on the bed, instead. The least we can do is make Mr. Carter comfortable, after what he's been through."

"Zach?" Knifing to my feet as the big guy lumbered past, I almost gagged at the stench. My theory about this dude not showering seemed to be right on the mark.

I glared up the stairs at Owen. "What happened? What did you do to Zach?"

Clenching my fists, the handle of Cal's Leatherman dug into my palm as I imagined grabbing the asshole by his collar and shaking him hard enough to cause serious damage. But the fantasy imploded when I noticed the ornamented leather vest Owen wore.

Dark stains coated the front of the supple leather I knew all too well. The vest was Treblow's. He'd been wearing that exact garment on the night he died. I remembered using the vining spell from that chain — that one, there, next to the third button down. And that empty space, the one a few inches below the right arm hole — that was where the kinetic spell plaits had hung.

Owen stripped that vest from his master's dead body!

Last night, when Zach and I stood over Treblow's bloody remains, the dead sorcerer hadn't been wearing that vest. I knew this for absolute certain. I distinctly remembered thinking that the victim couldn't be Treblow because he was wearing casual business attire instead of an elaborate robe.

If Treblow had been wearing this leather vest—with its dozens upon dozens of knotted plaits decorating virtually every square inch—you can bet I would have noticed.

It was too bad Owen had snatched it. And not simply because it was a powerful tool that a psycho like him had no business having. If I'd seen Treblow wearing this vest when Zach and I discovered his body, I would have noticed its strong resemblance to Owen's belt. I would have realized there was a connection between the two men. Who knows? I might have guessed that Owen had murdered Treblow.

"Let's just say he's been doing some snooping," Owen replied. "Unfortunately, the owner of this house was a little uptight about security."

Once Mr. Scruffy had deposited his payload and moved to the side, I rushed to the daybed, turning my back on Owen and Jacoby. I eyed Owen's thrall warily as I approached to kneel beside the bed. Thankfully, he stared into the distance without paying the least bit of attention to me. I grimaced. The smell was beyond disgusting.

I shivered as the baby hairs on the back of my neck went into porcupine mode. Talk about creepy, but I didn't think this guy's spook factor had anything to do with Owen's control spell. Jacoby had been under Owen's control, too, but he hadn't looked or acted like this Matthew dude—like an automaton with zero facial expressions and vacant, milky eyes.

Unease sucked me down like an anvil tossed into quicksand.

I had a bad feeling that I knew who and what Matthew was.

"Zach." Even though Cal's pocket knife was about as threatening as a letter opener, I didn't want to put it down. Using my left hand, I searched the edge of the mattress until I felt what turned out to be Zach's arm. After figuring out his orientation on the bed—hand to the left, shoulder to the right—I quickly ran my palm over his torso, taking stock. His skin-suit seemed to be intact and I didn't feel anything out of the ordinary. Reaching across his body, I found his left shoulder and gave him a firm shake. "Zach ... can you hear me? Come on now ... wake up. Please. Please wake up."

Treblow's memories told me that trying to rouse Zach was useless. He'd encountered the library's main defensive ward and because he wasn't keyed to it, the spell had siphoned his stamina. He'd be unconscious for at least a day, if not two, unless a healer lent him some of their energy.

"As touching as this is, I think it's time for round two," Owen said. "Lire, come up here. You can come willingly, or I can have Matthew drag you. It's your choice. You have to the count of three."

That voice. It grated. Never in my life had I wanted to hurt someone so badly.

But, first, I had to free Zach. I couldn't stand the thought of leaving him under the control of this slime ball for one more second.

Possessed by that thought, I slashed my palm with Cal's knife, slicing through the fabric of my glove and into my tender flesh.

"One ..." Owen called out.

Again, that out-of-body sensation rolled over me, as if I'd done this very thing over and over for hundreds of years. This time, though, I'd gone for maximum bleed. The cut was at least two inches long and stung like a son of a gun. Warm blood soaked into my glove, sticking the fabric to my palm and leaving an oblong dark spot that grew larger by the second. As I pushed the knife's memories from my mind, I pulled my fanny pack around to my front and dropped Cal's keys into Red's lap for safekeeping.

"Two ..."

I found Zach's left hand and wiped my now-throbbing palm around his wrist, not caring that I was probably smearing my blood all over his hand and skin-suit in the process. The absurd thought that I was coloring outside the lines went through my mind as the tell-tale snap of the completed magical circuit thrummed through me.

"Three. Time's up," Owen declared. "Matthew, grab the girl and bring her to me. Mind your strength, big guy, I don't want her too injured. Minor bruising is fine, broken bones are not."

Ontigan, I thought as I directed my stored potential into the crux of Treblow's stolen bracelet.

Mathew's hands clamped onto me, one at each armpit. Just before he yanked me upward, the control spell shattered beneath my gloved fingers, echoing through me with a subsonic pop.

Yes!

All the air went out of my lungs when my body went airborne and then slammed back-first into Matthew's hard chest, knocking the air out of me.

I sucked in a breath and immediately regretted it. The scent of unwashed human, smelly dog, and something far more putrid, coated the inside of my nose and the back of my throat. I fought not to retch as the creature towed me backwards across the room, the balls of my feet skimming the concrete floor.

"Jacoby, you will not interfere," Owen ordered. "You will sit on that drain and make no move to help Lire in any way."

I wanted to warn the Veepster not to reveal himself. There were things he didn't know, things I hadn't gotten a chance to tell him — like how Owen had used two werewolves to kill Treblow and that I was almost positive they were Cal's missing cousins. But, more importantly, this guy Matthew was one of them.

He was also very much dead. Or, undead, if you wanted to get technical. Which, incidentally, went a long way in explaining the stench and his general appearance.

It also explained why, on the night of his murder, Treblow's powerful spells hadn't stopped his two werewolf attackers. All but one of the sorcerer's chosen incantations had been intended for the living. His kinetic spell had worked to briefly deter the undead wolves only because that enchantment affected anything with mass — dead or alive.

If Treblow had known ahead of time that he'd been dealing with two undead werewolves, things would have ended differently. He would've had time to prepare. He would have selected different spells.

Even before I reached around behind Matthew's head, I knew what I would find. Encircling the undead werewolf's neck was a knotted, loose-fitting collar. However, unlike the control bands around Jacoby and Zach's wrists, this one didn't resonate with Treblow's essence. Instead, its enchantment undulated beneath my gloved fingertips like a malignant worm. I snatched my hand away as though I'd touched the wrong end of a blow torch.

As a nearly thousand-year-old ubhnati, Treblow had dabbled with all manner of sorcery, sometime weaving spells so destructive they had no business being invoked, but one class of magic he consistently avoided was black magic.

The enchantment around Matthew's neck was one that Treblow never would have woven because it was as black as any magic could get.

Matthew wasn't simply a reanimated corpse. He was a zombie, an undead slave, and creating one required a human sacrifice. Not a blood sacrifice — a *human* sacrifice — a deliberate, premeditated human death where its copious release of raw potential was needed to fuel a power-hungry spell. There was no greater wrong in our world. No wonder Treblow had recoiled when he'd discovered the proof of it around his attacker's neck.

Unlike Treblow's stolen control bracelets, I had no way to break this abomination. Worse, I knew from last year's MEW class that zombies were notoriously difficult to put to rest. They were impervious to most forms of magic. Short of shoving one into a giant wood chipper or a lake of volcanic lava, the easiest way to stop a zombie from fulfilling its handler's commands was by killing or incapacitating the person who controlled it.

Treblow would have killed Owen without batting an eye, and might have done so if things had gone differently that night. I knew this because he'd thought that very thing in his final moments. There were dozens of spells on his utility vest that could have ended Owen's life with minimal effort, and I knew where each one was located.

Problem was — I wasn't Treblow.

I despised Owen and what he'd done, but I couldn't simply haul off and kill him, not if there was another alternative. Somehow, I had to figure out a way to incapacitate him before he slapped a control bracelet around my wrist. And I had a good idea how to go about it.

Hidden from Owen by Matthew's bulk, I shot a meaningful glance at Jacoby and pressed my raised index finger against my lips. *Shhh.*

I looked into my unzipped fanny pack and whispered, "Get ready, Red."

Throwing my voice over my shoulder, I shouted, "Okay, dammit! You win. I'll come up there." I cursed when my heels smacked against the first step as Mathew started to back his way up the stairs. "Ouch! Come on, Owen. Tell him to let me go. This hurts."

"Matthew, hold up. Keep a firm hand on her, but allow Lire to stand and walk on her own. Follow her up the stairs."

Fortunately, I'd gotten my feet beneath me, so I didn't bounce down the step when the undead werewolf suddenly dropped his support from under my arms. He fastened his large hand atop my right shoulder, not so tight that it hurt, but tight enough to remind me that I wasn't getting away from him.

I circled to the right of my smelly escort and trudged up the stairs.

Glancing up at Owen, I scowled in disgust. How the heck did I ever think he was nice?

As I drew closer, I looked him over. Was he holding a leather control band in his right hand?

Doesn't matter.

When I reached the top step, I yanked Red from my fanny pack and thrust him out in front of me, wielding him like a cuddly sword pointed at Owen's stomach.

The effect was immediate and might have been comical if I hadn't been scared shitless.

Owen's demeanor went from haughty to frightened. As he stumbled away from me, I dove for the sixth plait down on the left side of his vest. Unfortunately, I hadn't accounted for Matthew's strength. Just as I made contact, the leather braid slipped from my bloody grasp when the obedient werewolf jerked me backward.

I screamed, reflexively dropping Red, as the undead's fingers dug mercilessly into the meat of my shoulder, pulling me upright.

Before I could think to forbid it, Red charged Owen, his black fuzzy form flashing across the stair's top landing as Owen shrieked and kicked his feet as though he was fending off a ravenous man-eating squirrel.

"Red!" I squirmed against Matthew's iron-like grip as I yanked and pulled on his unyielding fingers, which felt like they'd burrowed all the way down to the bone.

Behind me I heard Jacoby chanting in another language.

Something dark and vaguely snake-like slithered past me to tangle in Owen's feet. Owen, whose terrified expression and frantic shrieking hadn't abated, promptly fell backwards as he attempted to retreat from Red's revulsion spell while being confused as to why his legs weren't working.

"Take it!" Red shouted, suddenly at my side, shoving at my right ankle to get my attention. He held up a leather plait.

I stretched toward him as far as I could, but with Matthew's unrelenting grip on my shoulder, my outstretched fingers barely reached the level of my knee. The tips of my fingers tingled as my arm began to turn numb.

"You bitch!" Owen screeched, sitting up, his face red and mottled by rage. He threw the leather band in his hand aside and patted the front of his vest.

He's looking for a spell!

I knew precisely which spells were sliding beneath his greedy hands, even if he didn't.

None of them were good.

Red shimmied up my leg and I threw my body sideways, ignoring the searing pain that engulfed my shoulder as my skin and muscle tore through Matthew's stony, immovable fingers. My fingertips flirted with the leather plait, once, twice, before I finally got a firm grasp of it.

"Ontígan!" I screamed, directing the spell's unleashed potential at Owen with every scrap of will I could marshal.

Until that moment, I hadn't been sure if Red managed to steal the plait I'd been going for, but as soon as I felt the spell's resonance rip through me, I knew he'd gotten the right one.

If Owen had been untying the spell beneath his fingers, he never got a chance to follow through. His body contracted in an alarming way, shrinking in on itself as though I viewed him through the wrong end of a twisted telescope, until nothing was left except his discarded clothes.

"Interesting." Jacoby's cool voice echoed from behind Mathew and me.

Matthew, who'd switched to firmly clasping my arm after losing hold of my shoulder, seemed oblivious to Owen's transformation.

"Miss Devon, do you mind?" Jacoby prompted. "Please step into the hallway if you would. The atmosphere is getting somewhat thick, here, and this landing isn't wide enough abreast for the three of us."

With Red clinging to my ankle and riding atop my right foot, I cautiously moved forward a step, waiting for Matthew to haul back on my arm, but to my surprise the zombie werewolf shuffled along with me. If I moved normally, no diving or darting forward as though I was trying to escape, he'd simply follow along, just as Owen had directed.

I wanted to kick myself. If I'd figured that out sooner, my right shoulder wouldn't be burning in agony right now.

All too happy to get out of the basement, I moved into the hallway to the right of Owen's clothes, being careful to avoid stepping on them.

"My, my. What *have* you done?" Jacoby drawled, clearly enjoying himself.

"I didn't kill him, if that's what you're thinking." I backed away to keep Red's defensive spells from affecting Jacoby as he joined us in the hallway. *Drat!* If I leaned down to smuggle Red out of sight, I'd only end up drawing attention to him.

Matthew dutifully followed alongside me as I backed up. I pointed at the pile of clothes, hoping to distract Jacoby. "The murdering low-life snake is in there. You might want to catch him before he slithers away."

The Veepster stooped to pull aside Treblow's vest, revealing a three-foot gopher snake hiding inside the folds of Owen's polo shirt. He chuckled. "Aren't you the resourceful one?"

Jacoby grasped the writhing snake behind its head and straightened. "A transfiguration spell. I have to say, I'm impressed." He eyed me. "The question is: Did you know Treblow's knot contained this spell? Or did your familiar merely grab the first one that came to hand." He smirked. "Or, would that be 'to paw?'"

I masked my alarm with a shrug. "He's neutralized. That's all that matters. What I really want to know is how to get big guy, here, to let go of me."

"Why don't you ask Mr. Redborn? He's the necromancy expert."

"Because I'm supposed to keep him a secret from people like *you*." So much for distraction.

"People like me. How quaint. Do enlighten me. What am I *like*?"

"You're a member of the Council." *Duh.*

By slowly bending at the waist, I whisked Red onto my right shoulder without Matthew freaking out and squeezing my arm black-and-blue. With my hair stuffed inside my skin-suit's hood, Red pinched the fabric to avoid sliding off.

"Ah, yes, the dreaded Arcane Council," Jacoby said mockingly. "Criminals, to the last. We're not to be trusted, is that what you've been told?"

"Stop being such—" *A jerk.* "So condescending," I revised, scowling at his amused look. "You know exactly why I've been told to keep him hidden from anyone connected to the Council."

"Pity they didn't warn you about ethermancers, too—especially those who knew Grand Master Le Blanc or his familiar. Then, you'd have realized the futility of hiding such a thing from *people like me*."

I frowned.

"What is that school teaching you?" He clicked his tongue disdainfully. "Have you learned nothing about etherology?"

He sighed at my blank expression. "Auras, or more specifically, the study of auras and the various external forces that disturb them. If you possessed even a basic understanding, you'd know that I've been aware of John Redborn's influence since our first meeting." He raked me up and down with his arch gaze. "Among other things."

I narrowed my eyes at him. "What *other* things?"

"I'll save that for a later discussion. Right now, we're discussing your familiar."

"After saving you, the least you can do is swear by blood oath that you won't reveal Red's whereabouts to anyone."

His smile was razor sharp. "Of course," he said and then added, "provided you promise something in return."

"That's not how it works," I snapped. "You already owe us."

"Contrary to what you think, Miss Devon, I was never in any danger."

"I set you free, you ungrateful little ... *person*!" Only my deep rooted 'respect for one's elders' kept me from calling him something worse.

He laughed. "Now, now, let's not start saying things we'll regret." His eyes turned stony in stark warning. "Let me tell you how this works. Ideally, in a quid pro quo arrangement, the two sides should be balanced." He reached down to casually tuck Treblow's vest beneath his right arm. "Shattering an enchantment that I could have severed at any time doesn't throw much weight on your side of things. However, if you were to aid me in the task of securing Treblow's library for the Council, I believe I could find a way to keep Mr. Redborn's identity out of the coming inquiry into Treblow's death."

"Owen murdered Sorcerer Treblow. I have his memories. I know how he did it. Red doesn't factor into it. He helped save you!"

"Ah, yes. Thank you for reminding me. Yet another detail that the Council will be delighted to know—a clairvoyant who is able to get to the bottom of even the most gruesome of crimes."

Pain shot through my wounded palm as I reflexively clenched my hands into fists. "I should have left you down there, sitting on that drain. It's where you belong." *You selfish, conniving, rat-faced jerk.*

"Touché. But that's neither here nor there," Jacoby said. "Owen won't be the last, you know. Is securing Treblow's library from other power-hungry charlatans really so much to ask?"

"You're not asking."

"Neither are you." He regarded me steadily. "We each want something. To get it, we have to give up something in return."

"The problem with your proposal, Mister Vice President, is that your life isn't on the line if you decide to walk away. If I refuse and you expose Red, every corrupt magus desperate for power will look for ways to kill me so they can take him for their own. That's not a choice. It's blackmail."

"Something you're intimately familiar with, I believe."

I suppressed my choice expletives, but something larger and infinitely more powerful bubbled inside of me, threatening to break free. I squeezed the woven plait from Treblow's vest, still clenched in my right hand. There were other spells knotted into the leather, ones far more powerful than the transfiguration spell I'd cast upon Owen. Their individual resonances pulsed against my palm like the wings of a thousand angry bees.

Before I could do something stupid, deep, bone-jarring growls from the front of the house practically jolted me out of my sneakers. The booming growls turned into ferocious snarls followed by vicious barking, snapping, and a clamor of scraping claws.

Krissy, I thought. *The other undead werewolf.*

Owen's last command to her must have been to prevent anyone from entering Treblow's cottage.

Shouts in a language I didn't understand echoed over the animal's baying, followed by a series of resounding blows that shook the entire house. Then, after a particularly thunderous crash, everything fell into ominous silence.

Taking down a zombie wasn't impossible. It was just tremendously difficult. I stared past Jacoby, waiting for what might turn the corner at the hallway's opposite end, my heart beating triple-time while my own zombie steadfastly gripped my left arm.

Had the beast in the front room finished someone off? Or had someone, or some*thing*, taken out Owen's revenant?

Since Jacoby appeared untroubled, I wondered whether it was a contingent from the Arcane Council.

Blurred movement at my left tore my focus from the far corner toward something vaguely round as it thumped to the hardwood and rolled a few feet away from me.

Matthew's grip on my arm slipped and his decapitated corpse crumpled to the floor. His head, which had been ripped from his body, now lay inches from Owen's clothes, where it had come to rest.

Seemingly out of thin air, a dark-skinned phantom had taken up position next to me.

"What an unpleasant discovery," the creature announced.

I goggled at the newcomer, and not simply because his arrival was unexpected. I knew him! This was Alex—Alex the vampire, a.k.a. Hackervamp, the strigoi boy I'd defended against Skyler two years ago. His blond hair and eyebrows were a dead giveaway. They stood out starkly against the smooth black skin of his daytime form, the one that protected him from the sun's rays.

What the heck was he doing, here, of all places? And, holy shit, he had the ability to turn to vapor, in addition to being a day-walker?

Possessing two of the strigoi's most coveted and powerful gifts had to be unprecedented! It was rare for a vamp to have even one.

"A Council Vice President, two zombies, and — is that the power-hungry thief? What interesting company you're keeping these days, Clotilde."

If there was any doubt left in my mind, his familiar Midwestern drawl squashed it.

Definitely Alex.

Standing this close, I could see that his onyx-like skin was composed of fine scales, not unlike those of a snake. His eyes were wholly black, giving him a distinctly alien look.

Like a black mamba, but way more lethal.

If not for the tight quarters, I might have backed away. As it was, the wall to my right drew me up short.

When Mathew's headless body twitched and began to rise, Alex shoved it down with a well-placed boot between the zombie's shoulder blades and summarily tore its arms and legs off. All I saw was a blur of movement and the resulting pile of limbs. There was a surprising lack of blood and the little bit I saw appeared black and gelatinous, as though most of it had hardened to a thick paste inside the were's body.

I clamped my hand over my nose and mouth. From here on out, looking anywhere near the floor was to be avoided at all cost.

La, la, la, not thinking about it!

I repeated the mantra over and over until I got a hold of myself. Examining Alex helped. For a guy who'd been turned a few years ago, at seventeen, he was one majorly scary dude.

Alex blinked, rearing back as his nostrils flared. "You're bleeding," he snarled. "Are you hurt?"

I caught a flash of his fangs, deadly white against his black lips, and all rational thought dropped out of my head. "N-no," I stammered, clenching my fists as though it would cover up any lingering scent. "It's nothing."

Instead of succumbing to a blood-trance and falling on me in a fit of hunger, he turned to Jacoby. "She is ours!" Alex's roar cut through the stagnant air. "Is this how you honor the pact?"

"How dare you question my honor," Jacoby snapped back, unbowed. "The wounds are self-inflicted. Ask her yourself."

"Show me," Alex demanded, fixing me with his fierce glare.

It took me a stunned moment to unstick my tongue. "He's right," I practically squeaked. "I needed a sacrifice ... to break the control spells." I hesitantly showed him my palm.

"Control spells? Whose?" His gaze tracked to the snake in Jacoby's grasp. "The Council's low-life mole?"

I nodded. "Owen. He killed Treblow and stole his conjuring vest." I explained how Owen had used Treblow's knotted spells to control both Zach and Jacoby.

"Where is your friend, the occultum?" Alex asked sharply.

He knew what Zach was?

"He's in the basement, passed out on the bed. Owen forced him to break into Sorcerer Treblow's library. The defensive ward stole his stamina."

"Move aside, arcanist!" a deep, unfamiliar voice shouted.

"Jacoby, step to your right, if you would," Alex said. "Mr. Carter's father wishes to see his son."

Zach's dad was here, too? *Oh, no!*

"It's not Zach's fault that we got caught!" I blurted, hoping Zach's dad would pause to listen. "I passed out after reading Treblow's blood, so he had no idea that Owen was the murderer. Zach was trying to get us a ride back to school. So, uh, your son did a good job ... okay?"

"You both did," the disembodied voice replied. "And I have every intention of thanking you properly as soon as I tend to my son. Excuse me." His footsteps echoed on the landing as he started down the stairs.

"I broke the compulsion spell. You got that part, right?" I shouted after him. "So you don't have to worry."

Had he heard me?

Flustered, I bit my lip and straightened, coming face to face with Alex's black, impenetrable eyes.

"The Domn's right. You're a firebrand." He laughed at my expression. "Touching blood? Confronting murderers? Breaking spells?" Alex's left eyebrow arched upward. "That's not how most clairvoyants spend their time, especially ones still in high school. It's no wonder the Domn has his eye on you."

"Is that how you knew we were here? You guys have been watching me?" I wasn't sure I liked the idea that vampires were spying on me. It was creepy.

"Like a stalker? No, Clotilde. As fascinating as I'm sure that would be, we've better things to do than monitor your every move. I'm here because a lot of people are interested in Treblow's research. The Domn asked me to keep an eye on things to make sure the wrong ones don't get their hands on it."

"Like Owen and, uh"—I glanced at Jacoby before fumbling out—"others, like ... the elf king."

Alex's eyes briefly widened. "What do you know of the sidhe king?"

"Not a lot. Only that Treblow was obligated to him somehow." I frowned. "He was searching for some kind of gateway spell. He spent half of his life looking for it and was sick of Earth. The spell would allow him to go home to *Tír na hÓige*. He was obsessed with learning it."

"King Faonaín would like nothing more than to exterminate all humanity," Jacoby said. "Depriving him of Treblow's knowledge is paramount."

"And I suppose you think you're the one to take care of it," Alex sneered.

"Sindre Treblow was a founding member of the Arcane Council," Jacoby snapped, stepping closer. "As such, his life's work belongs to us."

"There are others who would disagree."

"Others?" Jacoby scoffed. "I know where your Domn's allegiances lie. The sidhe queen has no claim here, *dhêala*." He said the final word with such derision, it was practically a growl.

Alex hissed, his fangs on full display, reminding me of the day in the computer lab.

"It doesn't matter anyway," I said. When neither of them spared me a glance, I raised my voice and risked stepping closer. "You hear me? You're arguing over nothing! His library isn't here. Treblow moved it."

"Impossible," Jacoby retorted. "Your childish attempt to obfuscate will not stop the inevitable. With or without your help, the Council will take control of our rightful property." He shot a haughty glare at Alex.

He called me a liar, the arrogant son of a —

Fury, scalding in its intensity, heated my body, and I ranted inarticulately.

What the hell was wrong with me? Cussing out a member of the school's board of regents was a good way to get suspended!

Alex considered me with considerable shock, his fangs no longer extended. Jacoby glowered.

Crap.

"I did it again, didn't I?" I ducked my shoulders. "Old English?"

Jacoby nodded, a terse jerk of his chin.

"What did I say this time?"

"You called him a dung-eating son of an inbred cockatrice," Alex replied. "How is it you know East Anglian?"

Alex recognized East Anglian?

"Somehow, Sindre remains inside of her," Jacoby ground out.

"What? No." I waved my hands at them, fending off the absurd idea. "I have some of his memories. That's all. This only seems to happen when Mr. Vice President here, says or does something that pisses me off. It sort of … I don't know, it gets the sorcerer's memories all riled up in my head."

I glared at Jacoby. This was all his fault. "Treblow *really* didn't like you."

"The feeling was mutual, I assure you." He folded his arms. "Now that you have our undivided attention, please enlighten us. What is the current state of his library?"

"Like I said — he moved it. He discovered a spell that allowed him to shift things, into another dimension, I think." I frowned as I sifted through his memories. It wasn't easy, since most of them were mind-numbingly tedious. He'd done a crapload of translating and reading over the last four months. "This incantation wasn't the gateway spell, but he thought it might be related."

"Where is this spell?" Jacoby demanded. His calculating gaze lit on the discarded vest and he snatched it back. "Did he add it to his arsenal, like he did everything else?"

I wanted to thump him on the head. "Would you leave the combination to the Council's safe laying around for anyone to read?"

"You have his memory of casting it?" Jacoby's words challenged me, as though he assumed I was mistaken.

"Yes."

"And, afterward, you saw his library do what? Vanish? Just like that?" He snapped his fingers.

"Yes. He thought of it as—" I stopped to consider it, turning my attention inward. "It felt to him like he was ... sliding all of it sideways."

I didn't like either of their expressions. Alex glared at Jacoby, his eyes narrowed and chin stubbornly set. Jacoby looked ... I could only describe it as calculating. I could tell they were about to fall back into fighting again.

Hadn't they heard me? The library was out of their reach. What was there to fight about?

"She is the key," Jacoby said.

"Interfere with her and I'll rip your head from your body," Alex said, his voice low and disturbingly matter of fact.

"Meddling with your Domn's precious nonpareil is the last thing on my mind," Jacoby said coolly. "But King Faonaín is not bound to our pact. He will stop at nothing to attain the entirety of Treblow's library."

With the barest of tip of his head, Alex seemed to agree.

"Why, though?" I huffed. "There's no super weapon in Treblow's library, just a bunch of moldy old scrolls. And, I get that he wove a lot of dangerous spells that are stored in there, but why would this Faonaín guy even care? I mean, to be the elf king, he must already have magic up the wazoo, right?"

"Yes. But he lacks a crucial skill," Alex said. "He has a single gateway to Earth and can't create more."

"Which is all that stands between us and total annihilation," Jacoby said, his eyes hard. "And, now, it seems that *you* are the only living soul who knows what Treblow learned."

"You're talking about the spell he used to move his library?" I asked.

"Precisely. Not only do you have intimate knowledge of the spell, but you also know the location of his library." He folded his arms, leaning back on his heels. Owen writhed, still dangling from Jacoby's left hand. "You are the key. One that King Faonaín will do anything to get."

His ominous tone was enough to make my knees quake. "But that's stupid! It's not like I can *do* anything," I exclaimed. "I'm not a magic user."

"True. But there are ways to extract that information." Jacoby gave Alex a direct look. "Her life is forfeit if she's allowed to retain it."

"Yes," the vampire replied, staring at me impassively.

"It won't take them long to connect the dots."

"I know."

It was unnerving being talked about as though I wasn't in the room, especially about such a disturbing topic.

"I don't understand." Eyes wide, I looked back and forth between them. "You guys are the only ones who know! How would anyone else find out?"

"*Sard!* Do you ever use your God-given brains?" Jacoby snapped.

How was I supposed to think when he kept shouting and scaring the crap out of me?

He issued an exasperated sigh. "*Telepaths*, Miss Devon. The king uses an army of telepaths. Eventually, they will find you. As long as you possess Treblow's memories, the king won't be satisfied until every last one is ripped from your mind. Whether their methods turn you into a vegetable will be the least of his concerns."

Alex gently touched my arm, no doubt noticing my horrified expression. "Clotilde, the Domn won't let that happen, but before we get to that, how about breaking the wards on Treblow's study? We want to make things look less tempting. Burglars will show up and think someone got here first. Right?"

I wasn't sure how much good that would do once King What's-His-Name found out about the information in my head, but I nodded. "I guess it can't hurt."

Guided by Treblow's memories, I led the way to his study on the other side of the house, eager to escape the cramped hallway and breathe normally again. Unfortunately, one ill-advised glance at the front room had my hand pressed to my mouth for the second time in the last ten minutes. Large fur-covered chunks, which had once been Krissy the werewolf, lay strewn across the living room.

I hurried to the right, passing through the kitchen, and trundled down the two steps to the cottage's mud room. There, we were met by a glass-paned door that led outside and, to my right, a second door that looked like something out of a Spanish Baroque estate. Its rich mahogany stain and elaborate carvings spoke of a place far more interesting than a mere study.

Instead of issuing the command that would allow me to pass safely inside, I pressed my still-bloody palm flat to the wood. The magic emanating from a protective ward pelted my skin like a rain of static-charged feathers. Treblow's resonance vibrated up my arm, mingling with my own and opening my senses to the runed keystones that protected the room's perimeter. Again, the feeling of *déjà vu* quickly overwhelmed me, shrouding me inside its familiar fog.

Left palm still pressed to the wood, I traced a series of complicated patterns on the back of my hand, my right index finger serving as an imaginary pen. As I completed the outline of each rune, I infused it with my will until all four of the glowing designs danced inside my head like a psychedelic vision. Focusing on the ward's four keystones, I invested each brilliant rune with as much potential as I could muster and directed them into the matrix, commanding their spells to untie.

Ontígan!

The ward shattered with an audible *crack*, instantaneously draining my core of potential and pricking bright pinholes into my darkening vision. I swayed on my feet as everything fell to black.

I came to my senses sitting, slouched against a hard surface, my head resting on my left shoulder and Red's reassuring weight on my right. Jacoby's grim voice rumbled nearby for a time before I began to register his words.

"—Council will not allow her to retain such knowledge. Compel me all you want. It changes nothing. My influence will not be enough to protect her. You know what must be done."

"I cannot force it on her. This one is special. The Domn forbids it."

"Then you must do your best to convince her," Jacoby said. "I can do nothing in that regard. The ubhnati's influence poisons her against me. She won't trust a word I say."

"Standing by your unworthy charge hasn't done you any favors either. It was a mistake to take up her petition."

"Bound oaths aren't something one can ignore," he snapped. "As you know all too well."

"That, I do." He sighed. "Very well. Leave us."

A moment of silence passed, pierced only by Jacoby's retreating footsteps and the closing door.

Alex's whisper came at my ear. "I know you're awake."

I gasped and flinched up straight, opening my eyes to find him crouched next to me in his normal human form, his pale face a mere twelve inches from my own. When I bit my lip guiltily, he chuckled.

He had a nice smile, when his fangs weren't down that is, and his human eyes were a golden-brown, not blue, like I'd been imagining. He also had more freckles than I did. They peppered his nose and cheeks in a loose butterfly pattern. Even though we'd been in school together for my entire freshman year, until now, I'd never gotten close enough to his nighttime form to appreciate these things.

I looked around me. I sat on the cold floor of Treblow's study, my back against the wall to the right of the closed door. All the sorcerer's precious scrolls were gone, in addition to his tapestries and other knotted pieces. The items that remained were his monstrous oak desk, leather chair, two mostly empty bookcases, and several floor lamps. A stack of flattened cardboard boxes, three rolls of packing paper, and a tape gun were strewn in the far corner. Bits of paper, balls of discarded tape, and other debris littered the floor.

"Is it night?" I asked. "How long was I out?"

"A few minutes." He glanced around. "This room hasn't any windows," he said, returning his gaze to mine. "I thought my human form would make you less uneasy."

"The other's not so bad, once you get used to it," I said before cringing at how that sounded. "Sorry. That didn't come out right. What I mean is — "

"It's fine. I get it." He looked me over. "How do you feel?"

I shrugged, assessing the weight of fatigue that pressed down on me. "Totally slammed. Like I just finished a ten-mile run." In fact, I wasn't a hundred percent sure I could stand up without help.

"No wonder. Jacoby says you destroyed a ward that would have taken the entire Council a solid week to break."

"I knew the key." I tapped a finger to my temple, belatedly realizing that I'd basically echoed Jacoby's earlier pronouncement.

"Exactly." He shifted from his crouch to sit cross legged alongside my outstretched legs. "And there's the rub."

For a second, I could only marvel at the bizarre turn my life had taken. Never in my wildest dreams did I ever expect that I'd end up sitting on the floor in Treblow's mostly empty study, talking to Mr. Blond-and-Intimidating as though we were friends.

He propped his elbows on his knees and regarded me earnestly. "You heard some of our conversation, but I'm not sure you understand what's at stake. Do you?"

"I think so. Once the king finds out I have these memories, I'm toast. Not to mention anyone else who wants Treblow's stuff, like Jacoby and the Council." I banged the back of my head against the wall. "I never should have read his blood, but I was worried about Cal." I straightened. "You need to tell Zach's dad, I'm almost positive those two zombies were Cal's cousins, the ones Zach and Cal were trying to find."

He nodded. "Thanks to you, they'll be put to rest and their families will know they weren't to blame for Treblow's death. We all owe you a debt—the Domn, the Isangrim, the Council, the Doyen and, especially, his sons. If you hadn't subdued Owen, there's no telling how many others he might have killed or enslaved."

And, now, it seemed I'd be hunted down and my memories ripped from my head. Some thanks.

I sighed. "No good deed goes unpunished, I guess."

At least Cal would be released from jail. When it came down to it, I'd do it all over again, just for that.

"I can help you, Clotilde, if you'll allow it." His brown eyes looked deeply into mine.

"You need my permission. I heard you say so to Jacoby. Why? What is it you want to do?"

He hesitated, considering me. "I can make you forget what you learned today. When the king's telepaths read your mind, they'll leave you alone."

"You can do that? You have telepathy, too?"

Three rare gifts? That had to be a record.

He gave me a strange look. "All strigoi have that power."

I blinked, puzzled, and then my eyes went wide. He was talking about biting me! "But mind psychics are immune to strigoi saliva."

"Technically, you're not immune. Your mental shield protects you. For me to help you, you'd have to purposely lower it."

If I did that and allowed him to bite me, I'd become his thrall. He could order me to do *anything* and I'd comply without question. He could order me to kill my dad and I'd do it.

He took one look at my expression and patted the air between us. "Just hold on for a second. Before you freak out and reject me out of hand, hear me out. I'm not so hard up that I need a blood patron, okay? And since I can day-walk, a minion serves no purpose. But none of that matters. The Domn forbids me from doing anything that interferes with the course of your life. Like I told Jacoby, I can't do anything without your express permission. And the same goes if I bite you."

"What are you saying? Even if you have my blood and can order me around, you won't because the Domn won't let you? What if the Domn changes his mind?"

"That's not going to happen, but it doesn't matter because this will be a covenant between us. It'll take precedence."

"So, it would be like a blood oath, magically binding? Between you and me?"

"Yes. Exactly."

"And you'll swear only to erase my memories about Treblow?"

"Yes. The ones you acquired with your gift and probably most of what happened after."

"But what about Cal? If you delete those memories, I can't testify about witnessing what Owen did. He ordered those weres to kill Treblow."

"As soon as we're done, the police will be notified," he said. "They'll see the remains of the two zombies and put two and two together. Plus, the DNA will back that up. You don't need to worry about Mr. Mars."

Between Alex's use of 'mister' for Zach and Cal and the way he'd dismissed Jacoby with such authority, I had the strangest sense that I was talking to someone much older than eighteen. It had me believing the stories I'd heard about how the Domn spoke to all his subjects telepathically, no matter the distance.

Cripes. Did that mean the Domn could listen in, too?

I shoved the thought away before I got nervous and started stammering.

"What about Owen?"

"He'll face the Tribunal," Alex said, adding snidely, "if he lasts that long."

I frowned at that last bit, but it wasn't like I could do anything about it. Owen had chosen his path and, after what he'd done, I wasn't about to waste my breath pleading for his protection.

"Why is the Domn so interested in helping me?" I asked. "I mean, I get that you guys don't want the elf king to learn Treblow's secrets and stuff, but even before all this, the Domn stepped in to help me with that stupid stuff with Amanda." I glared at him. "I know it was him on the phone in Mr. Simmons' office. Don't try to deny it."

He tilted his head to the side, conceding the point.

When he didn't add anything to the sentiment, I scowled. "Come on Alex, tell me. Why am I special, like you said? Because jumping between you and Skyler in the computer lab doesn't seem all that amazing to me and that's the only thing I can think of."

"I'll tell you, if you promise you'll agree to our mutual oath."

I rolled my eyes. "Duh. Because you'll erase whatever you tell me, along with the rest of Treblow's memories, and I'll never know the difference."

His smile was so boyish and utterly unrepentant, I couldn't stay annoyed.

I thought about it. I trusted Alex way more than some faceless group of telepaths, that was for sure. And not remembering Treblow's horrific death certainly wouldn't be a hardship. On the other hand,

Cal would never know what I'd done to help him. But that was my selfish pride talking.

"What about my familiar?" I asked, reaching up to cup Red's cuddly body to the side of my head. "He'll know what happened, that you altered my memories."

"True, but High Necromancer Redborn knows how to keep a secret, especially those that might put his master in danger." Alex tipped his head genially at Red. "Magister Redborn, it's an honor to see you again."

"And you, Alexei."

My astonished gaze danced between them. "You two *know* each other?"

"Like I said, Magister Redborn knows when to keep a secret."

I gaped at him before coming to a bitter realization. Folding my arms, I slumped against the wall and frowned. "I finally learn all these amazing things and you're going to erase them."

Alex smirked.

I glanced at Red. "What do you think? Is this something I should do?"

"I know little of the sidhe king, so I cannot estimate the danger he presents. However, if telepaths are employed to remove these memories from your mind, the vice president is correct in voicing his concern. If care is not taken, considerable harm could come from such efforts. In regard to Alexei and the Domn, my past witness has always proven their word to be inviolate. You could do considerably worse than choosing to place your trust in them."

"Fine," I grumbled. "I'll do it. Not like I've much of a choice." I glared at Alex. "I'll agree to this oath with you, but I have one more condition. You or the Domn need to make sure that Jacoby never tells anyone about Red being my familiar. Since you know who he is, then I'm sure you also know there're people who would kill me to get him. If Jacoby spills the beans ..." I shuddered and had to stop myself from hugging Red to my chest.

"Agreed."

I eyed him. "Okay, now, spill. What's the deal with the Domn?"

Alex leaned back on his hands and gave me a singularly indulgent look. "I've been told that you'll be of great service to my Domn at some point in the future."

"It has nothing to do with my dad?"

He shook his head.

"Really? So … that's it? No details about this 'great service' or when it's supposed to happen?"

"All I know is that you'll be instrumental in saving the life of someone dear to my Domn's heart. No idea when or how."

"And the Domn learned this from a divinor or something?"

"Not just *any* divinor—a very old and esteemed oracle."

It was mind-boggling how much stock people put into divinations, even someone as powerful as the Domn.

I made a face. "Well, that was boring."

Alex laughed. The sound was so genuine and his expression so charming that, soon, I was chuckling too. Sometimes it was hard to remember that this cute guy harbored such a formidable alter ego.

"Could you seriously rip Jacoby's head off, like you said?"

His grin flattened to a ruthless flash of teeth. "Clotilde, I *never* bluff."

He'd do everything he'd promised. All these memories were as good as gone, but sometime in the future, I stood a good chance of meeting him again.

Until then, I'd have his protection.

But he'd also have my jot of blood.

CHAPTER 19

I've been wanting to do that for a while

THE circus surrounding our discovery in Treblow's living room was epic. Soon after my 9-1-1 call, the police arrived on scene to find the bloody carpet, disrupted living room, and me, sitting on the floor by the back door with an unconscious Zach's head in my lap — everything exactly as I'd described in a panicked voice to the unflappable emergency dispatcher, not ten minutes earlier.

The two officers searched the house, finding a grisly scene in the basement that I was sure I didn't want to know about, based on their markedly pale faces and grim expressions.

By the time Zach's dad showed up to take him to the school's infirmary, a fleet of police cruisers lined Sorcerer Treblow's driveway. I was forced to wait on the front porch, watching dozens of officers going in and out, before being questioned by a grumpy bald detective.

Since I was a minor, Mr. Gibbs had to be present during my questioning. He'd also been asked to help identify the bodies the police had discovered in the basement. Mr. Gibbs hadn't been a happy camper, but at least he'd told me that the police had found the remains of two werewolves. We both hoped they'd quickly realize that these two weres had been responsible for Treblow's death and drop the charges against Cal.

We didn't get back to campus until almost nine that night. And, to top everything off, I'd gone to bed thinking I might be catching something. I had a massive headache and my neck was sore. Plus, the cut I'd gotten while goofing around with Cal's pocket knife hurt like heck. I still couldn't believe I'd been so dumb as to be playing with it while walking through Treblow's clod-strewn fields.

Cal was released from jail the next morning, but Zach and I were too busy getting reamed out by Mr. Simmons and Mr. Gibbs to know about it. Afterward, Zach and I had slunk to our first-period classes, thirty minutes late, hungry for breakfast, and saddled with a week's worth of garbage duty.

The day brightened significantly, though, at the sight of Cal at our lunch table.

Ignoring the hushed chattering that accompanied my arrival in the dining room, I clutched my tray and rushed over.

I plunked my lunch on the table and slid onto the bench in one move, my eyes glued to the rumpled-looking were. If not for my darn gift, I would have hugged him. But that wasn't going to happen, so I had to satisfy myself with touching his arm.

"I'm so glad to see you. When did you get back? How're you doing? You okay?" Everything came out in a rush, and I gave him a half-apologetic half-sheepish smile.

"Oh, don't mind me," Zach piped up before Cal could answer. "I was only *unconscious* for ten hours. And then got kicked out of the infirmary at oh-dark early so I could make our wonderful meeting with Simmons and his sidekick. But I'm fine. Thanks for asking."

"You weren't in jail," I said tartly. "And if you hadn't insisted on snooping around Treblow's house instead of calling the police—right away, like I *told* you to — you wouldn't have been knocked out by Treblow's defensive spell." I scowled and leaned forward. "And thanks a lot for that, you big jerk. You scared the crap out of me! I had to deal with Mr. Gibbs and the police, all by myself, while you got to sleep it off."

I folded my arms and glared at him.

"Fine. You were right," he groused. "After seeing the blood and the messed-up living room, we should have called the police, instead of sneaking around. Go ahead and say it — 'I told you so.'"

"Well, maybe for just that part," I said, relaxing my arms. "But you were right about sneaking inside. If we hadn't done that, who knows how long Cal would have been stuck in jail." I turned to Cal and cringed. "Was it horrible?"

He shrugged. "It wasn't as bad as it could have been. They gave me my own cell."

"You look tired."

"Didn't sleep well. The bed sucked and someone was snoring like a frickin' foghorn." He shuddered. "And the food was terrible."

"That stinks." I gave him a sympathetic look. "So, uh, the dead werewolves that the police found in Treblow's basement. Were they … your cousins?"

He nodded. "The Isangrim confirmed it, last night."

"The police let you go, so that must mean they figured out your cousins are the ones who killed Treblow," I said.

He nodded.

"I'm sorry." Truly, I was, and not simply because it meant that my two best friends would be leaving. Although, I'd have been lying if I said it wasn't the main reason for my regret. "Does anyone know why they killed Treblow? Or how they ended up dead in his basement?"

"No clue," Cal replied. "It's weird, though. I guess the bodies were pretty messed up."

"Messed up? What do you mean?"

"Pop said they were in pieces."

"Jesus." I made a face. "Thank God Zach and I didn't go into the basement." I was also thankful I hadn't needed to touch the spot where Treblow died. All in all, it could have been a lot worse.

"I guess it's good that I got zapped, after all," Zach drawled. "If I hadn't, just think of what else we would've found."

"You're my hero, for sure," I said dryly. "Blasting yourself senseless and leaving me in that creepy house all alone, except for two dead bodies in the basement. Good job."

"You didn't know about the bodies," Zach said.

"True, but it was creepy as heck with the blood and the signs of struggle. Plus, I had no idea what'd happened to you! Waiting for Mr. Gibbs and the police to come were the longest ten minutes of my life."

"Yeah, well—"

"What the idiot isn't saying is thank you," Cal cut in. He peered at me with those crystalline blue eyes of his. "For everything. We won't forget it. If there ever comes a time that you need our help, we'll be there for you. You have my word on that."

I gazed down at my grilled cheese, which I'd lost interest in eating. "You're going to leave, now, aren't you?"

"Soon. Yeah," Cal said, his voice soft.

I nodded, biting my lip.

You will not cry. You will not cry.

"Pop's going to make sure you don't have to do garbage patrol, though," Zach said. "He's grateful to you, too. We all are."

I shrugged. I hadn't done much of anything. Just tagged along, hoping that I wouldn't have to use my gift on anything too awful. I'd called Mr. Simmons and the police. Big deal.

On the other hand, if I hadn't gone with Zach, he'd probably still be unconscious in Treblow's mudroom with no one to call for help. And Cal would have been stuck in jail for another day, or at least until someone discovered Zach and the bodies.

I looked up and smiled across the table. "Make me one of your drawings, on nice paper, and we'll call it even."

He chuckled. "No problem, but only if you promise to put it next to that dopey picture of Cal you've got hanging above your bed."

"It's not above my bed, it's on my wardrobe cabinet," I retorted, hoping my burning cheeks weren't noticeably red. "And it's a killer photo, so shut up."

"Whatever you say, princess."

"Do I get a photo of you, too?" Cal asked, briefly leaning closer to whisper next to my ear.

Smiling, I glanced away and shrugged. "I guess so ... if you want."

"I want. If I give you my address, will you mail it to me?"

I nodded.

"Hurry up and eat, slowpoke, or we'll be late for class," Zach griped.

"We? I thought you guys were leaving." I glanced his way as I pulled the protective plastic from my psi-free mineral water.

"Pop's meeting with Mr. Simmons and Mr. Gibbs, so we're stuck here for a bit," Zach said. "Plus, we want to say goodbye to Mountainside."

I forced myself to wash down a few bites of my lunch before the bell rang.

Professor Trapp was suitably shocked to hear about Cal's wrongful incarceration and what Zach and I had discovered at Treblow's house. Mid-way into the period, after we'd told him all that happened, including the truth about Zach and Cal's reason for attending Coventry, the call finally came from Mrs. McPherson, asking that both brothers report to the main office.

I knew this was the last time I'd see them.

I stood and watched while they gathered their backpacks. Zach's disappeared as soon as he touched it. Cal hefted his over his left shoulder and then stopped to consider me, his lips pressed together in a thin line.

"Hey, Prof, is it okay if Lire walks us out?" Zach called out from the door.

He waved us out. "Sure. Best of luck, boys. Lire, take your time."

Heart in my throat, I walked alongside Cal until we exited the building's back door and stopped beneath a nearby maple tree.

"Well, princess, this is it. Don't stay out of trouble. I expect regular updates with all the juicy gossip." He tugged a lock of my hair. "Don't disappoint me. It's all on you, now."

Eyes burning, I thrust out my hands, searching the air in front of me until I found him. I threw my arms around his shoulders and gave him a fierce hug. "I'll miss you." Jumping back, I scolded him through my sniffles. "Don't forget my drawing, okay?"

"I won't. Promise." He cleared his throat. "I, uh, I'm going to walk ahead. Okay, bro? I'll see ya 'round, Lire." He squeezed my arm and, in my ear, he whispered, "I'm going to miss you too, tiger. More than you know."

I had to bite my bottom lip to stop it from trembling as I listened to his retreating footsteps.

Cal regarded me with a serious expression. "I wish I'd gone to school here, instead of being tutored. You know?"

I nodded, not trusting my voice. For the dozenth time, I scolded myself to keep it together.

"Just ... whatever you do, don't change for them, okay?" He frowned, looking hard into my eyes. "Anyone who can't see that you're the most amazing girl in this whole school doesn't deserve your time."

I blinked, warmed by his vehemence. "I think you're pretty awesome, too. I'm going to miss you, Cal. A lot." My voice cracked, and I was reduced to biting my bottom lip again.

"Yeah ... me too. Uh, I'd like to ... I mean would it be okay if I—?" He shuffled his feet, looking distinctly nervous, and stepped closer. He held up his hands so I could see that he'd put on flesh-colored gloves, probably some of Zach's extras. "Can I, um ... I don't know ... give you a hug and, uh, maybe, a kiss goodbye?" His eyes widened. "If that's not okay, it's fine, I under—"

Before he could back away, I put my hands on either side of his waist and squeezed.

"—stand," he finished and then let out his pent breath in a minty, relieved gush. Moving closer still, his hands settled on my shoulders and he looked down at me with a shy grin that I wanted to devour whole.

He didn't make me wait.

He wove his fingers into the hair at the back of my neck and pulled me in, his lips a tantalizing brush against mine, touching off a kaleidoscope of butterflies that swirled through me. I gasped into his mouth, the sound muted by his lips as we each pressed closer to deepen our kiss. After a deliciously long moment while our mouths practiced this enticing new dance, his tongue flicked at the seam of my barely parted lips ... once ... twice ... and then, ever so briefly, darted inside to graze against mine, its slick warmth sending a jolt of excitement straight to my toes.

He tasted like peppermint gum and something else, something pleasantly forbidding that I imagined was unique to Cal. Everything fell away as his thoughts spiraled into my mind, bittersweet wishes and lustful yearnings that mixed with my own, heating me thoroughly until I didn't know where my thoughts ended and his began. But before I could get carried away on that wave of wanton desire, he broke the kiss and gently tucked my hair behind my right ear.

"I've been wanting to do that for a while," he admitted breathlessly, his voice rougher than usual.

"I know. Me too." I bit my lip, my body still humming, begging for more. If things had gone on, just a wee bit longer, I was sure he would have given me the tongue-tangling kiss of my dreams.

He suddenly looked worried. "Was it okay? I mean ... my thoughts ... when we were kissing like that I couldn't, you know ..." He cringed. "They weren't too bad, were they?"

I shook my head. "They were perfect." Smiling, I glanced away. "Especially once you stopped worrying about what you were thinking."

He ducked his head sheepishly before considering me with a devilish smirk. "Then I wish we had time to do that some more."

"Ditto." I sighed. "I guess that's not in the cards, though."

He looked sad. "No. I guess not. At least, not right now."

I nodded as I searched his face. "Maybe ... we could stay in touch?"

God, his eyes were stunning. I could happily stare into them for ages.

"I'd like that." He gave my shoulders a final caress and stepped back, depriving me of the heat of his body.

"Oh! Here." He bent down and rummaged through his backpack for a spiral notebook. He jotted something down and then handed me the ripped piece of paper.

It was his address and, even though I already had it, he'd written his cell number, too.

"Mail me that photo." He gave me a stern look. "You promised." Glancing down the pathway, he sighed. "I should go, but I'll text you later, okay?"

I nodded. "Okay."

He darted in for one more kiss, a quick peck on my left cheek, and backed away. "Bye."

Thankfully, the touch of his lips was so brief, I managed to coil his thoughts behind my shield and toss them away. I didn't want to experience them. I was sad enough already.

"Goodbye, Cal." Hugging myself, I watched as he strode away. I kept my composure until he disappeared around the corner with a fleeting wave.

When I finally dragged myself into Professor Trapp's classroom at 3:10 to pick up my backpack, after missing the rest of English and all of French class, he took one look at me and his expression softened. "You okay?"

I shrugged.

"They're good guys. I'm sorry to see them go." He tipped his head, considering me. "By the way, Zach wanted me to give you a message."

I blinked at him, puzzled. "He did?"

My teacher nodded. "He wanted me to tell you that you can thank him, later, for Desktastrophy. And not to worry. He gave Hugh a cash bonus for all the reassembly."

Despite crying in the bathroom for a good chunk of the last hour, I laughed.

I shook my head. Only Zach would be brazen enough to leave that kind of message with a teacher.

I couldn't wait to see the picture he promised to draw for me.

EPILOGUE

Life is a crazy roller coaster

Three months later ...

"GIRL! We're going to have some serious words if what I just heard about you is true," Diedra said as she slammed her English Comp binder on the table and collapsed dramatically into the empty seat next to me. She gave me her sassiest scowl. "I told you about my summer of doom and everything!"

I laughed, shaking my head at her. "Don't worry. If it's about me and remotely interesting, it's probably not true. Just saying."

"Shannon told me that you and *Zach* found two dead bodies at the beginning of the school year!"

I blinked. "Huh. Oh, yeah. I guess I forgot about that."

She gawked at me.

Ever since she'd started school, moving into the room next to mine in early-October, Diedra and I had become such fast friends you'd have thought we'd been separated at birth, never mind that she was half-Japanese. We were both clairvoyants, we both kept journals and loved manga, and, two months later, we both knew practically everything there was to know about the other. Mountainside had started calling us Thing 1 and Thing 2 after our Doctor Seuss-inspired Halloween costumes and because he seemed to think we were bound for mischief with the way we giggled and gossiped during our private English Comp class.

"Forgot?" She huffed. "You found two dead bodies and you forgot? Not to mention the sexy woodcutter was there, *too*, and you didn't tell me?"

She meant Zach. I was convinced she was more than half in love with him with the way she interrogated me whenever his name came up. After hearing about the drawing he'd sent to me, she'd begged for a full week until I gave her a copy of it. In it, I was a sexy Little Red Riding Hood watching avidly as the Big Bad Wolf stared at me. Nearby, a manly, broad-shouldered black silhouette leaned against a tree, a huge axe dangling from his hand.

Smirking, I wondered what Zach would think of Diedra's nickname for him.

Who was I kidding? The sexy woodcutter? He'd love it.

I shook my head at her. "You're making it sound *way* more exciting than it was. We didn't see any dead bodies, only blood and knocked over furniture." Cringing, I left out how Zach had gotten himself zapped senseless by snooping around. "The police were the ones who found the bodies, down in the basement. The whole thing was boring beyond belief, and then Mr. Simmons and Mr. Gibbs read Zach and me the riot act and gave us garbage patrol for a week for trespassing on restricted school property."

The Doyen ended up convincing Mr. Simmons to reduce my sentence to one day of kitchen duty, so it could've been worse.

"But Shannon said it got *bodalicious* Cal out of jail, so that must have made every garbage day taste like cupcakes," she finished in song, waving her arms gracefully in the air, doing her best impression of a sugar plum fairy while still stuck in her plastic chair.

I snickered, but inside, my stomach dipped at his name.

Cal.

I wondered for the gazillionth time when, or if, I'd see him again. He still sent me occasional text messages, so did Zach, but in the three months since their departure, the time between our exchanges had gone from hours to days to weeks. At this rate, it wouldn't be long before we stopped texting altogether. The thought cued the bitter-sweet heaviness in my chest that always came whenever I thought about Cal, especially when I remembered the captivating kiss he'd given me. My lips still tingled and I got all breathless whenever I replayed how sweet and intoxicating that brief slide of lips had been. I'd desperately wanted more, but at this point, anything better than a long-distance friendship didn't seem likely.

Still, you never knew. Three months ago, I wouldn't have dreamed that the day would come when Amanda got sent to another school, nor imagined Professor Everhart taking a job in Alaska of all places. *Or* that I'd end up going to the Homecoming dance with Ted (as good friends, amazingly enough) and, even more implausibly, that we'd be crowned King and Queen.

I guess all of that went to prove — life was a crazy rollercoaster ride and you never knew what surprises might be waiting around the next negative-G turn.

Especially for a teenage clairvoyant with a talent for trouble.

GLOSSARY

AENAI
A class of magic dealing with the manipulation of air and the weather.

ARCANE COUNCIL
The ruling body for all magic users (both witchcraft and sorcery) in the United States.

ARCANIST
A coarse term for a member of the Arcane Council.

BLACK MAGIC
A term used to describe a wide gamut of hurtful, demeaning, or otherwise negatively perceived enchantments. The most heinous 'black' spells require a human sacrifice to garner sufficient power to fuel them.

BLACK MAGUS
A spellcaster who practices black magic or whose soul has been compromised by a demon.

BROWNIE
A diminutive, roughly humanoid race from the Otherworld. Often mistaken for a hobgoblin, they are smaller, less hairy, and do not typically indulge in practical jokes. They have been known to inhabit human homes and perform household tasks in exchange for small gifts of food. Bread (especially brioche) and honey are said to be particular favorites. They work only at night and do not like to be seen. Of all the fae, brownies have been the most eager to reside permanently on Earth.

CIRCLE OF POWER
A ritually defined space, usually sealed with blood, used in spellcasting to control the flow of magic (and/or physical access) within its boundaries. See summoner, ward.

CLAIRVOYANT

A mind psychic who can read the psychic imprints (memories) associated with an object or person through direct physical contact.

CLEAN ROOM

An enclosed space that is completely psi-free, often within the confines of a psychiatric hospital.

COVENTRY ACADEMY

The private elementary, middle, and high school, located in Coventry, WA, dedicated to the education of children capable of spellcasting, possessing a psychic ability, or cursed by magic, including those affected by the strigoi curse (vampirism) and therianthropy.

CRYOKINETIC

An individual who can siphon ambient heat from the atmosphere or other physical objects. Also known as an icemaker.

CURSE

An enchantment that, by its very nature, imparts both positive and negative effects on an individual, location, or object. When applied to an individual, a curse is often (but not always) hereditary or transmittable via body fluids. Of all curses, therianthropy and the strigoi curse are perhaps the most well-known.

DARK ARTS/DARK MAGIC

A term used to describe a class of magic that deals with darkness and death. Sometimes used to describe the gray area between wholesome spells and those that are perceived to be unwholesome yet do not rise to the level of black magic.

DIVINOR

An individual with the gift of precognition, the ability to foresee the future. Also known as oracle, seer, or prophesier.

DOMN

Title given to the ruler of the United Convocation of Strigoi (vampires).

DOYEN
Title given to the chief of the Hidden (occultums).

ELF
In English vernacular, a term that refers to a sidhe, popularized by J. R. R. Tolkien in his high-fantasy books. Because 'elf' has, in the distant past, been used to describe invisible demonic beings and other unsavory (and often fictional) creatures, it isn't a term the sidhe favor.

ESSENCE
An individual's life-force, their soul.

ETHERMANCER
A sorcerer who has the power to read and alter auras.

FAE
An English vernacular term that refers to the many unique beings and creatures that inhabit the Otherworld.

FAERY
An English vernacular term for the Otherworld.

FAIRY
An English vernacular term for fae that has come to be associated with the fictionalized versions of Otherworld creatures found in European folklore. Often viewed as derogatory.

FAIRYLAND
An English vernacular term for the Otherworld. Often viewed as derogatory.

FIRESTARTER
See pyrokinetic.

GATEWAY
A magical conduit, or portal, large enough to provide physical transport from one place to another, often between dimensions or worlds.

GEOMANCER

A magus that has the power to manipulate earth and rocks.

GEOMANCY

A class of magic dealing with the manipulation of earth and rocks.

GLINDARIAN

A member of the Glindarian witchcraft sect. Glindarians are known for their dedication to healing and other restorative spells.

GOLEM

A magical being that is created from inanimate matter, often clay. It typically possesses limited intelligence and requires the continued direction of its creator to function.

THE HIDDEN

A secretive organization that is almost entirely composed of members afflicted by the occultum curse. If the rumors are true, they are frequently hired by governments and big businesses, using their skills for spying and espionage.

ICEMAKER

See cryokinetic.

ISANGRIM

Title given to the ruler of the North American Rout (werewolves).

KEYSTONE

One of at least three runestones used in the creation of a perimeter ward.

LEPRECHAUN

A diminutive, humanoid race from the Otherworld who are known for their skill in shoemaking and leatherworking. They are unrivaled in their ability to evade and escape capture, often by shape-shifting. If they are apprehended, a leprechaun will grant their captor one favor in exchange for release. Like brownies, they are content to reside permanently on Earth.

LEVITATION
The act of moving objects without interacting with them physically. See telekinesis.

LYCANTHROPY
The human-to-wolf transformation curse. See therianthropy.

MAGE/MAGIC USER/MAGUS
An individual with the ability to cast spells; a spellcaster.

MAGIC RESERVATIONS
Government owned compounds dedicated to the care and rearing of state adopted youngsters who are spellcasters, gifted with a psychic ability, or cursed.

MAGICIAN
Someone who does parlor tricks. Not a true magic user.

NECROMANCER
A magus with power over the dead. Many necromancers are also summoners. See black magus.

NORMAL
An individual who possesses no magical ability.

NORTH AMERICAN ROUT
The official organization of werewolves in the United States and Canada.

OCCULTUM
An individual afflicted with the occultum curse, a curse that renders its recipient completely invisible, including their shadow and, in some cases, any accompanying scent or sound.

ORACLE
See divinor.

OTHERWORLD
The world where the sidhe and other fae reside. Also known as Faerie.

PARANORMAL REGULATORY COMMISSION
An international organization of psychics that governs the conduct of the psychic community.

PIXIE
A diminutive, humanoid race from the Otherworld who are endearingly childlike and benign in character. They live in large clans, are tremendously fond of music and dancing, and often partake in mischievous but harmless pranks.

PORTAL
A magical conduit, most often forged during a summoning, that connects two different locations, providing access to another dimension or world. A portal may or may not be large enough for physical transport. See gateway.

PROPHECY
A prediction of the future.

PROPHESIER
See divinor.

PSI-FREE
Term used to describe something that is free of psychic (life-essence) contamination; an object untouched by humans or animals.

PSI-WARD
An area within a hospital that specializes in the care of those gifted with psychic or magic powers or individuals suffering from magic related injuries or curses.

PSYCHIC SHIELD
The mental construct that all clairvoyants and telepaths use to control the inflow of thoughts and memories into their own minds.

PSYCHIC
An individual gifted with a mind power, either telekinesis, pyrokinesis, cryokinesis, divination, truthsaying, or clairvoyance. Sensitives are also sometimes psychic. A psychic never possesses more than

one ability. (It is not understood why.) Telepathy is thought to be the rarest of the psychic abilities, followed by clairvoyance.

PYROKINETIC
An individual who can generate ambient heat. Also known as a fire-starter.

ROWAN
A member of the Rowan witchcraft sect, which is probably the most well-known of all the witchcraft denominations, second only to the Glindarian sect. The threefold principle is a guiding tenet for their members.

RUNE
A magical symbol often used in witchcraft to adapt, guide, or enhance a spell.

RUNESTONE
A stone marked with a runic inscription, often used in witchcraft to focus and enhance the magus' spellcasting.

SEER
See divinor.

SENSITIVE
An individual who can detect (and often identify) specific types of magic and/or individual spells.

SHADOW-MAGE/SHADOWMANCER
A spellcaster who has the power to manipulate darkness. See black magus.

SHIFTER/SHAPE-SHIFTER
A being that can change its shape and hold its new form, by virtue of magic or a curse. A werewolf is a type of shape-shifter.

SIDHE
An elder race that is arguably the most humanoid of all the magical beings that inhabit the Otherworld. The sidhe are known by other

sobriquets—aos sí, aes sídhe, daoine sídhe, daoine síth, and (perhaps least liked by the creatures themselves) fairy and elf. They are also sometimes referred to as 'the good neighbors,' 'the fair folk,' or 'people of the mounds.' Their Earth-bound gateways are typically encapsulated by a mound of earth or encircled by stones or mushrooms.

SILVEN
The language of the sidhe.

SKIN-SUIT
A thin bodysuit crafted from psi-free, moisture-repelling fabric, which is used to prevent contact between a clairvoyant and other individuals or objects.

SORCERER/SORCERESS
A magus who uses gestures for casting spells, their abilities are typically restricted to a certain field of magic.

SORCERY
Spellcasting performed by a sorcerer or sorceress.

STRIGOI
An individual affected by the strigoi curse; a vampire.

STRIGOI CURSE
The curse that causes vampirism. An individual afflicted by this curse is granted immortality, superior strength, and, in a limited fashion, the ability to shape-shift. Countering each of these boons is an equally powerful weakness. (This duality is the hallmark of all curses.) In the case of vampirism, the cursed individual's existence is restricted to the night—during daylight hours most are helpless and virtually comatose. To satisfy their thirst for sustenance, they must drink human blood. Precious metals cause great pain and weakness. The most powerful strigoi are almost always blessed with one additional gift that may or may not be offset by an additional weakness.

SUMMONER

A magic user capable of summoning a spirit being, usually from another dimension or universe, to a designated location, typically a circle of power. Because many summoners choose to work with demons, this branch of magic is often unfairly maligned. (It is important to note, however, that summoning is not synonymous with devil worship.) Summoning demons is extremely dangerous for the uninitiated and uneducated. As such, it is a practice best left to the experts. Necromancers are often (but not always) summoners.

TELEKINETIC

A psychic capable of levitating an object. A type one telekinetic can move only inanimate objects, a type two can move only animate objects, a type three can move both animate and inanimate objects. See levitation.

TELEPATH

A psychic capable of reading human thoughts without skin contact. Some (but not all) are capable of inserting memories into a human subject's mind. Fewer still can assume enough control to direct their human subject's actions. Of all the psychic abilities, telepathy is the rarest.

THERIANTHROPY

Term used to describe the curse of human-to-animal transformation. An individual afflicted with this curse is granted the ability to transform into a specific animal. Only rigorous training and self-discipline allows the cursed individual to retain their human consciousness during transformation. Depending upon their skill, this transformation can take place at will, however, during nights of the full moon, the transformation is compulsory. See werewolf.

THREEFOLD PRINCIPLE

The belief that the energy a magic user (or psychic) dispenses, whether it be positive or negative, will be returned threefold. You reap what you sow.

TÍR NA HÓIGE
The land ruled by the king of the sidhe. It means 'land of youth' in Silven.

TOUCHY
A derogatory term for a clairvoyant.

TRUE NAME
A being's intrinsic name, one which is bound so closely that it's tied to their essence. When pronounced with intimate familiarity, it can be used in a ritual to summon the being between worlds.

TRUTHSAYER
A psychic who can detect whether a person is being truthful.

UBHNATI
A magic user who is skilled in the art of magic weaving—the ability to store and invoke spells through woven knots.

UNITED CONVOCATION OF STRIGOI
The international society of individuals affected by the strigoi curse.

VAMPIRE
A colloquial term for strigoi, one that is viewed as somewhat coarse by those affected by the strigoi curse.

VARANGIAN COUNCIL
The Varangian Council is considered the progenitor of the Arcane Council. It formed back in the tenth century around the time of the Norman conquest of England.

VIRGE
A rod often used by witches and warlocks as a focal object for their spellcasting. In the past, virges were traditionally turned or carved from a single branch of a chosen tree. In more recent years, virges crafted from wood-infused resins have become increasingly popular. Unlike wands, virges can be retractible for more discrete carrying and storage.

WAND

A stick or rod, crafted from a single tree branch, often used as a focal object for witchcraft. A wand may be sourced from a wide variety of tree species known for their magical properties. Wands are traditionally finished to a high sheen but are otherwise left in their natural state, unlike virges, which are often carved. A wand is a type of virge. The two terms are often used interchangeably, even though a virge is not always a wand.

WARD

A type of ensorcellment that regulates (or prohibits) any magical or physical interactions that take place within its area of effect. Such spells are often (but not exclusively) used in conjunction with a magic circle, or within the natural boundary provided by a dwelling's foundation, and reinforced with runestones, otherwise known as keystones.

WARLOCK/WITCH

A magus who can only employ spoken or chanted magic. They use runestones and/or other focus objects (such as wands and virges) to power or strengthen their spells.

WERE

Someone who is cursed with therianthropy.

WITCHCRAFT

Spoken or chanted magic.

ZOMBIE

A human or animal corpse that has been raised from dead and animated by magical means.

AUTHOR'S NOTE

If you're anything like me, you're a rabid Scrooge when it comes to your free time. You carefully ration it and begrudge the need to spend it on ridiculous distractions like eating, sleeping, and shaving your legs. Okay, that could just be me. Even so, the fact that you spent your valuable time, reading something I created for enjoyment, means a great deal to me.

But if I don't hear from you, cherished reader, I'll have no way to know whether I succeeded or failed (or maybe just left you saying 'meh') in my attempt to entertain you.

I hope you'll consider posting a review of *A Jot of Blood* on the site where you purchased it. Reviews not only help other readers decide if my novels are something they might enjoy, but they also let me know where I need to improve as a storyteller. I appreciate all reviews, positive or negative. Let me know what worked for you and what didn't. You're also invited to visit and correspond with me on my website at www.katherinebayless.com. I'd love to hear from you.

ABOUT THE AUTHOR

photo © 2010 by S. Hamer

Katherine Bayless writes paranormal fantasy and romance for fun and occasional profit. When she isn't adventuring vicariously through her stories or playing chauffeur to her kids, Katherine crafts hand-made greeting cards, lays waste to the Scourge in World of Warcraft, and indulges her addictions to cooking shows, science documentaries, and digital photography.

In twenty-five years, she has moved eleven times, calling California, Oregon, Washington, and Illinois home at one time or another. She currently lives happily in view of Central Oregon's ancient volcanoes with her husband, three children, a sweet, shamelessly spoiled whippet named Patches, and Zeke, a cabinet-opening, treat-stealing commando who doesn't know his own name because everyone just calls him Cat.

You can visit her at

www.katherinebayless.com

www.ingramcontent.com/pod-product-compliance
Lightning Source LLC
Chambersburg PA
CBHW030554020726
47494CB00005B/1613